PLAS PHOENIX

BY

KYLE McGRAW

Cover design by Kostis Pavlou
www.kostispavlou.com

Interior design by Tara Mayberry
www.teaberrycreative.com

ISBN: 978-0-692-88371-6 (paperback)

PRAISE FOR PLASTIC PHOENIX

PRIZE WINNER—*New England Book Festival*

....

PRIZE WINNER—*Florida Book Festival*

....

RUNNER-UP PRIZE WINNER—*San Francisco Book Festival*

....

HONORABLE MENTION—*Midwest Book Festival*

....

IN PLASTIC PHOENIX, Kyle McGraw chronicles a thirty-two year-old gay man's odyssey through territory confronted on a daily basis in straight 21st century America, terrain fraught with the landmines of societal hypocrisy, romantic betrayals, and dysfunctional, hostile workplaces. Combining elements of campy exaggeration, perceptive insights, and compassionate, yet arch reflections on humanity's foibles, this novel is informed by a commanding authorial voice firmly in control of the narrative and the unfolding drama of all its characters, primary and secondary alike. Never before have I encountered a work so focused on an exploration of sexual exploits and the hollowness of what passes for mainstream morality and yet so poignant in its depiction of individuals routinely marginalized by our society. Readers, gay and straight alike, will be moved alternately by the raunchy, over-the-top antics of the main character, Kyle, and his outrageous, but endearing sidekicks, especially Melanie, the drop-dead gorgeous, fiercely loyal and kickass Goddess dominatrix, and the underlying motif—a haunting and impassioned plea for, yet

consistently uncompromising insistence upon, unconditional accep-
tance. PLASTIC PHOENIX is far more than a gay male's version
of "Sex and the City." In addition to making this "straight" female
crack a rib or two from laughing so hard at the riotously funny
escapades, McGraw's novel holds up a mirror to one indisputable
truth—regardless of our sexual orientation, we all long for inclusion
and to be loved despite our brokenness and imperfections.

*—Calder Lowe, widely-published author and the
former Editor of the award-winning Dragonfly Press*

To My Muses...
Leslie
Laura
Amanda
and Calder

www.plasticphoenixbook.com

CHAPTER ONE

TIFFANY BAG

You Never Know When A Tiffany Bag
Is Going To Save Your Ass.

IT WAS FRIDAY AT 5:01 P.M. and I decided to give up the ghost and head home. This had been an eventful day. At 4:45 p.m., a painful reminder of a bad episode from over three weeks ago had shown up at my office. I probably should mention that the guy, Aaron, was drunk. We'd been dating for a few weeks. He was attractive, fun in the sack, and for the most part interesting to hang with. Problem was he liked to drink. A lot.

He'd come into my place of work (more about that later) demanding I repay him for lost merchandise as the result of our last overnight escapade. It had gone down something like this: He'd had ten cocktails before coming over to my place. He'd parked his car in front of my building in Hollywood. He was stupid enough to leave in the backseat his leather jacket, iPhone, and iPad. Guess what was missing the next morning? I'd received an angry call from him when he got home to his landline, which I wish he had disconnected like the rest of the world. He blamed *me* for the loss because of the neighborhood I lived in. I found his lack of responsibility amazing. But then again, more and more people were pulling a Donald Trump these days and blaming everyone else but themselves. A couple of days later he called me wanting to get together again, I guess because he was horny or semi-remorseful, and while I have to admit the sex was amazingly good for an alcoholic, I gently told him it was time for me to move on because it wasn't working for me. Until today, I had thought things had ended on a relatively easy note.

Joyce, our stellar receptionist, was a white woman who at heart was a Pam Grier wannabe circa the *Foxy Brown* era from the early '70s. She even had an amazing collection of vintage polyester to pull off the look. She'd called me to the front lobby saying I had a visitor. When I got there he started shaking a fistful of receipts in my face demanding in a loud voice that I pay him for the replacement cost of everything he'd lost including the repair of his broken backseat window. He wobbled from side to side as he spoke which might have been humorous under different circumstances. Now, if you've ever tried to quiet a drunk you know what happened next. He started to shout at the top of his lungs which did a great job of dragging most of the entire office out of their chairs to come witness the commotion. After numerous attempts on my part to get him out of the reception area and away from co-workers, Joyce stood up to her full height of six foot two and jabbed one of her long fingers in his face. The clanking gold bracelets on her wrist punctuated her public displays of attitude.

"Listen mutherfuckuh," she said, laying on an accent she normally didn't have. "If you don't get your drunk ass outta of here right now I'm going to do it for you by kicking it down the mutherfuckin' street." It was almost an art form the way she said it.

It worked and Aaron left but not before he threw the fistful of receipts at me. I picked them up, wadded them into a ball and tossed them into the trashcan trying to look unfazed while inside I was completely humiliated. The crowd dispersed snickering and I headed back to my office.

As I threw my laptop into my new Gucci attaché that I treated myself to for no special reason last week, I felt aggravated. It was not so much because of Aaron's command performance; I had to laugh to myself because it was definitely a different way to end the work week. I was mad because I realized that Glenn, this studly stud of studs I had been dating for a while had not called today, which basically meant I was screwed in terms of any last-minute date possibilities for tonight. Whatever happened to "We'll talk during the week?" Well the week was over, and my patience had run thin. It would be a lot easier if men would just follow directions.

Not sure it's me. I mean, I'm a good-looking thirty-two-year-old Kinda-Hottie living in Los Angeles and you'd think that I'd at least have a date for Friday night. The problem is that Los Angeles is full of drop-dead gorgeous guys who are sitting alone on Friday nights because the competition is *that* tough. Still, I had to admit I did pretty well for myself so I'm not going to bitch. There certainly were uglier people who had less, but then again, when I thought of it, ugly people always seemed to be paired up. It's the above-average / average people who aren't getting any action.

I wandered out to the parking lot of Devore-Horizon Publishing, or as I affectionately refer to it, Shitty Books Inc. There was something about leaving on Friday after a tough week that made me think "What the hell happened along the way?" This was not part of the master plan I had envisioned for my life. By thirty-two I was supposed to be fully immersed in the romance of my life. Spending my time developing the next great adventure with someone just shy of perfection instead of wondering what I was going to do with myself, alone in my scruffy apartment. Aw screw it. That pipe dream was thought up when I was twenty-two not thirty-two. What the hell did I know back then? I could sit around whining about it or I could charge ahead like the weekend warrior I ought to be. I decided to charge ahead.

Determined to make the best of my night, I decided getting loaded out of my mind was the first and most logical choice for the evening but didn't want to be *too* out of it in case he did call. Is that pathetic or proactive? I thought back to all of the rah-rah comments of support I had dished out to friends about not letting this kind of garbage get to them. How they had to be strong and that it was all about *him* not calling and not about *them*. Boy, talk about a crock of crapola that nonsense is. Bottom line is your phone isn't ringing and you are headed to Gelson's to buy a bag full of limes to go with the Tanqueray and tonics you plan to down. It was pretty ironic as I thought back to Aaron the AA candidate that often it's the ones you don't want who are the most available.

I buzzed down Santa Monica Boulevard in my black-with-camel-leather-interior BMW M4, or as I like to refer to it, my $77,923 ego boost. Don't even think about calling it a penile extension. It's the one big splurge I've allowed myself. It was a choice between the car and a nice apartment, and in LA a nice car is a better marketing tool than a great apartment. It's easier to hide an address in a question-able building than a beater; you can always spend the night at his place but he's going to see what you drive up in when you meet at the restaurant. Same thing for business dates. It's all about your car.

I pulled into the Gelson's in West Hollywood. It's the grocery store that makes sense to shop at because I can usually see more than one hottie meandering the aisles or fondling vegetables. Oddly, there are still guys looking at *Grindr* even though they are standing in the best meat department in town.

This was the kind of Friday night that needed a distinct battle plan to maximize enjoyment. While getting blitzed sounded great, I decided I should buffer the effects of the Tanqueray by starting off with some sliced, slightly green Anjou pear and some aged Gruyère cheese, then fix some shrimp in a buerre blanc sauce, while I watched the Dodger game. I know what you're thinking, that with that kind of dinner I probably should be watching something instead of sports. My friend Mickey thinks I'm a lousy homo because I'd rather watch baseball than a documentary on Lady Gaga. What can I say? I like guys in tight pants and the crack of a hard bat.

I'm standing in the fruit and vegetable section molesting the pears. I notice a swarthy guy off to my left and slightly behind me who is checking me out. I catch him looking when I glance up from my pears into the mirrored wall of the fruit stand. He smiles at me and I smile back, then he looks back down at his tomatoes. I look back into the mirror noticing my own reflection. I had taken off my dress shirt and left it in the car, which left me shopping in a white wifebeater. My muscled shoulders and the dark brown hair on my chest looked good under the store's florescent lighting. I'd date me, especially with this tan and the cool scar I have on my shoulder from a car accident when I was seventeen. I've been described as the love child between a younger Dylan McDermott and Donald Trump Jr. This both flatters and disturbs me at the same time, but if it works, what the hell.

I catch the tomato fondler busting me for admiring myself. He rolls his eyes and walks away. I curse my own narcissism but then notice he walked up to his boyfriend anyway. He shouldn't have been checking out my pears that being the case.

I pay for my stuff and head to the parking lot.

Battle plan established. I feel some consolation that I've counter-acted a non-placed call from Glenn with a perfect evening including booze, baseball, and good food. Life is OK.

Maybe now is a good time for a side note about Glenn as I'm sure you're wondering what he's like. Glenn is six foot two inches of male…grade-A. Really hot with his big manly paws that are just the right mix of callous and softness, dark brown hair and ice-blue eyes you can lose yourself in. He's masculine to a fault with his hairy chest and an ass you could bounce quarters off of. He's the guy you'd pick out of the catalogue if only you had a Platinum Am-Ex to pay for him. He's got this great voice that sounds like a lone cello waft-ing through the midnight air on a hot summer night, and oh yeah, and he's got the best LTRD*

*LTRD (Long Term Relationship Dick: A dick that is big without being so big you can't imagine being able to handle it over the years. I mean let's face it, there're the cocks that make you gasp and your eyes go wide but is that what you want to do the deed with year after year? Didn't think so).

Just as I walk into my apartment my voice message indicator triggers on my cell. Crap, Glenn just called while I was in the elevator with no signal. Cool he called! Damn, I missed it! Wait a minute! He called three days late. What am I supposed to do in this situation, be angry or be happy? I stood there with the phone in my hand for a few seconds trying to quickly assess the situation. I decide to return the call. I'm not going to play those bullshit games. No answer. He *just* called me. That's so annoying. I start to hang up when his voice mail picks up. OK, leave a message and make sure you pace the gin and tonics so you don't slur your speech if he calls back this evening. That's the plan. "Hey, it's Kyle. I just missed your call and now you missed mine. Anyway, no big deal, I'm just here getting some work done (why do we always use this excuse when what we are really saying is we have no plans, but to say you have no plans is an admittance of defeat, so instead we act like we are so important at our jobs that we *must* forgo any fun and spend our free time keeping the economy afloat?) so if you want to give me a buzz, feel free. Later."

I start slicing a lime directly onto the counter because nothing could make it look any worse than it already does. The gin is next to me chilling down on its nest of ice. My phone rings. Cool, he must have been in the bathroom. Date tonight. That works because I'm super horny. I reach across the counter grabbing the phone but the caller I.D. cockblocks my fantasy. I pick up.

"Soooo? Are you headed out or what?" Glenn, no, Melanie (best friend—female, straight) yes. We'd met through a mutual friend whom neither one of us spoke to anymore.

"Oh hey, Mel, what's up?" Normally I love it when Mel calls. She is a fiery star in the constellation of life, the type of girl who could use the words thermal nuclear dynamics and pussy in the same sentence, and who always has a way of making me laugh at the hard stuff life throws my way.

"Don't act so disappointed. Clearly you're alone again from the sound of it."

"Thanks Mel. Your confidence in me is outstanding, but yeah, it's going to be a T&T night while following the Twitter feeds of my clients. He didn't call me all day and then I just missed him before I walked in the door, so I don't know what the hell is going on. I thought maybe…"

She's quick to interrupt. "Well, that bites. I just do not see why you are spending your time worrying about some guy who calls you last minute on a Friday night. Screw him, big pool or not." OK—the problem with giving advice to all of your friends when *they* are down is that your own words continually come back to haunt you. Maybe I should start listening to some of those old sessions I had with Mel during one of the many, many man-crises she's dealt with since I've known her. Besides, who is she to comment about the importance of pool size? She's the first to act disappointed with only getting to take a dip in a Jacuzzi.

"Well honey, I'd suggest we go to a movie, but this is one of our busiest nights at the club (now, please realize that Melanie uses the term "club" in the loosest possible way when describing what she does for a living) and a girl has rent to pay, you know." Don't I know it. I'm looking at a shocking AmEx statement staring me in the face and thinking how tempting it would be to do Melanie's gig for a while to get ahead. She's offered to hook me up but I don't have the balls to follow through.

"Listen, don't worry about me. I'm tired from work anyway and decided to treat myself to a night of killing my mind with gin and baseball."

"Oh Kyle...you are so straight sometimes, but I love you. Are we on for a quick Peachtini before I head into work tomorrow, provided you don't have a date by that time?" We decide the odds are good for meeting up and figure it's a done deal. See, I love Peachtinis so I'm not *that* straight.

I think back to the guy in the fruit and vegetable section as I whip up my Gelson-chow and sit down to a cold cocktail in front of my new 50-incher. Halfway through my fantasy of what it would be like to be in the locker room after the game a curve ball comes at me when my phone rings.

It's 9:32 p.m. I look at the caller ID. It's Glenn (thank God an upset stomach from the mess that was dinner squashed the desire for that last T&T because nothing is worse than slurring your words when trying to impress someone). So where was he tonight? He blabs on about some "quick" dinner with friends and had just walked out the door when he heard his phone ringing in his pocket, figured it was me, but didn't want to answer it. Why does he tell me this? I would have answered. But he makes a point of telling me he figured it was me and would just call me back when he had a full stomach. I love the assumption that he would find me home. I hate the fact that he's right. He asks me out for brunch the next day followed by some "afternoon time together." Well, we all know what that means. Fine-cool-good-I-forgive-you for not calling sooner but you sure as hell better be worth the wait. Eighteen hours to go until I get laid. I don't know if I can wait that long.

I head off to bed in need of a good night's sleep after the work week and the gin. I'm in a daze while brushing my teeth and taking out my contacts. Just as I put my head down on the pillow it dawns on me that I just pulled a Lindsay Lohan and accidentally took two Paxil versus one Paxil and one Ambien. Fuck. I drag my tired ass out of bed, swallow an Ambien, and crash.

Next morning I'm up at 4:45 a.m. I'm a deer in the headlights due to the accidental overdose of God's gift to antidepressants. Now what? It's freakin' early as hell, I'm so horny I could fuck a light socket, and I have no way of getting back to sleep without re-medicating which would definitely be a bad idea. So I decide to work out and run some errands. You'd be amazed at how much you can get done errand-wise by 7:00 a.m. on a Saturday morning in L.A. when there is no traffic. After an intense pre-date workout, I'm home, showered, and ready to head over to Glenn's Studio City Sky-Pad-Avec-Pool when he calls to:

A. Say he's going to be late and
B. Tell me he wants to come over to *my* side of the hill because his housekeeper is coming over to clean.

She's cleaning on a Saturday? Wait a minute. First, you're going to be late and now there's a change in venue? I'm looking out over the litter box I live in realizing I have exactly sixty minutes to get this apartment in "guest" condition and allow time to retake my shower. "See you soon," he says with a click of the receiver before I even have a chance to throw out an emergency substitute plan.

Heart pounding, my mind starts racing as I look around at the bombed-out mess I'm standing in. Pulverized lime carcasses litter the coffee table and there's a stain on the rug from where I knocked my ashtray over. It's then that it hits me. *I am so screwed.* I don't want him to think I live like trash. Time to triage. The adrenaline hits me as I tornado my sleazy lair. Dishes in dishwasher, dirty rug in closet, moldering throw pillow that has been on my list of things to replace for three months follows the rug into the closet. I have marveled many times at the advantages of coming out as it left me with a wonderful hiding place for my skeletons. I rummage through the closet trying to get the rug to stay in place so it won't pop the door open during an awkward moment. It is then that I have a revelation from God like a thunderbolt raining down from heaven pointing me in the direction of salvation. I see it tucked away neatly on top of some books...saved for just such an emergency. I pull the enormous Tiffany bag I had saved for a rainy day out of its archival spot. In one fell swoop I start throwing everything in. Bills, pens, lighters, limes...assorted bullshit galore. I drag the bag over to the corner of the room and can tell him it's a large vase I bought for a recently wed co-worker. Hmm, he might figure out its true purpose if he gets too close. So, I pull some white tissue paper from a drawer and pack it into the top of the bag. Cool. Clutter concealed.

I scan the apartment. Is there anything I don't / do want him to see? Pamphlet on how to avoid super gonorrhea from the doctor's office goes under the bed but the unread biography on Obama is left out on the coffee table along with a magazine about baseball. I figure they'll be either great PR in terms of making me look smart and studly. I start vacuuming like a coke addict trying to snort that last little dropped gem from the carpet and decide the living room emergency is finally more or less taken care of. It actually doesn't look half bad.

I launch the vacuum into the bedroom at full force, sucking up the usual bedroom floor litter in its path. With each evacuation of lint, bits of Kleenex and the tiny corners from condom packets that always show up at the wrong time, I get closer and closer to respectability. The one good set of sheets is already on the bed and I realize this is yet another hurdle toward making my afternoon lay session a quality one. Thinking quickly, I vacuum the dust and body hair off them as there is no time to throw them in the wash. Only one problem, even with the dust removed, it's clear they have been slept in at least four times. I go to the linen closet to grab fresh sheets and then start cursing myself that I didn't better utilize my time last night and at *least* do some laundry while I was pounding down those T&Ts. I stand in front of an empty cupboard with no clean sheets in sight. (Gay Scout Rule #7...*Always* have a backup set of linens in the lurch). However, there is an iron staring back at me so I whip it from its nesting spot and plug it in near the bed. I pick up a half-empty bottle of Arrowhead and pour some into the spout on top, wait til I hear a sizzle, and then start ironing the sheets on top of the bed. Like an infomercial targeting whores, the wrinkles start to disappear as the faint scent of salty sweat and cologne billows up with the iron's steam. I'm wondering whether there is a market for a gigantic iron to make wrinkle-free sheets a breeze when I see *The Picture* sitting there on my dresser. My pace stops because I feel a sense of guilt. It's of me and A.K. in London after getting caught in a rainstorm without the benefit of our umbrellas. Soaked to the skin, laughing our heads off, we got someone to take the shot for us. It was in some pub. Funny how things get fuzzy over time, but I think the name was something like the Brass Nail or such. It was the happiest day of my life.

A.K. was Andrew Kennedy. We had met on my birthday almost nine years ago and he had been, or maybe still was, the love of my life. I was the only one who called him A.K. He never let anyone call him Andy, always Andrew, but for me I was allowed to use a nickname. I liked the fact that it was only me who could do this. He liked it too. I wonder if I should put the picture away. It had gone in and out of a drawer many times over, but the permanent home was on top of my dresser. I never took it down for a date or someone I hooked up with, but Glenn was turning into something different. We had been dating for a while now. Things were changing and the sparks were starting somewhere deep inside me. It had been a long time since I had felt some of these feelings. Now that A.K. was gone, he was certainly no threat to him, but Glenn might not see it that way. I picked up the picture and held the cold frame in my hands. It was the only thing in my apartment I never let get dusty. I ran my fingers over the glass that covered A.K.'s face. I thought back to a time when glass didn't separate my touch. Had it been that long already? There are such mixed emotions because there was so much happiness, discovery and adventure with him. But then there was that summer day where my world came to a stop. Winter had set in that July and the life was poured out of me. Pain, grief and longing had replaced my happiness. Someone once said to me that love is something that happens over a great deal of time; that it's not possible to love in only two or three months. Infatuation definitely, deep caring maybe, but true love proved itself over the years. The time I first heard this I had just met A.K. and thought it was a total crock, but now, all these years later, I realize how wise that individual was. I opened my top dresser drawer and carefully laid A.K. and me to rest.

The reality that time is running out pops back into my head and I realize I have to throw my sweat-covered bod into the shower. While the water is pounding on me for a second time this morning, I begin to compliment myself on a remarkable job well done of turning my litter box of an apartment into a stabbin' cabin. It's amazing what one horny homo can do in twenty minutes of time. I think back to the first time A.K. came over to this very place with me racing to get a shower on time. The carpet was new back then, wasn't even ratty.

I'm re-washed and re-dressed and now I get to sit here like an idiot waiting for him to show up. The clock ticks away. I turn on the TV to look for a distraction but find it's hard to focus on anything since he's due to arrive any minute. I check CNN, *Facebook*, *The Onion*. Since a lot can happen with Donald Trump in the time it takes to peruse *The Onion*, I recheck CNN for updated headlines. He's even later than he said he would be. This shit drives me crazy. Waiting for people to show is the biggest waste of time. What project can you possibly start in five minutes?

• • •

But before I know it…I find myself sitting across from him at brunch later that day. His strong face, moustache, and brown silky hair looking sexier each time I see him. We are at my favorite little bistro in the mini neighborhood that's crammed between Doheny and Robertson. Such an odd journey to get to this country-French-toast haven.

We could barely get through our food fast enough before we were back at my litter box ripping the clothes off each other. This was great.

We lay there on the sweat soaked sheets (they are *definitely* heading to the wash later) while a summer breeze rattled the cheap vertical blinds blocking the afternoon sun. He turns to me, flashing those eyes. Two blue eyes that seem like they could melt away the frustration and chaos of life and he says, "I was thinking a weekend in Palm Springs would be a good thing."

As the breeze continued to play with the blinds, things sort of stopped for a moment. How many times had my friends heard me say that all I was looking for in life was an accountant who was stable, and liked me for the inside as well as the outside? Someone who had a house and a Golden Retriever, a nice pool. A guy who preferred spending time together watching movies in front of the fireplace instead of convincing me we were missing a third person from our relationship. Someone who was fun to be with, easy to talk to and wanted to buzz off to Palm Springs on a whim? I just didn't expect him to be seventeen years older than me when I constructed the fantasy.

CHAPTER TWO

MELANIE

Patent Leather Peachtinis

I CAUGHT THE REFLECTION of Melanie's knee-high-white-patent-leather boots on my Peachtini glass. She clicked up behind me, bent down, and gave me her signature nibble on my earlobe which sends shivers down my spine and leaves me totally willing to do anything. It was early Saturday evening at The Abbey; an outdoor gay bar filled with wall-to-wall gorgeous people drinking overpriced but extra-big martinis. This was for over two years now a weekly ritual for us minus any extraneous dates or other complications.

The bright sun was setting through the trees and it provided Melanie with the most perfect lighting. The world was her runway; her hair like liquid obsidian. The purest, shiniest black you can imagine and it cascaded onto her shoulders caressing the tiny straps of her filmy, low-cut, raspberry-colored dress. Her skin was lightly tanned but not too much. She was someone who wasn't afraid of a future wrinkle to look good today but knew how not to go overboard. She had fine elegant features and graceful hands with long fingers and a perfect manicure. She looked like a model but carried herself like a CEO. She set a small Gucci clutch that matched her boots onto the table.

Looking over at the bartender, I saw that he'd already started our round of drinks the minute he spied Mel. She took her seat; ready for me to spill all regarding what had happened since we spoke last night. She picked a tiny leaf off her Kleenex-of-an-outfit as I spoke.

"He wants to take me to Palm Springs."

Her jet-black eyebrows rose.

"How'd you find that out?" She impatiently looked around for the waiter and our drinks.

"It just came up at brunch today. Can you believe that?" The waiter approached with our liquid meds and started to fire up the heat lamp next to us. As usual, Melanie came severely underdressed considering the warm sun was setting and the cool LA marine air was rolling in. The waiters at the Abbey also eagerly anticipated her needs; this was the magic she had over men as they gave deference to her. They even let her smoke in an otherwise no-smoking city. Mel took a swig of her drink and looked me in the eye.

"Kyle, there's something I just don't like about this one."

Melanie's love and protection for her friend Kyle...love it. Melanie's disapproval for about everyone I've ever gone out with... well, this drives me crazy. "Why don't you cut me some slack, Mel. He could be a great fit for me. He's solid, grounded, and his life could use someone like me." There was an awkward silence as she fished around in her purse for her pack of Winstons ignoring the fact that smoking was illegal. A Peachtini ritual as well, she lit up two, handing me the second one. I'd learned the hard way to wipe the excess lipstick off before taking that first drag. One time, after spending thirty minutes trying to impress this cute guy, I went to take a leak and realized I had Estée Lauder Dusty Rose #4 all over my lips. (Gay Scout Rule #13… *Always* keep looking in a mirror to head off any facial / nose disasters). We exhaled in unison and then she started in on me.

"You know, it's just that…the thing that bothers me is where you met this guy. Hardly a good place to encourage a lasting romance."

"The garden center at Target? Come on Mel, what in the world is wrong with that? I mean talk about innocent."

"Kyle, that's exactly the point I'm trying to make. It's too innocent and excessively boring. I mean for God's sake how corny. 'Our hands touched as we both reached for the same rhododendron.' Where can this possibly lead?" Melanie's logic always intrigued me. In its own twisted way it had an unnerving sense of truth to it. I was there buying plants for my balcony and he was there buying plants for his pool area. That *is* rather boring and dull, but there was also something kind of romantic about it even if it was at Target. Melanie would have preferred I met him a leather party or a sex club so that she knew his sense of adventure was intact.

"Kyle, he's an old man spending his time laying plants." She flicked a wayward ash off the table.

"Hey, hold on Mel. He's also spent a good amount of time laying me." I had an afterglow flashback to this afternoon and how glad I was I had ironed those sheets. "It's not like his plants are his main concern in life. Taking care of your home is a good thing. And he's not an old man." She rolled her eyes.

"You said he was something around thirty years older than you." She stubbed her Winston out with a vengeance.

"Seventeen," I shot back.

"Seventeen, twenty, thirty, forty. What difference does it make? You should be dating someone your own age. I know these things after all. Men are established perverts once they hit forty. It's a known fact."

Melanie's research also intrigued me. She based 90 percent of her psychological findings from her work experience at The Black Door, an underground "lounge" for off-kilter men who had a severe need to be dominated by beautiful women.

"Kyle, the key is to find a man in his thirties and then try to train him into his forties. It's a lot like remodeling a kitchen. Start with a fixer-up that's had some use but has a layout you like. Then mold it so that by the time you're finished he's exactly what you had envisioned. That way he's broken in with use and experience but has a shiny new surface with upgrades." She had a point. "Once past forty they're set in their ways and there is no changing them," she continued. "It's all about them and nothing about you. Look at how he drags you along; calling you at the last minute and then you come running."

Ouch.

That stung.

But admittedly because of the element of truth in it. I never wanted to think of myself as someone who is desperate but instead as someone whose perennial sense of hope gave him the ability to keep on trying. I had to give it to myself that despite past history I didn't give up. In fact, I refused to give up.

"Did he say he'd pay for the trip?" Melanie's sense of practicality kicked in. She hates the fact I'm seeing this guy but does see the value in a free trip to Palm Springs. "I mean, if *he's* suggesting Palm Springs then he should be footing the entire bill. Besides, you're hardly the one pulling in the big paycheck from Warner Brothers. Don't lay down a cent, especially when he'd most likely have been paying for a rent-boy if he went without you, so by taking you, it's a bargain. By all means you need to find out these kinds of details in advance." She offset the semi-harshness of this commentary with a wry smile that set the record straight between us. Her disapproval came from a place of caring and twisted humor. (Gay Scout Rule #3...You can either laugh or cry so make sure you laugh).

We sat there a little while sipping our drinks and checking out the guys.

"I'm feeling things I haven't felt since A.K., Melanie." That froze her. She sat there staring at me with a loss for words. Her face registered a quandary of emotions and I could tell she was rapidly trying to sort through them before saying something — a rare event for someone known to blurt out whatever is on her mind. She turned her head away, shifting uncomfortably in her chair. This was the first time she had heard me say this and she now knew it was a whole new playing field.

"Oh." She toyed with the cherry at the bottom of her glass.

Maybe I should change the subject. "So how was work last night?" Melanie's job was a surefire way to break the silence and confusion we both were feeling.

"This guy had me use him as an ottoman again last night. Same old same old." Believe it or not, this kind of scenario was run of the mill for Mel when she was at work but how can you tire of hearing about it? The world was full of over-forty perverts who were ripe for a beating.

"What's the price of being furniture these days?" I asked.

"The price I pay or the client?" She pursed her lips for emphasis and I leaned forward in anticipation.

"Typical accountant from the Valley. Balding with those funky little half-glasses when he reads." (What exactly he was reading during all of this was beyond me. Maybe the price list?). "Paunch. Nothing to look at that's for sure. He has the hairiest ass. It's actually a pretty easy gig though." She loved making me beg for more details, a holdover from her professional life.

"Come on Mel, keep going." I knew when to play into her sense of the dramatic.

She lit up another Winston and then kicked it into high gear. "He secretly wants to be an ottoman. All I have to do is sit on the couch in the employee break room and watch TV for an hour, he specifies the show. He strips down and then gets on all fours in front of the couch and has me put my feet up on him. When I took off my shoes, he got very upset and said I must keep my heels on so as to 'dirty' the bad ottoman's nice upholstery. I've noticed I get a bigger tip if I have mud or gum on the bottom of my shoe." I couldn't believe it. Melanie was a portal to some of the most bizarre examples of human beings on Earth. It never failed to amaze me the new places she could take me. She paused, took another long draw on her Winston, and then blew out the smoke in a slow exhale before beginning again. She looked skyward as she did this and her face had a look of contentment mixed with sardonic mischievousness.

"Anyway, he sat there very still while I watched Sean Hannity on Fox News. But here's the trippy part (as if this wasn't trippy enough). Every time Sean went to a commercial break I had to pick up a ping-pong paddle and smack him on the ass and say 'Bad ottoman!' 'Bad ottoman!' He'd squirm and then bleat out an apology, promising to be better during the next segment. Then, and this was the tricky part, as *soon* as Sean mentions Barack Obama or Hillary Clinton I had to give him one really hard smack and yell 'STAY STILL!' Then I would kick back again until the next beating. Sometimes he likes me to flip through the latest *Wall Street Journal* while doing this but not always."

What do you say to someone after they've just told you this?

"Oh, I forgot about the pizza; that's the best part," she said excitedly. I didn't know at this point if I wanted to know how pizza played into a hairy-assed-accountant-turned-ottoman's fantasy or not, but

I knew curiosity would get the better of me anyway. "Oh Kyle, he *insists* that I order a pizza before we start his scene. He waits in the lobby until it arrives before we can begin. I'm to munch on it during the show and talk in great detail about it. It *has* to be pepperoni. That's one of his requirements. One time they accidentally delivered a vegetarian pizza by mistake and he was beside himself. So, I sit there and the sexual tension builds in him as I work my way through each piece, carefully describing what it's like in terms of taste, texture, and especially the spiciness of the pepperoni. He starts to breathe faster and faster as I continue to eat which is kind of annoying because my legs go up and down each time he inhales and exhales. Jesus, he about shot his wad when I bounced an uneaten crust off that bald head. What a freak."

Many times I had tried to justify the meager funds I pulled down at Shitty Books Inc., working a career I felt was respectable despite it being its own kind of torture, while Mel was pulling down a fortune eating pizza and ping-ponging an accountant from Tarzana. Who was truly prostituting themselves, me or her? It didn't take a genius to figure that one out. Just look at the cars we drove. "I have to tell you though, Kyle, all that paddling does wear you out, and it was hard to fully enjoy the show as I had to be ready to smack him exactly at the right time and last week I broke a nail."

Mel looked at her watch and shot out of her chair. "I didn't pay attention to the time. I have to be going. The Milkmaid has an early flight to Pittsburgh so he can make some HR conference." She threw her cigs into her clutch, swirled what was left of her Peachtini down her hatch and smacked a quick one on my cheek before flying off on the wind. So typical of Melanie. In one ear and out the other before you had any idea of what hit you.

CHAPTER THREE

MISS MAGGIO IN THE HAY BALES

Tequila Noon-Rise

I UNSUCCESSFULLY TRIED TO SLAP MYSELF AWAKE. Sundays
have the ability to be incredibly brutal especially if you follow three
Peachtinis with an evening with Mickey Maggio who Melanie affectionately calls "Hay-Bales" because he lost his virginity in the
back of his father's barn. My nickname for him is Miss Maggio because I met him while he was an accountant for Victoria's Secret.
My intent had originally been as follows:

> *PLAN ONE: Leave the Abbey after two-and-a-half cocktails
> with Mel. The half Peachtini left in the glass would be an exercise
> in self-control. Hit gym on way home (this would be the second
> time that day because I was feeling extra studly after my after-
> noon work-over compliments of Glenn. Light dinner followed by*

early bedtime. Early Sunday morning jog. Breakfast with Mickey at 10:00 a.m. Accomplish at least eight items on my to-do list.

Reality was...

PLAN TWO: Run into Mickey Maggio while finishing third Peachtini. Breakfast moved up to 2:14 a.m. after Saturday night mayhem. Screw the to-do list. It ain't happening.

I looked at the clock. 11:46 a.m. At least I was alleviated of some guilt by the fact I'd experience fourteen minutes of morning. I stood looking in the mirror doing a quick damage assessment of my face followed by a cargo check at my crotch. I was too wrecked to do anything about my morning wood, but it's still good to at least verify its existence with a quick squeeze and ball count. (Gay Scout Rule # 4...*Always* make sure you don't leave anything behind). I pulled on a pair of blue plaid boxers from their resting place on the floor and padded out to the living room.

Slowly regaining consciousness, I spied a pink toe poking through a sock at the end of a blanket-covered lump on my couch. Further investigation jogged my memory that at some point Mickey had been assigned to the couch and not the drive home. I mentally scratched off "jog" from my list. The list hadn't specified it couldn't be mental. Now was the time to salvage what I possibly could from this day.

I headed toward the kitchen when I was reminded that pain is God's way of making us conscious of our surroundings. Stepping on an upside-down bottle cap in your bare feet slaps you into instant awareness. My piercing shriek woke the deadened horizontal blob as well.

"What the hell you doin' Kyle? Yuh know how early it is?" he said in his Midwest drawl from underneath the blanket. I extracted the demonic bottle cap from my foot.

"Hey! *You* were the one drinking the Coronas last night. How many times have I told you to not leave your caps on the floor?"

Mickey's head popped out from his bedding like a turtle coming out of his shell. He scratched his blond curly hair and bounced off the couch. He had an amazing ability to come to life no matter what had transpired the night before. I think this was in part because Mickey was raised on a farm in southern Illinois and was used to getting up early and having to harvest an entire crop before breakfast. He was a little over six feet tall and while overall he was somewhat lanky he clearly had been corn-fed most of his life. Life in LA had developed a simpler sort of muscularity in Mickey from his days of farmhand prowess. He's shown me pictures of him back on the farm when he was lifting hay bales and plowing fields. At that time, he was really built with eye-popping biceps and a chest you could have bounced a hog off. He admitted he was lazy these days, yet he still maintained a great body despite doing very little work on it. He had a light dusting of blond hair on his legs and forearms but was smooth everywhere else. Mickey wasn't the smartest guy in the world, but he knew the value of being a cute farm boy in the big city. He was big, dumb and loveable and a great friend who was a lot of fun to hang with. At least I should say he was dumb on the outside. Inside, Mickey was pretty shrewd.

"We should do sumpin' today," he said as he stretched energy into his perfect body. While he stretched, I did a quick check of my love handles to make sure they weren't getting over the recommended weight for carry-on baggage. My to-do list came back to the top of my head. Sunday was fast disappearing and I needed to have crossed at least one of the chores off. "I haven't seen Mel in a while. Maybe she'd like to join us for some brunch." I wasn't sure if I could handle a recap of Mel's work night with a queasy stomach. I had dreamed a bald pizza delivery guy had spanked me with a tennis racket last night and knew I had Mel to blame for putting the thoughts there in the first place. Still...

• • •

Mickey and I sipped our third cup of coffee at Makin' Biscuits while we waited for Mel to show up. This was his favorite place because he said it tasted like his mom's cooking. Plus, it was cheap and Sunday morning loaded with carbohydrates and fat always makes sense after a night of heavy drinking. Some of the same crowd from The Abbey were there albeit looking a little wiped out due to the previous evening's libations and God knows what else. I was growing impatient. Of course, Mickey was his usual calm, go-with-the-flow self, continually scoping the room for potential conquests. I was surveying the parking lot, ready to go ahead and order when I finally saw Mel's red, always spotless, Mercedes convertible swoop in. She did a quick check of her makeup in the driver's side mirror then got out and strode across the parking lot. She was wearing a low-cut, breezy, floral, dress. A Little Whore on the Prairie motif so to speak. She came into the restaurant, spotted us and headed over.

"Hey guys." She planted us with her trademark hug and nibble oblivious to the fact she was over forty-five minutes late. But hey. That was Melanie. You couldn't be angry at her no matter how hard you tried or what she did. She was born with a walk-on-water ability to remove all negativity from those around her. You loved her for her quirks as well as her qualities. Mel Shanghaied my coffee. "Breakfast is on me, guys. I had a great night."

Miss Maggio and I were more than willing to accept a free meal. Especially one that came with what we both knew was going to be a great story. I contemplated the menu but as usual ordered exactly the same thing I always did, French toast with bacon. A part of me wanted to go for the huevos rancheros or Greek omelet but in the end, I always chose the safe, predictable bet that went well with khakis and a button down shirt.

As it turned out, Mel's HR man, who we jokingly referred to as The Milkmaid, had come in earlier than expected last night so he could catch the redeye to Pittsburgh. He was attending a convention on compensation benefits. I imagined planes full of mild-mannered businessmen stuck in boring jobs and had to wonder how many of them led the kind of freaky lives that most of Mel's clients did. The Milkmaid's trip had to do with Mel filling baby bottles, squirt guns, and water bottles with milk, preferably whole, definitely not non-fat, and then a variety of activities would begin. He was a regular, only showed up on Saturday night, and was what Mel referred to as a bread-and-butter client. I thought it was interesting that someone like The Milkmaid could be thought of as dependable. Each week he would come to The Black Door carrying cartons of milk and assorted paraphernalia. He would then change into crotch-less lederhosen while Mel put on a Swiss Milkmaid outfit. The dirndl was missing from her dress so that her boobs hung free. She would then pour milk into the receptacle of his choice and the fun would begin.

"It was squirt guns last night," she began. "You know those cheapy lime green kinds you had as a kid? He had the big ones. They were very hard to fill and he got upset when I spilled some of the milk as he had only just enough since he was headed to the airport and not back home. I mean, with all of his planning you'd think he'd have thought of some kind of funnel or something."

"Maybe he was just stressed he had to catch a flight that night," I piped in. Mel took her work very seriously and never appreciated a stern word from any client. It was her job to criticize and no one else's.

"That could be. You know how men are when they get into business mode. Anyway, once I got the damn things filled, I had to hold them up to my tits and then fire away while he ran around the room trying to dodge the streams. Can you fucking believe this?" Mickey snorted into his coffee.

"What's wrong with people these days?" she cranked. "I mean at exactly what point did America just go down the damn toilet? And you two wonder why you can't meet any eligible men? I'm telling you, Fox News and too much internet porn is a terrible influence. Hurry up, because once they're past forty it's worse."

"Hey, I meet good ones all the time. Don't mix me up with Kyle, Mel."

"Thanks, guys. You both suck," I said.

"Did Kyle tell you he's dating a virtual skeleton, Hay Bales?" At least she said it with a smile. OK, (Gay Scout Rule # 5...Learn how to dodge a bullet).

"No, but I'm sure you could tell me how to squeeze cash out of the bone marrow of one of your customers," I shot back. She playfully stuck her tongue out at me.

Mickey and Mel chattered on while I sat there with my mind wandering. I was feeling restless today and wasn't sure why. I wondered if Mel was right about guys being worse after forty. Did I miss my chance with A.K. and now it was going to be a life of dysfunctional accountants and HR men the older I get? In one respect I have always felt love is like Las Vegas. Everyone steps up to the games but only a few people hit the jackpot and the rest crap out. I'd hit my jackpot once already. That it didn't last was something I never planned on. Still, I had to hope that casino lightning would strike me twice. Maybe I should concentrate less on being cynical and more on French toast.

The chow finally arrived just as we were about to pass out from hunger and for the first time in a little while we three sat in silence. Simple silence. Like when you are really in love with someone and it's OK to *not* do anything. Just exist with them. That was the rest of brunch. We three friends.

CHAPTER FOUR

BMW

Leaking Hoses

"THEY HAVE CUTE MECHANICS HERE," said Mickey as he pointed to the guy who was looking at the underbelly of my cranky car trying to figure out what was going on.

"Maybe it's a BMW thing, to make you feel better about the screwing you're going to get with the bill." We were in the glass fishbowl waiting room and could see the repairmen working on the cars in the bay. Considering it was a Sunday afternoon it was quite a production with people coming and going and out-of-control kids running around while their parents waited for an oil change.

"I slept with that one over there," said Mickey pointing at a swarthy guy who looked like he might have been Russian or Czech. The mechanic had a buzz cut and very angular facial features. He looked like he could kill you in hand to hand combat.

"Seriously?"

"Yup...I think...It was dark at the time."

"Is there anyone you haven't slept with?"

"Probably not," he laughed. "Boy's got needs."

My mechanic motioned for another mechanic to come over and look at my car. After a few moments, the second guy began to scratch his head and it looked like they didn't have a clue. This was going to cost me.

"Does what Mel say bother you at all?" Mickey looked at me with a puzzled expression.

"What do you mean? Bout the sex stuff?"

"No, I love her sex stories. I mean about her comments that all guys over forty are messed up."

"I don't know. Don't know I really care t' be honest."

"It kind of makes me feel uncomfortable sometimes. For instance, I was filling her in on Glenn yesterday and she was saying that someone his age is stuck in his ways and that I'm getting into something that I shouldn't. That bugs me because I don't agree with her."

"Sex good?"

"Yeah."

"Then what you worried about?"

"There's more to life than sex, Mickey."

"True, but in the meantime while you're figrin' out if he's a loon or not you're gettin' it good. *Thaaaattttsss* the point I'm tryin' to make."

His fucked-up logic made sense.

"You know what Kyle? My whole growin' up was always lookin' to the future. Would the crop grow right? Would next season be a good or bad? Is it goin' to rain for what we need? Is the tornado goin' to hit and kill us all? That's all I ever heard was worryin' about what was comin' instead of what was goin' on right now. I don't think much of the future. If it happens it happens. My spendin' time worryin' about it aint goin' change nothin'. So instead I figure I spend my time worryin' about today and what I'm doin' right now. Are you happy right now?"

"Yeah, for the most part I guess."

"There you go. It's not that complicated."

I felt like this advice should have come with peach cobbler.

My mechanic came into the fishbowl and walked over to us.

"No big deal, Kyle," he said. "Just a hose problem that we can replace easy." (Gay Scout Rule # 28…Beware of leaky hoses). "Just give me thirty minutes."

"Thanks," I said.

"You're welcome," said Mickey.

CHAPTER FIVE

SHITTY BOOKS INC.

The Bad Omen

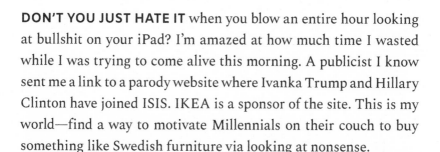

DON'T YOU JUST HATE IT when you blow an entire hour looking at bullshit on your iPad? I'm amazed at how much time I wasted while I was trying to come alive this morning. A publicist I know sent me a link to a parody website where Ivanka Trump and Hillary Clinton have joined ISIS. IKEA is a sponsor of the site. This is my world—find a way to motivate Millennials on their couch to buy something like Swedish furniture via looking at nonsense.

I swig down the last of my coffee, do a quick brush of the pearlies, nose and face check (see previous Gay Scout Rule #13), and I'm out the door to Devore-Horizon Publishing, or as I've already told you, the monstrosity I prefer to call Shitty Books Inc. Devore-Horizon is the largest publisher of non-fiction books on the West Coast. A mini-giant so to speak as most of the big boys are located in NYC. It's non-fiction so that means we run the gamut from cookbooks to relationship manuals to self-help-New Age-from-outer-space type stuff.

The publisher is actually proud of the fact that we have five different psychics under our wing. She should have been a carnival barker.

Don't fool yourself about publishing. The only glamorous thing about my job is the drive to and from work as it takes me through Beverly Hills. This morning as I wait for the light to change at Rodeo and Wilshire, I wave at the doorman in front of Tiffany & Co., fondly remembering how glad I was I bought that Bloody Mary set last year and that it came in that extra large bag. I turn my head to the right and cruise a hot looking gardener in a beat-up old truck. He smiles at me just as the light turns and makes his right turn while I cross through. I debate about turning around to follow him down Wilshire and give him my number but since I'm running late, I figure this is one time I'll have to forgo self-promotion. Our office is located in a tiny building south of Wilshire in south (slums) Beverly Hills. One block further down and we are in Beverly Wood which is just a bullshit name for a run-of-the-mill neighborhood that happens to be Beverly Hills adjacent. Adjacency is a big deal in LA. It's not being something that necessarily counts just being near something or someone better than you are. Sort of a class by geographic association thing.

As I pull into the parking lot of "SBI" I wished we were in the porn biz. It would be so much more fulfilling than some of the "life saving" stuff we market to the soul-less, hungry and needy. Oh yeah by the way, that's my job, slinging hash to the masses…also known as marketing and promotions.

I prepare myself for the heavy smell of incense, scented candles and generic cigarettes. Clean air in the workspace laws be damned; the publishing world could give a rat's ass. I realized after gasping for several months that somehow editors thrive off stuffy, stale-air environments. It reminds them of their days working in NY or getting laid in the stacks of some moldering library. Now they were in

LA, an open window away from at least a fresh blast of pollution, but preferring a musty, dusty, cigarette-laden fog that stuck to the walls. I go into my office. In this instance God had smiled down on me and I lucked out getting the corner office which is located the furthest from the incense burners. I tuck away my jacket and put my lunch on my bookshelf. I'm very methodical about my lunch. One Lean Cuisine, a piece of fruit and a little container of lettuce with no dressing. It's the French toast of my workweek. I sit down, turn on my computer, and check my e-mails. The first one is from some editor at *Holistic Life.com* wanting a review copy of a book we are publishing on dog astrology. Oddly, there is also a message from a guy I dated about six months ago wanting to see if I'd like to hook up for some trouble. Not sure why he was emailing this to my work. He had been a wild one in the sack but was also a dating vampire, sucking the life out of me with his endless demands and high-maintenance style. I finally couldn't take it anymore and had stopped returning his calls like a big pussy instead of just leveling with him that I needed him to back off.

I sit in the solitude of my office listening to my computer hum and click. I feel motionless on Monday mornings and I'm an example of inertia at its worst. The inside of me expects the outside of me to take the lead and vice-versa. Instead I just sit there. Usually on Monday I promise myself to party a little less and sleep a lot more. But by Friday I can't wait to let loose and before I know it I'm back in resolution mode.

I have a mountain of work that needs to be taken care of but I can't seem to find a starting place. None of it interests me this morning. I decide that a cup of Java might do the trick to energize me, so I wander out to the coffee station and start a fresh pot. The incense lovers had put on a pot of decaf per their routine, but I needed something more invasive to give me a jump start. I stand

there listening to the stream of black fluid sail into the carafe waiting for the first possible moment that I can steal a cup before it's
completely finished. The publisher just hates when someone takes
a cup before the whole pot is done so I find this act not only daring
but satisfying as well. If you can believe it, this was actually one of
the line items on our weekly meeting agenda last week.

I head back to my office. It's a nice office all things considered.
Cramped, but I do have plenty of shelf space and a window that
looks out onto the top of a palm tree. Sometimes I watch squirrels
humping in the palms, a highlight of any day.

Thirty minutes later I'm dead again. The coffee didn't work.
Next weekend I'm not going to drink one single drop.

What Mel said is still bothering me and I know I need to get over
it and move on. I admit I've been on the dating merry-go-round for a
long time and keep wondering when I'm going to get off. It shouldn't
be that hard to meet a cool guy, settle down, and just *be*. Be next to
each other doing nothing. Being. I jotted "being" down on a pale
blue sticky note and posted it to the side of my monitor. That would
be my Zen thought for the week to get to a simple state of being.

But that doesn't seem to be the case with me, nor with a lot of
guys I know. So many looking for the same thing but seemingly
dumping their lives into anything that will take their minds off
the fact that they are alone. I'm definitely someone who likes to be
around other people.

"What the mother-F-ing-hell are you doing?" I'm jolted out of
my thoughts by Lucy Arnot. True to her pretentiousness she uses a
faux-French pronunciation but considering she has a mouth like a
truck driver I don't know why she bothers. There she stands in her
cheap pumps and with a foul-smelling generic cigarette dangling
from her lip. Notice I didn't say lips. Lucy's cig always seems to be
permanently fixed to her lower lip where it hangs and smolders

until it's replaced by a younger brother. Her face matches her personality; a beat-up novel that maybe had some appeal back in 1987 but is severely dated now and best used to help balance a broken coffee table leg.

"I'm sorry?"

"Tammy and Tom are going to be here in ten minutes. Don't you have some materials to gather?" She glares at me as she spins around on her pointy-yellow-leather heels. I hate Lucy. Hate her with a passion with the one exception that she loves baseball. It was the only point in life that I not only agreed with her on but enjoyed talking to her about. We had even attended several Dodger games together which says something as I was able to put my hate aside for her seats behind home plate. How can you hate anyone who appreciates the hotness of baseball players? When our favorite Dodger was traded to the Cubs, she and I both drowned our sorrows at a sleazy sports bar near the stadium. It was a loss we could bond on.

"I'm ready." What a lie. How could anyone be ready for a future train wreck? I had spent part of the weekend reading the manuscript and understood why the managing editor, Dave, had spent so much time cursing and fighting with Lucy. More than one coffee mug had been hurled across the board room recently. According to Dave, this book was a loser. According to Lucy, it was a relationship masterpiece put together by two loving geniuses who happened to be married to each other. Dave was also infuriated at how this whole project came about, completely under the table without any input by the editorial staff. You see, Lucy used to bunny-hump Tom way back when, so when he found out she was in publishing at Devore-Horizon, he came running and voila a book deal with an extra-large check appeared. Now there were three questions on everyone's mind.

How the hell did Tammy and Tom get a sweetheart advance for a piece of shit idea? You can do the math. He was still a pretty good-looking guy and Lucy had been long overdue for some action. She was an easy target.

Did Tammy know about the negotiation process or the past love affair?

If Tammy did not, who would be the lucky bastard who got to tell her, preferably at some pinnacle moment like the launch party of their book? That, my friends, was the real question.

It was bizarre that I was going to meet people who openly wrote about Tom's premature ejaculation problem and how at first Tammy used to chastise him but over time grew to accept it as something to love about him. My favorite line from the book had been..."Many times a Bounty paper towel had come to the rescue for cleaning up after Tom's well-intended yet misdirected efforts."

I was the last to arrive in the board room. All of the publishing suits were on one side of the table with Tammy, Tom and their agent, Leanne Bixner, on the other. Let's start with Tom the jack rabbit. In his 50s, salt and pepper hair, good looking guy but at some point got too much sun along the way. He looked like he had played endless games of tennis. You could tell he still worked out and if he was gay, he wouldn't have any trouble working the daddy scene in Palm Springs. He'd be a big hit amongst the hustlers because they could collect their $200 a lot faster than usual due to his hair trigger. Leanne Bixner looked like the bitch she was with unkempt and wiry hair. Unfortunate outfit and if she ever smiled, I swear she would break. The type of woman who is so uptight she could crack walnuts with her vagina. Then we come to Tammy. Tammy was a woman in her late fifties who was trying to hold onto what she could through face-lifts, too much Botox, cheap-pink-acrylic nails, bleached teeth and a helmet of dyed red hair that had been processed far, far too many times. (Gay Scout Rule # 6...Whatever you do, never, NEVER over-process). A fake smile was permanently plastered on her face while she kept one arm coiled around Tom's forearm. I would learn that for the duration of the meeting Tom would never get out of her clutches.

After the obligatory round of cheerful "Nice-to-meet-yous" we got down to business. Tom started in.

"Tammy and I are very excited about our new project *How to Keep the Fire Burning Even if You Are Divorcing.* Did everyone read our breakthrough bestseller *Kissing Kingdom?*" It was another meeting with morons. I could only imagine how long this torture would last.

OK, I'll get you up to speed on all of this. Let's see. Which piece of garbage should I start with first? *Kissing Kingdom* actually was a bestseller though I'd hardly call anything about it breakthrough. It was one of the semi-pamphlet books like the *5-Minute Manager* series that were popular in the late eighties. The premise of the book was you could solve any problem just by kissing for seven solid minutes. In the middle of a knock-down drag out fight? Start kissing. Walk in on your husband screwing the housekeeper? Start kissing, although due to their incompetent writing it was never clear as to whom you should start kissing, the husband or the maid. That brings us to the masterpiece for which we are going to kill trees as well as add to the jumble on Kindle. *How to Keep the Fire Burning Even if You Are Divorcing* was a "how-to" book on divorce with a twist. Divorce, according to Tammy and Tom, was no reason to stop the passion and sex. Isn't loss of passion and sex the reason so many people divorce in the first place? Or they realize that their partner is having passion and sex with someone else? It was pure genius!

Off in the distance I could hear the whistle blowing; train wreck dead ahead. The meeting went something like this. Everything Lucy suggested Leanne Bixner shot down, shook her head in disagreement at, or sighed out loud to in a big showy way. Or she'd throw in some comments like "I don't know about that."

Every time Tom started being a bit too vocal with his opinions Tammy would vice grip his forearm until he shut up. It was her personal volume control for him.

Tammy's tactic was cooing a compliment to someone in the room before presenting some demand. Tammy, very simply, was the one to watch out for in this group. At least you could see Leanne Bixner coming at you with that wiry hair and angry puss. Tom seemed like a typical nice guy who had been whipped into shape. Tammy shielded her evil with a coat of pink frosting. It's the frosting I'm wary of. It hides everything but after only a few licks you realize it's made with Crisco instead of butter and you're just biting into a turd cupcake.

I said nothing. I just sat there soaking it in and scanning my brain for the top ten media outlets I thought would be good fits for this puke. How the hell would this ever appeal to Millennials? When it was finally my turn to throw something into the ring, I of course threw out the usual stuff like *Today, Good Morning America, The View.* Shows I thought they would chomp on. I spoke all of this while my insides were screaming. This was going to be a nightmare media campaign. Producers would be laughing in my face when I pitched this one to them.

The meeting dragged on for approximately three years until Tammy suggested that Tom might need to use a restroom as he didn't have the same bladder control she did. He thanked her for giving him the opportunity then got up and went out of the room. The rest of us sat in complete silence. I wanted to run. Dave the editor kept shifting in his chair. Bixner clearly wanted to get out of there because she didn't make any extra money while Tom was pissing her time away in a urinal down the hall. Tammy and Lucy just stared at each other as if they each knew *exactly* what the scene was since they both had handled Tom's tennis racket. The tension was thick in the air. This is the hell that is my life.

CHAPTER SIX

GAY MAN S TUG-O-WAR

(Gay Scout Rule # 22…Friends Don't Play This Game)

THE MEETING WITH TAMMY AND TOM left me with a bad taste in my mouth. I had a foreboding feeling that this would be a situation which would end up causing me trouble. The combination of an author whose co-author-husband slept with your boss doesn't position itself to be very promising. Because it ran so long, I ended up having to stay late to finish some expense reports. I resented my evening being eaten away by Tammy and Tom. I hated them already. After a diligent hour of work on the reports I figured I had done enough and decided to head home.

I live in a four-story, rather large apartment building in Hollywood. It's a bullseye for starving actors, rockers, and an eclectic assortment of just about everything else. Like most of LA, my building occupies a location that used to have a historic building on it. True to LA form it's an example of history by adjacency as opposed to the real thing still being there. I can't remember now what that famous building was, but the landlord used it as a selling point when she showed me the place. When I first moved into the apartment it was a cheap deal because the neighborhood was still on the questionable side. But endless redevelopment projects had pushed the rents higher and higher. I was now paying a fortune for a shoebox in LA's version of Times Square. I had gone from cheap, hip and shaky, to expensive, hip and congested.

I pass my Nazi neighbors in the hallway and they smile and say hello like they always do. For Nazis they are very friendly. They are both from Georgia. I can never remember their names, but he is older with dyed hair and she is in her 20s with half her head shaved and a mullet down the back. She wears on a daily basis combat boots, camouflage pants and a white wife-beater. Tattoos run up and down her arms with various slogans and symbols sort of like a walking billboard for white supremacy. She has remained in touch with her feminine side however, as her accessories change regularly. She vacillates between swastika necklaces, skull and crossbones earrings, and a variety of other hate-wear like "White Power" scarves or bracelets. One time in the elevator with her, I was discussing conflict breaking out in the Middle East. She turned to me and said, "War makes me horny." I wanted out of there fast.

The male Nazi has a terrible body. I accidentally saw him naked on his balcony one day while I was leaning out to clean the outside of my bedroom window. Trust me...I paid a price for a spot-free shine. His tiny penis was hiding in an enormous jet-black bush that hadn't been whacked in ages. It was revolting.

The worst stench possible hits me in the face when I open the door to my apartment. I curse myself for not grinding the morning's eggshells down the disposal. I walk over to the sink and start to shove them into oblivion, adding a huge squirt of lemon Joy to make things smell better. You know, while my building is kind of the pits, my apartment isn't all that bad provided I remove rotting garbage. It's old and shabby but I've done some stuff here and there to make it look better than it really is, like painting the walls each a different color. Sort of like putting lipstick on a pig, though, because while the walls look cool, there's no hiding the old carpet with its cigarette burns and spilled wine stains. I turn on the Dodger game and then check my phone for texts. Nothing. Hmmm. I guess I went from getting a glowing review on the *How Did I Do?* form (which I keep in a handy dispenser above my bed) to not even getting a call or text? Men are weird.

I debate about texting Glenn an impromptu dinner suggestion but decide I might look desperate. I forgo my no games rule and decide to play it cool for a while. Just then my phone rings and I smile when I see who it is.

"Hey you, come out with me tonight." Glenn no, Tyler yes. Tyler and I met at a singles event when I first came to LA. He's older than me, totally crazy, but can be a lot of fun to hang around with. We never dated but hit it off as friends.

Tyler is the perfect solution to keep me from sitting around spending my evening sifting through Internet porn offerings in-between innings. "Meet you at the Mother Lode in thirty minutes." I hang up the phone, quickly change clothes and am out the door.

I eat a banana in the car. I figure it will provide the necessary nutrition I need for dinner yet allow me to have four beers and still keep within my calorie count for the day. When I arrive at the Mother Lode, an institution almost like Tyler, I spy him across the bar getting a jump on his first Bloody Mary.

Tyler's age is a bit of a mystery but most of us peg him to be somewhere in his fifties. Tonight, he's dressed in a loud Hawaiian shirt covered in magenta and yellow hibiscus flowers, white linen pants and crisscrossed leather sandals. His hair and beard are dyed a deep black and provide a striking contrast against his deeply tanned skin and bleached teeth. Gold bracelets dangle from his right wrist and on his left wrist is a gold Chopard watch with diamonds. Around his neck is a medal of St. Anthony on a gold chain. Two diamond studs are skewered into each earlobe. I often think that Tyler would have made a perfect Mr. Club Med 1976. He's handsome, looks like a player and has an international air about him. He's also one of the smartest people I know. Tyler was the son of an American diplomat and got to grow up in Brussels, Paris and Madrid. I was the son of an Army Captain and grew up in places like Fort Bragg, Fort Rucker and Fort Eustis.

It's always an experience with Tyler. You have to go into an evening with him with no expectations. Just let him lead you on the adventure or rather the mis-adventure as the case has been many times. Since he retired early in life he's always up for going out during the week when other friends like Miss Maggio are napping because they are too tired from their work day to have a quick cocktail.

There is a problem however with Tyler as a fellow bar hopper… getting dragged into a round of Gay Man's Tug-O-War. You see, gay men go to great lengths to avoid this nightmare situation as it has been the demise of many a friendship over the years. Even the most jaded queens will shudder at the mention of it. That's because Gay Man's Tug-O-War is when two friends are attracted to the same guy and all hell breaks loose.

There is great strategy used to avoid this. Careful screening of preferences amongst friends regarding height, skin color, background, profession, hair color, age etc. are mutually discussed at the beginning of friendships so you know who is a safe bet to take to a bar. For instance, my friend Mickey is a safe bet because I prefer my Twinkies wrapped in cellophane while he prefers them wrapped in sheets. He likes young blondes with air in their heads and no air in their spare tire. I don't mind a little spare tire as long as it comes with some experience in the sack, an in-depth conversation before hand, and the ability to pay for their own dinner. On paper Maggio is a perfect fellow hopper. Only problem is Mickey loses steam by eight thirty on weeknights which leaves us with either bingo halls or nursing homes for possible places to pick up single men. Tyler on the other hand likes exactly the same kind of guy I do which is a major issue when you happen to meet two guys at The Mother Lode bar who are in the US Navy. Always one to be patriotic, I was more than happy to talk to the thirty-three year-old named Jeff. Jeff it turns out was an oral surgeon for a Naval hospital in San Diego while Billy the forty-year-old was closer to Tyler's age and waist size I might add. The Tug-O-War began when Tyler decided he wanted the dentist as well. Both had great personalities and absolutely mind-blowing stories of sex on the high seas. I started thinking of the money I could make taking Jeff and Billy on a gay lecture tour, dispensing stories of getting blow-jobs underneath the flight deck of an aircraft carrier while warplanes were taking off overhead; Admirals and sea Captains clearing the dossiers and ship logs off their desks to jump on the nearest Ensigns; and a laundry list of hazing events that always seemed to involve getting covered in axle grease and being hosed down naked on the flight deck. Six months at sea seems to turn even the butchest homophobe into a pawing horn-dog. Tyler and I were slack jawed. For once the porno scenarios were actually true and we were in the presence of two men who just received exalted status for their tales of adventure.

The award went to Jeff however and that was for his tales of doing dental surgery on Navy Seals. He began telling us that when a man goes under anesthesia your body relaxes and you pee on yourself so they insert a catheter. But, did you know that after they knock you out they have to masturbate your penis until it's hard so it's easier for the nurse to get the tube in? Jeff went further to explain that when scheduling patients for surgery he would assign the retired Admirals in their seventies to be done by the other dentist on duty and made sure that all Navy Seals were on his watch. He described having to really concentrate on not getting too turned on in his loose-fitting scrubs when the nurse pulled back the surgical sheet to reveal one of God's gifts to creation lying naked and passed out in the dental chair. She would then slap on some gloves and go to work whipping that Seal into shape before she lubed the tube and hosed the hose. Personally, I think this would be an ideal time to send nurse Ratchett out for a coffee break. Then they stick a thermometer up the guy's ass to take his temperature. No wonder people feel an odd sense of "cheap" and "violated" along with severe pain after jaw surgery. We couldn't freaking believe it. Jeff said the first time he observed this surgery he about died realizing the same thing had happened to him when he had his jaw worked on. How humiliating. True or not it was a good story and they told it with conviction.

Tyler and I stood there stunned and enamored by Jeff. I don't know what it is about military guys but even the dentists have a certain sex appeal that's hard to beat. Now the game began. Tyler and I both trying to ply Jeff with our charms, funny bon mots and personal sex appeal. Billy was interested in Tyler but no, Tyler has to go after the guy that I am sure is interested in me. Every time I start to tell a good story an ever-drunker Tyler interrupts with some slurring commentary. I was getting agitated. The thought crossed my mind that if I had come alone I would not be dealing with this cock blocking but then I remembered that if Tyler had not called this evening I would be home on the couch.

As if the verbal jockeying wasn't enough, Tyler then started to physically get me out of the way. He pulled out a $100. "Kyle, I'll buy the next round if you'll be a sport and go get them. Guys what will it be?"

Damn him. Before I have a chance to quick think my way out of this ploy, Billy and Jeff have given me their cocktail orders. Tyler hands me the bill with a wicked smile and a "Beat that one Bitch!" grin that clearly puts him in the lead. I smile, grab the $100 and head to the bar.

It's an endless wait for the bartender as the place is wall-to-wall pecs. My head rotates back and forth between trying to catch the bartender's eye and seeing what Tyler is doing. I wouldn't put it past him to suddenly get them to leave and head off to another bar him telling them that he will tell me where to meet them on the way out. Finally, the bartender lumbers over and fills my order.

"$40.00 dude." I take a big swig of my T&T since as long as Tyler is paying I might as well order something pricier than beer. I give the bartender $10.00 in tip and pocket the change.

To my relief I have not been ditched as I'm jostled by the horde of guys that has now taken over the Lode. T&T, Screwdrivers and a Bloody Mary are getting sloshed down my arms. I look like a sticky, bleeding mess by the time I make it through the crowd.

"What the hell happened to you?" as he stands there looking annoyed. "What a mess Kyle, you're wearing half our drinks."

I shoot him a look of death making sure that only he can see me. "Give me a break, the crowd is killer in here tonight. Besides guys, I ran into a producer who works at Universal, so we chatted a bit. Sorry it took so long." What a lie, but it worked. Something told me these guys were the star-fuckers of the high seas.

"You know a producer?" asks Jeff, wide-eyed and thrilled now to be talking to me again. I could only imagine what story Tyler had regaled them with while I was gone. "Do you know any stars?"

"Oh sure, a bunch. I work with them all the time." Although I did work with producers Tyler knew I was lying about chatting one up. He knew it would take forever to get drinks as busy as this place was tonight. I was back in the lead. He interrupted.

"Kyle sweetie, don't forget my change now."

"Oh, Jack was telling me he was collecting money for the NBCUniversal Children's Fund for underprivileged kids, so I gave him a donation from both of us. I hope that was O.K." Got him again. More points for me.

"That's so thoughtful of you Kyle, thinking about children and all," says Billy. Score! Tyler is clearly annoyed. He knows there is no producer, needy kids fund, or a chance in hell that he will see his change. On top of everything I just made $50.

The evening ends with an exchange of numbers, plans to meet again in two weeks when the sixth fleet is back in West Hollywood, and an angry Tyler who I guess could be termed collateral damage for my good fortune at being the one the dentist would prefer to give an oral exam to.

The walk to the parking lot to get our cars was an uncomfortable event. I laughed to myself that I had ended up not spending the evening thinking once about Glenn but now had an angry friend to deal with. Still, he knew the rules. He had a sure bet with Billy but took a chance on moving in on my mark which I felt was unfair. The silence was finally broken when we reached my car. We said our good-byes with a slightly bitter undertone along with the hug. So, I had won this round. Who knew if the dentist would ever call anyway? It was just one of those things that happen sometimes between friends. The slate would be cleaned by the next time we went out.

CHAPTER SEVEN

BUSTIER

Black Leather Has Its Moment

THE RINGING OF THE PHONE BLEW ME OUT OF BED. My heart was pounding as the racket pierced into my soul, into my bones, into my…what the hell time was it? Clock. Where are you? 3:06 a.m. Damn. Who the hell? I can't see my phone without my contacts, if this is Tyler calling drunk to rehash everything I'm going to…

"Hey." Melanie. Didn't she know what time it was?

"What are you doing?"

"Mel, it's the middle of the night, I was sleeping. What's going on?"

"I need you to come over."

Now, many people would hate a friend who would call in the middle of the night, wake you up and then ask you to put on your clothes and drive over to their place. But that's the kind of friendship Melanie and I had. A middle of the night phone call was important, and you didn't need to justify any request. It was just an understanding that went unspoken between two friends. (Gay Scout Rule #8… You are *there* for your friends)

"What's going on?"

"Just get over here. I need you. I'm in a lot of pain right now."

My mind raced. Please tell me some freak didn't hurt her. Please no. I pictured Melanie black and blue, raped, beaten. I know she felt empowered by what she did for a living and that it was her choice but deep down in the pit of my stomach I knew that some day some fucker would mess her up.

Everything was blurry. Contacts. Shoes. Car keys. I was more awake now; curiosity flowing through me like a river. I zipped down Hollywood, left on Fairfax, right on Fountain left on Kings. I got to Melanie's condo and pulled into the red zone because it was the only place to park. I pressed her apartment code. Ringing. More ringing. More ringing. Where the hell was she? I reached for my cell phone, ready to call her when I realized I had left it back in the apartment as well. The intercom finally came alive.

"Kyle?"

"Yeah, let me in." The door lock clicked open.

Even luxury condos have creepy hallways at night. Something doesn't feel right to be the only one awake knowing that behind each door people are snoring away. I got to her apartment. She had cracked the door for me and I walked in.

There was Melanie, standing in the middle of her living room in a black leather bustier. Mascara was smeared down her reddened, swollen face.

"Don't just stand there like staring like an idiot. Help me out of this thing."

"What's going on? What happened? Did someone mess with you?"

"What? No. Kyle, hurry. I can't get out of this thing. The lace knotted up and it's cutting off my circulation."

This is one of those moments when crystal-clear reality hits you. There was no rapist, no freak, no broken bones. Just a damn knot.

"Mel, are you fucking kidding me? *THIS* is why you had me come over here?" She looked at me like I was insane.

"Kyle, so help me God. If you don't get me out of this thing, I'm going to kill you. The knot is stuck, it's cutting into my skin, and I'm swelling up. I've been working on this for over an hour and I need help."

I went over and looked at the knot. It was exceptionally taut. I mean, like it was glued together. "How did you get this so tight?" I worked and worked on it.

Melanie wheeled around and looked at me with a fierce glance. "I can't believe I'm stuck in this damn thing. Get it off of me! Later today, at eight, I'm being picked up by my Construction Worker, for a real date, for *the* date, and right now I am being branded like a cow. I have a date with a *real* guy. With the kind of guy who doesn't use peanut butter as foreplay. Do you hear me?"

She was right. This was a crisis.

Cutting the laces was out of the question as they were so imbedded into her skin that I'd risk cutting her too. The design of the bustier was that it was all pulled tight by one knot, in back, which somehow Melanie had managed to pull tighter and tighter by her impatience.

"How did you get into this in the first place?"

"I put it on at the club and Carla laced me up. I didn't think it was going to be so hard to get out of."

I started shaking my head and the tears started flowing down her face. I was letting her down. She was still a prisoner of Trashy Lingerie. (Gay Scout Rule # 11...What would Martha Stewart do?). I went into the kitchen.

"Where the hell are you going?"

"Just a minute I think I have a solution." I went riffling through her kitchen drawers until I found it. I brought the corkscrew back to the living room, took the pointy end and tried putting it through the knot. I struggled and the corkscrew slipped, nicking her skin, causing her to scream. I winced when I saw the drop of blood trickle to the surface.

"Damn it! I'd like to be alive for this date if you don't mind."

Working again with the corkscrew I finally got it through until I had enough leverage to pull. The knot came free and Melanie's tits popped out like two pink Jack-in-the-boxes. She pulled the bustier off and ran around the living room like an un-caged nudist chicken.

"Thank you, Jesus, thank you." She started to frantically rub the red marks on her skin. Wow, she was really, really marked. I could see crisis number two coming down the pipeline. Melanie went buck naked to the mirrored closet doors in her bedroom. She gasped in horror as she saw a road map of the bustier perfectly etched into her flesh.

"NO! Damn! My God, my date tonight! Look at my skin, it's a mess."

The tears started flowing again. Even Martha would have a hard time removing those tire tracks in her flesh not to mention the stab wound I gave her. I realized something. One knot had caused so much pain. Technically, it was just a knot that was in the way. But in the scheme of things it was so much more. That knot represented a block to happiness. This was a woman, who despite her job, her attitude, her hardened exterior...she just wanted to be loved. She was tired. Tired of all the losers who had come before the construction worker, the guys who had let her down, left her feeling demoralized, and left her alone. That knot was getting in the way of finding that one soulmate in life to just *be* with. That person to untie life's future knots for you.

In a stupid kind of way later today was the date she had spent a lifetime preparing for. This was the guy she had held out for, who she was falling in love with, who she had been looking for all those years. And tonight was the night she was going to sleep with him for the first time.

And that knot had stood in her way.

"What am I going to do?" The tears started flowing again.

"Let's get you in a tub." I went into the bathroom and started a hot bath figuring warm water might be the best thing to get the marks out. At the minimum it would help calm her down. I threw in some pink powdery stuff she kept in a bowl by the edge of the tub and swished it around with my hand. The smell of gardenias was overpowering. Yikes. How can women stand this? I'm definitely not the kind of guy who wants to smell like a florist. Give me sweat and beer breath any day over flowery stuff.

She crawled in the tub while I went into the kitchen. I found some Stoly in the freezer and made us a couple of cocktails with a lone can of ginger ale. While I was making the drinks, I noticed a bunch of loose photographs lying on the kitchen table next to an unfinished scrapbook album. I walked over to steal a look. The pictures must have been of Melanie when she was a little girl, and in them, she was dressed up in all kinds of pageant wear. Fluffy dresses and sparkly crowns. In some of them a woman I thought must be her mom was wearing a matching outfit; both of them wearing sashes that said Mother –Daughter First Place. Mel looked like JonBenét except with black hair. I'd never seen pictures of Melanie's family before and I felt like I was invading her privacy but found it hard to look away. Nowhere in Melanie's condo were there any pictures of her family or past unless they were of her friends and life in Los Angeles. The picture album was leather bound and looked expensive. She had taken obvious care to put each picture in its place with perfect spacing between them. Melanie had never mentioned being in pageants when she was a little girl and we'd joked about JonBenét before. I wonder why she didn't mention it. But in some ways that made sense. Melanie talked about her family back east but not much. She had the same kind of contentious relationship with her parents that I did with mine so in some ways it was less painful to discuss it.

I went back into the bathroom, sat on the edge of the tub and handed her a drink. She took a long gulp then just sat there looking at me. Dejected.

"The marks will come out Mel, they just need some time." She surveyed her stomach, frowning.

"I'm so frustrated Kyle. I really want tonight to be great."

"I know you do but, maybe you shouldn't put so much pressure on yourself to make everything perfect. Things happen."

"I don't know why but I feel like so much is riding on this guy. Why is that? The stakes seem to get higher every time I meet a good one. It's seems to be so rare of an occurrence that when it actually happens, I feel incredible pressure to make it work."

I knew exactly what she meant. We weren't in our 20s anymore and the time for trial and error had elapsed. Each birthday was clicking off a mean-spirited biological clock. For Mel it was about getting married and having children. For me it was crossing that gay boundary where I'd be forever single. Which birthday would be the one that would define me as off the market?

There was no logical reason for either of us to feel this way. We were two funny, smart and good-looking people who had a lot to offer. We each had two failed long-term / live-in relationships under our belt, knew what the potential in life could be, but damn-us-both-to-hell we just kept striking out. We were still alone and that frightened the hell out of us.

The years since had been filled with bad dates, broken hearts, and the frustration she spoke of. When someone of quality did come along, which seemed like once in a blue moon, we felt the pressure, incredible pressure that mounted each time we stepped up to the plate. When was it going to be our turn to hit the homerun?

I knew one of the reasons Mel wanted me to back down from Glenn was because she knew that I knew there was potential there. It was her way of helping to alleviate some of the pressure that the relationship, or I, might fail again. We understood the art of trying to be the perfect date without putting up a false front. We were both smart enough to know you have to be true to you who are but at the same time finesse the reality of life so that it didn't seem so bad to the other person. I wasn't in debt. I had just paid a financial price for being able to live a carefree life and that's why I was the age I was and still not a homeowner. This in a land where material wealth was a critical factor for desirability. Mel wasn't a dominatrix. Instead she was an enterprising businesswoman who was taking advantage of her natural assets to get ahead in life. My professional life was about promotion and spin and we applied those same principles to our personal lives as well.

"I wish I had some answers for you Mel but I'm just as clueless as I ever was." You'd think the trial and error period lasting for the past fifteen years would have given me great wisdom. But it only made my lack of it all the more frustrating.

CHAPTER EIGHT

GLENN

Sexy Puzzle

BY THE TIME I HAD FINISHED RUBBING cold cream into Melanie's lash marks it was time to get ready for work. I would have made it on time if my car hadn't been towed from the red zone in front of her building. It took me almost an hour to find out in which impound lot it ended up. Then another hour getting there and standing in line with a bunch of angry people. It was a rude awakening for all of us.

I sat at my desk wondering how I was going to manage on the 1.5 hours of sleep I had caught between fighting with Tyler and fighting with a bustier. I was so out of it.

Phone.

"Come have dinner with me tonight."

Of all nights. I had planned to hit the sheets early so I could make it through the rest of this week without dark circles under my eyes. I also could hear Melanie's lecture in my head about how I always came running when he called.

"Um, tonight's not the *best* night for me, any chance we could meet tomorrow?" I was proud I threw that out there.

"Business dinner tomorrow. Can you hold?"

Before I could answer I was hearing audio spots for the latest Warner Brothers flicks. You have to hand it to Hollywood as they don't leave any promotional opportunity unturned.

Click. "Sorry, back again. Yeah, tonight's really the only night that would work for me during the week. It's crazy here because we have shows running over budget. I was thinking you could drop by my place at eight and we'd go from there."

So basically, I either follow Warner Brothers' schedule, or I don't get the date I'd been hoping for until the weekend or next week. I decided momentum was the best choice and despite being dead tired I was feeling pretty squirrelly. "OK, I'll see you tonight then. What kind of food do you want to grab?"

"Oh, I don't care. Let's see what we're in the mood...sorry but there's a problem here. I'll see you at eight." Click.

The rest of my day was a complete mind-screwing-blur. I floated through my work wishing I had the talent that one of the manuscript readers had. She was able to prop herself up with her head looking down into the pages, close her eyes, and fall asleep. She looked to be deep in thought reading away. I wasn't so lucky. I had to tap into my energy reserves and try to figure out how I'd pull it together by eight.

The day just kept glacially grinding along until it was finally time for my escape. I'm putting stuff in my bag when the phone rings and I stupidly pick it up on a reflex.

"This is Kyle."

"Kyle?" I hear two voices in unison and reel back in horror. I realize I have just been caught in the Tammy and Tom trap. "Tammy *here*." "Tom here."

No! I need to leave. "Hi, uh, what's up?"

"We wanted to go over the *media* plan you sent us," cooed Tammy. "You know I can tell you worked very *hard* on this but (OK, she was just about to slam me) Tom and I just don't feel this is comprehensive *enough* for *HKFBEUAD* (*How to Keep the Fire Burning Even if You Are Divorcing*). It took longer to say the acronym than it did to say the whole damn title. Moron.

"I don't understand why you think it's not comprehensive enough. That plan is about twenty-five percent larger than our usual campaign." Lucy had told me to bump up the amount of media outlets I hit. The budget on this book just kept going up and up. Accounting must be screaming.

"Tammy and I feel…"

"*Tom*, let *me* finish please. What Tom and I want to say is that this kind of plan might be appropriate for your other, *less important* titles, but it is clearly not going to be the caliber of plan we expect for *HKFBEUAD*." Expect?

"It's not that Tammy and I feel you have failed in any way, bud, and we want to make sure you feel that." Thanks for the words of encouragement.

I quickly realize an advantage to the fact I was just walking out of the office is that Lucy had left early. "Tell you what. Lucy has left for the day but first thing tomorrow I'll go over this with her. I'm happy to reevaluate it for you." That should shut them up.

"We would *appreciate* that. Goodbye from Tammy"

"Goodbye from Tom."

The freak show had ended. I grabbed my keys and headed out the door. Traffic across town by this point was a unbelievable nightmare. Each minute that ticked off was one less minute of restorative repair I would not be able to make on the damages from the night before. I tried to calm myself because hellish traffic makes me a raging lunatic. I looked around at my fellow miserables and noticed other people doing their stress management techniques. Meditation, yelling at the Uber driver, or texting. Anything to compensate for the time that was being ripped away from their lives. Unfortunately, there was no ice in my car to start in on those dark circles.

I finally reach my apartment building. When the elevator arrives, Diane, the rocker chick from down my hall, steps out.

"Wow you look like terrible. Tie one on last night?"

"You could say that. Have a nice evening." One sentence with Diane had the potential to turn into a forty-five-minute conversation so I've learned to end the conversation after the first response. As long as you physically kept moving you could usually escape. Once inside the elevator I looked at my reflection in the metal button panel. I did look bad.

Reaching my front door, I realize I only have one hour to get ready and maybe grab a quick cat nap. Damn. It's times like these you have to refer to the manual. (Gay Scout Rule # 17...*Always* keep two sized-to-your-eyes spoons in the freezer). Stretching out on my black leather couch I flip on CNN, lay back, and apply the spoons to my eyes. God it feels great to just stretch out. I mentally go through my closet putting my outfit together while Anderson Cooper carries on. My brain vacillates between what to wear and wondering what Anderson looks like naked.

When I woke up not hearing any familiar droning, I knew I was in trouble. Clock? *Damn!* I now had ten minutes to get ready and get there. No need to slap myself awake on this one, the adrenaline was pumping new life into me as I shot into the shower in record speed. Thankfully, I had at least not fallen asleep until I had pre-planned what I was going to wear. Indigo-gray cotton shirt, French jeans that make me look like I'm hung like a bear, and black Euro-trash shoes. I was in a sudsing frenzy. Rinse. Rinse. Shower off. Grab my towel. Was almost dried off when I find a bunch of soap still under my balls. Cursing, I throw the towel on the floor, get back in the shower, re-rinse and then as I'm stepping out of the shower the wet spot on the floor causes me to come crashing down against the side of the tub. I'm rolling around wet, naked, and in an incredible amount of pain. My right shoulder, elbow, ribs and hip cry out in agony. At least I was getting dry as I rolled around on the discarded towel; a time-saving technique I hoped I'd never repeat.

Grabbing the countertop I pull myself up. *Slowly.* I catch my reflection in the mirror and forget my pain for a moment when I see how well the cat nap and spoons worked on my face. The pain shoots through me again as I stand completely up. Oh my God. Deep breath.

Hobbling into the bedroom I do my best to get the ironing board set up. Bending down to plug in the iron was another adventure in torture but I notice that the more I move around the better I become at pain management. I pull it together pretty fast all things considered. It's 8:01 p.m. I start to reach for the phone to tell Glenn I would be late when I decide against it. Let him be the one waiting around this time. Besides, he's only fifteen minutes away.

I pull off the freeway into Studio City which is one of the only acceptable places to live if you have to live in the valley. The Studio City hills overlook both Universal Studios, Warner Brothers and in the distance, Disney. It is a neighborhood of choice for those working in high-paying jobs on the movie lots.

My car burps its way up Chisolm Lane (It seems like it should be running better considering I just had it in the shop) until I make the turn onto Leaf View Terrace. On one side are homes overlooking the San Fernando Valley and on the other side is mountain sagebrush containing coyotes, rattlesnakes and scorpions. I can handle things with fur but the other two are definitely downsides of living this high in the hills.

Pulling into the roughed-granite (as Glenn describes it) drive-way I hoped my car wouldn't leak while parked there. I imagine a furious gardener with a can of Ajax and a toothbrush cursing me tomorrow afternoon. When I turn off the engine, I realize I didn't bring my contact lens case with me. Luckily, I keep a spare in the glove compartment along with a stash of sleeping pills and breath mints for these kind of situations. (Gay Scout Rule # 2...*Always* be prepared). Now, you may have just chastised me for not having a stash of condoms in there as well, but as all you sluts out there know, never store a condom in a place where the temperature soars above 98 degrees. Ambien and Altoids have a much better glove compart-ment shelf-life.

As I slide out of the car, I re-live my shower disaster all over again and it takes me a moment to work the kinks out. While I stretch, I notice that all of the flowers have recently been replaced along the driveway and in the pots by the door. The old ones were flourish-ing last time I was here but if you have money in the land of false impressions then it's normal to regularly change your landscaping each month. Why keep something around just because it's blooming?

It's nineteen after. OK, I'm still relatively on time. I press the intercom button and wait trying not to look into the surveillance camera. Another LA rule is always act cool in front of cameras. Glenn's voice crackles that he would be there in a minute as he is out back by the pool. After a little bit I hear him clomp through the house. He unlocks the vintage door, salvaged from an old monastery that was being torn down to put up a mini mall, and pulls it open. There are those blue eyes again. They pop out against the ice-blue short-sleeved shirt he's wearing. His shirt is somewhat silky, and it shimmers about his waist un-tucked. The best part is that it's unbuttoned just enough so that his chest hair is toying with me. His strong forearms are tan and covered with a masculine dusting of dark hair that runs down to nice big hands one of which is collared by a James Bond-type Omega watch. His lower half is poured into a pair of casual European-cut pants that frame his crotch like a piece of priceless art before cascading down his legs to a cool pair of Italian shoes. He is casual, classy and sexy all rolled into one package. I can't wait to get him out of those clothes.

"I was beginning to wonder if you had gotten lost." Cool. He had been getting anxious about my arrival. "Come here." He grabs me and pulls me in for a hello kiss. I thought I was going to pass out from the pain. How was I going to make it through this night?

"I just need to fetch my keys and we can go. We'll leave through the garage." He bolts the door, punches a code into the alarm, then goes into the kitchen on his key hunt. I stand there looking around his living room, an odyssey in white, beige and a very light, dusty gray. There are several pieces of bronze sculpture, and the painting on the wall is an original someone. I can't quite make out the signature, but it looks like de Kooning. I'm too embarrassed to ask but am still impressed at how many of my yearly salaries are hanging on his walls. There's also a Picasso somewhere because he mentioned it one time. I remember him telling me something about the housekeeper not dusting it correctly. I had never seen it but would be able to recognize Picasso's style and signature in any event at least better than de Kooning. The TV was non-existent unless you looked up at the cherry wood panel that ran across the ceiling. When you turned on the TV the panel opened and an eighty-five-inch QLED lowered from the ceiling. I don't know which was cooler: the TV, the un-seen Picasso or the alleged De Kooning.

A few minutes later we're buzzing down the hill in his Cherry-Red Astin Martin with hand-stitched-camel-leather seats. The car matched him perfectly. Pretty hot. I figure I won't comment on how great it is; deciding to play it cool since I was feeling a bit out of my element. *His* car didn't burp, and if it ever did, cash probably came out instead of transmission fluid. I sit there starting to plan a strategy for the sex that is sure to come later. I figure the bruising won't show up until tomorrow. Maybe the best ploy is to mask my cries of pain into grunts of ecstasy. When you think about it sex sounds and looks like torture anyway. Pay attention when someone is having the Big O; my God you'd think you'd just shot them with their eyes rolling back in their head and a grimace on their face.

We pull up to Astra; a hot little bistro in the Valley that is frequented by the locals. It specializes in blond wood decor, wood-fire pizzas, and a mixture of various gay and straight couples out for the evening. One thing I love about LA is the mish-mash of gay, straight, whatever. No one cares who you're sleeping with, only how you are connected to the industry.

· · ·

Glenn is funny. I like that. He catches me off guard more than once during the evening with his commentary. As I relax into the meal, I forget the pain in the side of my body, Tammy and Tom, and my burping car. I just have fun. I start being more who I am, countering his funny lines with some of my own. It's a natural cadence that I love. A wonderful sense of peace comes over me. This is what it's about right? That person who removes the bad stuff from your life so there's room to breath and laugh and smile. It feels easy once you get there but the journey is anything but.

The night chill has set in outside. The warm glow of the fire pit bounces off the cozy walls of the restaurant. It's sort of a late-night magic hour. That hour before sunset where your skin glows and you look fantastic. His blue eyes bounce the firelight back to me.

· · ·

A warm smile during the drive home. Complete quiet as the Astin purrs its way up the steep hill.

We're silent too when we enter his house; the sound of our footsteps resonating against the marble floor. The ambient light of the city below, and the moon up above, lights his living room. We stand there just kind of looking at each other in the quiet. He gently puts his hand up to the side of my face just kind of holding it there... suspending the moment in this Valley of solitude. Our eyes lock and there is that smile on our lips that runs right to the center of our souls. A smile so deep that it makes me forget all the pain.

CHAPTER NINE
MORNING BREATH

Morning Puzzle

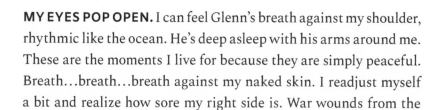

MY EYES POP OPEN. I can feel Glenn's breath against my shoulder, rhythmic like the ocean. He's deep asleep with his arms around me. These are the moments I live for because they are simply peaceful. Breath...breath...breath against my naked skin. I readjust myself a bit and realize how sore my right side is. War wounds from the dating front.

Last night had a certain magic quality to it. The sex rocked, there was no doubt about that. This guy knows how to move. Just something cool about it all. The moonlight, I guess. That always seems to add something, even to a meaningless one-night-stand, which this certainly wasn't. This had been a real date, the kind where you spent the night and weren't handed your pants and watch at 1:00 a.m. with some lame excuse about an early morning meeting or a plane to catch. Everything had just flowed along naturally, and nothing was forced. I looked at good sex and some romance as mini vacations from people like Tammy and Tom or problems like how to get the landlord to replace the moldering carpet without raising the rent.

The rising sun was beginning to shed some light around the room allowing my eyes to rove around my surroundings with the benefit of being able to see more details. His bedroom was rather simple. Not many personal photos or items which I thought was kind of unusual. Then again, a "less is more" theme seemed to permeate his interior plan, so I guess they were tucked away in the office or what have you. I had never been given the official tour of the house as it was divided into two distinct areas. The rooms I had seen, including the master bedroom and bath, were all located on one side of the floor plan. According to Glenn the other rooms were guest rooms, laundry, den, office, storage etc. and I didn't ask for a tour since he didn't offer it up.

The room was big with a king-sized bed and a minimal amount of furniture. White and putty were the predominate colors of choice. I admired the closet space as the room had three double-sliding-door closets. You could literally have a closet for business / formal, dressy / casual, and casual / gym. I imagined how liberating it must be to not have to break into a sweat by cramming clean clothes into an already over-stuffed single closet. A friend in Florida had turned one of his spare closets into a mini dungeon so my mind really started to churn as to what was behind those doors. Rows of suits and Ralph Lauren or jackboots and a whip? This is the wonder of dating someone new as you never know what is going to pop out from behind door number three.

Glenn shifted and stirred a bit then rolled over onto his left side. I followed suit and we spooned in the opposite direction. Now it was my breath on his shoulder. The completion of the equation. Contentment.

The clock said 6:03 a.m. Cool. I had enough time for us to snuggle and go another round because morning sex is just about the best possible way to start the day. I'd be able to drop into Hollywood by doing the Cahuenga / Mulholland / Outpost route that would bypass the Highland mess. Then I'd be home, do a quick change and head down to mid-Wilshire and be at work with time to spare. Geographically, this relationship was in tune with my agenda.

Glenn started to stir again so maybe that next round wasn't too far off. I tasted my mouth and puffed into my cupped hand to get a reading on the oral quality of my being. Problem. I also need to piss like a racehorse, so I slide across the Egyptian sheets and onto the floor. He snoozed away while I popped into the bathroom.

While urinating into his Italian toilet I notice how neat and tidy the bathroom is. No random clutter all over counters like my place. I walk over to the sink and look into the mirror. I can see bruising down my side, but I am nonetheless looking pretty hot with my tousled hair and sleepy eyes. I re-tousle my hair so it looks like I just woke up on a movie set and then figure I need to solve my breath issue.

Now, the beauty of this kind of bathroom is that everything is neatly in its place, but when you need some mouthwash or tooth-paste and don't want to wake the hottie that's asleep in the next room, it's a bit of a problem. I'd have to start rummaging through the medicine chest or drawers to find what I need, and I didn't want him to hear that because he'd think I was snooping. I stand there trying to figure out what to do. I decide the medicine chest is too personal, so I'll try the little drawer by the sink. That would be the most logical place to store the toothpaste especially since it's on the right-hand side of the sink and he's right-handed. I slowly pull on it but it's stuck. I wiggle it but it won't budge. Damn. I yank it ever so slightly and it pops open making a crackling noise.

Rats! It's completely empty with the exception of a stapler and a box of Q-Tips. Why would you keep a stapler in a bathroom? It was the first warning sign he may be crazy but then again, we all have our quirks. I slid the drawer shut and rinsed my mouth with water while using one of the Q-Tips as a toothbrush. I figure it would at least be an improvement from where I was five minutes ago.

Glenn was awake when I went back into the room. I hoped he hadn't heard me struggle with the drawer.

"Hey sexy," he said in a gravelly morning voice. He added a smile to go with the compliment. "Come here."

I hopped under the covers grateful I had pre-planned my mouth issue which was now in a state of natural freshness. He pulled me into him, and our mouths met. Now I felt pain not only in my side but in my taste buds. He tasted terrible but was intent on continuing the kiss. Pulling back, he smiles and reaches into the bedside drawer. I figure he's grabbing some morning sex supplies but instead out comes a pack of Big Red chewing gum. He pulls out a piece and hands it to me.

"Have some gum." He doesn't take one for himself. Great. I'm getting pinned for having the nasty breath when I'm not even the culprit. Like when you are in an elevator with someone and they fart as they exit to their floor; incriminating you at the next stop when someone gets in.

I started chewing and kissing at the same time so he'd get the benefit of the lone stick. (Gay Scout Rule #12...Conserve critical supplies). Half an hour later with a wad of gum jokingly stuck to the headboard, we accepted the fact our jobs were looming.

"I've got to get going," he says, standing up to stretch. "Do you need to shower here?"

Need? "No I'm cool. I have to head home anyway on my way to work. Wouldn't have a cup of coffee in the plans would you?"

"Oh, you know, I don't do the coffee and OJ thing. I have some cans of V8 if you want to take one of those." While I appreciated his trying to find an alternate solution, I'm a big believer that tomato juice is only drinkable when accompanied by Stoly, Tabasco and an outdoor brunch location.

"No thanks, I'll grab a coffee on my way in to work." I threw on my clothes with him standing there monitoring as if he wants to get me out of there, cross me off on his to-do list, and then proceed with his shower. I could tell this guy was into line items on a daily agenda. He has the same smile on his face that a nurse has when she calls you and says the doctor will see you; it was just kind of plastered on but did have a note of sincerity to it.

We headed to the front door and he replaces the nurse smile with a rocking good-bye kiss and then grins at me with genuine warmth. "Last night *and* this morning were absolutely great," he says. "I'll call you to do something this weekend."

Stepping outside I hear the wooden door bolt behind me. Before getting into my car I check for leakage, but it looks like I hadn't left any damage. A definite plus.

As I drove the drive of shame, of which I felt none, I was on perma-grin. Mornings are best when you are on your way home after a great night and an eye-popping morning. The sun seems so much more cheerful, as if it's inviting you to the wonderful breakfast buffet of life, and you don't mind that you didn't get the amount of sleep you normally prefer. My mind played with possibilities of where all of this could go.

Once home I raced through my shower and was heading out the door when my phone rang. I was surprised to see it was Mel this early in the a.m.

"Hey, can you meet me at Makin' Biscuits on your way to work?"

"What the hell are you doing up at this hour? How was the date with the construction worker?"

"Incredible, that's why I'm up. He had to get up at quarter to five to go install doorframes. Pretty cool huh? Come on, can you grab a quick one?"

Actually, I was already running early despite having worked sex and the drive home into my morning schedule. "OK, I can be there in ten minutes.

"Fab. See you then."

What's amazing about LA is how a place like Makin' Biscuits is busy even on a weekday. Many of the patrons are dressed for a day in the sun or the gym instead of an office. When do these people earn a living? Mel was already there, a possible first in our friendship. She was wearing jeans and a T-shirt, her long black hair pulled back in a ponytail.

I slid into the booth wincing in pain.

"What's the matter with you? Sex too rough?"

"I slipped in the bathroom last night. I'm lucky I didn't kill myself."

"I told you sex in the shower is a bad idea."

"It was at my place as I was getting ready. I was rushing around because I fell asleep on the couch. Anyway, spill it. Tell me about the construction worker."

"Oh Kyle, I have to tell you, I think I'm falling in love with the guy."

"Really? Wow. I take it the sex was good."

"Beyond good but that's not the only reason you moron. It's just icing on an already wonderful cake. I have to tell you Kyle, this guy is different. There's just something about him, I can't quite pin it down, but something that tells me I have a chance for this to go somewhere."

"Mel that's fantastic."

"He's caring and funny. Sexy as all get out and can carry on an intelligent conversation. Plus, he made me feel like a million dollars."

I was happy for her. Things seemed to be changing for the both of us. Had we finally reached that line that divided our single lives from our relationship lives?

"What about you? Did the cadaver deliver the goods?"

"Will you stop? Yeah, he delivered the goods all right. But first we had the most romantic dinner. The romance has finally kicked in. I love when that happens. I can tell there's a spark there. It was just right you know. Not a mind-blowing time but just right, comfortable, and relaxed. I slept like a baby too."

Mel just looked at me. I could tell that while she wants to see me happy her gut feeling was she didn't like Glenn. Would she ever?

"I can see myself living with this guy." Another odd look.

"Kyle, is that because of the house or because of him."

"Give me some credit Mel. I mean I might joke around about wanting a great lifestyle, but I wouldn't sell *myself* just to have a nice car." The minute I said it I regretted it. She got a steely look on her face that she was trying to cover up. I had hit a chord in her. It wasn't meant the way she was taking it but I know that she was hurt. Damn. There was some silence while I tried figuring a way out of this.

"Everything's a compromise," she said. Let's order.

CHAPTER TEN

EMOTIONAL JOGGING

Getting Off the Treadmill

DESPITE OFFENDING MELANIE AT BREAKFAST, I was on cloud nine most of the day. Things were looking up for me. Tammy and Tom's seven phone calls didn't seem to get on my nerves as much as they normally did, my boss left me alone, and I had this great tan-like glow to my face. It's amazing what some romance and good sex can do for one both inside and out.

I was looking forward to tonight. Melanie, Mickey and I had plans to meet at nine for a late dinner. Mel was pulling the late afternoon / early evening shift and Mickey and I would be through with our workout by then. Mickey was dying to try a new BBQ place called When Pigs Die that had just opened so we all agreed to forgo the diets in search of fatty pork product. Mickey and I allowed ourselves to do this since we had agreed to add an extra thirty minutes to the workout this evening.

Jogging side by side at the enormous 24 Hour Fitness located at ground zero in West Hollywood, we chatted about our day and I told Mickey about the offending comment I made to Mel.

"For Pete's sake Kyle. It's not like you said somethin' that wasn't true. I mean after all, Mel doesn't exactly pull in your normal paycheck."

"Yeah, you know I have no issues with how she makes her money, but it came out all judgmental."

"Kyle, she squirts naked HR men with milk from squirt guns. That's the reality of her retirement plan. If she doesn't have a problem with it I wouldn't worry about your comment."

"That's just it. By the look on her face I think she does have an issue with it."

"Then she should switch businesses. Melanie is plenty smart to do anything she wants. Let's face it. She drives an astronomically expensive car and pays for that luxury condo because of what she does. And to be honest, when I'm sittin' there countin' beans for PricewaterhouseCoopers, ready to scream from the boredom, I wish I had someone to paddle, or squirt or cover in mayonnaise. Then I could at least say I had an innerestin' day at the office. I envy her sometimes."

Mickey did have a point. While unconventional, Mel's job did have the great advantage of being interesting and something different. Her "same-old, same-old" was someone else's never in a million years.

We kicked up the pace on the treadmills to a run. Mickey has amazing stamina so it's always a challenge to keep up with him. He pushes my limits and never lets me slack.

"So, what's up on the datin' front. Seen Glenn lately?"

"Yeah, last night. It was great. I don't know, Mickey. This one could be a keeper."

"Even as old as he is?"

"You know, at first it kind of bothered me, but then the more I thought of it I figure why should it? If someone is caring, hot and a good catch doesn't that outweigh the age difference?"

"I guess. Mel would say no of course. I don't think she likes him at all."

"She hasn't even met him yet. Talk about judgmental."

"She's just concerned for you, Kyle. She doesn't want to see her best friend go down the emotional sewer again. Me neither for that matter."

"Well add me to that list but if I don't put myself out there and let myself be vulnerable then what am I ever going to gain?"

"OK, you need to stop watchin' old reruns of *Oprah*. Kyle, just fuck around until it all falls into place. You think too much about all of this stuff. Just let life happen."

"I don't watch old *Oprah* shows."

"Go with the flow."

"You know, I've always noticed that people who say "go with the flow" want you to go with the flow as long as it's *their* flow. Total control sentence."

"Maybe. That's something I think Los Angeles could learn from farm country. People here think they are all relaxed and such, but they are really uptight."

"You're probably right."

"Kyle, men are clueless. The majority of them are emotionally unavailable and let's not even get into the internalized homophobia and fear of intimacy statistics."

"That's what I like about Glenn. So far, he's passed the alcoholic test and doesn't seem to be afraid of the close stuff. In fact, he kind of checks in with me to make sure I'm not going to freak and run."

"Well, I'd expect someone his age to have dealt with those issues but keep your eyes peeled. You never know when that skeleton is going to come dancing out of that closeted past. He is out isn't he?"

"Not completely."

"Oh Kyle, have you forgotten the first lesson on how to avoid homo-tragedy?"

"I know, I know."

"I mean come on. Do his parents know?"

"He said they would have to know but that they've never actually had The Conversation. He said he feels that's just more of a political thing to be running around saying you're out blah blah blah."

Mickey hit the emergency stop button on his treadmill. "And you believed that horseshit? Kyle, when are you going to start learning from the bullshit men you've dated in the past? Someone who is 52 years old and isn't out to his parents or with people other than close friends.... Come on!

Mickey shook his head in disgust. I came to a stop as well and we left the treadmills to hit the showers. Mickey could only hold his silence for so long before he started up again.

"You know as well as me and every shrink on this planet that any 'mo who can't be truly honest with his family, that doesn't have the balls to admit who he really is, has a bunch of bad stuff inside. And we all know what that means."

This was a lecture I didn't really want to hear but had remembered giving to others more than once.

"You're going to keep going down this path with him falling hard and getting emotionally entangled and then out of the clear blue sky it's all going to come crashing down on you in one of two ways."

Here it comes.

"One, he's going to start feelin' somethin' real and then FREAK OUT, running away because those real feelings make him feel ashamed and not so good about himself, OR, two, you end up in a relationship with someone who has you move into the spare bedroom when the parents come over or refers to you as a roommate to his family. Is that what you want in your life Kyle, to be a fucking ROOMMATE!"

I stopped in the middle of the stairwell. The people coming up the stairs gave us a look when Mickey started raising his voice.

"I don't want to talk about this right now."

"Kyle, you can't run away from the facts."

"No, you know what Mickey? Maybe I can face the facts and help him through those issues. God knows I did it with A.K."

I started back down the stairs.

"Look where that got you."

I wheeled around. My throat clenched up and I could feel the anger in my eyes. "Fuck you!" I headed down the stairs to go out towards the pool. Mickey was right on my heels.

"Kyle I'm sorry, I shouldn't have said that."

"Mickey, you're one of my two best friends and I love you to pieces but drop this. I don't..." I was so aggravated I didn't even notice the hot, naked Italian guy with the cool tattoo on his left thigh just above the knee, toweling off next to me.

"Kyle, I said I was wrong. Listen, I know that you are a very caring person and God knows you had all the patience in the world with A.K. but, you can't be the emotional 911 for every fucked-up guy that should a been in therapy years ago. It's not fair for you."

Why does the truth have to sting?

• • •

I stood under the spray of the shower letting it cascade down from the top of my head. Deep down I knew Mickey was right. The logical side of me said I should see the warning signs and set all of this aside since statistically it would fall apart. I had worked hard to feel good about myself as a gay man so would getting into a relationship with someone who obviously had issues in this area, well, was that a good choice? Glenn might think he had it all together, and he certainly expressed to me that he did, but when someone says that aren't they covering for something? Maybe I should be looking for the guy who had the sense to set his ego aside and say, "I'm a little fucked up here and there but I'm always working to be a better person." That would be refreshing. Who doesn't have at least a few issues?

The water felt good as I tried to sort this one out. I definitely fall for the uber-masculine-cocky guys who looked great on the surface but had deep problems inside. Still, I couldn't deny how I felt when I was with Glenn. I felt great and that was a feeling that seemed to trump logic.

By the time I had toweled off and had gotten dressed Mickey had gotten the phone number from a visiting Cuban fresh off a 787 Dreamliner from Miami. "Locker adjacency" worked just as good as being Beverly Hills adjacency when at this gym. (Gay Scout Rule # 4 … *Anywhere* is a good place to meet men).

I waited patiently while Mickey said his goodbye and off we went. When Pigs Die was just a short jaunt over to La Brea. It was a warm night, so I put the top down on the M4 and took a deep breath of the sweet night air. We left the car at the valet. You have to love LA for even having valet parking at a place that serves pig knuckles.

To both of our surprised eyes was the sight of Melanie already there drinking a cocktail. First to arrive twice in one day. Something was up.

CHAPTER ELEVEN

THE RETURN OF THE OTTOMAN

Cream Puffs & Pizza Tins

"HEY GUYS," SHE SAID AS SHE CLINKED THE ICE around in a nearly empty highball glass. Mickey and I sat down and started scoping the scene for any hot guys and hopefully a server to get us caught up with Mel. One of the great things about my friendship with Mel was that we did not have to rehash this morning's bonehead comment. We'd learned to just let that stuff go.

"So what's up?" I said. "How was work?"

"I'm exhausted. The Black Door was absolutely slammed so it was back-to-back clients. Then the Ottoman showed up unexpectedly."

"Isn't he Saturday?" chimed in Mickey. He and I had heard enough of Melanie's stories to know what her tentative whipping schedule was.

"Exactly. His mother's coming to visit him this weekend, so Saturday was out. I kind of look forward to his Saturday appointment because I'm kind getting into that Sean Hannity show which is on Fox Saturday evenings so that's when I schedule him. He was very upset that he'd have to wait until next week, so we worked him in."

The waitress finally came around and took our drink and pork orders. Mel continued with her Stoly tonics while Mickey and I opted for Dixie beers. If you're going to do the white trash dinner you might as well go all the way with matching beverages. (Gay Scout Rule # 14…Don't Forget to Accessorize).

"So, what did you watch instead of Sean?" I inquired. When you thought about it Sean Hannity was an interesting fit for ping-pong-paddling. I should call the producers and pitch a show on The Black Door.

"Judge Judy and then Jeanine Pirro. He got very agitated with Judge Judy because it reminded him of his mother." She swirled the ice around in her glass some more. "When she started yelling at someone, he made me switch stations which was irritating because there was nothing good on."

A soccer mom dressed in dusty pink was eating with her carpet monsters at the next table. She was giving Mel's low-cut outfit the once-over and doing her best to eavesdrop. She was in for a treat.

"It was very frustrating for me. I like his appointment because it gives me a chance to kick back and be paid for watching some TV but with his incessant channel surfing, I was getting irritated. On top of that he was fixated on the shoeshine thing again."

Mickey and I did a quick pick of our brains to remember the details on the Ottoman. He was an accountant from the Valley who liked to be paddled, yelled at, and most of all pretend he was purchased at Ethan Allen. In accordance with the whole foot theme, he was also into shoes and enjoyed spending his after-glow time buffing Mel's stilettos.

"Today he brought a creampuff and wanted me to squish it with my shoe during the commercial break and then yell at him to lick it off." Our next-door neighbor looked appalled.

"I had a brand-new pair of Jimmy Choo's on today," she said with a helpless look. "I wasn't in the mood to get a grease stain on them but sometimes you have to be accommodating to the client, know what I mean?" Yes and no. It might be fun to have Tom lick my shoes while I paddled Tammy. I hadn't really thought of how liberating that might be. Though enthralled with Mel's story, Mickey was flirting with the waiter at the next station.

"I told him I thought we should wait until next time because I didn't want to get the carpet messy in the break room. Wouldn't you know it he had brought a pizza tin with him to put the creampuff on."

"A horny man is always thinkin' ahead," chimed in Mickey, clearly disappointed that the waiter he was eyeing was now focused on someone else.

"So, he put the creampuff on the tin, I grabbed the ping pong paddle and..."

"Excuse me, but I *don't* think this is an appropriate restaurant conversation." We all turned. It was our neighbor and she had a haughty look on her face. In a grand gesture of appellation, her hands were covering the youngest child's ears. Mel turned around.

"What did you just say?" said Mel. Mickey and I could feel our faces getting warm.

"I think you should save your conversation for the toilet where it belongs. I have my children with me, and even if I didn't, I don't want to hear sewage like that."

"Listen sister, I've had one hell of a day at the office so if I want to talk about it I am and if you have a problem with it then you can just blow it out your ass. You've got some nerve telling me what I can and cannot talk about." The woman was taken aback.

"There are children present."

"That's not our fault lady." Mel turned around and the woman signaled the waiter for her check. "The *balls* of some people. Can you believe her?"

"Keep going with the story Mel." Anything to distract her from going another round with the mother which at this point was very probable since she was cocktail lubricated.

"Oh screw it. I don't want to talk about it anymore. She made me forget where I was anyway."

"Hey guys," leave it to Mickey to change the topic. "What are we going to do for Tyler's birthday?"

As if nothing had just happened Mel's face lit up. She loved any opportunity to throw a party. "That's right, we have to do something cool for him. What number is this anyway?"

"You think Tyler is going to cop up to being anything over 30? Come on. Just put "Happy 30-60th Tyler" on the cake. That will work yet still bug him at the same time."

The haughty one made sure she shot Melanie one last dirty look on her way out the door. Mel ignored it since she was happily consumed with a party to plan.

By the time our pig selections had arrived we were able to hash out some of the major details such as what color Melanie would build the party around (she had her whole apartment repainted Smoked-Ecru for my last birthday) and also to confirm a day with Tyler. See, not only did Tyler not let on how old he was but he had never told anyone the exact day either. We only had the actual astrological sign to work with, so we just picked a time that best fit our calendars and went from there. It was going to be two weeks from this Saturday.

Melanie started to make a guest list while Mickey and I called out various names and whether we felt they deserved to be invited. Tyler had some very unusual friends in his circle so a lot of concessions had to be made in the taste and tacky department. When he threw an event you always had the feeling you were walking into a carnival as the guest list could just as easily contain an ex-con, witch, or taxidermist as it would a doctor, lawyer or banker.

"So now the big question for you two," smiled Mickey. "Will you be bringing your respective men to this?" He was half serious, half joking.

"Well we know you'll have trouble deciding which trick to wear but yeah, I think my tool-belted trophy could handle it, Tyler's friends and all." Melanie turned to me.

"I don't know," I responded. Lame.

"Why, are you worried he's too old for this crowd? Most of Tyler's friends fit the 60+ plus category." She couldn't resist.

"It's not that, it's just…I don't know that I really want to throw Tyler and his crowd at Glenn all at once. That's a bit on the overload side. This is still pretty new."

"Not as new as Melanie's relationship," chimed Mickey. He had me in a corner and he was loving it. "Come on Kyle, when are we going to meet this guy anyway?"

How do you tell your best friends you don't want to screw up your relationship by having the man you are dating meet them? Was I a complete louse for feeling this way? I loved Mel and Mickey to pieces, but I just couldn't see the four of us sitting down to brunch yet.

"*Kyle?*" Melanie was looking right at me. She wanted an answer.

"I don't know." I was ashamed I was being a traitor. Would it be possible for me to keep these two lives separate? I just didn't want Glenn to go up against two important people who would love to see him go away. How could that be productive on any account?

"What are you ashamed of, Kyle?" She was going in for the kill.

"I'm not ashamed of anything." Liar. "I just feel it's kind of early in the game for meeting the friends; that can be intimidating for anyone.

"If you are worried we'd say anything, you can relax," said Mickey. "Right Mel?"

She didn't answer him but just looked at me with her "I know what you are really thinking and you're a twat for sitting there thinking it in front of your two best friends who would do anything for you." A visual lecture.

I was saved by the waitress stopping by to clear the plates. I picked up the check before they had a chance to react; a minor attempt to alleviate some of my guilt.

Mickey and I said goodbye to Melanie in the parking lot and climbed into my car. On the way back to his car I kept waiting for him to bring it up, but his chatter seemed to go in the normal fluff and puff direction: hot guy waiting for light, Katy Perry, etc. I pulled into a tow zone across from the gym to let him out. He turned looking at me.

"You're embarrassed to have Glenn meet us, aren't you?"

"Come on Mickey, that's not fair."

"I didn't say anything about fair. I'm just saying the truth. What are you afraid of?"

"Mickey put yourself in my place. You've listened to your best friends hammer away on the guy you are dating and then they want to know when they are going to meet him. Would you feel like that's the best dinner party fit?"

"You know we would never say anything…"

"Mickey, you don't have to actually say anything. One of Mel's looks can say it all. I'd be sitting there the whole time waiting for her to either make some wise crack or shoot one of her scowls that would make her opinion very clear. She's not one to hold back. You're aware of that."

Mickey got out of the car and shut the door. Turning back to me he said "It's getting chilly. Maybe you should put the top up for your drive home."

And with that he crossed to the other side of the street.

CHAPTER TWELVE

CHEESE GRATERS

Who Knew?

IT WAS THE NEXT DAY AFTER WORK and Mel had asked if I would join her while she shopped. She was looking for some work equipment…we were in Williams Sonoma. What was a cook's paradise to some was a pervert's paradise to others. Melanie carefully inspected graters.

"Do you think this is too sharp?" she asked as she carefully ran her fingers over the nibs of a tiny nutmeg grater."

"For what?"

"This guy from Kentucky. I don't know. I think I'll go with this parmesan grater instead." I didn't want to know.

She threw the cheese grater into her shopping basket which already contained a large rubber spatula, two different wire whisks, and a wooden spoon. All of which she said were perfect for spanking. She'd also found a bulb baster she thought the Milkmaid might enjoy as well as a wooden mallet she thought had potential for a Republican appeals court judge. She picked up a jar of specialty cinnamon.

"What's that for?" I asked as I imagined her pushing it up the nostrils of some poor bastard wearing a leather hood.

"Snickerdoodle cookies," she said as she put it in her basket. "OK, I think that about does it. Do you want to grab a cup of coffee?"

"Sure," I said. Mel paid for her accoutrements and we walked to the Starbucks next door. We got some iced lattes and found a table in a quiet spot.

"It feels good to sit down. These heels are killing me today," said Mel as she flipped off her right shoe and rubbed her foot.

"Any ideas for dinner?"

"Something spicy. Tacos sound good. I need to swing into Home Depot because they are having a sale on chain link and light bulbs. Since we'd be on the East side we could hit that place in Silver Lake if you want."

"Works for me." I wondered if the light bulbs were for work too.

We sipped on our coffees a bit until I said "Mel, I have to confess something."

"What?" she said, her concern clearly showing.

"Well, the other night when you were in the tub and I was getting cocktails for us. I sort of looked through your pictures on the kitchen table."

"Oh," she said. "I wondered if you saw those."

"It's you and your mom, right?"

"Yeah. How embarrassing."

"You were quit the little JonBenét weren't you?" I smiled.

"Kyle, I swear to God. If you tell anyone you saw those, I'll kill you."

"Why are you so ashamed? I thought it was cute."

"It was a long time ago but it's still mortifying."

"Was this in Connecticut?"

"No. It was while we were living in Atlanta for a few years. Other mothers of the neighborhood we lived in had their kids in these pageants and my mother, the WASP of all WASPS, got hooked if you can believe that one." Melanie came from a very proper socialite family from Darien. Her mother was the epitome of an uptight protestant Republican and was obsessed with proper behavior and social standing.

"That's hard to believe from what you've told me."

"Let's just say that the pageant circuit was my mother's crack cocaine. She hauled us all over the Deep South and the more I won, or we won if it was a mother-daughter competition, then the more crazed she would get to enter another one. This went on for the entire five years we lived in Atlanta."

"You looked like you were having fun."

"I was, actually. It was really the best time I ever had with my mother because it was just the two of us. My sister was at boarding school already. But it all ended the day we moved back to Connecticut. I remember my mother crying as she packed up boxes of our trophies, costumes, and tiaras. She refused to let the moving company touch any of it. I remember thinking how excited I would be to show my friends all that we had won back to Connecticut. But when we got back to Darien those boxes never arrived."

"The movers lost everything?"

"That's what my mom said but I think she threw them away. You see, it was expected that my parents would have a loveless marriage, that my mom would fuck the pool boy, and that she'd numb herself with vodka at regular intervals. But only trash do pageants. Her Junior League friends would have laughed her out of the state. The first time my mother overheard me telling a friend about our pageant life she became furious and slapped me in front of my friend saying I was horrible for telling lies like that. Later that night she apologized and said that if I told anyone about our secret life it would ruin the magic of it."

"Why didn't you tell me any of this before?" I asked.

"What can I say? She trained me well."

"It's like I just found out your secret identity is a superhero."

"Would you like to meet my family?"

"Yeah, right."

"I'm serious, Kyle. I've been meaning to ask you for some help but wasn't sure how to approach this."

"I'm not sure I understand."

"My sister Alison is getting married in a few weeks and I want you to come to the wedding with me. As my boyfriend.

"Are you kidding me? Why don't you take your real boyfriend?"

"You can't be serious, Kyle. You don't understand. I can't show up in Darien with a construction worker boyfriend. My parents would be nightmares."

"So, you're going to show up with a homo instead?"

"That part we can work with. They don't know you're gay."

"It's an interesting detail you left out when describing me to your parents."

"They only know that Mickey and Tyler are gay. They sort of know you as the straight successful one." I shot her a look knowing more was to come. "That I've been dating for the past two years."

"Nice, Mel."

"Kyle. If you do this for me, I swear I'll do anything you want. I'll pay for everything. It won't cost you a cent and after it's over I'll treat us to a few days at the Waldorf-Astoria."

"In the bridal suite?"

"It's not funny," she said in an anguished voice. "Please, just promise me you'll think about it."

What could I do? A friend was in need. I just wondered if she'd be packing her bustier.

CHAPTER THIRTEEN
PHONE TAG

Medicate Now

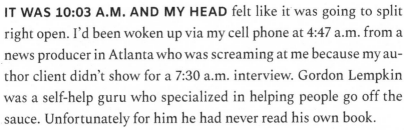

IT WAS 10:03 A.M. AND MY HEAD felt like it was going to split right open. I'd been woken up via my cell phone at 4:47 a.m. from a news producer in Atlanta who was screaming at me because my author client didn't show for a 7:30 a.m. interview. Gordon Lempkin was a self-help guru who specialized in helping people go off the sauce. Unfortunately for him he had never read his own book.

By now he had missed all eight interviews I had set up for the pre-lunch part of his day. Atlanta was burning down around me, and I could pretty much figure I wasn't going to be booking that market for a long time to come. Lucy and I had gone back and forth over half a pack of her cigarettes trying to decide whether to scrap the rest of the day by canceling his tour and giving producers time to book last-minute replacements or hope he had dried out enough to call in and show up. Endless phone calls to the hotel, including one where I had a front desk person bang on his door, produced no Gordon. When I finally convinced the hotel manager they needed to open his room to make sure he was alive, all they found were his clothes strewn about and an empty mini-bar.

"*You booked a goddamn lush into a room with a fully stocked bar?*" The veins in Lucy's forehead were pulsing. Smoke billowed around her head complimenting the evil dragon impression she does so well. "Do you know how much this is costing us? How fucking stupid are you?"

I was frantically going through hotel emails to find the one that would confirm I had requested a no-alcohol room. Just as Lucy started in again the receptionist buzzed me.

"Kyle, Tammy and Tom on line five." Our Front Desk Empress was a master at hanging up the intercom before you could say you couldn't take the call. Never mind trying to page her back to request a message be taken. She would ignore my plea for help and later say she had stepped away to the bathroom.

I looked up at Lucy for some guidance. Leave them hanging and let her keep screaming or pick it up and hopefully she would shut up.

"Get those fuckers off that line as fast as possible," barked Lucy as she lit up another one.

Pain shot through my head as I picked up the call. "This is Kyle."

"*Kyle*, this is Tammy." I waited to hear a buzz in from Tom but nothing. This was a first. "There's a problem I need to discuss with you."

The intercom buzzed again. "Kyle, someone named Glenn on line four." Click. How could I even be excited that Glenn called with Lucy's disapproving stare and Tammy yapping like a poodle on the other end? It pained me to watch Glenn's line blink and blink and blink while Tammy blathered on. One of those times I wished he'd just texted me.

"I wanted to *call* you by myself because it's concerning the picture of us that is going to go on the cover."

"What do those morons want?" hissed Lucy form across the room. She began to re-arrange my bookshelf while she waited. Her nervous energy was contagious.

"What's wrong with the picture, Tammy? When I talked to you and Tom yesterday you *lovvvved* the photo shoot." I enjoyed putting her words back on her.

"Well Kyle we did love the photo *shoot. That* was a very enjoyable experience. It's just that I *personally* don't think these are the right photos for the book."

Glenn continued to blink while my agitation mounted. "Tammy, let me put you on hold for one moment…"

"*NO*, don't do that. I need to have this conversation while Tom is in the bathroom. I only have a few minutes because he eats a lot of fiber." My next opportunity at dinner / movie / sex continued to blink away. Damn her!

Lucy held up a note that said, "GET THAT BITCH OFF THE PHONE!"

"Tammy, what's the problem with the photos? I have three calls holding I need to make this quick."

"I'm not in front of Tom; he's in front of me. I think I should be the one in the front of the picture with him standing behind me. One can hardly see much of me don't you think? It would make for a much prettier cover."

Amazing. She was jockeying for better placement over the man she claimed to love. What the hell difference did it make? They were married and did everything together with the one exception of taking a dump it seemed. Actually, I was surprised she wasn't in there wiping his ass. Glenn went from a blink to a dead light. Rats.

"OK, duly noted. I'll bring it up in our production meeting this afternoon."

"But *Kyle*. I'd appreciate it *much* more if you'd go ahead and try to get an answer for me this morning. When you call me back, before noon Pacific Time mind you, make sure you don't mention this call but that it was decided on *your* end to make the change and redo the cover."

"Tammy, I can't promise anything. A lot of money has already been spent..."

Her tone changed. "Kyle, I'll tell you what. You just forget I called, and I'll take this up with Lucy, *personally*. Thank you for what you are trying to do but I don't think you understand the importance of from *where* I'm coming."

Lucy shook her scribbled sign at me again and I got off the call. "What's that bitch up to now?"

"She wants the cover re-done. She thinks she should be in front of Tom on the picture so she's more prominent."

"Dominant you mean. What a pussy he always is. Rolling over for her every time she barks." It was evident that the benefits of the office sex Tom used to close this deal had long since worn off for Lucy while irritation at an ongoing nightmare marched onward. She picked up the mock-up copy of the book. "Pussy, pussy, pussy!" she hissed. Was she drunk?

"Tell her to take her idea and shove it up her ass." The intercom squelched again.

"Lucy, are you back there?"

"What is it?" she barked.

"Tammy on line two for you." Lucy was the only person the Front Desk Wonder would take a message for.

"Tell her I'm in a meeting." She punched the disconnect button on my phone before any possible retort.

"Fuckers!" She grabbed her cigs off my desk with one crushing sweep and then marched down to her office leaving me to continue to mop up the morning.

I rummaged through my desk drawer looking for an Excedrin. I threw the empty bottle in the trash but remembered I had spilled it once and thought maybe there was a stray jumbled in with the rubber bands. To my relief I found one, along with one Advil-looking thing, so I dusted them off and swished them down with some cold coffee. (Gay Scout Rule # 15 ... Take as Needed).

Glenn. I rang his office.

"Glenn Wycoff's office."

"Glenn please."

"Who's calling?"

"Kyle from Devore-Horizon," I replied, trying to make it sound like a business call.

"What is this concerning?"

"I'm returning his call."

"Regarding?" Jeepers. Just give him to me, would you? It amazed me how many layers certain people had covering them at the studios.

"Personal business." I tried to sound intimidating. She put me on hold, and I listened to some track by a new fourteen-year-old artist named Misty Dwyer. Glenn had said she already had a heroin problem and they were concerned rehab would screw up her pending concert tour. He had green-lighted a remake of *The Bodyguard* starring Misty and he was counting on getting some stock footage of her tour.

"This is Ms. Jackson."

"Huh? No, I was holding for Glenn Wycoff."

I'm Mr. Wycoff's senior assistant. What can I do for you?"

"I'm trying to get hold of Glenn. I'm returning his call."

"Regarding?" I was tempted to say dinner and cocksucking.

"I'm a friend returning his call. He just called *me* ten minutes ago."

"Please hold." I put her on speakerphone and started going through e-mail. Two additional Misty tracks later I was at the end of my rope, ready to hang up, when the line picked up again.

"He's going to have to return."

"Fine, he has the number." I hung up. My intercom beeped.

"Kyle lines three and four. Gordon Lemton and..." Click. Huh? In her race to avoid a response she cut herself off. Unbelievable. Which one might be Glenn? I picked up number four.

"Kyle here."

"Kyle it's Gordon Lempkin," the gravelly voice spewed.

"Gordon, thank God. Where have you been? Hold on while I get rid of this other call. Under no circumstances hang up." I picked up line three.

"Kyle here."

"Kyle it's *Tammy*. Lucy is not returning my call."

"Tammy let me get off the other call." As if I would pick her back up anytime soon. She could sit and rot.

Click. "Gordon what the hell happened? I've been besieged with angry calls this morning."

"I *am* sorry, Kyle. I wasn't feeling very spry this morning so I called in sick."

"To whom? You weren't in your room. I had the manager open the door to see if you were alive."

"Oh, very much alive. I admit I didn't make it back to my hotel room last night but stayed with a friend." Or a hooker probably. I had been warned that in the past Gordon had submitted a receipt for a call-girl service. I spent the next hour assessing what we could save from the mess that Gordon had made. During that time Tammy tried to reach me four different times but I refused to talk to her until I got Gordon hooked up with our "legitimate" tour escort and out the door to the rest of his day. I listened to the pile of messages on my voice mail. Number seven was a simple one.

"Glenn Wycoff's office returning." Click. Very studio. I couldn't believe he had his secretary leave the message.

"I rang back."

"Glenn Wycoff's office."

By this time, I was too exhausted to sound intimidating. "Kyle for Glenn."

"Please hold." Hmmm, no grilling. I was surprised by how fast he picked up. "Hey you."

"I can't believe you had your assistant leave me a message. How Hollywood of you." It was fun to tease him.

"Oh, sorry about that my cell was about to die so I had her ring you. It's a force of habit with her when she doesn't reach the person we are trying to call. What are you doing tonight?" Cool, impromptu date. "Putting a gun to my head, banging you, or having some dinner. Want to pick two out of three?"

He laughed at my twisted sense of humor. He got me and I liked that. "Hmmm, well, I definitely don't want you to shoot yourself because that would make you stiff in the wrong way. Howzabouts some food and you spending the night?"

"That works for me." I was trying to be casual but deep down I was really excited he had called. It made up for this morning.

"Cool. My place at eight sharp."

"See you then."

"Kyle?"

"Yeah?"

"Just thought I'd let you know I've missed you."

And with that the line went dead.

CHAPTER FOURTEEN

GLENN REVISITED

Poolside Chatter

I KNOCKED ON THE MONASTERY DOOR and waited for him to answer. A little squirrel was digging in his potted hydrangea and I wondered if that would cause an imbalance in Glenn's otherwise perfect universe.

Pad Pad Pad. The door opened and my date officially began.

"Hey there," he said. "How goes it?"

"I found my missing alcoholic and managed to avoid marital hell by not returning Tammy and Tom's calls." Glenn laughed. I filled him in on the reality of author drama while he returned the favor with great inside gossip from Warner Brothers. It was worth dating him just to find out which star was headed to Betty Ford next. I loved his stories of out-of-control divas on their way to being the train wrecks of the century.

As we walked into his living room, I admired the muscularity of his shoulders which were nicely defined under the tight shirt he was wearing. "How about something to drink? Beer? Wine? Whatever?"

"I'll take a beer." He went into the kitchen and I wandered around the living room. Over by the fireplace there were three new sculptures side by side. Each about a foot high and they were made of alabaster and in the shape of strange-looking people.

"Hey. I like the new art." I heard some bottles clink and the sound of beer being opened.

"What?"

"I said I really like your sculptures over here by the fireplace." He walked back in.

"Oh, Michael put those there." The Ex. Glenn got a funny look on his face as soon as he had said it.

"Oh." The funny look transferred to me.

"They were there before. You just didn't notice."

OK, now one thing I am is observant (Gay Scout Rule # 16... Pay attention to details) and I'd been in this living room enough to have remembered these sculptures. I could swear they weren't here before. And if there were why didn't Michael take them with him when he moved out? Maybe I was wrong. Time to switch the subject before my mind became my own worst enemy.

"So, what's up for chow?"

"Well," he said as he walked up to me and put his arm around me. "Since we both had tough days, I was thinking we could do the Jacuzzi thing and order in. How's that sound?"

Won tons and a whirlpool. It could be worse. "I don't have my suit with me," I said coyly.

"I'll get you something to put on." He went into the back room. Nuts. I was hoping he'd suggest skinny dipping. Whose suit was I going to wear? One of Michael's leftovers? Two flashes later he returned with two huge white Turkish bathrobes and his cell phone. Cool.

"Follow me," he commanded. I grabbed our beers. We walked out the glass wall and onto the patio. It was an amazing evening with warm air and an orange sky. He set the robes and phone down and stripped off his clothes. I watched his shirt being peeled from the muscular back I fantasized about only ten minutes earlier. God he was hot. Buck naked he turned and smiled at me. So sexy. Damn. Damn, damn, damn, damn, damn.

"Well? Are you standing or dipping?" He picked up his beer and got in the Jacuzzi. While I was undressing, he fiddled with the remote control for the Jacuzzi and got the bubbles whirling. I did my best to look hot while I stripped. Might as well take advantage of the outdoor stage to make an impression. He smiled in approval. I picked up my beer. It was so cool to drink out of real glass poolside... so renegade. No plastic for this man.

"Hand me my phone, will you?"

I handed him his phone and he looked up the restaurant's number. While he waited for them to pick up he smiled at me. Wow, what a smile. He looked incredible surrounded by the rising steam of the water.

"We're having Willow on MacGregor tonight." Willow on MacGregor—impressive. I couldn't believe it. Here I thought we'd be eating Dominos or some greasy Kung Pao slop and he was ordering from the restaurant at which every wannabe in LA was trying to get a table.

"This is Glenn Wycoff. I'd like to order dinner please. Yes. Something for the grill. Two Kobe fillets. Yes. What do you suggest tonight? No. Yes. Great." He hung up. I noticed he didn't have to give his address.

"They need thirty minutes. Any suggestions as to how we should fill the time?"

He came over to my side of the Jacuzzi and we began to make out. There was something about the way he kissed. Incredible. Don't think it was just the beer and bubbles — this guy had something going for him. OK, maybe the beer and bubbles added something to it but regardless he knew what he was doing.

It seemed like we had just come up for air when the front door rang. "Damn. Gotta take a break. Don't stop looking incredible." With that he hopped out of the Jacuzzi and put on his robe, tying the sash really hard to cinch in Glenn Jr. He opened the front door and the delivery man came in with two bags of food. What the hell did he order? The delivery man went into the kitchen to set the bags down. I could hear him rustling around. Glenn came back outside and picked his beer up.

"Are you going to stay in or get out? Now's the time to do it."

The jets of hot water felt great and I was beginning to feel the buzz from the beer on an empty stomach. "I'll stay in for a few more minutes," I teased. Might was well let Glenn serve it up.

The delivery man came out to the terrace to get paid. So I thought. Instead he walked over to the gas grill and lit it up. I was confused. He went back in the kitchen and came out with a tray of steaks, peppers, salad and a bevy of other accoutrements I couldn't make out from my vantage point in the water. He seasoned the steaks and put them on the grill then began fiddling with the salad.

The water was warm. Very, very warm and it was time for me to get out. But I was naked, and the delivery-man-turned-chef was right there in front of me. I was getting hot. I could feel my face lobster and I was sizzling along with the steaks. I don't look good with a red face. Why didn't I get out when I had a chance? Glenn sipped his beer over by the table and was looking at me with a grin on his face. He could tell I wanted to get out and he looked over at my robe on the opposite side of the patio. The bastard. He was enjoying this. His grin increased with my discomfort.

Damn.

Damn he's cute.

Damn...I'm falling for him.

Damn.

And that was the moment. You know, that little "click" that happens when you suddenly realized that a spark has started you down the path of falling in love. The scary path that means you have it all on the line, that you're vulnerable again, and that this person has your heart by the balls. That wonderful click which in an instant makes you realize you are alive. So alive.

Damn. It feels good to be alive.

"How would you like these, sir?"

"Medium rare for me and, Kyle?"

"Thanks. Same. Medium rare." Screw the steak, I was well done. How the hell was I going to get out of this?

"Excuse me, sir?"

The chef turned to me. "Do you think there might be some kind of BBQ sauce you could put on mine while it's on the grill?" He was clearly appalled that I was going to torture a Kobe with K.C. Masterpiece. Nonetheless he headed to the kitchen.

"Nice move," laughed Glenn. "I'm impressed."

"No, you're a son-of-a-bitch," I said as I hopped out and quickly got my naked ass over to the chair with my robe. I smiled at him as I put it on and snuck in a quick kiss just before the chef rounded the corner.

"I'm sorry sir but I couldn't find any sauce." He did have two fresh beers with him, however. Thinking ahead but a liar nonetheless. I had seen a bottle of BBQ sauce in the fridge last week.

"Oh, no problem, just wondered."

I took a fresh beer and shot a look over to Glenn. He was having fun teasing me and impressing me I'm sure. I could only imagine how much this was costing him.

While I watched the chef toss our salads, I thought about mentioning Tyler's party to Glenn. Maybe he'd be cool with going. I wanted him to go. This felt right and if it felt that way then it made sense to have him meet the gang warts and all.

"My friend Tyler is having a birthday party Saturday after next. It should be a lot of fun."

"I'll feel sorry for you. I hate birthday parties. I guess that means I won't be seeing you that night?"

Yeah, I guess you won't be. Damn.

CHAPTER FIFTEEN

HAPPY BIRTHDAY

Many More Unhappy Returns

DESPITE ALWAYS CARRYING A PHONE Melanie insisted on honking her horn when I ran behind. She and Mickey were downstairs, and I was still trying to decide which shirt to wear. After the third honk I went out on the balcony and shouted down."

"I'm coming!"

"Jesus, you don't even have your shirt on yet. Hurry up!"

Originally, the party was going to be at Melanie's, but Tyler protested due to the fact he was nervous the three of us would edit his guest list. Who knew what kind of evening we were in for? With Tyler at the reins of who was invited and who was not you could expect anyone from a voodoo priestess to hunky firemen. I went back to my closet mirror and held up the two choices; finally deciding to go with the new Hugo Boss that had been sitting in my closet for the right debut opportunity (Gay Scout Rule #17…Wait for the right opportunity to debut a great shirt). I had thought about saving it for a date with Glenn, but it was on the mod side and I usually went the more conservative route with him. I didn't invite him to the party figuring he made it clear he didn't want to go. Maybe this would be a relationship I'd have to keep separate from my friends. One last face and hair check and I was out the door.

As I hopped into the back seat of the Mercedes Mel threw me one last dirty look. "What the hell where you doing? And by the way that shirt makes you look completely hot."

"It does doesn't it."

"Mr. Modesty in the back seat," flipped Mickey. He sounded and looked unusually tired.

"Late night Miss Maggio?"

"Nights would be more like it. Houseguests from back home that don't know when to say no."

"You should have brought them," said Melanie.

"Please. I need some relief. I'm completely over entertainin' them. I just want a nice peaceful party where I don't end up with my head in a toilet at the end of the evening."

"I doubt you'll find that at Tyler's," I said. "What did we buy him?"

"A $150 gift certificate to the Pleasure Chest."

"Are you serious?"

"What's wrong with that? You can never have enough condoms."

"Or whips," said Mickey.

"I don't know," I said. "It just seems like kind of a tacky gift."

"Kyle," said Melanie, "Look who is having the birthday. He's not the Queen of England."

"Besides, Kyle, Melanie and I like the practicality of it. He's got something of everything already."

They had their points. We pulled into Tyler's Hancock Park neighborhood and saw that it was a complete parking lot.

"My God, he must have invited a thousand people," she said. "The streets are jammed with cars." We crept along trying to find a spot big enough for the Mel-Mobile. When we finally found one it was five blocks away and Mel was incensed.

"See why I wanted guest list control if it was going to be at my place? He's invited every goddamn person he's ever met in his life to this thing." She clicked along in her six-inch heels; not a good choice when you don't get rock-star parking.

The noise from the party could be heard down the block and two blue-haired matrons were whispering and pointing towards Tyler's house when we walked by. I had to wonder how long it would be before the police showed up. We were a few houses away when I saw a new blue Toyota Prius with "4THEDOC" on the license plate. I stopped dead in my tracks; my throat clenching tight.

"I can't believe this." Mickey and Mel stopped to look.

"What's that one doing here?" asked Mickey.

"Miss Maggio's right. See what I told you? Asshole Tyler *has* invited everyone he's ever come in contact with. I can't believe he did this to you Kyle. I'm using that gift certificate." She put her cigarette out on the side of the car and threw the butt in the gutter. "He's got some balls for doing this." She stared at the car with complete contempt.

"Lookit that car," said Mickey. "Brand new but still had to transfer that tacky plate. God, I hate people who use a "4" in the plates. 4 David, 4 Mary, 4 Shit-for-brains as far as I'm concerned."

I stood there not wanting to go any further. It had been about three years since I'd seen "THEDOC" and I had hoped we'd never cross paths again.

"I can't believe this. A.K.'s Ex."

I had walked out the door feeling excited about this evening and now I was facing a piece of my past I just did not, under any circumstances, want to deal with right now.

"Do you want to leave?" Mickey waited for my answer.

"No worries. I can be a man and handle it. Just duck if anyone starts throwing things."

We marched up to the front door of the Tudor mansion with its long slate walkway and perfectly manicured topiaries. From the windows we could see the place was beyond packed and under the front eave two women with henna tattoos on their faces were in the middle of an argument. Tyler had made a fortune in the stock market during the 80s and thanks to careful investments was able to retire sometime in his late 30s by best estimates. The outside of the house was fantastic with amazing grounds and a beautiful pool. There was great attention to detail right down to perfectly spaced rose bushes bordering the walkway so that small clusters of various flowers could grow in between. The inside didn't match the exterior however as Tyler had old carpet and the tackiest collection of furniture you could imagine. Still, it was great for a party because if you spilled anything it would go with the many stains left by wayward Bloody Marys and vomiting guests of the past.

"For God's sake can you stand out of the doorway so we can get in?" Melanie had arrived and it was time for people to clear the way. We pushed into the living room and tried to work our way to the backyard where Tyler would have a bar. Walking through his living room was a complete sideshow experience. Just about every type of person imaginable was crammed into any available crevice swilling cocktails. One guy was swigging from a bottle of Patron. A lesbian with a bone through her nose was pouring her drink into the belly button of her date and licking it out as another woman giggled uncontrollably. The coffee table had been removed from the living room and a mass of bodies pulsated to dance music blaring over the house sound system. It was madness and the air was a haze of pot smoke, tobacco smoke and incense.

The dining room table had been set up as an enormous buffet with just about everything imaginable on it. An old lady who was completely nude minus a well-placed shawl and cheap flip-flops was yakking with a police officer (real or not it was hard to tell) who was rolling a joint. Along with the turkey and roast beef Tyler had thoughtfully placed a rather large amount of pot in a silver Tiffany bowl. Next to the bowl were packs of rolling papers on a silver tray. The room was lit with huge candles that dripped wax everywhere...on the carpets, down the side of the table, and onto an antique sideboard.

As we squished our way down the hallway, I felt someone feel up my ass. I turned to try to figure out who it was just as we finally broke through and stepped out onto the patio. I spotted Tyler over by the bar helping a naked bartender with an astonishingly large tool blend margaritas. He saw us when he looked up.

"Kids, over here!" he screamed at the top of his lungs.

"Happy birthday," we all shouted.

"Oh, screw all of you! I hate getting old, damn it all to hell." He was already lit.

"This place is a madhouse. How many people did you invite to this thing?"

"More than you would have Melanie. Have a cocktail and relax." Tyler handed her an icy margarita while the bartender started another batch. Two drunken women hanging off of an upstairs balcony threw a strawberry at the bartender. It's bounced off his ass and they screamed with delight. Mel shook her head in disgust.

"I'm so glad you guys made it. Did you find a place to park?"

"What do you think?" shot back Melanie.

I surveyed the patio scene and noticed a hippie-looking woman who had once been on a sitcom during the 90s. I couldn't remember her name but thought the guy she was talking to was pretty hot. He was fawning and gushing so it looked like he had been a childhood fan and he just creamed his pants when he realized he was at the same party with her. I could see her try to back away slowly from him, but he kept moving closer to her not about to let the catch of his day get away from him. I imagined him on the phone the next day calling everyone he knew with his "Guess who I met at a party last night!" declaration. That was one of the odder things about LA as you never knew when you'd run into someone who you grew up idolizing on some show when you were a kid. It was always disillusioning to have your childhood fantasy wrecked when you were close enough to see the crow's feet and bad skin that had taken over your favorite sitcom star.

"Hey guys, I need to go take a leak. I'll be right back." I handed my drink to Mickey and went in the side door and through the kitchen to the bathroom located near there. Unfortunately, the line was a mile long. So, I went down the hall to the back staircase and then upstairs. At the top of the stairs I went into one of the guest bathrooms figuring there wouldn't be a line. Good choice. No one was waiting outside the bathroom but when I pushed the door open two women were snorting cocaine off the back of the toilet. One of them was topless and the other one was dressed in latex. I wondered if they were coworkers of Mel's.

"Oh, sorry," I said.

"Don't worry honey we won't bother you. Line?"

"Sure, why not." I figured I might as well help them clean it up if I was going to get to use the john. I bent down and snorted the line she cut. It was good stuff.

"Nice."

"So big guy? Wanna fuck?" The topless one started playing with her nipples and looked over at her friend in latex. The coke had made me horny and they certainly seemed ready to roll.

"Uh, actually, I just need to use the bathroom."

"We strike out again. You're the third guy up here that would rather take a piss than some pussy."

Latex did another line off the toilet and handed me the straw. While I put another one up my nose, I thought about screwing around with them. It was tempting and would definitely make a good cocktail story. I was instantly crawling the walls from the blow but there was just something about getting it on in the bathroom at Tyler's party that seemed to be a little on the tacky side for me. Not that tacky can't be a good thing under the right circumstances.

"You know," the topless one cooed, "I think you just need a little coaxing."

With that she unzipped my pants. I was high from the coke and was getting hard as a rock. Before I knew it, I was looking in the mirror at two cokeheads on their knees blowing me. (Gay Scout rule #9...Never turn down a blowjob). I leaned back against the wall and thought of Bradley Cooper.

Just as Bradley was crying out in ecstasy Melanie and Mickey walked in.

"For God's sake Kyle," said Melanie. "We need to use the bathroom." Mickey started laughing as I quickly pulled up my pants.

The women were put off that they had been interrupted. "Who's this bitch?" the latex one said.

"I'm his wife you tramp. So, if you know what's good for you you'll get the hell out of here before I kick your ass all the way down the stairs." Melanie was convincing in the role of scorned spouse.

The women shot to their feet and hustled out the door. Melanie picked up their purses and threw them after them.

"Out of here you whores!"

Then she turned to Mickey and me and the three of us burst out laughing as I took my drink from Mickey.

"Honestly Kyle, you'd let anyone blow you."

"When in Rome," said Mickey as he did a line the women had conveniently left.

"You'd better finish that off before they realize they left it here," said Mel as she turned down the straw from Mickey.

"Don't worry I locked the door," said Mickey. He turned to me instead. "Kyle, you take the last one as a finder's fee." When in Rome.

"Turn your heads I need to take a leak."

"Are you kidding us? We just saw you getting a hummer."

"It's not like we both haven't seen that thang a million times," added Mickey.

"Yeah, but not while taking a whiz." They indulged my modesty and while I was mid-stream the pounding on the door began.

"Open this door damn it." It was the kneepad girls.

"Just a minute," said Melanie. We all started laughing again. I zipped up and Melanie opened the door and snarled at them.

"Enough with the pounding already we needed to use the restroom."

The two women almost knocked us over trying to get back to their stash. By the time they were in the back part of the restroom where the toilet was, we were halfway down the back stairs laughing our asses off.

Hard as it was to believe, the crowd had actually grown during our bathroom extravaganza. We pushed our way to the bar in the kitchen and helped ourselves to some more booze. It was a fun party. We were hanging with a group of investment bankers; two of whom were hitting on Melanie simultaneously. After repeated tries to get her to take off her clothes she told them she had a boyfriend.

"Where is he anyway?" I wanted an explanation after the hell she gave me for not inviting Glenn. I had thought about mentioning it again and telling him it would mean a lot to me if he came but I hadn't really talked to him much since the BBQ night. We'd only seen each other one time since then and he hadn't returned my last two phone calls. I refused to call him again. My gut feeling was something was up, but I wasn't sure about what.

"He got hurt on the job and needed to rest his back. He didn't want to spend the night standing." Good enough of an excuse, I thought. But I did wonder if she had ever truly asked him or if she also felt the way I did about exposing him to all of this.

"Oh, hey, look who's across the room," said Mickey. We both looked over and saw A.K.'s Ex looking back at us. It was an awkward moment. We locked eyes, froze for a moment, and then both of us looked away uncomfortable.

"Well this is awkward," I said.

"When was the last time you saw that twat?" Melanie took a long look at one of the people she hated the most.

"I think it's been about three years. Listen, you guys stay here, I'm going to get some fresh air out back." I wasn't in the mood to party anymore.

I went outside and walked down to the pool area which was at the back of the property and somewhat secluded from the house. Tyler had some big redwood chaises and I plopped down in one of them. I looked up at the stars; at least what you can see of them when you're in the city. Tyler had a nice life. Beautiful house, tons of friends, and he didn't seem upset to be single. In fact, I had never known him to ever be in a relationship. He dated a lot but nothing serious ever seemed to come of it.

I heard someone behind me, and I turned my head to see if it was Mel and Mickey. There she was, A.K.'s Ex-wife Daniella.

"Hi Kyle." What the hell is she up to?

"Hi."

"Do you mind if I sit here?"

Why did she follow me down here? I wasn't in the mood for another fight. Last time we spoke to each other she spewed invective at me while throwing a beer bottle at my head. It had all taken place at SkyBar years ago and it was not a pretty sight.

"Go ahead. What's up?"

"I owe you an apology." Is she kidding me?

"Huh?"

"The last time I saw you I behaved like an idiot. You didn't deserve being treated like that. Especially the beer bottle thing." I noticed she had a bottle of water in her hand this time. I wondered if she had stopped drinking.

"Thanks, but you don't need to apologize. It's all in the past."

"No, you do deserve an apology. I was having a hard time dealing with a lot of anger at that time. Especially stuff surrounding Andrew, and you came along at the wrong time."

This was uncomfortable. I really didn't expect to be sitting here having this conversation tonight or any other time. It sounded like she must have joined AA and was working that step where she has to make amends to everyone she's ever wronged. A definite disadvantage to knowing alcoholics is that when they sober up you get to relive all the icky times again but none of the fun ones.

"Daniella, I know I've never told you this and you probably won't believe me, but I didn't know you and A.K. were together when I met him. I would never have started dating him had I known he was married."

She just looked at me for a minute. "I believe you," she said.

More awkward silence. The evening had taken an uncomfortable turn.

"You know Kyle, I thought you were the one to blame for so many years, and I know I took it out on you every chance I got. But the person I was truly angry with was Andrew. I also hated myself for letting him get away from me or at least getting involved with him in the first place. It took me a long time to accept the responsibility he and I had in everything."

It sounded like someone had done some serious therapy. I flashed back to the many times Daniella had made my life a living hell when I was with A.K. The rocks that were thrown through my windows. The hate letters and messages on my phone machine. The gossip she spread through the PR community. Not to mention the guilt I had felt for breaking apart someone's relationship. By the time I had found out about her I was in love with A.K. I remembered how angry I was he hadn't been up front with me, and it almost broke us apart. So many times I had felt I should have walked away from the relationship with A.K. because it had started with dishonesty on his part but I stayed on. I couldn't deny the feelings I had for him. Such a stormy beginning and end to that story.

"Do you still miss him?" I asked.

"Yeah, what about you?"

"Yeah, more than I would like to admit. I still wake up some mornings and expect to roll over and see him lying there. I have a hard time accepting he's gone."

"Well, he definitely had a huge impact on both of us. If it's any consolation it does get easier over time."

I hoped she was right. My logic side said more than enough time had passed for me to be able to not feel anything anymore. Sometimes I actually fooled myself into thinking that but then there was a picture or some memento or something that jarred me from my false sense of recovery and raw grief.

"You know Daniella, if it makes you feel any better, I never had a chance to say goodbye or anything like you did. I woke up to one life and went to bed to another. There was no chance at closure. He was there one moment then gone."

She nodded in agreement and we just sat there in silence. That we were bonding on this issue was very odd; mortal enemies laying down the swords. I regretted my guilt over her. Maybe I could have done something back then that would have made it easier, but I don't know.

"He would have loved this party," she said. "Crazy people stuffed to the rafters." We laughed in agreement.

"Kyle, thanks for letting me get that off my chest. I need to go now."

"Thanks. I do appreciate it and I am sorry for my part in all of it. It's been something I've always felt bad about."

"I understand. Take care."

She got up and headed up the path to the house. I thought of how odd it was that someone like A.K. had the most positive and most negative effects on both of our lives. Did that mean it balanced out to zero? No, because at least with zero I would feel nothing. Grief doesn't let you feel nothing. But often wished I did.

CHAPTER SIXTEEN
SILENCE

The Hike To Hell And Back

I LOOKED AT THE TIME FOR THE ZILLIONTH TIME. He was forty-five minutes late. Looking around the parking lot at Griffith Park I tried to see if his car was one of the ones turning in either of the two entrances. No sign. I'd already texted him fifteen minutes ago and didn't want to appear to be some psycho by leaving another or calling. Where the hell was he? Some way to spend a Sunday afternoon by baking away in the heat with nothing to do. Making things even more irritating, a homeless man wouldn't stop staring at me with a creepy look in his eyes.

The first hike had been scheduled for Saturday morning which was cancelled last minute per Glenn and then rescheduled to Saturday afternoon which he also cancelled. Today at eleven-thrity, was the third time chosen and now the clock had pushed it into afternoon. Should I just get in my car and leave? I wanted to and it would serve him right. Just leave and let him finally get his ass here and not be able to find me. The trouble is I really wanted to see him. It had been ten days since we'd seen each other, and I knew something was going on but I couldn't figure it out. After the Jacuzzi BBQ we had a great date sharing a bottle of wine by the ocean. It had been a really romantic, fun, and relaxing evening. We'd gone back to my place and had mind-blowing sex and then he just went silent on me after that. He didn't return my calls and I eventually got some lame text that he had been swamped at work. Maybe that was true, I don't know. People find time to do what they want to in life. It made me feel really insecure which you probably figured out by now.

Fifty minutes late. At what point does my self esteem take over and say this is bullshit? Mel would have left after fifteen minutes if not five. I hesitated then got back into my car, started the engine but then turned it off. Then I started it back up again. Screw it. I don't appreciate this. More to the point screw him. I put the M4 in gear and circled the enormous lot to see if somehow I'd missed his car. Nope, not there. I pulled out and headed back down the road. There was another lot near the golf course, not the designated ranger station locale, but I figured he may have gotten confused and thought I should check. He wasn't in that one either.

I pulled out of the park and made a right onto Los Feliz Boulevard. I'd basically thrown away my entire weekend for this guy by being blown off three times. This was really confusing. Everything had been buzzing along just right and then it all seemed to fall into some messed-up place.

When I got home, I figured I should at least make the most of a wasted morning by getting something done. I had a stack of crap that needed to be sorted through.

Phone. It was him on the caller ID.

"Hello?"

"Where the hell are you?" Is he joking? What an ass.

"I'm back at my apartment. Where are you?"

"Where do you think I am? I'm in the park where we said we were going to meet."

"Hey, I waited for almost an hour and you weren't there. Are you by the ranger station?"

"Yeah, I ran late. I can't believe you left." He can't believe I left? I noticed there was no apology for his running over fifty minutes late and now he had an issue because he was the one doing the waiting.

"I waited for fifty minutes and tried calling your cell. Out of curiosity how long did you expect me to sit on my ass wondering if you were going to show?"

"I said I was sorry I ran late." He did? "Anyway, are you coming on this hike or not?" Part of me wanted to tell him to stick it up his ass but the other part of me had looked forward to seeing him and wanted a chance to assess what was going on.

"I'm leaving now. I'll be there in ten minutes."

"It's hot out here. Why don't you bring some bottled water."

"Sure, see you in a few."

Mixed emotions. Strength or weakness? I couldn't decide or maybe I was just in denial. I loved the fact that I was also the errand boy for this date. Chilled beverages in hand I rolled up next to his car. He had a vexed look on his face.

"Did you remember the water?" Well, hello yourself asshole. I handed him a bottle and didn't say anything. No hug I noticed. I was regretting showing up. There was tension between us. This is the shit I hate about dating.

"Come on," I said as I pointed in a certain direction. "This trail is a good one." It was also the hardest one on the mountain. I was going to hike this fucker into the ground. One thing I have is an extreme tolerance to heat, plus I'm in great shape, so I was going to make this a hike he'd remember.

I started off at a brisk walk and he was right with me. There was just a bunch of silence at first; the only sounds were the birds above and pine needles crunching under our shoes. What I wanted to say was 'I can't believe you're bitching at me today when you are the one who not only cancelled on me twice yesterday but then was an hour late today.' What I did say was "Pretty day." Pussy.

"Yeah, beautiful."

We kept hiking. The trail had a medium grade to it which isn't bad except it never let up. Uphill all the way. I could hear his breathing start to get heavier, but I kept mine controlled and steady. I didn't want him to suspect I also was feeling the hill, so I quickened the pace.

Sweat was dripping off our foreheads as we rounded a bend that took us to the hardest part of the trail. The grade went from medium to very steep. Here's where you separate the men from the boys. I attacked the side of the mountain like it was nothing even though my heart was pounding away.

"Isn't this a great hike?" I asked as I looked behind me at a now, very sweaty, Glenn. I took great pleasure in watching rivulets of glistening sweat run down his pained face.

"Great," he gasped. His titanium ego was not about to let him admit he needed to stop for some water. I kept plowing forward despite feeling the burn in my thighs. God, I wished he would cry uncle soon because I needed a break myself. We kept on climbing; both of us breathing hard by now. I turned my anger at him into energy and picked up the pace. I could feel his irritation at my decision to kick it up a notch.

"Do you need a break?" I asked in a condescending tone.

"I'm OK," he lied.

"Because we can stop if you need to rest."

"I said I'm fine." Liar. I'll teach you to leave me standing in a parking lot getting stared at by homeless people for an hour. We kept on up the trail winding along the mountainside. LA is a remarkable place in that you can literally hike to the top of a mountain in the middle of it. The heat wasn't letting up and if anything, it was getting hotter.

Hike, hike, hike. What if I accidentally killed him? It's a possibility after all. Just because someone is built doesn't mean their heart is in good shape. We continued side by side still in silence. What was I going to say to break that? Why doesn't he throw something out himself? We kept on going and came to the first overlook. It was built on an outcrop of rocks and the view was amazing.

"Do you want to stop and enjoy the view?" I was giving him an out.

"If you do." Ego to the end.

We walked to the end of the lookout and sat down on a rock. There was no one else around. The only thing either one of us could hear was the effort we were making to catch our breath. A good five minutes must have passed with nothing said. I finally caved.

"So, what's going on?" I said.

"Huh? Nothing." Nice, I give him a chance to open up this conversation and then he closes it back down again.

"I meant with us."

"Huh? Nothing." Great. The Master Communicator was in my midst.

"It's just you've been pretty unavailable and everything, I don't know."

"Kyle, I have a big job that requires a lot of me. You're going to have to accept that." Ouch. Put me in my place. More extended silence. It was really hot, and I was completely uncomfortable. This was supposed to be a fun time and instead it was just tense and awkward.

"This was a good idea. Very pretty day." I guess this is his attempt at either avoiding the subject or trying to make me feel better.

"It's hot. Do you want to head back?"

"If you do." No, I don't. Who needs a hike like this? Without saying anything else I got up and he followed. We didn't say two words to each other all the way back down the hill. It was a long forty-five minutes and I was relieved when we arrived at the parking lot. What was I going to do when we get to our cars? Should I just give him a curt goodbye, hop in and drive off?

When we reached our cars, I decided to take control. I barely looked at him. "OK Glenn, have a good rest of the weekend."

I started to turn to open my car door and he turned me back around. "Hey, thanks so much for coming, Kyle, I really appreciate it." His smile was warm, and he gave me a nice hug to go with it. What the hell was going on? I'm completely baffled.

"Sure," I said. I unlocked my car and got in, started up the engine, and pulled out of the lot without looking at him.

CHAPTER SEVENTEEN
TORTURE CHAMBER

Tammy And Tom Come Unglued

I WAS STILL IRRITATED FROM YESTERDAY'S HIKE when I walked into work this morning. Nothing like starting off Monday morning with the bad taste of relationship drama in your mouth. After leaving the park I went home and did nothing except watch baseball and brood. It makes no sense and I was aggravated that I was dealing with it to begin with. Only a few weeks ago, I was on cloud nine but this morning I had woken up to confusion.

To make matters worse, Tammy and Tom had another stick up their ass today. Lucy had given me a dirty look when I walked by her office. Had she not been on the phone I'm sure the look would have had some commentary to go with it. When I got to my desk there was a post-it on my computer screen that said we had a phone meeting with T&T at quarter to five. This was not going to be good...I could feel it. It would definitely not be the best way to end the day and I'm sure the meeting had been planned on Tammy's part to maximize the destruction of any happiness I would feel this evening.

I started sifting though my e-mails…watching the clock click towards impending doom. My lunch should have been delivered by a priest and a warden as it would have been appropriate for what I was going to hear. Let's face it; my head was going to roll.

During a *quick* coffee break, because I didn't want to appear to be a slacker, a co-worker commented that when they ripped me a new one a second asshole might have its benefits. She thought it was funny. I didn't.

At 4:40 p.m. Lucy walked into my office, closed the door, and sat down. "We need to have a pre-meeting before we have this phone meeting." She just stared at me. Damn. Couldn't she at least let me off the hook by not forcing me to say the next line?

"So, what is this about?"

"Like you don't know."

"To be honest I really don't. But I can imagine it has something to do with Tammy and Tom not being happy with…"

"No, they aren't happy. That's the understatement. This is an important book and you're screwing it to hell and back."

"Lucy I've been working very hard on this…"

"Yeah? Well let me tell you something. You haven't been working hard enough. There hasn't been enough coverage on this book and there's only one person to blame for that."

"Come on. It's bullshit. No one wants to touch it and you know that." I couldn't believe I said it but it just came out. Lucy glared at me with that look that she uses to freeze dry humans.

"Kyle…do you like working here?" I couldn't believe she actually used that old and extremely tired line. The only thing is that when it's used on you it feels uncomfortably fresh.

"Of course. I like my job very…"

"Then you'd better get your shit together and I mean fast because if I get one more call from Tammy and Tom about you then you're going to be on the unemployment line." Another cliché but I could tell she meant business. Fuck this shit.

"Dial them up." I punched in their phone number and put them on speaker phone.

"Hello. Is this Lucy *and* Kyle?" It was Tammy in her bullshit-phony-cheerful voice. I hated her so much I wanted to beat her to death with her hardback. Lucy equaled the sugar in Tammy's voice which was even creepier. I guess she was Tammy's new best friend.

"Hi Tammy. Is Tom on the line?"

"Of course he is. Say hello Tom"

"Hello, how are you today, Kyle?" Hmmm let me think...I'm on a conference call that is meant to humiliate and emasculate me down to your level you dick-less ass.

"I'm doing OK," I lied. How do I even respond?

"Kyle," said Tammy in a stern voice. Her tone had certainly changed in the blink of a fart. "I asked Lucy to call this meeting because Tom and I are not happy with your performance as our publicist. We *feel* that you have basically *dropped* the ball. This is a serious matter and I, I mean *we*, *hope* you realize the importance of you getting *back* on track."

"We have all the faith in you bud," added Tom. Was he serious? You know, I think he was actually a sincere guy who had gotten involved with a viper. But even so, shouldn't he take responsibility for his bad decisions and still be blamed?

Lucy gave me a look of death that said I needed to mop up this situation and quick. She was pointing at her watch in irritation. Already her patience was spent after two minutes of Tammy.

"Lucy and I had a very long talk today." God, I hated this. I was good at what I did, and it wasn't fair I was being screwed like this for these two losers. I bit into my lip and looked Lucy right in the eye.

"I'm sorry and I guarantee you things will be different." Lucy sat back in her chair with a nod and a smile.

"We are *very* glad to hear this because we have *not* been happy." What a bitch. Despite my apologizing she just couldn't help saying it one more time.

"Now that *that* is understood we would like to see us booked on *Candy.*" Was she serious? These two expected me to get them the number-one hardest booking in North America? I was screwed. Candy, born Constance Williams in a small town in Arkansas, was an alcoholic ex-rodeo queen who fell on hard times. At her low point, she was working as a lot lizard, a down-and-out prostitute who climbed up parked semis, offering ten-dollar blowjobs to truckers. After getting raped and beaten by a rough group of rednecks, Candy was found bleeding in the bushes by an elderly itinerant preacher named Ross Davis. Davis nursed her back to health and Candy credited Davis with helping her to turn her life to God's work, praising him at his funeral as the father she never had. She traveled the Bible belt preaching at various revivals and that's where her fortunes turned. Supposedly, one misty day during her last year on TV, Oprah Winfrey was driving incognito by herself through the farmlands of southern Illinois on a soul-searching road trip. Like Willy Wonka and his chocolate factory, she was trying to decide to whom to turn over the reins of her business when she stumbled across the tent revival. Oprah was instantly enamored with Candy. After years of touting spiritual gurus like Deepak Chopra, pop psychologists and celebrities, Oprah in the end chose a carnie to take her place. Candy was an instant success. She had a down-home manner like Dolly Parton that was hard not to like. She appealed to a wide range of people who were drawn to this redheaded American success story. But she was especially loved by millions of middle-class women who had money to spend—she was a ratings bonanza.

"If anyone can get you on *Candy*," said Lucy. "Kyle can." Where did this assurance come from all of the sudden?

What had happened to my life? It had gone from things going well, falling in love with a hot guy, and now it was just a soured mess and moldering hope that I would remain employed. I was so grateful the M4 was paid for since it might be my permanent address. Then it hit me. As far as Lucy was concerned, I was a blackened banana left to die a terrible death in the back of the refrigerator. There has to be something more to life than this hell. I mumbled a goodbye as Lucy reached over and clicked the phone off with her claw. She gave me one more silent dirty look then left me alone. I wanted the hell out of there.

Stopping by Gelson's on the way home, I bought a meatloaf and a bottle of gin. Mabye some red meat with a Martini chaser might make things feel better. I couldn't wait to go home and anaesthetize myself. But on the way home my plan was foiled by a film premiere at the Dolby and I was stuck in an enormous traffic mess. Thousands of motorists jammed the streets of Hollywood and I prayed I would make it home soon before I lost it.

Ten minutes later I had only moved half a block. I hated living in Hollywood. I went to call Mel but realized my phone was in the trunk with my laptop. Great. Should I hop out and get it? The minute I did I knew the traffic would creep five feet and some twit would force their way in front of me which would simultaneously infuriate the person behind me. I needed to accept that I was a trapped rat.

When I finally reached the garage, my nerves were shot. Thank God I had pre-planned the gin. I was never so glad I had stopped off at the store. I parked, grabbed my loot, and headed to the elevator.

A piece of my mail dropped onto the floor when I pulled out the pile that had been crammed in there by the mail woman. I bent down to pick it up.

And there it was.

A postcard.

I just stood there unable to move. The elevator arrived. The doors opened and I let them shut as I just stood there, not sure how to feel. I just kept looking at it. It was one of those stupid cards with cartoon movers carrying boxes into a shiny new house.

I've Moved!!!
New Address is:
Andrew Kennedy
1967 Lakeshore Drive, #17
Chicago, IL 60657

CHAPTER EIGHTEEN

SHELLSHOCK

Regroup And Come OUT Fighting

"A.K. JUST MOVED TO CHICAGO."

The stunned look on their faces said it all. After everything that had happened none of us had expected this one. Mel, Mickey, Tyler and I were halfway through our Jambalaya at Southern Comfort; a Cajun / Creole hot spot that was a welcome change of pace to Southern California cuisine. Everything was extra greasy and extra spicy including hot southern waiters who'd been shipped in from Louisiana. You had to appreciate the authenticity; only a gay owner would think of that one.

"This is unbelievable. He left New York?" Mel was the first to comment.

"That's the first thing that came to my mind," I said.

"What an ass. I'm sorry Kyle but you deserved a phone call for that news instead of some mass-mailed postcard."

"Tyler's right," said Mickey. "Why would he do that?"

"Come on guys. He left me with no notice. Why is this such a shocker?"

"Because you expect people to eventually grow up." She had a point. I did expect that one day A.K. was going to grow up and realize what a huge mistake he had made. But what did that get me? Maybe I was the one who needed to grow up and let go of all of this.

"Kyle, one of the best things you can do is to forget about A.K." Tyler pushed his Jambalaya around with his fork on the hunt for one last shrimp. "The smartest thing I ever did was to stop trying to make things happen with relationships in my life. They either work or they don't whether it's romantic, friends, or sex. But regardless of the outcome it shouldn't dictate your happiness."

"Tyler that is such bullshit and you know it," said Mel. "Honest to God just because you like being single doesn't mean the rest of us do."

"Well Melanie, maybe you should accept that fact that I have some wisdom in this area. I am older than you as much as I hate to admit it."

"No one will argue that," shot Mickey. Tyler threw the rest of a half-eaten hush puppy his way which Mickey caught mid-air and popped it into his mouth.

"You ass," laughed Mickey with his mouth full. "So tell us Kyle, did you have a meltdown last night or what?"

"Leave it to Mickey to soften the blow," said Melanie. "But I have to admit I was going to ask it if he didn't."

"I just stood there. I didn't cry. I just felt completely confused by all of it. I mean, let's go back to that wonderful day when I came home and found out he'd moved all his stuff out. And he left me with one paragraph explaining he'd taken a dream job in New York and that he needed to go back there and be on his own again. That he just couldn't handle being in a relationship anymore and that he belonged in New York and that that was the only place he could ever really live. Yet he ends up in Chicago. Talk about shellshock. I knew he was having a hard time and didn't like living in LA but to just bail like he did."

This subject always set Mel off. She'd been the one who had the biggest responsibility mopping me up after A.K. left. "I have to tell you Kyle, why you care at all for this person is beyond me, especially after what he did to you."

"Melanie is right," said Tyler. "You should have put his photo on the bottom of a cat box long ago."

"Yeah, but this was the love of his life. It's easy to say hate someone when you weren't the one that loved 'em." The scary thing about Mickey was he could actually be a philosopher once and a while. "We all loved A.K. when he was around. He was impossible not to like."

The waiter came by to clear some plates. He pushed up against me a bit more than usual when he reached in to get mine. There's something disarming about having someone pick you up when you are in the middle of an emotional hurricane.

"Did you see that?" Melanie had a sharp eye.

"How could we miss it," said Mickey. Go for it Kyle. You could use some somethin' Cajuny in your life right now. Get yer mind off this mess."

"Mickey, how come your answer to everything is to get laid?" Although I had to love him for the simplicity of his philosophy.

"Works for me."

Melanie laughed. "Kyle, screw A.K. You've got something going on with Glenn that's good. Just go with that." Wow, did she just say something positive about Glenn?

"I can't. It's not going on. I don't know what the hell is happening."

Tyler sat straight up. For someone who didn't believe in relationships he was always the first who wanted the scoop. "What's this?"

"You tell me. Things got really weird with Glenn on Sunday when we went on a hike. He was a total ass and I haven't heard from him since."

"And now it's Thursday."

"Thanks for reminding me Mickey."

More advice from Mel. "Well don't call him. Let him apologize before you do anything more."

"I seriously doubt he'd ever apologize for anything. He's got an ego that could crush a building."

"No one's going to argue that point," said Tyler as he signaled the waiter. "Sweetie. A bread pudding, a bananas foster, and four spoons please."

"And another round," added Melanie as she waved the magic manicure over our drinks.

"Let's do an inventory," said Mickey. "Your job is on the line, A.K. is still fucking with you long distance, and the Glenn thing is off kilter. All in all, I'd say things are looking up."

I had to laugh. We all did. When the truth hurts it's time to apply the rule of laughing versus crying. I'd cried enough and what had it got me? Just smeared emotional mascara.

"I have to hit the head." I got up and headed to the back of the restaurant. On route I asked the hostess where it was, and she pointed me to a hallway.

"All the way back, a left and then a right."

I hit the hall, to the right, then left and came to a door. It was unmarked but I figured it must be the outer door to the restrooms. I pushed it open and found myself in a stockroom loaded with cans and boxes of supplies.

"Can I help you?" I almost hit the ceiling. I wheeled around and saw our waiter behind the door on top of a step ladder.

"Oh, sorry, I was looking for the bathroom and got lost." His crotch was at my eye level. There was something to be said for Louisiana's exports.

"This isn't the bathroom," he said with a smile and a cheesy southern drawl that made me stir in a cheap kind of way. He was looked right at me...intently. "Anything else maybe I could help you with?"

"Um, I..." (See Gay Scout Rule #9).

He stepped down and walked over to me. Pushing the door shut he locked it and jumped me. Wow! How the hell did this happen? What a fucked-up week. He pushed me back against the shelves and some of the cans rattled. He was all over me. I had had the kind of week that justified going at it like alley trash with only a few minutes to spare. I unbuttoned his shirt as fast as I could. Incredible body...I have to head south on my next vacation. I could hear belt buckles coming undone at light speed and before I knew it he was on his knees. I gulped and played with the back of his hair with my right hand. I leaned back and looked up at the rows of corn meal boxes. I had never thought of corn meal as sexy til now. Did that mean I'd get a hard-on from here on out every time I saw someone bite into a corn muffin? I don't know where this guy learned to do what he was doing but all of the sudden my eyes were rolling back in my head.

"Oh God, I'm going to blow." I pushed back too hard against the shelf unit behind me and while I was coming cans of tuna fish came flying down like meteorites. One of them bounced off his head.

"Gawd daaammmmmnit that hurt," he said, rubbing his head.

"Not for me it didn't." We both burst out laughing.

"I've got to go. I'm sure I have food up by now." He pulled up his pants as I did mine.

"Wow, thanks."

"No, thank you, that rocked," he said. He opened the door and directed me towards the restroom. Getting head on the way to the head. Not bad.

I pissed as fast as I could and went back to the table.

"Where the hell have you been?" said Mel. "Do you have diarrhea?"

"No, just met someone I knew and chatted a bit."

Mickey gave me a very knowing glance. "I wonder why our deserts are taking so long."

Just then my Louisiana home-grown came up with our drinks and desserts. We smiled at each other and I did a quick raise of my eyebrows in gratitude.

CHAPTER NINETEEN
S.O.S.

The Hour Of Death Is Near

FRIDAY. THANK GOD this week was almost over. At least I would have the weekend to regroup and sort some stuff out. I had poked around on Indeed.com looking at some other job possibilities as I knew I was close to getting tossed on the trash heap. Stressed? I was beyond stressed. How I had gone from the darling child to the unwanted child was beyond me. It just seemed to come from nowhere in the form of two horrible individuals campaigning against me. God bless 'em to hell.

I had also not heard from Glenn all week and that bothered me as well. Surprised? I thought about calling him today but then decided to screw it; if anyone deserved a phone call it was me. I wasn't going to be the one who caved. Still, if that was my philosophy, then why didn't I line anything up for this weekend? I hated to admit that I had kept it open in case he called at the last minute. I should go to Palm Springs and jump in a pool with a bunch of hot guys. That would be the perfect way to recapture my week.

I dialed the direct line of my contact at *Candy* for what had to be the zillionth time today. I couldn't risk just leaving a message; I needed to at least get some feedback from her. It was a long shot, but I had put together thirty different pitches on how to sell Tammy and Tom to be on the show. Talk about pulling something out of my ass in the nick of time. It was a miracle of PR that I actually came up with one legitimate idea let alone thirty. Sometimes shit can sell. It just has to be packaged as roses.

The line rang. One more ring and it would go into voice mail and I would hang up.

"Megan Chalmers."

"Megan, it's Kyle from Devore-Horizon."

"Oh, hi Kyle. Can you hold real quick?"

While on hold I took time to say a prayer. Please Megan, God will be good to you if you just do this one enormous favor for me.

"Back again, sorry. It's been a complete zoo here today due to a guest canceling on me. I'm completely frustrated."

"Sorry to hear that." Damn, hurry up and tell me the verdict.

"So, listen Kyle, the show proposals you sent over were great." (!!!) "But we are going to pass on this one," (#@!!%~!@#).

"Rats. Can you tell me why?"

"You really want to know?"

"I can handle it."

"It's nonsense. Not your proposals but the material. Honestly, have you actually read this thing?"

"Believe it or not from cover to cover."

"It's absurd don't you think? The idea is catchy but once you start into it…well, it's just worthless.

"I understand." I was crestfallen and very possibly out of a job. There are deal breakers in life and this was one for me.

"I'm sorry Kyle. I wish there was some way we could do something with it but there just isn't, and it's not just my opinion, I had some other people look at it and our thoughts were unanimous."

"No problems Megan. I really appreciate you taking time with it. I know you're swamped."

"Well, luckily I had read it before this show I was working on fell apart. It's alcohol awareness week next week and I had the grandson of the actual Bill W. coming on the show until he panicked and bailed on me this morning."

Was this Deus Ex Machina? In my hour of need were the Gods reaching down from heaven to save me?

"Megan, I have a great person that we can build a show around on alcohol. Gordon Lempkin."

"I forgot you repped Gordon. Candy's a huge fan of his books."

"Then why haven't you done anything with him yet?"

"I don't know. There's a lot she's a fan of so we can't do everything. Can you get him last minute?"

"For you no problem." When Candy calls you respond regardless of anything else. One appearance on the show can mean nearly one million book sales. It's an incredible machine to reach the masses.

"We're doing a live show one week from today."

It was happening! All would be forgiven from Lucy re: Tammy and Tom if I got anyone on Candy.

"Kyle, let me go run this by our exec producer and Candy. I'll call you back as soon as I have an answer. This could be a great replacement show."

The clock stopped at that point. When I had to go to the bathroom I had someone stand at my desk and monitor my phone. I couldn't miss this call no matter what.

About an hour later the call finally came through.

"OK, it's a go on our end. You and I need to put together the show structure. In the meantime, I'll have our travel department get flights for you and Gordon. What city does he live in?"

"He's in Taos."

"Cool. I need to finish some things here first. Can we do this in about an hour? I'll call you and we'll work on it together."

"That works on my end. Megan, I owe you big time."

"Hey, you made my life a lot easier. It just worked out."

I hung up the phone and shot down to Lucy's office. She was in the middle of a meeting with the editing suits. I knocked on the door frame and everyone turned to look at me.

"Kyle, we're having a meeting. Is this important?"

"Yeah, I just spoke to Megan at *Candy.*"

"You'd better have some good news for me."

"They don't want to do Tammy and Tom. They looked at the materials and feel it's not a good fit for them at this time but maybe later down the road. It's being kept on the back burner." What a crock that was.

"Damn it that is *not* what I would call good news, Kyle."

"No wait." I could feel my left leg trembling in my pants because I was so excited. "The good news is I convinced them to book Gordon Lempkin for a show on alcohol awareness week next Friday. It's a go!" Everyone cheered. This would mean massive amounts of money coming into the coffers especially since Gordon had not one but three books on booze that we published. I had taken back my title of Wunderkind. Even Lucy cheered.

"I knew you could do it Kyle." Another crock.

After some glad-handing I went back to my office floating on my success. Even if Candy cancelled, I still had saved my ass by getting the booking. I'd have to get a good gift for Megan for making this happen. (Gay Scout Rule # 20...*Always* grease the machine).

The rest of the afternoon zipped by in a happy haze and I knew I was going to have a great weekend enjoying my *Candy* afterglow. Even the Friday evening traffic didn't bother me as I inched my way home. Life was good and I could sigh a sense of relief.

As I stuck my key into my door lock my phone started ringing in my pants. Damn, never fails. I fumbled trying to get the lock open, zipped in, and fished it out of my pocket. Glenn.

"Yeah?"

"Hey." About time you called me.

"Hey." Pause. Silence.

"What's up, you sound out of breath?"

"I just walked in the door."

"I tried reaching you at work, but you'd already left." Another awkward pause. I wasn't going to say anything.

"I wondered if you'd like to have some dinner tonight?" Now what? Deep down I wanted to see him again, but I was still upset from Sunday.

"You there?"

"Yeah, I'm here," I said. "You know Glenn, this isn't a good night for me." I did it. Hooray for me.

"What are you doing?"

"I have plans." More silence. I'd better think of something quick in case he asks me what my plans actually are. I could tell by the third pause that he was sensing my coolness.

"I was hoping I'd see you tonight." Well buddy, you aren't. "What's your weekend like?"

"I kind of left it open, I'm not sure what I'm going to do. Thought I'd play it by ear."

"Maybe I could give you a call tomorrow and see if you want to do something." It was a statement more than a question. I could feel myself starting to cave.

"Tell you what Glenn, why don't you call me in the morning after I get back from the gym and we'll figure something out."

"OK, that sounds good." I was semi-fuming.

"Listen, I need to get going."

"Oh, yeah no problem, have a fun night and I'll talk to you tomorrow."

"That works. Later, bye."

"Bye." I hung up the phone. Nice attempt at an apology. I had to wonder if he even felt he had done anything that constituted saying he was sorry. Such an ego. Maybe I was being a hard-ass but I didn't think I was so out of line expecting some acknowledgement from him ruining last weekend.

OK, points for standing my ground and not caving but there was still one problem. I was left with nothing to do on a Friday night.

CHAPTER TWENTY

REDEMPTION

Call Me An Idiot; But This Is Why I Love Him

I HAVE TO ADMIT THAT I WAS SURPRISED there were not one but two messages from Glenn when I returned that morning after the gym. I had left my cell at home. It was completely out of character and I have to admit I was loving it. I'd rattled the lion's cage with my coolness the night before and I needed to make sure I remembered the effectiveness of being a cooze. I had gotten an hour's worth of sun by the pool and figured that 11:27 a.m. wasn't too early to call him back. He answered before the second ring—had he been waiting by the phone?

"Hello?"

"It's me, returning."

"So, what's up?"

"Sweat, sore muscles, and stinky armpits. What about you?"

"I was wondering if you wanted to go boating with me today? I thought we'd buzz out on the water, get some sea air, and watch the sun set." Wow, talk about a great offer for a date.

"I don't know."

"Come on Kyle. I'm dying to get on the boat and it's a lot more fun if someone else is there. I'll take care of everything all you need to do is be ready in thirty minutes."

"Pick me up in forty-five." Before he could respond I hung up the phone. It was going to be different from here on out. We were playing by my rules now.

After my shower I smeared some reduced fat Jif peanut butter on a cold cinnamon English muffin and wondered into my bedroom. While I picked out the raisins and ate them one by one, I pondered what to wear on a boating expedition. I did have a pair of plain white canvas sneakers that looked cool without socks. I put those on with some walking shorts and a nifty white Cuban shirt that I picked up in Miami the year before. I grabbed a sweatshirt for when it got chilly later on and also some sunscreen. Once I had my clothes in order, I finished my muffin while reading a magazine. I was getting restless waiting for the forty-five minutes to go by. Reality was I could have easily been ready in twenty. I walked into the bathroom and brushed my teeth. When I was done my cell phone rang. It was him, early. So impatient.

"You downstairs?"

"Ready to roll. What about you?"

"Yup, be right down."

Glenn was waiting for me in a brand-new dusty-black Range Rover. I guess this is the car he uses for boating. I hopped into the passenger seat and he flashed me a wavering smile. Instead of a kiss he tousled my hair and scratched me behind the ears. Was he nervous?

"I'm glad you're here. This is going to be great."

The ride down La Brea on route to hit the 10 was filled with mindless chatter on everything from the Dodger game the night before to a future desire to rummage through the antique stores lining La Brea. He spoke quickly. He *was* nervous. You'd have thought he was on a first date, but he wasn't this way first time we went out. This was something quite different. Glenn *always* exuded confidence. I was intrigued.

"It's really hot today," I said. "I like the heat." It was around ninety-five in Hollywood and when we pulled onto the freeway Glenn raised the windows and blasted the air. He continued to babble on while we buzzed west towards the Marina. I had never seen his boat, or ship, or whatever you call it. I hoped it wasn't some dinky sailboat that looked easy to fall out of. I'm no pussy but I didn't want to end up like Natalie Wood after three beers.

He pulled into the lot and we hopped out. The ocean air did feel good even if it was tinged with the smell of rotting seagull poop and gasoline. Glenn opened the back of the car and pulled out an enormous ice chest. I enjoyed watching his muscles bulge and his face grimace in pain up when he lifted the chest out. Clearly it weighed a ton.

"What the hell did you put in there?"

"Chow and some stuff to drink. Did you think I wouldn't feed you?"

He smiled, and to be honest, I felt myself begin to relax because this is the way it's supposed to be. He threw a large duffle bag at me and then slung a second one over his shoulder. He locked the car and we started down the dock. There was an interesting collection of boats in the marina. Old and new, and big and small. Finally, he dropped the chest and bag down.

"Here's she is."

We stood in front of the *Eclipse*. She was definitely not a dingy, but she wasn't quite a mega-yacht either. She was however, a beautiful sailboat bobbing under the blue sky. Two sailor-looking guys were busy fixing ropes and preparing things for our sojourn. As soon as they saw Glenn they jumped onto the dock and grabbed the ice chest and our gear. I stepped onto the boat and started to get some sea legs. I don't know why they call sailboats "she" when they are clearly masculine beings. For God's sake, the big mast juts straight up; it doesn't get much more phallic than that. Everything about the boat was male, from the dark cherry wood to the shining brass knobs that glistened from a vigorous rubbing. Everything was hard and strong and made to handle the elements. Glenn threw me a bottle of water while he and the crew continued to get things ready. After what seemed like endless preparations, Glenn signed some paper they had given him and then the two guys jumped onto the dock.

"Aren't they coming?"

"No, I can handle it myself. They just get everything ready."

I quickly looked around for where the life jackets were kept. After all, I didn't really know how accomplished Glenn was on the water and I didn't want to end up dead from some stupid date. But before I could think too much about it the motor was putt-putting us through the marina and out to sea.

"How long have you been sailing?" I asked.

"Since I was ten." He looked over at me. "Are you nervous?"

"No, I just wondered." I have to admit I was glad to hear his answer. I guess it wasn't like being flown in a single-engine Cessna where he could have a heart attack and we'd plummet to earth. I'd have a chance out on the water. The ice chest he brought along had food to last at least a week I'm sure. Or at least enough to throw a reception for the rescue crew if they found me in time.

He smiled at me. "I'm glad you're here," he said.

When we got far enough out on the water he shut off the engine and began barking orders at me. My delusion that I was going to recline with a glass of wine while he skippered the boat was replaced with a crash course in ropes, knots, and other sailing accouterment. I quickly found out it was a lot more complicated than it looked.

Before I knew it though, the sail caught wind and off we went. It was amazing as we sped along in the water with the sea spraying our faces. I watched his strong forearms when he turned the wheel. You had to hand it to Glenn...definite power-stud.

"Look over there!" I looked down into the water and saw dolphins swimming alongside the boat.

"Wow, how cool is that?"

"Pretty darn cool." He reached over and pawed me behind the ear again. I was getting to like that.

We buzzed around on the water for an hour then Glenn dropped both the sail and the anchor. Once we were more or less stationary, he began fiddling in the galley. Before long he came to the back of the boat where I was. He had wine bottle and glasses in hand. A guy could grow to like this.

"I'm glad you're here." OK, how many times has he said this to me this day? He opened the bottle and we sat back soaking it all in.

"I come out here when I want to completely unwind. This is my idea of paradise."

"It's not bad," I admitted. "It really is peaceful." We listened to the sound of the boat rocking on the water.

"Kyle, have you ever lived with someone?" O.K., where did that come from?

"Yeah, one guy."

"What happened?" Now this is one of those moments when you have to make a decision very fast. Are you honest and cop to the fact that your lover left you without any notice? Or do you gloss it over and make out like you're the one who decided to call it quits?

"It just didn't work out." Chicken.

"Why?" Was this therapy?

"I don't know. We had two different game plans and they just didn't mesh." Yeah, that's it. My game plan was to stay in a relationship and A.K.'s was to dump my ass.

"Relationships are hard." That was vulnerability. All right, what was going on with him?

"I sometimes think they are God's joke on mankind because you're right they *are* hard. They can be the greatest thing in the world and then everything can just go sailing down the drain at light speed." OK, maybe I should lay off the honesty a bit.

"Would you ever live with someone again?" What the hell was he up to? How does this guy go from being Mr. Icy to Mr. Hot? I was feeling a bit off kilter by all of this.

"Yeah, I would. If it was the right guy." That seemed to shut him up. He looked away out towards where the sun would eventually set.

"What about you?" He just looked back at me with no expression on his face. I'm not exactly sure why he was so blank. Then he gave me a quarter-smile and turned back out towards the ocean.

"It feels comfortable with you, Kyle." Before I could say something, a seagull plopped down on the edge of the boat and looked at us. Glenn chuckled. The bird flew off and Glenn's attention returned to me. He put his hand up to the side of my face and just kind of kept it there while he looked at me. Quiet…the boat in the water. He pulled me closer until our mouths met…it was a really nifty kiss, soft and lingering. He pulled back and kept looking at me.

"I sometimes wonder what it would be like living with you." I was speechless. I didn't know what to say yet felt compelled to verbalize something. Had I thought of living with Glenn? Yeah, of course. But I didn't know the answer to that one. It was still pretty new and confusing and all.

"There would be boxers on the floor."

"Huh?"

"I leave my boxers on the floor. I'm terrible about picking up my dirty laundry." OK, well, not the most poetic response but it was the first thing that came into my head I felt I could cop up to.

He just laughed, which broke the tension and then I laughed too.

CHAPTER TWENTY-ONE

SEASIDE SANITY

Hey Sailor!

AS THE BOAT SWAYED THE MORNING LIGHT breached between the gap in the curtains and struck my eyelids. Fighting waking up was useless with the sun on the opposite team. While I struggled to get my bearings, I realized the bed was rocking. Ah, that's right, Glenn's boat. Rock, rock, rock. It was complete tranquility. It had taken me a bit to fall asleep the night before, what with my fear of drowning and such, but once I did, I slept like a log. Inhaling the salty air, I backed up against Glenn's chest. He was sound asleep, and I could feel his breath on the back of my neck. God, I loved that. This was so nice and simple. What the hell had happened yesterday? I mean, he just kind of came around didn't he? He'd been such an ass only days before. I didn't get it. But maybe I needed to stop finding answers to his idiosyncrasies and just relax. Relax. That was easy this morning. Being careful not to wake him I rolled over so I could lie face to face. I just stared at his face, at the pores and the stubble, and the lips that were the most incredible mix of gentleness and masculinity. I stroked his face with the back of my knuckles, and he stirred a bit. At least if I woke him it would be a good way to come into morning. There was some salt mixed in with the pepper and that was pretty hot. He inhaled a deep breath. He was deep in peaceful sleep.

My hand went down to the top of his chest, the part just under his neck. It creeps me out to touch someone's collarbone but that part of the chest where the pec begins is so incredibly hot. Fuzzy. Muscular. Simple.

My stomach alerted me that I was starving. Too bad he didn't bring some cookies into his captain's quarters last night. That would have been cool. I could have nibbled on them while I pondered his chest hair. A slight purr erupted from his lips and buzzed along with his dreams. I just lay there and wondered if it was possible to have a life with this guy? He was so much of what I had been looking for, and while he certainly had his downside, I had to wonder if I could do better.

This time his eyes opened when he stirred. "Hey."

"Morning."

He smiled and took a deep breath in then exhaled. His hand came up to my face and he stroked the back of his fingers against my morning stubble, just as I had done while he slept.

His eyes darted around, surveying my face and tousled hair. "You look really sexy right now," he said.

Say it again. I smiled, and for once, just didn't say anything.

"Aren't you glad you came out here with me?"

"Yeah, it's been great."

He snickered, "Especially last night."

"Yeah." Now it was my turn to smile. It was the kind of sex where the afterglow carries you into the next day.

"We make a pretty good team, don't we?" It was a statement more than a question, and it came from his heart. He just kept smiling at me and I just felt...I just felt great. Because I was ready to be part of a team again. Let's be honest. I was sick and tired of being alone and I knew I was ready to attack life with someone by my side.

"Yeah, we do. Thanks." I pulled him into me, feeling his hairy chest against mine. There's something incredibly beautiful about holding another man, that melding of muscle and sweat, and fuzz, and stubble and smooth skin. Pulled together under the caress of a giant's gentleness.

We held each other close; feeling each other breathe in and out.

And that's all that mattered right then.

CHAPTER TWENTY-TWO

DRY LAND CONFUSION

Love Should Come With A Guidebook

MELANIE'S LEFT RING FINGER TAPPED against the side of her plate while I told her about my weekend with Glenn. Hunger had hit me by the time I got back home so I gave her a call to see if she wanted me to download the whole experience over some falafel.

She didn't say much while I gave her the details. She just kept tapping away. Now I had come to the end of my story and we were just kind of staring at each other while I waited for her to respond.

"I'm glad for you Kyle."

"No, you're not."

"Is it that obvious?"

"Yeah."

"I don't know. He seems like a great guy on one end, but I just don't get a good feeling about it. I don't know why that is. Maybe I'm just being a jealous bitch."

"I doubt it myself sometimes, but Mel, it was incredible."

"I'm sure it was Kyle. Who wouldn't have wanted to be out on the water on a boat? I'm just concerned about other things."

"Yeah, I know what you mean. But has it ever crossed your mind that maybe you and I are single because we are too picky? I mean there's something wrong with everyone and maybe we are just waiting for Mr. Too-Perfect."

"I'd buy that if Glenn called you more. He just seems kind of infantile at times. It's the egomaniac in him, constantly needing to be fed, or whipped I bet. I know about these things you know."

"That's what bothers me." I bit into my falafel and a big glob of yogurt sauce ran down my chin. Mel grimaced.

"Shades of this afternoon?" she said as she mocked a blow job into the air.

"Actually, last night, this morning and this afternoon if you really want to know."

"Damn. Forget what I've been saying and marry the bastard. I didn't realize old men could get it on like that." I very ungracefully continued with my sandwich, using the back of my hand for a napkin. Mel picked away at her salad; wheels turning in her head.

"I know I haven't been very supportive of all of this, Kyle."

"I understand. You're just looking out for my best interests."

"Yeah, that's true, but…well to be honest I guess I've been a little scared."

I was slightly confused. Mel's bravery usually took a front seat to any fear in her life. It's what gave her the ability to look at chains, whips, and a stockade as a nifty challenge instead of something to run from.

"I just don't want to lose you. I suppose that with everything happening with Glenn I felt it was a possibility."

"Mel, come on. I didn't drop you while A.K. and I were together. What makes you think it would be any different with Glenn?"

"Because A.K. loved the fact I was a dominatrix and Glenn would be disgusted. That's why."

"How do you know he would disapprove?"

"Are you telling me you've actually told him?" She was looking right at me. What should I say? Truth of the matter is I hadn't said anything to Glenn about what she did for a living because I *didn't* want him to disapprove. In some ways it had been easy to avoid because he had never asked me one question regarding any of my friends.

"When you and A.K. got together I was really happy for you. You both brought out the best in each other. He made you a happy person and you opened a world for him that he only dreamed of. I can just tell that Glenn is the type who has preconceived ideas of what makes a person worth hanging around."

"I'm sure you'd charm the pants off Glenn."

"Maybe. But he wouldn't respect me and that's a big thing in my book."

She was right. Glenn would be polite to Mel but deep down he would probably see her as a circus freak and not the wonderful person I knew her to be. It made me think again. If I was in a relationship with Glenn how would my friends fit into the equation? Would he be one of those guys that would slowly push me away from them until I was only with him?

"So I'm happy for you Kyle but I have to admit I wish it was you getting back with A.K. like it should be and not with someone else."

"That's not going to happen, Mel."

"Well maybe it should."

"How?" This conversation was beginning to irk me. Here I had just wanted to bask in the afterglow of my weekend with Glenn and it was turning into a therapy session.

"That's for you to figure out. I mean come on Kyle. Clearly he had a reason for letting you know he moved to Chicago."

"It was a stupid, mass-mailed postcard, nothing more." Who even uses those anymore?

"I don't think so. If he didn't want to hear from you he wouldn't have sent you anything. The two of you haven't spoken since he called you a month after he left. I'm telling you Kyle, this is his way of reaching out to you."

I didn't want to hear this. It had taken me a long time, but I'd finally put A.K. to rest in many ways and was moving forward in my life. Yeah, I wondered why he had sent the postcard. It was kind of peculiar that he would do that instead of just picking up a phone and saying hi. Was he scared to talk to me? How did two people who loved each other as much as we did end up only being able to converse via a three-by-five-inch card?

My irritation was turning into exhaustion at this point. I was tired and just wanted to mellow out after an emotionally charged day. I didn't want to be reliving painful emotions.

"I'm telling you Kyle that..."

"Mel can we please drop this?" She looked caught off guard.

"I'm sorry. I didn't mean to anger you."

"I'm not angry. Maybe a little. It's just...look...things are finally going well with Glenn and I want to focus on that. I spent enough of my life trying to figure out what the hell A.K. was all about."

"I'm just saying..."

"Stop it!" I had raised my voice enough to embarrass myself. Mel looked down at her plate. "If A.K. wanted to be with me he wouldn't have left me, understand? It's very simple when you think about it. His postcard is an afterthought. It had a goddamn computer printed label on it. I'm sure he just printed out everyone in his address book and threw mine into the mass mailing with the rest." She looked up at me, clearly sorry that she had brought this up. I just sat there burning.

"Goddamn it Mel, he didn't even take the time to write one... fucking...personal line on it." My voice cracked when I said it and I felt my eyes water. I pinched my eyes with my fingers and tried to concentrate on not losing it in the restaurant. I was tired, I'd had too much to drink, and this was not the conversation I had the wherewithal to tackle.

"Let's get the check," I said. Mel signaled and reached for her purse. "Let me get this."

"No, it's my turn."

"Kyle, it's the least I can do, I ruined dinner." She handed me back my credit card and I decided not to fight it. She threw some cash on the table and we got up to leave.

The walk across the restaurant had that feeling to it as if the entire world had been listening in on our every word. Once we were out the door, we walked along the sidewalk in silence until we got to Mel's car.

"OK, I'll call you tomorrow, Kyle."

"Sounds good."

"Oh, crap."

"What?"

"I forgot to bring this up earlier. Now's probably the worst time to ask but I need to make arrangements before tickets go up at midnight."

"Oh, that's right, your sister's wedding."

"Did you make up your mind as to going?"

"Yeah, sure."

"I really appreciate it. I'll take care of everything. Thank you."

"Not a problem." She slid into her car and I waved goodbye then walked down the street towards mine.

The drive home was one of those where I don't want the radio on because I'd rather be tortured with my own thoughts. There was a lot running through my mind. I tried to focus more on the earlier part of the day and how great it had been with Glenn out on the water. He was a good guy even though he was a bit tricky at times. I needed to stop bitching and remind myself of what was good about him.

I knew things would be cool with Mel in the morning and that we'd probably discuss this in further detail when we were both sober and not tired. At this point in time though I didn't know if I really ever wanted to discuss this subject. I was so frustrated.

I parked my car and gave a slight nod of my head to a neighbor who waved at me. It seemed like an eternity before the elevator finally came. I watched the number click from one to the next until I was home at my floor

Walking into my apartment I went over to the dining room table and picked up A.K.'s emotionless postcard. Refusing to look at it, I went into the kitchen and tossed it in the garbage where it belonged.

CHAPTER TWENTY-THREE

CANDY AHOY!

Chicago Here We Come

AFTER SITTING ON THE RUNWAY FOR FORTY-FIVE MINUTES the plane finally climbed into the sky. I looked out my window and watched New Mexico get smaller and smaller. I sat up straight and looked back a few rows at Gordon. He was fast asleep in his seat. I envy people who can sleep on planes.

It had already been an interesting two days. I'd flown into New Mexico the night before so that I could personally keep an eye on Gordon, and more importantly, escort him onto this flight. I'd taken his Starbucks into the men's room stall with me and poured half of it in the toilet. Then I spiked it with four miniatures of vodka. I didn't find out until the last minute that Gordon had a severe fear of flying. One that he felt could easily be cured with a few stiff drinks. I had envisioned someone calling the *TMZ* and spilling the beans about a tipsy charlatan on the flight, so I thought I'd better keep up appearances and load his coffee in privacy. He'd swigged it down before we boarded and now it looked like he was sleeping it off.

I'd come a long way to get this close to Candy and I wasn't about to blow it. In twenty-four hours, we'd be done with the show and I would pour Gordon back on a plane to Albuquerque.

Everything was running like clockwork. We'd land in Chicago and head straight to the hotel where I would stay in the same room with Gordon. I wasn't taking any chances by letting Gordon have his own room. It was funny; he was like a little kid in some ways. When he knew someone was watching him, he behaved himself. Give him too much leeway and you were in trouble.

I pushed my face up against the scratched plastic of the window, feeling the plane's vibrations against my cheek. Life is odd. One day you're going about your business and then you happen to run into someone in a casual way. That encounter then changes your life forever. There's never a grandiose introduction to the people we fall in love with or the ones who wreak havoc on us. They just happen to have stopped at the 7-Eleven exactly when you did to pick up a pack of smokes. Then they caught your eye across the aisle, smiled, and then that's when your life changed. It had all come down to a split-second craving for a cigarette that led to me meeting A.K. and I almost skipped going to Target the day I met Glenn. It made me wonder what other ordinary event was going to bring me to someone who would have tremendous impact on my future.

"Tired?"

"I'm sorry?" The woman next to me had decided it was time to talk.

"I said are you tired? You had your head against the window like you were trying to take a nap." Then why did you start talking to me? Perhaps it was her attempt to make sure I suffered the same sleepless flight that everyone in the center seat would experience.

"Just thinking."

"Planes are a good place for that aren't they?"

"Yeah. I suppose so. Do you live in Chicago?"

"No, just going to visit my daughter. There's a *celebrity* on this flight." She whispered the word celebrity which I found endearing.

"Really?" I said. At least now she had something interesting to say. "Who?"

"Gordon Lempkin," she whispered again, despite the fact he was completely out of earshot. Jesus. This was going to be a long flight.

"He's a famous author. Have you heard of him?"

"Yeah, I have."

"His book saved my life."

"Really?" Now I was interested.

"Yes. I was able to stop drinking after reading his first book. It was a miracle. I wonder if I should say something to him."

The thought of her trying to talk to Gordon and then possibly smelling alcohol on his breath was something I thought she could do without. I decided to protect the image of her hero for her even though Vodka is the best bet for sober-smelling breath.

"You know, I hear he's a very, very, private man. Extremely humble and he hates having people say something to him." Maybe this would keep her from talking to him.

"Oh, that's probably true. I wouldn't want to be a pest. It's just that he helped me so much."

"I know what you mean."

Ironic. The man who had helped millions of people kick their addictions couldn't make it through the day without succumbing to one of his own. It was hard to imagine Gordon ever being sober. Most likely he had written all of his books loaded.

For whatever reason she became engrossed again in her *OK!* magazine. This was the brilliance of our world and in a twisted way what I loved about PR. An alcoholic who couldn't kick the sauce if he wanted to had helped countless others do it. It had also made him a rich man in the process. All that mattered was people like this woman next to me believing what they read in a magazine or saw on TV. The truth was inconsequential. It was the perception that mattered and perception that kept people like me employed. At times I wondered about the integrity of it all but just look at her... Gordon had indeed helped her even if he was a mess himself. You couldn't argue with that.

Gordon didn't wake up until the plane bumped down on the runway. Looking back again I saw him trying to come to life. If only the rest of the trip could be this smooth, then I'd be home free. Everyone at the office was waiting on pins and needles for tomorrow. The show would go out live in certain markets and then run off tape later in the day for the rest of the country. By nightfall tomorrow a staggering number of viewers would have seen Gordon and be purchasing his books. The latest book he wrote was about making any kind of change in your life, not just stopping drinking, so it had fantastic mass appeal. Every available copy of Gordon's books had been shipped from our warehouses to Amazon and various distributors and chains. This one appearance was going to make a small fortune for Devore Horizon and would simultaneously make me the hero of the office. I imagined a ticker-tape welcome when I got back.

Once inside the terminal I wrestled with the luggage while Gordon waited for me on a bench over by the side of the baggage area. When I finally found the last piece, I headed over to where he was sitting.

"Did you find them all?"

"Yeah, all six. You don't travel very light do you?"

"Be prepared for everything my boy. Plus, I brought some goodies for the producers and Miss Candy that I picked up at a Taos art fair this week. Just some tacky cheap shit that looks expensive."

"Excuse me, Mr. Lempkin?" It was the woman next to me on the flight. She'd finally swarmed in on her target.

"Yes, I'm Gordon Lempkin." She turned to me with an excited grin on her face.

"You sly dog. Are you traveling together? You were so coy acting on the plane." Gordon had a quizzical look on his face obviously realizing he had missed something while lost in cocktail-lubricated slumber.

"Busted. Gordon is going to be on *Candy* tomorrow. I'm his publicist."

"How exciting! I have to tell you Mr. Lempkin, your book simply changed my life. I haven't had a drop in six years now!"

"Bravo young lady, bravo!" said Gordon. He grabbed her hands in his.

"Thank you. Thank you so much for everything," she gushed. Tears were welling up in her eyes and in Gordon's too.

"You must be my special guest at the show tomorrow," said Gordon. "Kyle here can arrange for you to sit in the audience. The woman squealed with delight while I cringed inside. This was not my show to produce and now I had one more logistic to deal with. After getting her contact information and handing her my card with my cell number on it, I loaded Gordon into the limo that the show had sent.

Once we were settled into the back seat and on the expressway, I looked over at Gordon. He seemed to be lost in thought looking out the window. He let out a big sigh.

"Well then," he said.

I wondered what was going through his mind. How many times a month did someone recognize him and tell him what a difference he had made in their lives. Did it make him feel like a sham knowing he couldn't get through the day without a fifth by his side?

We sat together in silence for the rest of the ride. The Chicago skyline drew closer. Aside from one layover at O'Hare years ago this was my first trip here. What had drawn A.K. here from his beloved New York? Maybe there was another man in the picture now and he was living with someone.

"Kyle?"

"Yes Gordon?"

"Are you hungry?"

"Starving."

"Would you mind if I showed you around Chicago a bit? It's one of my favorite towns. I know a great place that serves corn-fed filets that are out of this world. It would be so much nicer than spending the evening in a lonely hotel room."

"You're right Gordon. That works for me." (Gay Scout Rule #3 ... Appreciate a nice cut of meat).

"Then an evening soaking up the best of Chicago it is."

CHAPTER TWENTY-FOUR
TITTIES AND BEER

Life On The South Side

THE HOTEL SCREWED UP THE RESERVATION so instead of a two-bedroom suite Gordon and I had to share a regular room with two double beds. They offered an extra room, but I thought it was best to keep a close watch on him.

Once we were unpacked, I sat in one of the barrel chairs near the window and gazed out onto the city. The chair was covered in that kinky hotel fabric containing a mix of colors you'd never use in your own home but is designed to hide what the last guest was up to. I puffed away on one of Gordon's Dunhill Reds while waiting for him to finish in the bathroom. He'd been in there a good twenty minutes with terrible flatulence that I could hear as clearly as if I was sitting next to him. Finally, he emerged with beads of sweat dotting his forehead.

"Remind me to *never* mix vodka and Starbucks again."

"You OK?"

"Nothing some red meat and a baked potato can't fix. Are you ready?"

Jumping up I grabbed my jacket. Gordon carefully arranged a silk scarf around his weathered neck before putting on his navy-blue jacket. He patted his sides then shoved his gold-plated lighter, cigarette case and reading glasses into the offending pockets. Odd that Gordon protected his cigs in a casket of precious metal while his glasses had the hell scratched out of them from being tossed in the same pocket.

"All right then young man. Let us paint the town red!" And off we went.

We piled into the cab in front of the hotel and Gordon tapped on the back of the passenger headrest.

"Have you heard of a restaurant called the 'Little Luck'?"

"On the south side?" the driver asked, almost incredulous that anyone would want to go to that part of town if they were staying at our hotel.

"That would be the one my friend." The cab pulled out from the curb and zoomed away.

"Kyle, my friend. This night's on me. You haven't lived until you've spent an evening at the 'Little Luck'." Gordon had the same expression a fourteen-year-old boy does when he finds out his parents are going to be gone for the weekend and he'll have the house to himself.

"What kind of place am I in for Gordon?

"Just you wait and see my friend."

After driving until what I thought had to be Indiana, the cab moved along a scary street that had seen better days. Large brick Queen Ann town homes whose beauty had faded years ago struggled to retain some sense of decency; some of them darkened from abandonment. In the middle of the block was an oasis of light and activity.

A restaurant with heavy green velvet curtains in the windows and two stone maidens flanking each side of the stoop. This was going to be interesting. We hopped out of the cab and Gordon walked up to the hulking piece of flesh guarding the door.

"Mr. Lempkin, it's been a while."

"Yes, it has Charles. How is the wife?"

"Doin' good sir." And with that he opened the door onto the wildest steakhouse into which I would ever set foot. In the corner was a jazz pianist banging on the keys of well-polished upright while an old African American chanteuse croaked away and kept the crowd cheering for more. Sawdust covered the creaking plank floor and cigar smoke filled every corner of the room. A gorgeous blond hostess whose tits were spilling out of her dress showed us to our table once she was done flirting with Gordon. We weren't seated for a minute when a waiter came by with two glasses of water and what looked suspiciously like a bourbon and something.

"Hello Mr. Lempkin, how are you tonight?" He put the cocktail next to Gordon.

"Wonderful, wonderful. I'm going to be on the *Candy* show tomorrow."

"Oh, good for you. And what is your friend going to have."

"I'll have a gin and tonic please."

"No, he won't, it's his first time here. He'll have an Old Style." Before I could protest the waiter was gone.

"It's a must your first time here my boy."

"Why is that?"

"You'll see." He winked at me and stuck the tip of his tongue out the side of his mouth.

I looked around the room while the music and singing blared on. You had to hand it to alcoholics...they know how to have a good time.

"Oh Kyle, here's your beer," said Gordon with a sense of glee.

Turning to face the waiter I was instead greeted by a pair of breasts that belonged to the same hostess who had seated us. She had my beer in her hand.

"Well hello there," she cooed. My face was getting red.

"Hey."

She gave me a big smile and started to put my beer down in front of me. I thanked her and then when I reached for it she snatched it away from me.

"Oh wait. I can't let you drink it like that."

Maybe I was confused but I realized I was the only one who felt that way because all the tables around us were looking over at Gordon and me.

"Why is that?"

"This is your fist time here, right?"

"Yeah."

"Hey everyone," she bellowed as the music came to a screeching halt. "This is his first Old Style at the 'Little Luck.'" The crowd cheered and I sensed I was in trouble. It didn't take a genius to figure out I was going to have to earn my beer tonight. Gordon was cracking up. "So big boy, do you want this beer or don't you?" She held the side of the bottle up to her cheek. The crowd laughed.

"Uh, yeah."

"Should I give it to him like this?" she asked.

"NO!" the crowd shouted back. Oh God, what was coming next? I could feel my face getting red and sweat starting to bead on the back of my neck. She looked me straight in the eye and then put her foot up onto the edge of my seat so that one leg was propped up. The crowd was hooting and hollering. She reached down to the edge of her skirt and started to pull it up on her thighs.

"Yes, yes, yes, yes!" hollered the crowd.

With her other hand she made a big gesture with the beer bottle and ran it up her thigh and then under her skirt. The crowd went nuts. She pulled her skirt higher and higher while following it with the bottle. Finally, she got to a point that only I could see between the edge of her skirt and the bottle. I was also the only one that could see she had no underwear on.

"What do you say baby, do you want it?" She looked right at me. It was too bizarre. Here I was sitting in front of this truly incredibly good-looking woman. She was the kind of a woman a straight man would die for and here she was exposing herself to me. I felt bad that this experience was being wasted on someone who would've rather seen the bartender's unwrapped package.

"Uh, ok, yeah."

"Yeah he says!" And with that she put the neck of the bottle in the last place I expected to see a beer bottle go that night. Gordon was rolling in his chair.

"Oh baby, give it to me nice and hard and COLD!" she wailed. I watched the neck of the bottle slide into her pussy. I felt bad for her. And I wished I was anywhere but here. But I acted like it was great.

"Yeah, fuck that bottle baby!" I shouted. The crowd went nuts and she pulled the bottle out of her twat then set it down on the table. She grabbed my face with both hands and then stuck her tongue in my mouth. Once I got over my surprise, I realized I had forgotten what it was like to kiss a woman. So soft and different...no scruff.

When she finished with the kiss she stood up and kept looking at me. I didn't know what to do. Everyone was intent on my next move.

"Thanks, that was great," I lied, trying to soak up the adulation of my adoring fans...it was then I realized she had not brought me a beer glass.

"Well?" some whiskey-voiced woman shouted from across the room. God, what was I supposed to do? I could feel my face get hot. I started to reach for my wallet to tip her when the crowd and the waitress broke into laughter. I was completely lost so I looked over to Gordon. With his hand he mimed that I should drink the beer.

"Come on!" hollered a fat guy at the next table. "Do it!"

"Drink, drink, drink, drink..." went the crowd. I just sat there feeling like I was back at the cafeteria in junior high.

"Aaaaah, he's going to puss out on us!" It was the same guy. Screw him. Grabbing the bottle, I chugged down the beer. The crowd went nuts again and the loudmouth leaped out of his chair smacked me on the back.

"That-a-boy," said the loudmouth. I looked over at Gordon who had a perplexed look on his face. The bartender took a Polaroid and told me he would put it on the men's room wall.

Before long the crowd went back to their steaks and chops and the music started up again. I was no longer the marquee attraction. Something had clearly gotten to Gordon though as he was unusually silent for several minutes. Before long he was chattering away trying too hard to keep the conversation going.

The rest of the meal was thankfully painless. I mean, it's hard to top a waitress sticking your drink in her pussy and then a crowd cheering you on to drink it. I'll say this too, he was right, it was the best steak I'd had in a long time. Once dinner was over, I thought it was a good idea to get him on the road before he got out of control. It took fifteen minutes for him to make his rounds; saying hi to old friends and staff. Something told me his cover wouldn't be blown as I couldn't imagine anyone wanting to cop to the fact they had been at this place.

We got into the cab. It felt good to be heading back to a soft bed. I hoped I wasn't in for a night of continual farting on his part.

"Did you enjoy your meal?"

"I did Gordon, the steak was amazing."

"I'm sorry about the whole beer bottle thing."

"It's OK."

"No, I could tell you were uncomfortable."

"Just caught off guard."

"I guess I just assumed you would get a kick out of it."

"Don't worry about it."

"Stupid custom when you think about it. I don't know why I like to go there."

"Clearly a regular from the treatment we got."

"Since I went to college at De Paul if you can believe it. I hung out at some rough places. Quite the drinker in my day."

"Can I ask you a personal question?"

"After the ordeal I put you through tonight I think you can ask me anything."

"Were you ever sober?" Gordon paused and fiddled with his scarf a bit. My question had caught him off guard.

"Yes, while Evelyn was alive. My wife."

"When did she die?"

"About six years ago. She was in the medical corps while I was in Vietnam. Nursed me back to health after I'd been shot up. Isn't that a cliché?"

"I was thinking it was kind of romantic."

"Having someone you have the hots for wipe your ass because your arms are in casts is not in *any* way romantic."

"God, I guess not."

"Getting a hard-on though when she went to sponge-bathe me, now that was. Ha! You should have seen her face." We had a good laugh.

"We got married after the war was over. I drank pretty hard until she left me. That's when I stopped. I would have done anything to keep her. She came back and we had the best life together."

"How'd she die?"

"Cancer. I didn't touch a drop until the day she died. Then I figured what the fuck? Who gives a goddamn at that point?"

"Yeah, but what about your career?"

"Oh, I suppose, huh? It's amazing I've never been outed as a closet drinker. You must think I'm the biggest sham."

"Not really."

"Oh, come on and admit it."

"I don't know. You clearly helped that woman on the airplane."

"True. But she was such a mess it wouldn't have taken much to help her don't you think?" We laughed again. "Who says I can't help others just because I'm a mess myself?"

"That's true."

"Oh God Kyle. Who cares about any of it anyway?"

"Then why do the show tomorrow?"

"Jesus, my boy. I have to have some way to pay for my habits," he laughed. "It's a good distraction I suppose. And I guess that deep down I do feel at least I'm doing something productive."

The cab pulled up to the hotel and we went up to the room. I called the front desk and asked for two wake-up calls. The extra one was in case we fell back asleep and my phone alarm didn't work. I was taking no chances.

Before I knew it, I was lying awake listening to Gordon snore. Here I was lying in the same room with Gordon; killing time until we went on *Candy*. Career-wise this was huge, but it seemed kind of ridiculous when I thought about it.

I debated about going into the hallway and calling Glenn. He would still be awake in LA. Then again, maybe I should just try to fall asleep. I didn't want him to think I couldn't make it a day without talking to him. Let him wonder what I was doing anyway. Still, the last thought on *my* mind was what was *he* doing?

CHAPTER TWENTY-FIVE

CANDY LIVE!

Inside The Candy Dish

PRE-SHOW JITTERS LEFT ME LYING AWAKE a big part of the night while Gordon snored away. As long as *he* was fresh and energetic that was all that mattered. As jaded as I had become in public relations, I had to admit that this was pretty exciting, and I felt proud. I had gotten the biggest booking there was and the entire show was going to focus on my client. It was a PR coup. Fans of Gordon's had been Twittering all week about his appearance.

I was ironing my shirt while Gordon was taking a shower. Thankfully, he wasn't wrecked from last night's escapades. I had kept a close eye on him and the number of cocktails he had downed. My phone started ringing and I saw it was Mel.

"Are you nervous?"

"Hey. Yeah, I have to admit I am a bit nervous, or excited. Not sure which."

"Same difference. I can't wait to see it."

"Yeah."

"How's Gordon?"

"Great. He's taking his shower and room service is bringing up our breakfast any minute. You won't believe where he took me last night"

"Boobie bar?"

"Worse. It's a long story but let's just say I'll never look a beer bottle in the eye again."

"Oh my, this sounds good. I can't wait to see you to get the blow-by-blow. We have to do a celebratory dinner with the guys."

"Line it up. Did you have a date last night?"

"Yeah. It was great. We did the stupidest thing though."

"What?"

"Played Ski-Ball at the Santa Monica Pier."

"You're kidding me? Can't picture you doing something that corny."

"I know. I must have something wrong with me."

"You're falling in love my friend."

"Yeah, I think you're right. Isn't it great that this is finally happening to us? Not like we didn't deserve it. Kyle, I want you to meet him." I didn't think I'd be meeting him this early on in the game, so I was a little surprised.

"Definitely. Pick a night and we'll do it. Do you want to invite him to my post-Candy bash?"

"I thought about it. But I think I'd rather you just meet him by yourself before he meets the rest of the gang."

"Got it." A knock came from the door. "Hang on Mel, breakfast is here." I opened the door and let in a cute waiter who was poured into his uniform; the brass buttons on his waistcoat shined in the morning sun. He rolled the cart over to the window and gave me a smile.

"I should let you go so you and Gordon can have a romantic breakfast together."

"That is so far from reality you have no idea." I signed the bill and added on a big tip. Gordon popped out of the bathroom only wearing a towel. His sagging titties being the last thing I wanted to see this early in the morning.

"Oh wonderful, breakfast!" The waiter gave me a wry smile as he left.

"O.K. Mel. Keep your phone by you today and I'll call you as soon as I can."

Gordon sat down and I tossed my iPhone on the bed and joined him. He had done the ordering and, by the looks of it, he was hungry *and* thirsty.

"My favorite part of staying in a hotel is having breakfast in the room."

"It is a luxury isn't it," I added.

We had just enough time to wolf down our food and send out some Tweets. Gordon made one last trip to the bathroom to finish dressing while I packed up two tote bags with the assorted goodies he had brought for the producers and Candy. Once I was satisfied that everything was in order I went over to the window and looked out onto the city. Which part of Chicago did A.K. live in?

"Are you ready my boy?"

"Works for me, Gordon." I called the concierge to make sure the car was ready for us and then we headed down to the street.

Gordon was non-stop chatter all the way to CandyLand Studios. It was odd that something with so much caché had a creepy ring to its name. But while Oprah's studio was the usual nondescript building that every television show seemed to be taped in, Candy had requested that her studio be painted dusty pink. Rumor had it that she'd had Swarovski crystals ground into the paint which in turn had created an effect that made the whole studio look like it was covered in lip gloss. A production assistant greeted us and took us to

Gordon's dressing room which was also done in a pink motif. I got us settled and within a few minutes Megan Chalmers came in and we did a round of "Good-to-Meet-You-Finally-in-Person" that publicists and producers always play. Megan looked completely different than I had expected. On the phone her gravelly voice made me visualize an overweight chain-smoker who never had a date and whose hair was unkempt. Instead I stood before a striking woman impeccably dressed all in gray minus the pink shoes on her feet. Her hair was pulled back tightly, and her makeup was perfect. I introduced her to Gordon, and he was his usual charming self; working in at least three flirtations in one minute flat. Gordon must have been quite the ladies' man in his day.

"OK," said Megan. "Here's the drill. Candy's going over some last-minute prep for the show. Gordon, you're going to be the key guest, the first segment will focus on your own life story with pics and clips from the past, the second segment will focus on your work over the years, the third segment will look at your new book. Then the rest of the show you are going to do some work with a few guests we have chosen from letters that have come into the show. All of them are alcoholics who have failed with other methods of quitting and Candy wants you to work with them. If they stay dry over the course of six months, we'll look at bringing back the success stories for a follow-up show."

"Wow, that's great!" I said.

"Yeah, Candy really likes your books Gordon. Especially the new one so there's definite repeat possibilities here. Any questions?"

"I think you've covered them my dear," said Gordon.

"Good," said Megan. "Julia will be back in to take you to make-up. Once she's finished with you, we'll have about ten minutes before air-time. Remember, we are live in certain markets then tape delay for the rest so if you screw up just keep going. Anything drastic they will edit for the later broadcasts."

Megan left the room after another round of shaking hands and then Julia appeared quickly thereafter. We were walked down a long hallway to hair and make-up. Gordon sat in the chair and the make-up artist who looked like a grandmotherly truck diver tucked Kleenex into his collar so she wouldn't get powder on his shirt. Gordon sat there silently, and I looked at my watch. In a short while Gordon would be beamed around the country and the sales would begin. My phone rang. The office was calling.

"This is Kyle." It was Lucy.

"Kyle, how's it going?" I could tell she had me on speaker phone with the suits. They chimed in a quick hello.

"Everything's great. Gordon is in make-up right now and we'll be on the air soon. Did the books hit the distributors in time?"

I could hear Lucy exhale smoke. "Yeah, they're back in the system and depending on rush orders we have his latest going down for another printing tomorrow. Are you there with Gordon?"

"Yeah he's right here."

"Put him on." I handed the phone to Gordon.

"It's Lucy Arnot."

"Oh," he took the phone. "Hello Lucy, my dear."

Gordon was silent while she talked. Her voice cracked away but I couldn't make out what she was saying.

"Yes. Yes, I see. Thank you. Yes, thank you." He hung up and handed my phone back to me. The make-up artist began applying powder while her bald assistant worked over Gordon's hair. All of a sudden Gordon pushed their hands away from his face, swatting at them like flies.

"Stop it! Stop!" We stood there stunned. Gordon ripped the Kleenex out from his collar and clamored out of the chair.

"I need to get out of here!" He started down the hall and I chased after him leaving the hair and make-up department with their mouths hanging open. Gordon sprinted past people lumbering in the hallway; the heels of his dress shoes clicking on the polished floor.

"Exit! Exit! Where's an exit?" he spouted. A production assistant pointed towards a door and he shot through it. I was in hot pursuit. The door opened up onto a parking lot filled with trucks and expensive cars. A guard came over to us. Gordon was doubled over panting and holding his side.

"What's going on, is he OK?" asked the guard.

"He'll be fine. Just pre-show jitters." I motioned for the guard to go away. "Gordon, what's wrong?"

"I can't do this," he said.

"What?"

"I can't do this. I can't do the show." Oh my God. We were just ten minutes until airtime and Gordon was panicking.

"Gordon, you can do this. What are you scared of?"

"I need a drink. Kyle, I need a drink right now. I can't do this. They are going to find out I'm a charlatan. I'll be the laughingstock of the world. I don't need this. I have enough money to get me to the grave." I put my arm around him.

"Gordon, it's going to be..." He broke free from me.

"Get me out of here!" Gordon started running for the guard gate.

"Gordon come back!"

"No, no. I can't do this."

"Grab him!" I shouted to the guard who leapt into action and held Gordon in place. The clickety-click of Jimmy Choo's on pavement got closer and I turned to see Megan followed by the hair and makeup people.

"What the hell is going on? Is he OK?"

"He's just having some pre-show nerves." What in the world had Lucy said to him?

"Megan, let's just get him back in the dressing room. I can get him calmed down." We walked a now shaking Gordon back inside and down the hall to the room. The whole staff was watching the spectacle that was going on. Gordon grabbed the casing of the doorway.

"I can't do this, Kyle I need..." I wasn't about to let him blow this. "STOP IT!" I shouted. The guard, Gordon, Megan and several staff members who had followed us into the room all looked at me with mouths wide open.

"Kyle, I..." he stammered.

"SIT DOWN *NOW*, GORDON!" He took his seat like a frightened child. "Everyone out of here!" I pushed them out the door. Megan protested but I told her to give me five minutes with him. I shut the door and turned back to Gordon.

"Kyle, I need a drink. I can't do this." Why had I been so stupid to not pack more booze? I was worried that he would screw up on camera so I had limited his intake to two screwdrivers at breakfast thinking it would be enough to get him through the show.

I grabbed him by the shoulders shaking him. "Listen to me!" I hissed. "You're not going to fuck this up for me do you understand?"

"I don't need the money," he whimpered.

"I don't give a goddamn, Gordon." I squeezed his shoulders so hard he was wincing. "Look me in the eyes!" I gave him another hard shake until he was looking right at me.

"A lot of people are depending on you to get your ass out on that soundstage and deliver. My job is on the line here. Do you understand?" He just looked at me so I gave him another shake and I could feel that I had a look of death on my face. "Do you understand? Do it for me if you aren't going to do it for yourself!" He swallowed hard and I let loose of him while I stood up straight. I was at my wits end.

"What did Lucy say to you that got you so upset?"

"She said 'Good luck.'"

"*That was it?*" I couldn't believe this.

"Yes. What time is it?" I looked at my watch. Megan was knocking on the door.

"We have four minutes to air Kyle. We need you out here now!" He looked at me, and I let out a big sigh. He slicked back his hair and got up from where he was sitting.

"Well, let's do this then. She can't be all that scary now can she?" He opened the door to an ashen-faced Megan.

"Are we a go?" she pleaded.

"Yes, O.K." he whispered.

We raced to the set and frantic technicians scurried to get his mic on in time.

"Places everyone. One minute!" a voice boomed. A frantic make-up and hair team did a last-minute fix powdering down the sweat which coated his face.

"Rolling...five, four, three, two, cue music, and we're live." The studio filled with the Candy theme song and out she came. The crowd went wild. Megan and I stood off stage watching it all unfold.

"What the hell happened?"

"Severe stage fright," I answered.

"How'd you get him out here?"

"To be honest I don't know. I just hope he makes it to the end of the show." Candy introduced the show and then Gordon. The crowd gave him a standing ovation and he waved to them. His knees were shaking, and he looked like he was going to pass out.

"Oh my God, this is going to be a train wreck," said Megan. She'd clearly seen guests have meltdowns while on stage.

Candy introduced the short biography of clips they had put together. From where I stood, I was able to see Gordon's expression while it played on the giant screen behind Candy and him. It was a great reel on him, starting off with humble beginning in Nebraska, going to Vietnam, and then his struggles and triumphs with alcohol. I could see Gordon's hands shaking like leaves. This wasn't going to be good.

The piece ended with a montage of home movie footage of Gordon and Evelyn at their ranch in New Mexico. There was a close-up shot of Evelyn. Her head filled the screen. As soon as her face smiled down on him, I noticed his hands stopped shaking. The final shot was of the two of them holding hands and laughing together. A friend must have taken it for them. The screen went black and then the lights came up on Gordon and Candy.

"So, what goes through your mind Gordon, when you see those clips?"

Gordon took a long pause and I could feel the tension in the air as Megan and I held our breath. I could feel the blood pumping through my body and sweat break out on the back of my neck. Gordon remained silent as he looked out into the audience with a funny look on his face. Candy started to look bewildered, unsure what was happening. He took a deep breath and paused. Then he bellowed at the top of his lungs, "LET'S…GET…SOBER!" The crowd went wild. He was back.

CHAPTER TWENTY-SIX

CHICAGO REVISITED

Wind Blowing Through My Mind

"WELL MY YOUNG FRIEND, I think that about does it." We were standing outside of the hotel while the driver put Gordon's luggage into the car.

"You did great Gordon. The show was a huge success."

"Do you think so? I'm glad it worked out OK."

"It was amazing. Your latest book shot to number one on Amazon fifteen minutes into the show. Absolutely incredible."

"Well, I have you to thank."

"My pleasure."

"No, I'm serious Kyle. I realize that I was a complete pill to deal with, so I want you to know that I really do appreciate everything you've done." The driver opened the passenger door and patiently waited for us to finish our conversation.

"That's appreciated."

"I don't know how you publicists do it to be honest with you," Gordon said. "Dealing with neurotic authors, agents and producers all the time."

"We're a nutty breed."

"Now, since you're not returning right away to Los Angeles, what are you planning to do here?"

"This is my first trip to Chicago, so I thought I'd check it out and see what the fuss is all about."

"Well, after your experience at the Little Luck and dealing with me, I'm sure the rest of your stay will be much easier."

"Ha, well, I hope so anyway."

Gordon got into the car. "Goodbye Kyle, see you soon." The driver shut the door and I waited for them to drive off. Gordon turned around and waved back at me. I gave him a big smile and a wave then watched the limo turn the corner. Now I could breathe a sigh of relief.

Amazingly, the show had been incredible. I had to hand it to Gordon. For someone who fell apart at the last minute he came through like a champion. He was flawless and during the after-show taping he showed a different side altogether. Candy, Megan and everyone else gushed afterwards about how great both Gordon and the show was. Lucy had tracked the response on the book, and it looked to make Devore-Horizon a major chunk of change. It was time to revel in the glory of my achievement.

I went back into the hotel and grabbed a drink in the bar. It felt good to kick back with a scotch and to just let it sink in. I was tired yet exhilarated at the same time. Gordon was an exhausting person to deal with, but you couldn't help but love him, and in his own way, he deserved admiration. Despite being a mess himself it was hard to deny how many people he had helped. He'd spent close to an hour shaking hands and signing copies of his book after the show.

So here I was in one of the greatest cities in America and I figured I should decide what to do with my time tonight. After swilling down my drink I headed upstairs to my room. Once there, I pulled back the drapes and looked out into the evening sky. I just stood there soaking it all in. It was a beautiful cityscape that lacked the overkill New York seemed to have.

I went over to my carryon and rummaged through until I found a piece of paper. I picked up the phone and dialed.

Ring.

Ring. I felt my chest get tight.

Ring. "Hello?"

I took a deep breath and jumped out of the airplane.

"A.K.?"

CHAPTER TWENTY-SEVEN

A.K.

Why Did I Call? Yikes!

"KYLE?"

I hesitated. Now that I was really speaking with A.K. I was having second thoughts. I hadn't planned what I would say to him if he actually answered.

"Yeah."

"Oh my God, how are you?" He sounded upbeat and excited I had called.

"Pretty good. How are you?"

"I'm great." Wrong answer. "I guess you got my card that I'd moved."

"Yeah." It was difficult to say much.

"So how's life for you? Are you still working at Devore?"

"I'm in Chicago."

"You're kidding me, seriously?"

"Yeah, I had a client on *Candy* today."

"That's great." He seemed a little too enthusiastic about my success.

"Actually, the whole show was built around him."

"How long are you here for? We should grab some dinner or something."

"I leave tomorrow."

"Oh wow, I have plans tonight."

"That's O.K. I should have given you some notice. It was a last-minute kind of thing." There was a part of me that was relieved he wasn't free.

"No, no, I want to see you. It was just going to be something with friends who I see all the time anyway." You made friends fast didn't you?

"I'll call and cancel with them and we'll go out instead. Where are you staying?"

"I'm at the Drake."

"OK, you're not that far from me. I'm just north of there. Why don't you come over to my place and we'll go to a restaurant over in boys town and knock around there. You have my address?"

"Yeah, I have the card with me." Should I tell him it was stained from old coffee grounds when it landed in my kitchen trash? I felt weird when I dug it out after throwing it away but I'm sure I wasn't the first person who had done something silly like that.

"All right, well, the place is a mess, but you can come over whenever you're ready. I just showered, so you tell me."

"Let me clean up a bit first."

"No problem. I'll see you soon. This is so cool."

"Yeah. See you in a bit." After hanging up the phone I had mixed emotions. The conversation went alright, I guess. What was I expecting anyway? Five minutes ago, things were completely different and now here I was standing in a hotel room in Chicago about to get ready and see the one person who had single-handedly broken my heart worse than anyone. Why in the world did I call him? My face was all hot and flushed and I felt nervous. Yet I had to admit that I also felt a certain sense of excitement mixed with curiosity.

Stripping down, I got into the shower. The hot water came crashing down on me and it felt good and energizing. What would happen when I saw A.K.? Would he try to kiss me or just act like I was another friend at this point? Then again, how should I act? I guess there really isn't any protocol for seeing your ex for the first time in ages. It felt a little overwhelming.

After a few minutes of discernment, I pulled out a black button-down silk shirt and a pair of black dress pants from the closet. I looked good when I did my last check in the mirror. Hopefully A.K. would look like hell. I fantasized that he would be fat and bald. I imagined a burned-out apartment building with moldy ceilings and the smell of grease and baked beans embedded in the walls.

I made one last check in the mirror next to the elevator while I put on my jacket. Before I knew it, I was in an Uber heading north to A.K.'s.

Disappointment overwhelmed me when the cab pulled up to 1967 Lakeshore Dr. A.K.'s building was *anything* but seedy. It was a twenty-floor, pre-war masterpiece with manicured flowerbeds behind cast-iron grates and a brass plaque with 'The Kennington' stamped on it. Across the street was a beautiful mini park and just beyond that was Lakeshore Drive and then the waterfront. The building was fronted with two massive double doors covered in ironwork that looked like ivy winding its way across the beveled glass. I pushed his apartment number on the security panel and a few seconds later I heard a buzz and then the door clicked open. The lobby had marble floors and a large French chandelier in the foyer. A bead of sweat swam down my back while I waited for the elevator. This was stupid.

My mouth went dry as the car climbed up to the ninth floor. My feet were greeted by plush carpet as I stepped out of the elevator and went to his apartment door. As soon as I knocked, I felt each second of time click away like the timer on a bundle of dynamite.

When he opened his door, I saw a slightly different version of what had walked out of my door, in what seemed like a lifetime ago. He was a bit thinner around the middle and more muscular around his shoulders, chest and arms. I could tell this by the spray-on shirt and jeans he was wearing. The same pair of sexy feet were still waiting to get some socks and shoes, and while he now had a beard, the pair of eyes looking at me were the same eyes that I had looked into countless times as we lay in bed together. Eyes that I thought I would grow old looking into.

"Wow, it's you," he said.

"Yeah, hey." What do I do?

"Well come here you little bastard." A.K. opened up his arms and pulled me into him for a big bear hug. He squeezed hard.

"Kyle, it's so good to see you again." He pushed me back away from him and I was a little unsure about all of this. This wasn't steady ground.

"You look good," I said.

"Come on in, I just need to get some shoes." He didn't comment on my looks even though I was looking amazing today. I put myself on emotional autopilot and crossed the threshold.

There was a disappointing lack of flaking wallpaper in A.K.'s apartment. It was sleek, modern and hip. Everything looked like it was recently purchased; very expensive and extremely Italian. I remembered he said the place was a mess but there were no signs of anything being out of order.

"Come on back. I'll show you the bedroom." We walked back through a hallway where different pieces of artwork were hung. I noticed there were no photos of family or friends. In *our* place, A.K. had an entire wall covered with photos of people he cared about. Pictures of events, trips, parties; you name it. We walked into the bedroom. Against the wall was the most fantastic cherry wood sleigh bed I'd ever seen. I wondered who he'd been fucking on it.

"Great apartment."

"Do you like it?"

"Yeah, you must pay a fortune in rent."

"No more renting for me. I bought it when we moved."

We. In the entire apartment I noticed *one* picture of a person and it was in a silver frame. It was near the bed and I picked it up to take a look at it. The guy was a total Latin stud with the whole chiseled-face-smoldering-eyes thing going on. He wore no shirt in the picture and his chest was completely hairless. I thought that was odd since A.K. always said he liked hairy guys.

"Who's this?" A.K. beamed at me.

"The reason I moved to Chicago. His name is Marco."

"Oh...you have a boyfriend."

"He's more than a boyfriend Kyle, we're married now." It went through me like a knife. I felt hot, uncomfortable and thirsty.

"He lives here?"

"Of course."

"Oh, O.K."

"He's at work right now."

"What does he do?"

"He's preparing for a case tomorrow so he's working late tonight." I hoped he was fucking a clerk. I also hoped he was one of those lawyer-personality types who had to argue about everything and *always* had to be right. I hoped he was a living hell to be around. I hoped he farted in bed.

"How long have you been together?" (Gay Scout Rule #32 ... *Never* ask a question that you don't want to hear the answer to). "I met him right after I moved to New York. He was on vacation there." Jesus, our relationship wasn't even cold, and he'd found someone else. Did I mean that little to him? I'd spent all this time alone until recently and A.K. just slid right into something great. I regretted being here. It was a mistake and I wished I'd flown home with Gordon.

A.K. finished dressing, grabbed his wallet, and we headed out the door. I could tell it was going to be a long night.

CHAPTER TWENTY-EIGHT

THE FOOD SUCKS AT THIS PLACE

So Did My Attitude

I PUSHED THE SOGGY POLENTA AROUND WITH MY FORK. In a city known for amazing food he takes me to this dump which A.K. insisted we eat at because it was "Marco's favorite trattoria." Fuck him. McDonalds that had been sitting under a heat lamp for hours would have been better than this shit. "You'll just love it Kyle," he had gushed. I hated Marco. What a stupid name anyway. I also hated being in the place that was the first restaurant A.K. and Marco ate at together in Chicago. Why was he taking me here? To rub it in?

Dinner had been a painful experience. I'd spent the last hour and a half listening to how great A.K.'s life was. The wonderful job, the big bonuses, buying the condo, moving to Chicago after meeting the man of his dreams, blah, blah, blah. I remembered a time when

I was the man of his dreams at one point and I would at least have known the difference between good and bad Italian.

I was stuck in a bad dream. Should I start screaming in the middle of the restaurant that the person he was gushing about *used* to be, and *should still have been* me, not some douchebag from Argentina whose parents were in cattle futures.

On and on it went, and the longer it went on, the angrier I became.

"So, Kyle, tell me about what's going on with you? Have you met anyone yet?"

Finally, it was my turn. While A.K. had blathered endlessly I'd been compiling notes in my head for my counter salvo.

"I'm dating a studio executive."

"Really?" He was intrigued from the start. This was going to be easy.

"Yeah, he's with Warner Brothers." When A.K. lived in LA he had always wanted to get involved in the film business but had failed miserably.

"Is he hot?" Hmmm, was he a little jealous?

"Very. He looks like a Colt model." A.K. loved Colt men.

"Damn. Good for you Kyle."

"And he has a huge cock." O.K., that was tacky, but I liked the fact this conversation had turned in my favor. Plus A.K. wasn't that well packaged so I have to admit it was a bit of a barb. What was Chicago turning me into?

"That must make *you* happy," he said laughing.

"Well, he's more than just a nice dick. He's incredible in the sack. Really a lot of fun." Now I could tell I was hitting a sore spot. A.K. looked a little uncomfortable and I was feeling empowered.

"What's his name?"

"Glenn."

"One n or two?"

What a question. "Two."

"Oh, I just hate that. It's so unnecessary." Who are you kidding, what the hell does it matter how someone spells their name? "Where does he live?"

"He has a gated estate in Bel Air." I can't believe I just lied like that.

"Oh." He was clearly taken aback. "New or old Bel Air."

"Old. Part of his backyard connects to Cher's house. She's really sweet once you get to know her. Her chef makes the best chocolate chip cookies." If you're going to lie don't forget the details. A.K. was also a huge star fucker so I could tell he was envious that I knew a megastar.

"Sounds serious."

"Yeah, it is. He asked me to move in with him, but I told him we need to wait a bit longer."

"I'd think you'd want to jump at that."

"Why, because I'm desperate?" Damn, why did I say that?

"No, I didn't mean it that way. He just sounds great."

"Well, great or not, I'm not rushing into another relationship until I know he's going to stick around." I looked down at my plate giving my polenta a crushing blow with my fork. The air was tense, and I felt a tad ashamed.

"Do you want dessert?"

"No, I'm pretty full," I replied. I figured I'd spare hearing about some wonderful time he and Marco had over runny tiramisu.

"O.K." He signaled the waiter for the check. We both reached for our wallets.

"Let me get this A.K."

"Kyle don't be ridiculous. You're the visitor here."

"No seriously, I want to pay."

"No Kyle, I'm not going to let you." He snapped the bill from me and handed it to the waiter with his credit card.

"O.K., well, thank you."

"It's the least I can do when you are visiting."

On the way out we stopped in the men's room. A.K. took the urinal next to mine and there were no privacy dividers. Even though I'd seen his and he mine a million times prior it did seem a little peculiar.

"Check this out Kyle." I looked down and saw that he had had his cock pierced.

"Oh my God. Why did you do that?"

"Isn't it hot? Marco has one too." I should have guessed. I was glad we were the only ones in the men's room for this discussion.

I zipped up and washed my hands. A.K. washed his in the sink next to me and we looked at each other in the mirror. This was all so oddly civilized minus the cock-ring show and tell. Once we were outside, I realized the evening had finally come to a close. I was grateful because this had been more than I had bargained for.

"Kyle, it was so good to see you."

"Yeah. Different huh?"

"I guess." We just sort of stood there, neither of us knowing what to say next, I guess.

"Next trip you'll have to meet Marco." I looked at A.K. and felt my face get hot with anger.

"No."

"Huh?"

"I have zero desire to meet Marco, A.K."

"Well that's rude."

"Really? Well, too bad. Do you really think I want to meet him? Huh? Do you?" I was furious.

"O.K. Kyle, I've had enough, I don't need to listen to this."

"OH YES YOU DO YOU MOTHERFUCKER!" I shouted at the top of my lungs. A.K. was so stunned he was motionless. He had a stupid look on his face. Everyone in front of the restaurant was slack-jawed. I was stunned at myself for participating in this homo-tragedy.

"Kyle..."

"No, you listen to me and I don't care if you don't want to hear it. You walked out on me with absolutely no notice. You fucked my life up beyond comprehension. You *owe* it to me to listen." I was furious and I could feel myself shaking.

"I did what I had to do, Kyle."

"You're an asshole, A.K. How could you have done that to me?" He just stood there.

"How could you have just walked out without even clueing me in to what was going to happen? Did I mean that little to you?"

"It was just the opposite. Because I cared about you so much, I thought it would be easier if there was a sudden break."

"Are you insane?" He continued to stare at me. "Answer me, *are you insane*? Did you really think that was going to help me? Do you have any idea of how freaked out I was, how disoriented I was? You asshole! After everything I did for you? I was the one who was there through all of your shit and as soon as it got good you threw it away."

"I did what I had to do Kyle."

"Exactly, what *you* had to do and fuck everybody else in the process. FUCK YOU!"

I turned and walked away towards the end of the block, not looking back to see if he was following me. I was so glad I finally had the chance to let him have it and give him what he deserved. It was fantastic and liberating. But I still felt angry and confused and bottled up. When I turned the corner out of site I ducked into a doorway and started to cry.

CHAPTER TWENTY-NINE

FLOODGATES

Trying To Wash It Away

MY BACK WAS AGAINST THE BED. I was sitting on the floor and I was crying pretty bad. Why is it that when you have a complete breakdown the floor seems like the place to end up even though it's the most uncomfortable choice? Mel was on the other end of the phone listening to me sob. If I had been able to just isolate one emotion and deal with it, I would have been a lucky man. Instead I was a salad bowl of emotion. The weight of the world and my life seemed to be pressing down on my chest and shoulders, wringing the tears and the life out of me. And I just kept crying.

It's impossible to remember a time when I cried as hard as I did now. Even when A.K. left me there weren't tears like this, just cold shock. Yeah, I cried, and I cried hard and many times. But this time it was different. These were tears of pain and sadness. Of what I wanted it to be and the reality of what it would never be. Clearly a part of me had never accepted reality.

And most of all I was just tired.

"Just let it go Kyle."

"Oh Mel."

"I know. Just let it out."

So, I kept crying. Stupid when you think of it. I mean come on. A.K. and I had been broken apart, smashed to bits, for a long time now. Yet all of this was happening in my Chicago hotel room after the first time I'd seen him. The last time had been the morning of the day he had left. I can still remember lying there, praying the snooze alarm wouldn't go off for another year, watching him sleep, just enjoying the moment. Watching his chest expand with every breath. Listening to his breath go in and out of his nostrils. Watching the morning light as it tripped its way through his chest hair. How many times had I reveled in the innocence of that morning yearning to be back in that place nine hours before life as I knew it ended.

But this was life as I knew it now and the scratchy hotel carpet was digging into my ass and it hurt enough to finally make me stir and shift myself. I blew my nose into my shirt sleeve and then looked at the mess I'd made.

"O.K. I'm done now."

"Got it all out?"

"Yeah, I just blew my nose into my Ike Behar shirt."

"Kyle, forget that fucker. Think about what you have with Glenn."

"You're right—time to stop the pity party."

I could hear the Construction Worker ring her doorbell. She kept talking while she let him in. There was a muffling while she explained to him that she was dealing with a snotty crisis. I could barely make out something about helping himself to a drink while he waited.

"Kyle you're going to make it through this."

"I know. Thanks for letting me wallow."

"Go to bed. When's your flight?"

"Not til two."

"Good, at least you can get some sleep. Take a valium but make sure you don't sleep through your alarm. Do you want me to pick you up at the airport?"

"Yeah. That would be great, but don't you have to work."

"Don't worry about that. Call me before you board and I'll make sure I'm there for you."

And I knew she would be.

CHAPTER THIRTY
PINK BOOTS

God Bless Los Angeles

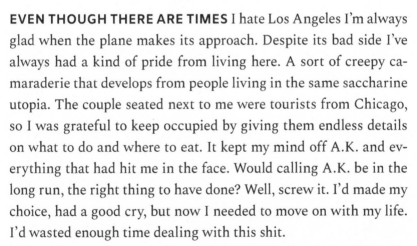

EVEN THOUGH THERE ARE TIMES I hate Los Angeles I'm always glad when the plane makes its approach. Despite its bad side I've always had a kind of pride from living here. A sort of creepy camaraderie that develops from people living in the same saccharine utopia. The couple seated next to me were tourists from Chicago, so I was grateful to keep occupied by giving them endless details on what to do and where to eat. It kept my mind off A.K. and everything that had hit me in the face. Would calling A.K. be in the long run, the right thing to have done? Well, screw it. I'd made my choice, had a good cry, but now I needed to move on with my life. I'd wasted enough time dealing with this shit.

Getting my bag was the usual LAX hell. Tired travelers suddenly gained Herculean strength when the first bag burped its way into eyesight. Everyone started pushing and shoving. Once I found my errant child, I fought my way to the curb. Just as I was reaching for my phone to call Mel along came her convertible Mercedes in all its glory. Mel was dressed in a white halter top with matching hot pants. Her hair was pulled back and tied with a gold ribbon. Her eyes were shielded by a pair of white Gucci sunglasses, and her legs were encased in the most awesome pair of pink, patent-leather, thigh-high boots I'd ever laid my eyes on. She looked amazing and I was never so glad to see her as I was just then.

"Hop in sexy," she said. It's easy to obey a dominatrix. Especially when she's your ride back to Hollywood. As I got into the car, I noticed a group of businessmen watching me and wondering what I did for a living that this was my girlfriend.

"Thanks for picking me up."

"Like I was going to leave you hanging."

"It's good to be back home." She pulled into the traffic and we were silent as we squished our way onto Century Blvd. Leaning my head against the leather headrest I smiled.

"Feeling better?"

"I am."

"It's just residue from when he left you. It means nothing."

"It's amazing how much that crap can hurt sometimes?"

"That's how life fucks you in the ass my friend." She had a point.

"Just because something happened a while back doesn't mean it can't come back to haunt you today."

"This is true but it's time to move on."

"Good for you. Focus on the fact you have Glenn in your life. He's better than A.K. anyway." O.K., what the hell was happening? Mel was pimping Glenn.

We came to a stop light and she used the opportunity to check her makeup. "What are you doing tonight Kyle?"

"I don't have anything planned. What were you thinking?"

"Well, I talked to Peter and since he doesn't have to be on a job site tomorrow, he's available to go out tonight." Peter was the

Construction Worker and time had come for me to meet him. While I wasn't in the best mood maybe it would be a good project to keep my mind off of everything.

"Sure, I'm up for meeting him."

"O.K. Why don't you come over to my place at seven-thirty and we'll have a drink and then we could walk down to Café La Bohème. Did you want to drop by work?"

"No, they aren't expecting me til morning. Just home. I think I'll try calling Glenn and see if I can line something up with him."

"Great idea. Anything you need to do to keep your mind off that Chicago twat. Be glad you're done with him Kyle. He's had a hold on you for a long time now."

"Yeah." I wanted to change the subject. "So are you ready for me to meet the Construction Worker?"

"Of course. I'm excited. Why wouldn't I want him to meet my best friend?"

"I don't know. It's always kind of nerve-wracking isn't it?"

"I guess. I mean it would be if Tyler and Mickey were along tonight but not when it's just you. He's a wonderful guy Kyle. I know you're going to love him."

"Well from what you've told me I don't see how I couldn't."

"Yeah, and I know you'll think he's hot. He's your type."

"God bless construction workers everywhere."

"I'm up for that," she laughed.

"So am I. It'll be fun."

Traffic was light all the way up Fairfax. Before I knew it Mel was dumping me at my front door and I went upstairs."

When I got inside, I dropped my suitcase by the door and looked into the fridge for some much deserved hunger relief. While I was scanning for something good I looked at the clock. I had plenty of time to call Glenn and unpack before getting ready to meet Mel.

I rang him up.

"Glenn Wycoff's office."

"Kyle from Devore-Horizon for Glenn."

"Oh, hello Kyle, one moment while I get him." Huh? Had he given instructions that all calls from me were to be cleared?

"Hey sexy," he purred. God, I loved that voice. "Back in town?"

"Yeah, and in once piece believe it or not."

"How was Chicago?"

"I have to say it was an experience. I'm glad I'm back. The show went great. You should have seen it."

"I did."

"Really?"

"Of course. Did you think I'd miss your first *Candy* coup? I watched it here in the office. Gordon delivered. Excellent job. You can PR me anytime."

"That's cool you saw it. Yeah, I was really proud. I'll have to tell you the backstage drama next time I see you."

"Which will be tonight right?" O.K., I could get used to this.

"Can't tonight. I'm meeting Mel's boyfriend for the first time." The thought popped into my mind to invite Glenn with me. Sort of an I'll show you mine if you show me yours kind of thing. I hesitated but then canned the idea. Why set myself up for him saying no?

"What are you doing tomorrow Glenn?"

"Trainer, but I'll cancel him. I'd rather see you. I need to take a day off anyway."

"How about seven at your place?"

"Works for me sexy. See you tomorrow. God, I'm so horny I think I'm going to jump you in the driveway."

"Go back to work, horn-dog. I'll talk to you later."

Well, Chicago may have been a shitstorm but at least LA's forecast was looking great. Fuck A.K. I went into the bedroom and took

A.K.'s picture off my dresser and stuffed it at the bottom of my sock drawer then decided that was too good a place for it and tossed it in the back of my closet next to dirty laundry.

While the water was cascading down on me, I thought about how disorienting it is coming back from a trip. A.K.'s life is going on in another part of the world while mine is going on in L.A. I guess there's a part of us that just assumes life is only happening where we are at that given moment. It bothered me that I was so upset from seeing him. It would have been better if I'd been able to keep my cool and not lose it around him. What did I gain from all of that? True, it had been great telling him to go fuck himself but maybe I should have been cooler and just acted like none of it bothered me. I don't know; I was glad it was over.

What's the best outfit to meet the straight construction worker boyfriend of your best friend? I hoped he wasn't homophobic. Mel hadn't mentioned anything along those lines, and it was hard to believe she would ever put up with someone who was. Still, he wasn't exactly in the most gay-friendly business. I opted for tan linen pants and a button-down Ralph Lauren shirt. Pale blue.

I got myself psyched up on the way over to Mel's. I didn't want to be nervous on what was an important evening for her. Admittedly, I was looking forward to meeting Peter. She was clearly in love with him and I was glad for her. Thankfully, Mel and I knew that despite our marital status we would always be great friends. Though past relationships had come and gone our friendship had remained steadfast. It was unshakeable, unbreakable and it would endure.

I pulled up in front of her building just as she was pulling into her garage. I locked my car and shot into her garage just before the gate started to close. When she got out of her car, I almost did a double take. She was dressed in a beige Ann Taylor suit with matching shoes and bag. Her soft hair gently fell against the side of her face. There stood before me not Melanie...but a Republican.

"Well?" she said as she held out her hands and modeled the outfit for me. In her right hand was a Gelsons bag."

"You look beautiful." I skipped over the fact that I felt like I was in Colorado Springs.

"I was out of gin, so I buzzed down to the store. Peter is upstairs already."

"Cool."

"You look nice."

"Yeah," she said while eyeing my outfit. "Two conservative peas in a pod."

"Oh this, well, you have to admit I look great."

"Yeah, it's just so not you though."

"I should say instead that it's just not what I'm used to seeing you in." She smiled and we went upstairs.

"I'm thrilled you're getting to meet him Kyle." We stopped outside her front door and she handed me the gin while she did a quick fix of her hair.

"Okay," she said. "Time to meet Mr. Wonderful."

She opened the door and we walked into the living room. Melanie was in front of me and when she stepped aside I could see that on the couch sat Mr. Wonderful — Peter the construction worker.

The first thing that came to mind was "Holy Shit."

CHAPTER THIRTY-ONE
CONSTRUCTION BOOTS

Living Nightmare

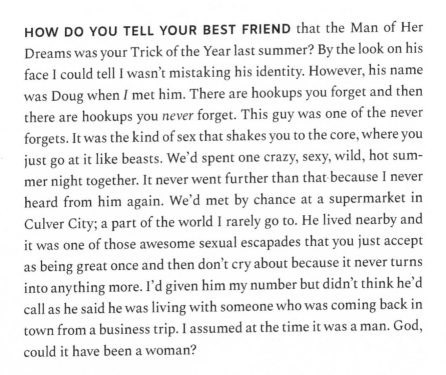

HOW DO YOU TELL YOUR BEST FRIEND that the Man of Her Dreams was your Trick of the Year last summer? By the look on his face I could tell I wasn't mistaking his identity. However, his name was Doug when *I* met him. There are hookups you forget and then there are hookups you *never* forget. This guy was one of the never forgets. It was the kind of sex that shakes you to the core, where you just go at it like beasts. We'd spent one crazy, sexy, wild, hot summer night together. It never went further than that because I never heard from him again. We'd met by chance at a supermarket in Culver City; a part of the world I rarely go to. He lived nearby and it was one of those awesome sexual escapades that you just accept as being great once and then don't cry about because it never turns into anything more. I'd given him my number but didn't think he'd call as he said he was living with someone who was coming back in town from a business trip. I assumed at the time it was a man. God, could it have been a woman?

"Kyle meet Peter, and honey, meet Kyle." Melanie beamed as she squeezed his arm.

Peter / Doug got up off his perch to shake my hand. I felt a million beads of sweat surface on my skin. It was time to go on auto pilot and just shake the guy's hand. Pull it together and act as if it's all normal. Only it wasn't normal. This was hell.

"Hey, nice to meet you." Great, now I'd just lied to my best friend.

"Hi Kyle, good to see you." Slip of his tongue? Memories of his tongue and my armpit started to haunt me. He looked me right in the eye as if to say, "Don't blow this for me dude."

"Let's have a drink before we go to dinner," said Mel. Perfect idea. Anything to anesthetize me. "Peter, do you want to do the honors?"

"Sure." He went over the bar where a bucket of ice sat, and he began fiddling with the drinks. When his back was to us Mel mouthed 'Isn't he hot?!?' to me. At least I could agree with that. I felt like I was going to vomit.

I plopped down in one of the white-leather Mies van der Rohe chairs she had in her living room. She sat on the matching couch, facing me. Behind her was Peter / Doug, mixing the cocktails away. His back was to us and I was looking at his ass filling out those dress pants. I remembered he was solid muscle when I screwed around with him and that he had one of those funky farmer-tan things going on. Oh yeah, he had a tattoo of Snoopy on his ass. I wonder why Mel had never mentioned that to me before. I thought it was kind of different for a guy that butch, but it worked on him. On anyone else it would have been weird instead of cute.

I looked over at her and she was beaming the beams of someone who is incredibly in love and getting to show off their boyfriend to her best friend. Peter turned around and served us our drinks.

"I hope this is how you like it, Kyle."

"Thanks," I said. I took a sip and it was pure gin with maybe a drop of tonic if anything. He must have figured I was a little nervous.

"Isn't this great?" said Mel?

"Yeah," I said. What do I say?

"Mel tells me you work in books," said Peter / Doug.

"Yeah. For the last four years," I said. What I wanted to say was 'What the fuck is going on here you liar?'

The conversation might well have been in Turkish as I was completely detached. The only thing I could focus on was my drink and the internal conversation that was running through my head. The question wasn't *whether* I was going to tell Mel it was how and when. There's no way I couldn't let her know the truth about this guy. Was this going to be the end of our friendship? The rattle of cubes in Mel's glass brought me back to reality.

"Kyle, are you O.K.?"

"Huh?"

"You were drifting off?"

"Oh, no sorry. I think it's just some jetlag."

"How was Chicago?" asked Peter / Doug. "That can be a wild city."

"I think I can say this has been one of the most eye-opening weeks of my life," I said.

"Kyle had a client on *Candy*."

"Very cool, congratulations," he smiled.

"Alright guys. I'm going to use the little girls' room and you entertain yourselves. I'm sure you can carry on the conversation without me for five minutes."

"No problem babe," said Peter / Doug. Mel gave him a quick peck on the cheek then sauntered off to the bathroom, a noticeable bounce in her gait. I felt like trash.

The minute we heard the door shut to her bathroom the meter started running.

"I guess this is a little awkward," said Peter / Doug.

"Gee, do you think? I walk in to meet my best friend's boyfriend and find out I fucked him last summer. What the hell is going on?"

"Nothing's going on. Mel's a great woman."

"I know that. I just want to know what you're doing with her?"

"Why, do you think I should have ended up with you?" said Peter / Doug.

"What? No. Don't fuck with me. Did you tell her you like guys as well?"

"It hasn't come up. If she asked me, I'd probably tell her."

"If she asked you. Otherwise you just let her assume..."

"Mel's a big girl Kyle, you should know that. Jesus, look at what she does for living. I hardly think she'd have a problem with someone taking it up the ass now and then."

"I can't believe this. I've had sex with my best friend's boyfriend."

"It's not that big of a deal."

"What world are you living in Doug, oh excuse me, Peter?"

"Doug is my middle name."

"Your gay name you mean."

"Look Kyle, I don't know why you're so upset. Is this because I never called you after we sweated it up that time? That was completely hot by the way."

"Aren't you listening to me? This is a serious problem."

We could hear the door to Mel's bathroom open.

"It's only a problem if you make it one Kyle. Cut the drama queen shit."

I should have thrown my drink at him. Mel came into the living room with her purse in hand.

"O.K. boys, what did you talk about?" God, if you only knew.

"Baseball," said Peter, formally known as Doug.

"We have to go to a Dodger game together. Wouldn't that be fun?"

"Fab," I said.

We headed out the door and down the street.

• • •

It was impossible to enjoy dinner as my mind was focused on the disaster at hand. I tried my best to be cheerful and put on a good front even if it did feel like I was lying to Mel. Should I just blurt out what the truth was right then and there? Mel deserved to know but I didn't want to be the one to tell her because face it; she would blame me for bringing it all down. That's human nature.

The waiter cleared our plates and Mel excused herself. "I'll be right back guys, pick some good desserts out for us."

Once she was out of earshot Peter started in. "I don't see why you are so upset Kyle."

"You don't? How would you like to be in my situation?"

"I don't know. It could have its advantages."

"What do you mean by that?" I shot back. He looked at me with a slight smile on his face.

"I know what you've been thinking of this whole night Kyle, and it's not your friendship with Mel."

"Come again?"

"You can't keep your mind off what it would be like to have sex with me again. Admit it."

"Fuck you."

"Exactly. That's all you've been thinking about. I can see it in your eyes. You remember how hot that was that night last summer; working up a sweat like we did."

I hate to admit it but I couldn't get the thought out of my mind. He *was* hot. That night was hot. Incredibly, incredibly hot, and I have to admit that the thought of him naked again had given me more than one erection during dinner.

"Come on Kyle, think about it. How fun would it be for you and me to just go at it like dogs again?"

My cock was getting hard and I felt a combination of shame and lust.

"I wouldn't do that to Mel."

"Why not? It's not like you'd be breaking any rules or anything. She and I don't have any kind of commitment or bullshit like that. I can fuck anyone I please. Including her best friend."

"Sure Doug, or Peter, or whatever you real name is. You might think that would be cool, but something tells me she'd have a bit of an issue with it."

"See, you've proved my point."

"What?"

"That you want me. What's stopping you is that you think Mel would mind. You didn't say you wouldn't do it."

"You're twisting this around."

"It's true"

"I said stop it!" The volume was just enough for the busboy near our table to turn his head.

Doug leaned into me real close and with a sly smile slapped across his face said, "I bet you're hard right now."

Rock hard to be specific. Before I could come back with something Mel walked back from the restroom.

"Did I miss anything good?"

"Kyle was telling me about his erection."

Mel looked stunned. Time to cover.

"Ha ha, very funny," I said. What an asshole. How did she end up with this guy? O.K., I know the answer to that one. He's pure animal magnetism that would make any hot-blooded American sweat.

"Why Kyle, you dog you. Did you tell Peter how big it is?"

"You've seen it?" said Peter. He looked intrigued. Probably hoping that a three-way was in his future.

"Kinda," said Mel. "Just kidding you. So, are we having dessert?"

"I don't know, I'm pretty beached at this point," I said. I wanted to get the hell out of there.

"I'll get the check," said Peter. At least he was picking up the tab. He paid the bill and we walked back to Mel's place. When we got to my car, she gave me a hug goodbye.

"Thanks so much for coming tonight, Kyle," she squeezed. Her mouth was right near my ear. "I'm so glad you got to meet him, isn't he just great?"

"Yeah, he's a find alright." She broke loose.

"Nice meeting you Peter," I said as I held out my hand. In a quick move he grabbed my hand and then pulled me into one of those "tough-guy" hugs that are acceptable amongst "straight" men.

"It was great Kyle, can't wait to see you again," and with that he gave my ass one hard squeeze.

CHAPTER THIRTY-TWO
SLACK JAWED
...*With Cotton Mouth*

MICKEY AND TYLER WERE STARING BACK AT ME with their mouths open. I had called for an emergency breakfast at our favorite hangout. I spilled the whole story the moment after we ordered.

"This would only happen to you, Kyle," said Mickey.

"Are you going to tell her?" asked Tyler?

"I think I have to, don't I?"

"Absolutely," said Mickey.

"Not in a million years," said Tyler. "Stay out of it. No one likes to be told what to do with their romance." He scowled at what was obviously a dirty piece of silverware.

"He fucked her boyfriend, Tyler."

"Regardless, she doesn't need to know that."

"I think I have to tell her. I mean come on; he's not being truthful with her."

"I agree," said Mickey. "If he's lying to her about screwin' around with guys he could be lying to her about all kinds of things. He might even be positive and isn't telling her."

"That's jumping to an awfully big conclusion," said Tyler. "Mel's a big girl. My God, if anyone wouldn't care it would be her."

"That may be true," I said. "But think about it. Even though she'd go to the mat for her gay friends doesn't mean she'd want one for a husband. She draws a line for what she wants for herself."

"Another assumption, Kyle,' said Tyler. God, it made me wonder what it would take for him to tell something like this.

"Do you think this is going to bust up your friendship?" said Mickey.

"I don't know, what do you guys think?"

"Yes," said Tyler.

"Probably at first," said Mickey. "Thing is though, you guys are so close, I'm sure it'll eventually blow over."

"The fact of the matter is this." said Tyler, "You'd better be ready to lose her as a friend if you're willing to tell her this. Why don't you take advantage of her past track record and let the relationship fizzle out on its own? She'll never be the wiser and you won't be risking your friendship with her."

"At least you haven't lost your good sense in that department," said Tyler.

"I don't know Kyle; I think you really need to tell her." Between the two of them I felt Mickey was probably the one whose advice I should listen to. "You need to think about what is best for her; put that above the risk that you might lose a good friend."

"She should be happy I told her," I said.

"Who are you kidding?" said Tyler. "No one wants to have their love-bubble popped no matter how sincere the messenger."

"Do you think he'll tell her on his own?" asked Mickey.'

"I doubt it. He seemed too wily to screw this up by disclosing something he didn't have to."

"I bet he gets off on all of this, Kyle," said Tyler. "I know his type. He knows you are sitting here anguishing over the right thing to do and it's probably giving him the biggest hard-on he's ever had. Power maniac guaranteed."

"I think you're right," I added. "You should have seen him last night. He loved twisting my words around and screwing with my head. He was trying to get me back in the sack again too."

"Like I said, power hungry."

"Would you?" said Mickey.

"Sleep with him again?"

"Yeah."

"Are you nuts?"

"I don't know. It's not like you aren't in over your head already. Why not some fun for old time's sake."

"I could never do that."

"Sure, you could," said Tyler. "That's why you're so bothered by all of this. I can tell you're partly guilty because he still turns you on."

The waiter came by and refilled our coffees. I waited until he was gone before I continued.

"O.K., I admit I was turned on."

"Told you," said Mickey. Tyler had a big grin.

"He was a great lay."

"You're such a whore, Kyle." Tyler stirred some more cream into his coffee with his knife.

"I'd never do that to Mel," I said.

"Of course, you wouldn't," said Mickey. "Still, there's no harm if some good masturbation fantasies come from it."

"So when should I tell her?"

"Are we back to this," said Tyler? "Never. But since you insist you might as well get it over with sooner than later."

"I agree with Tyler. Give it to her straight and get it off your chest. You know there's always the possibility that she won't get as upset as we all think she will."

"Yeah right," said Tyler. "What're the odds that'll happen?

CHAPTER THIRTY-THREE

DRY WELL

Sometimes It's Better Not To Ask

I DROVE UP TO GLENN'S HOUSE AND PARKED my car in the driveway. I got out and rang the door. No answer. After a minute or two I gave it a ring again. Still no answer. Was he in the shower? I looked at my watch so I could time a five-minute wait because at this point, I figured that was all he deserved. What a pain. If I sit down on the step I'd get my pants dirty, so instead I stood there like an idiot.

Crazy day. Work had been hectic, and I couldn't get the whole Melanie fiasco out of my mind all day. I needed to think this one through very carefully and make sure that I didn't screw it all up although I felt that was probably inevitable.

At the five-minute mark I rang again. No response. There was a security intercom in the bathroom plus the living room *and* kitchen so even if he were dripping wet, watching TV or making a sandwich he could still buzz me that he'd be right there. Where the hell was he? It was five minutes til eight. He said to be here at seven thirty.

I took out my phone and rang his cell. After a few rings his voice mail came on, so I left a message.

"Hey, it's me. I'm outside and you don't seem to be home. Call me and let me know what's going on."

Weird. Firing up the car, I pulled out of his driveway and headed down the hill. I turned onto Cahuenga and started to head back to Hollywood. Just as I was going by the Hollywood Bowl my cell rang. It was Glenn.

"Hey, where are you?"

"I'm headed home. Where are you?"

"I'm home."

"Just now?"

"No, I've been here since six."

"Why the hell didn't you answer the phone?"

"Don't get snippy. Sorry, but I fell asleep. Turn around and come on back." He hung up before I had a chance to respond. Oh well, as much as I wanted to hate him, I guess it was an innocent mistake, although why did I feel like I was the one that was supposed to put forth an apology?

Traffic was a nightmare in the reverse direction, so I didn't find myself back in his driveway until a quarter to nine and by then I was starving. I rang the bell and waited impatiently. He finally opened the door with a less than sorry greeting...typical.

"Hey," he said. What the hell happened to you? I'm starving."

"Hey, *I* was here on time *and* awake I might add. I was all the way back in Hollywood when you called, and traffic was a mess on the way back."

"I went ahead and ordered Chinese food, no MSG per your past demands." He smiled at me but seemed to be in a quirky mood. I wondered what was up.

"Great."

"Beer?" he asked as we padded towards the kitchen.

"Sure." The phone rang but he ignored it. He pulled two beers out of the fridge and handed me one of them after he screwed off the cap with his sinewy paws.

"You can answer that if you want."

"That's OK. I don't need to talk to anyone." He looked down at the floor for a brief moment then back up at me. "Well, anyone except you of course." His smile was there but something behind his eyes said different.

"You OK?" I asked?

"Yeah, why?"

"You don't seem to be yourself." He looked at me then took another swig from his beer.

"I got sesame chicken extra spicy and tangerine beef. Will that work for you?"

"Yeah, sounds great."

"I know you like sesame chicken and I remembered that last time when you were looking through the menu you commented on the fact that you'd like to try tangerine beef sometime."

"That was nice of you to remember."

"I also got some egg rolls and I made sure they included the hot mustard that we both like."

"Thanks." He took another gulp of beer, followed by a deep breath. "I need something different."

Oh my God, this was why he was acting this way. He was breaking up with me.

"You're kidding me."

"I think I'm getting stagnant." This set me off.

"That's what you think of me? That I'm causing you to rot? You son of a bitch, I can't fucking believe this."

"Huh? No, Kyle, I was talking about my job." All right, so even if I look like a complete asshole right now at least he's not breaking up with me.

"Oh, OK, well…"

"Did you think I was dumping you?" He had a smirk on his face and that annoyed me.

"What would you've thought if I'd said the same thing?"

"Well, you'd *never* break up with *me* so I would of course know you meant something else."

"Oh ha, ha. You're a dick." I was half-angry but kind of joking at the same time.

"Oooh…a little ticked now aren't you?"

"Don't try to change the subject."

He set his beer down and grabbed me starting to tickle me.

"Stop it, damn it. I don't like to be tickled." He was relentless now.

"Oooh, now you're really ticked."

I squirmed and squirmed but he was getting the best of me. My anger was getting erased by the laughter until I cracked my elbow on the corner of his counter.

CRACK!

"Auuuugggghhhhh! Oh my God, fuck, fuck, *fuck!*"

"Oh shit, Kyle, are you OK?" I was consumed with numbing pain shooting up and down my arm. It hurt so bad I could feel it in my balls.

"Oh Kyle, I'm sorry, shhhh." Glenn pulled me close to him, gently rocking me in his arms til I started being less of a baby and more of a man. We slinked down to a sitting position on the tile floor.

"You OK?"

"Yeah, I whimpered. That really hurt."

"I know it did. It's OK." He just held me and it felt nice. The two of us sitting there, listening to the soft purr of his refrigerator. It felt nice.

"I love you Kyle."

"I love you too."

He pulled me close and I felt his lips against the back of my neck.

We sat there holding each other for a moment and then the doorbell rang. It was time to eat.

CHAPTER THIRTY-FOUR

WEDDING AHOY!

LAX Bound

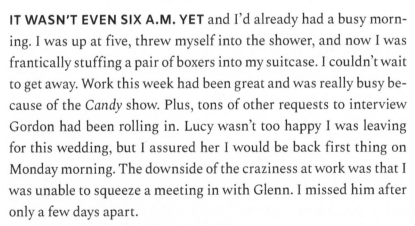

IT WASN'T EVEN SIX A.M. YET and I'd already had a busy morning. I was up at five, threw myself into the shower, and now I was frantically stuffing a pair of boxers into my suitcase. I couldn't wait to get away. Work this week had been great and was really busy because of the *Candy* show. Plus, tons of other requests to interview Gordon had been rolling in. Lucy wasn't too happy I was leaving for this wedding, but I assured her I would be back first thing on Monday morning. The downside of the craziness at work was that I was unable to squeeze a meeting in with Glenn. I missed him after only a few days apart.

The phone rang and I picked it up.

"Your car is waiting for you downstairs," said the electronic voice.

I grabbed my jacket, wallet and keys off my dresser then zipped up my suitcase and headed downstairs. When I walked outside a long double-stretch limo was parked in front and the driver was waiting to help me with my bag. When he opened the door, Mel was already inside waiting.

"I thought we might as well travel in style today as long as my father is paying for it," she said.

"Look at you," I said. "Did you rob Ralph Lauren last night?" Mel was dressed in a pale pink blouse, beige slacks and conservative shoes. Her hair was tied back into a ponytail and around her neck was a simple strand of pearls.

"Did I over do it?"

"You know I always like a good pearl necklace."

"They belonged to my father's mother. Last time I wore them was at her funeral. You look perfect by the way. I'd mistake you for an uptight WASP any day."

"You can thank the dress memo you emailed me yesterday. Just how Brooks Brothers is this weekend going to be."

"*Very*," she stressed.

"Let me see if I got everyone's name right. Your sister Alison is marrying Randal Thompson Kemp."

"Correct, but everyone calls him Rand or sometimes Tin Tin."

"Tin Tin?"

"His nickname from when he was on the Yale rowing team."

"And I address his parents as Mister and Mrs. Thompson-Kemp?"

"No, just Mister and Mrs. Kemp. Thompson is Rand's middle name. Address my father and mother as Mister and Mrs. Allingsworth unless they ask you to address them as William or Margaret which at some point, I'm sure they will do. Just make sure you don't call my father Bill."

"Got it." I noticed there was very little traffic at this time of day.

"Then there's my grandmother who is still alive, my mother's mother. She's Mrs. Wellington but I guarantee you she won't let you address her as grandmother until we get married."

"Tell me you didn't say we are engaged."

"No of course not. That would have been stretching the truth too much."

"As if you haven't already."

"Alright now. I know it will be difficult, but you have to let go of the gay sarcasm this weekend," she said as she poked me in the ribs. "It's a dead giveaway."

"Are you nervous about all of this?"

"Yes. I had trouble sleeping last night." She shifted uncomfortably in her seat despite the fact the limo was cradling us in comfort.

"Don't worry. It will all work out. I can be the perfect straight man for you."

"Yeah. Try not to check out the caterer's ass OK?" She said it with a weak smile. It was her attempt to mask the fear underneath, but it wasn't working.

"Are you always uptight like this when you go home?"

"I think it's extra bad because of this stupid wedding."

"Is your sister going to have you wear a hideous taffeta dress? Please say yes."

"Of course not. No, Alison is the epitome of refined taste. Even the bride's maids' dresses are Vera Wang let alone her own gown. Trust me. This spectacle will look like something out of *Town & Country*. Everything will be perfect and in its place. My family specializes in appearances."

CHAPTER THIRTY-FIVE

WELCOME TO DARIEN

Bloody Marys

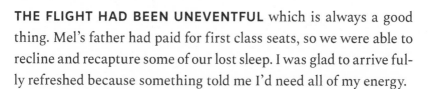

THE FLIGHT HAD BEEN UNEVENTFUL which is always a good thing. Mel's father had paid for first class seats, so we were able to recline and recapture some of our lost sleep. I was glad to arrive fully refreshed because something told me I'd need all of my energy.

Melanie was unusually quiet as her father's Bentley wound its way through wealthy enclave after wealthy enclave. She was definitely uptight about all of this and I was glad I didn't say anything about Peter/Doug even though at one point I almost brought it up.

The scenery was impressive. Massive estates behind iron gates were nestled amongst the dense foliage. It was quite different from what I was used to in LA...palm trees don't give much coverage. The car began to slow down considerably.

"Here we go," said Mel quietly as the chauffeur turned into a stone driveway and pulled up to a large, black iron gate supported by red brick columns. The driver hit a button on his dash and then the gates swung open allowing us through. I couldn't see much due to the towering trees until we made it into a clearing and pulled in front of an incredible Georgian mansion built of red brick. Four massive pillars held up the front cornice which covered the front entry. The house had two main floors with a third floor sprouting dormer windows out of the slate roof. On each side of the house were wings. The house was even longer than it was tall.

"Oh my God." I said.

"Welcome to my childhood home," said Melanie with a certain sense of resoluteness. Mel had never hid that she came from money. But I had no idea it was *this* kind of money.

The driver got out of the car and opened the door for us. Once I stepped out, I looked up at the house looming down on us. High overhead the front steps hung a wrought iron light fixture that looked like it could crush us all if it fell. We walked up the front steps where a smiling, older Black woman stood in the open doorway. She was dressed in a charcoal-colored maid's uniform and her silver hair was pulled into a neat bun.

"Miss Mellie, welcome home!" Are you shitting me? I felt like I was on the set of *Gone with the Wind.*

"Hi Lottie," said Melanie as she gave the old woman a huge and loving hug. "It's so good to see you."

"You're a sight for old eyes Mellie. And who's this handsome young man with you?"

"Lottie, this is Kyle."

"Welcome, Kyle. Come on in." As we crossed the threshold into the front hall we went from the front steps of Tara to *Architectural Digest.* A staircase of white balusters with a dark railing curved its way to the second floor. The sunlight danced amongst the pendants of a breathtaking crystal chandelier hung above an inlaid maple table on which sat an enormous spray of fresh flowers. The floor was patterned with creamy shades of marble and must have been made up of thousands of individual pieces. The white paint of the wainscoted walls shined as if recently painted and large pieces of art hung in gilded frames. The driver brought in our luggage and set it by the front door.

"Melanie." I turned and saw Melanie's mother. Margaret Allingsworth was a woman who was both handsome and elegant at the same time. It was easy to see where Mel got her sense of grace, style and fortitude. She looked to be in her late fifties and was dressed in a smart Chanel suit that was a dusty light-blue. Her chestnut hair lilted onto her shoulders and around her neck was a strand of pearls not unlike Melanie's but larger. On her suit jacket was a pearl and diamond brooch that seemed like a throwback to another era.

"Mother," said Melanie as she gave her mother a kiss on the cheek and a gentle hug. It didn't go by me that Lottie had received the better of the two greetings.

Mel's mother turned to me. "You must be Mr. McGraw." She held out a hand weighted down by an enormous ring. Something told me she didn't have to worry about dishwater dulling it.

"Please to meet you ma'am," I said as I gently shook her delicate hand.

"Melanie's told me so much about you." She said it in a way that had a hint of disapproval to it.

"All good I hope." Her lips made a pursed little smile as she expertly retrieved her hand; letting it gracefully rest on her hip.

"May I call you Kyle?"

"Yes of course Mrs. Allingsworth."

"So glad you could join us." She turned to Melanie. "We're having Bloody Marys. Do you need to freshen up first?"

"No, we're fine, mother." I nodded in accord.

"Lottie will see to it that your luggage is taken upstairs. Melanie, you'll be in Alison's room with her. Kyle, you'll be sharing a room with Rand."

"Why can't I stay in my old room?" protested Mel.

"Because I put your Aunt Clarice in there with her new husband Donald. Rand and Kyle will be in the south guest room." She turned back to me with a pained look on her face. "I'm afraid it's a full house this time so you'll have to double up."

"Not a problem Mrs. Allingsworth."

"I knew you'd understand."

She turned and we followed as she walked into the adjoining living room. Or drawing room I guess you'd call it. It was as remarkable as the entry way; everything in its place. Expensive fabrics, antiques, fresh flowers and artwork were everywhere. In the corner was a concert grand Steinway and in another corner was a harp. Despite its size the room seemed warm and inviting. Margaret crossed to the other side of the room, into a hallway, and then entered an even larger salon. Similar to the first room in its grandeur but even larger in square footage. It was equally immaculate but slightly less feminine with a portrait of a rather cranky looking man staring down at us from above the fireplace.

On a settee were Alison and Rand. I recognized them from a picture Melanie had shown me. Alison's hair wasn't as dark as Melanie's but you could definitely tell they were sisters. Alison, however, had a certain innocent look that Melanie did not have. She certainly fit the picture of a young and proper Connecticut bride. Her fiancé Rand was a good-looking guy. He had short blond hair and a nice square jaw. He wore a jacket with no tie, tan slacks and preppy shoes. Despite the jacket I could tell he was built. In a big chair was Mel's father. He was the kind of man who looked like he was born in a suit. He was distinguished, conservative and handsome.

His black hair was mixed with a smattering of grey; he looked like a banker or the CEO of an oil company. Across from him was Mel's grandmother. I thought it was ironic that her dress was the same charcoal grey as the maid's. However, this old dowager looked like Cartier had dipped her in glue and rolled her in diamonds. Collars of diamonds encased her skeletal neck and left wrist. Her spindly hands were covered with rings like passengers on a crowded bus. She was holding a Bloody Mary and her lipstick was the same tomato red as her drink. They were a sharp contrast against the deathly pallor of her over-powdered face.

Melanie introduced me to her clan and overall, I received a welcome that was both warm and proper. A houseman, or butler guy, brought me a Bloody Mary and I took a seat in a chair across from Alison who sat next to Rand and Alison. I prayed I wouldn't spill my drink on anything in the room. I could just imagine their antique rug looking like a crime scene due to one clumsy move on anyone's part.

Melanie's father took a deep sip of his Bloody Mary then looked at me.

"Melanie tells us you are in publishing Kyle."

"Yes. I work for a company called Devore Horizon."

"How nice," chimed in Alison.

The old lady looked at me from her perch with a sour look. "Are you a Catholic?" she spat. I was a bit taken aback.

"Grandmother!" Melanie interjected. "He's not practicing." The old lady muttered something under her breath and stirred her celery stalk around her Bloody Mary. The afternoon sun hit the diamonds on her wrist like a disco ball and I couldn't help but think this had to be one of the most surreal experiences I'd ever had.

As if on cue to help interrupt the current topic, the houseman appeared at my side holding a tray of appetizers.

"You must try a canapé, Kyle," said Margaret. "Mrs. Harper has outdone herself."

I assumed Mrs. Harper was the cook and took one. I was grateful for the distraction and made a mental note that so far I'd counted four servants.

"Melanie told us she redecorated your condo." Huh? I could see Melanie's face tense up at the realization she had forgotten to fill me in on her supposed career.

"Hardly what I expected for my daughter after paying for four years at Vassar," cranked Mr. Allingsworth. "Seems like a servant's position to be decorating people's homes."

"I think it's quite respectable," said Margaret.

"She should leave decorating to the homosexuals," said the Grandmother. "She should find a respectable man to marry like Alison." Uh, hello. I'm in the room. This was going to be a long weekend.

"My sister married a man whose cousin is a decorator. Queer as they come," said Rand as he motioned the houseman for a refill.

"She's quite good you know," I said. I figured someone had to come to Mel's defense so it might as well be me.

"Really?" said her father sounding somewhat hopeful that if she was going to waste her life as a decorator at least she was good at it.

"Absolutely."

"She didn't send us any pictures. What did she do in your home?" inquired Margaret.

"Well, she has an amazing eye for leather pieces." I said. I could see a tight smile on Mel's lips.

"That's not what I would have expected," said Alison. "She seems like the type who would go for chintz."

"She's really good at what she does. I know for a fact that she leaves her clients simply gasping for breath because they are so overwhelmed by her talents."

"Really," said Mrs. Allingsworth. "She always did have an eye for the esthetic."

"I still don't approve," said Grandma. "Are you two getting married?"

"Grandmother! Please." I just kept my mouth shut because I figured it was best to let Mel take the lead on these questions.

"I'm simply saying," said her Grandmother as she took her celery stalk on another trip around the rim of her glass.

"Too bad you weren't here last weekend for my bachelor party, Kyle," said Rand. If he only knew how grateful I was I missed it although after my experience with Gordon at the Little Luck I suppose I would have fit right in. I noticed Rand was already halfway through his fresh drink. The boy could put them down. I also noticed that Melanie seemed like she was an actress playing a character unlike her own self. This whole scene felt like something out of a stage play and I wondered how the first act was going to end.

"What is the plan for this evening?" asked Melanie.

"The cars will be here at seven," said her mother.

"I should help Kyle get settled."

"Sure you don't want to stay for another drink?" queried Margaret, holding her Bloody Mary up for inspection.

"No, I've got a bit of a headache and need to lie down for a bit," said Mel.

"Oh, I hope you'll be feeling better by this evening," said Alison.

"I'm sure she will be," said Mr. Allingsworth. "Just travel nerves."

I thanked everyone for my drink and followed Melanie out of the room.

"You don't have a headache at all do you?" I whispered.

"Of course not, I just need to get away. I thought I was going to scream. Come on." I followed her up the staircase. At the top of the stairs was a sitting area adorned with antique chairs, consoles and a small loveseat. On either side of the sitting area was an impressive hallway and I noticed another staircase that went to the third floor off of the left hallway.

"This place is huge."

"Ridiculous isn't it?" said Mel. "Sometimes I'm ashamed I grew up here." She walked down one of the hallways.

"I wouldn't be complaining. It's pretty awesome."

"Yeah, I guess so, but I don't feel like I fit in here."

We came to the end of the hall and Melanie opened the door. We walked into a large guest suite. The walls were pale yellow and the curtains and bed linens while bright and cheerful didn't fall on the side of frilly thereby giving the impression this is where male guests were put. Over the carved mantel of the fireplace was a painting depicting a hunting scene, complete with the requisite hounds and men in red riding jackets, white pants and shiny black boots.

"Tell me that's not what we are doing tomorrow after the nuptials," I said, pointing to the painting.

"Very funny. I'll have you know that there are no riding crops involved this weekend."

"That'll be a switch for you now won't it?" I smirked. She gave me a playful slap on the arm and got down to business.

"OK, Lottie will have had everything unpacked for you so look in the armoire for your things. When my mother said the cars will be here at seven that means we should be dressed and ready to go by quarter til. I'll meet you downstairs. A reminder that tonight is for your tuxedo. I'm sure Lottie already had Philip steam it for you but check to make sure, so it looks right. Whatever you do don't be late. Mother would be incensed."

"Will do."

"You have time for a quick nap, but you might want to get your shower now because don't forget you have to share the bathroom with Rand."

"Looks like that's not the only thing I'll be sharing," I said as I patted the bed.

"Oh yeah, well. Sorry it's not king size but you'll have to make do," she said in a terse and stressed voice.

"Mel, I was just kidding. I'm fine with it although it's a bit odd."

"Welcome to old money. We do things differently here."

"Hey, are you alright?"

"No, not really," she said with a helpless look in her eyes. "Kyle, I don't want to be here. I don't relate to any of these people."

"It will be fine."

"No, it won't. This isn't right. A person should be excited to come home to see her family not dreading it. I feel like everyone has their eyes on me in a disapproving way."

"I didn't see that. They seemed genuinely happy to see you. Well, maybe not your grandmother, at least on the outside. But I'm sure she's happy on the inside."

"She's not big on smiling," said Mel. "I'm so sorry I got you into this but thank you so much for being here. I never could have done this without some help."

"Don't worry about it," I said. "It's kind of entertaining. I don't know people lived like this outside of the movies."

"I think I'm going to take a hot bath and try to relax. Meet you downstairs later on?"

"Sure."

"Alison and I are in the room directly across from this one so if you need anything just knock."

"I'll walk you home," I said. We walked across the hall into the other room. It was bigger than the one Rand I and were assigned and as I expected, this one was done up in floral everything. It was very feminine and even included a canopied bed.

"Very girly," I laughed.

"When I was a little girl, we used to try to count the different kinds of flowers on everything. It's impossible to get them all."

"Alright, go get your shower. By the way, since we are a couple should I hold your hand or kiss you in front of your parents?"

"Hell no, said Melanie. WASPs would never do that."

CHAPTER THIRTY-SIX

ROOMMATES

Don't Drop The Soap (Gay Scout Rule # 21)

BACK IN MY ROOM, I WAS LOOKING out the window down on the backyard. Workers were erecting white chairs and tents. It looked like there was going to be a big crowd tomorrow. Gardeners were busy making sure everything looked perfect and were racing against the setting sun. I could only imagine what all this cost.

Things had gone well so far despite the uncomfortable-ness of it all. At least everyone was more or less friendly and the Bloody Mary certainly helped relax me. I opened the armoire and saw all of my clothes hanging neatly on one side. The other side contained clothes I assumed belonged to Rand. I opened the drawers on his side and found silk plaid boxers. No surprise there for Tin Tin. The other side contained my socks and boxers and the experience wasn't nearly as interesting as rummaging through someone else's. All were carefully laid in the drawer. I pulled out my tuxedo and gave it a once over. No one would've been able to tell it had been smashed into a garment bag for most of the day. In fact, it looked perfect.

The bathroom was the same scenario. All of my toiletries laid out on one side of the vanity and Rand's on the other. It was odd to have strange toiletries commingling on the same counter as mine. Taking Mel's suggestion, I took my shower and shaved so that Rand could have the bathroom when he was ready. I threw on some casual pants and a shirt; I'd put on my tux last minute so that I wouldn't wrinkle it. Since I wasn't sleepy enough for a nap, I got a book and sat down in an easy chair by the window. Just as I settled in then there was a gentle knock on the door.

"Come in," I said. The door opened and the same man who served me a cocktail earlier stuck his head in.

"Is everything to your satisfaction sir?"

"Thanks, I'm good," I replied.

"You'll find your dress clothes hanging in the armoire. I steamed them and gave your shoes an extra shine as well."

"Thank you, that's very kind." Was I supposed to tip him?

"If you require anything, simply lift the phone and press the pound key."

"Thank you. I'll remember that." He nodded then closed the door. To think of the times I thought about having a staff of servants and now they were only a touchtone away. Just as I wondered if I could get room service during the middle of the night the door flew open and in burst Rand.

"Hello Mr. Los Angeles," he said with exuberance as he flopped himself down on the bed. He raised his arm in a sweeping motion. "So, what do you think of this place?"

"Pretty incredible," I said.

"The old man did all right for himself eh?" I nodded in agreement. "We'll be sitting in the catbird seat soon enough won't we?" said Rand.

"Huh?" I replied.

KYLE MCGRAW | 251

"Come on bro, I'm not stupid you know. Alison and Melanie are pretty and all, but they look a lot sexier when they're standing in front of a crib like this."

"Oh, I don't know about that," I said, not exactly sure how to continue this conversation and amazed he was saying what he was. Rand got up off the bed. As he walked by me towards the bathroom, he gave my hair a tousle.

"Oh, all right. I get it. Wink, wink." He went into the bathroom and I could hear him turn on the shower. "Mind if I clean up?"

"No. Go for it." I said, grateful he was distracted with getting ready. From where I was sitting, I could see steam rise from the behind the shower curtain. He'd left the door partially open and I caught myself wondering what he looked like naked. I didn't usually go for Rand's type, but he looked pretty built and I had to admit rather hot.

Despite his endless singing in the shower I soon found myself engrossed in my book. It was a sleazy detective novel set in the bowels of Tijuana. I barely registered the sound of the shower being turned off.

"So, when are you going to pop the question to Melanie?" I looked up to see Rand standing in the bathroom door…buck naked…unless you count the pale blue fluffy towel that moved from one part of his body to the other and was currently working over his eye-popping bicep. I think my mouth was hanging open.

"Come on, don't act so surprised. You know you're going to ask Melanie to marry you." Actually, I was agape at the candlestick Alison was receiving as a wedding gift. Rand put his foot on a nearby chair to dry his toes. His balls were swinging back and forth like pealing wedding bells. As difficult as it was to turn away, I stared down at my book.

"To be honest, it really wasn't on my mind to marry Melanie. We're kind of taking it slow. You know how it goes."

"That's not what I hear from Alison, Tiger. Grrrr." He chuckled after saying it and I realized I had no idea what was running through his head. God, what had Melanie said about me, about us?" Rand turned and walked back into the bathroom. I caught a nice shot of his ass as he threw his towel into the tub. His time spent on the rowing team had served him well. It was getting late, so I got up to put on my tux.

"I'm actually looking forward to settling down," said Rand from the bathroom.

"Yeah?" I said somewhat surprised as I hopped into my trousers.

"Ready for some babies and the suburbs." He came back out of the bathroom wearing a pair of boxers. I wondered if they were the same ones he'd taken off when he went in to take his shower because he didn't get them from the armoire.

"You don't strike me as the suburbs type," I said as I buttoned up my shirt.

"I am when they look like this," said Rand as he once again made a grand gesture with his hand around the room. He would have made a good real estate agent. I shot him a smile and we finished dressing.

Once I was all ready, I told Rand I'd see him downstairs. He was busy texting someone and nodded in agreement. As soon as I got into the hallway, I felt a vibration in my pants that this time wasn't caused by Rand. I pulled out my cell and saw that it was Glenn.

"Hey!" I said. My voice was laced with excitement that he called.

"How goes the impending nuptials?"

"It's been interesting. You should see this place."

"Tacky?"

"Immense. If you pick up a phone and press the pound key a servant is at your beck and call."

"You must be in heaven."

"It's actually a bit uncomfortable." Not to mention the fact that I am sharing a bed with the groom, but I thought I'd leave that tidbit out of the conversation.

"Rich people are their own breed." I wondered if he included himself in that grouping. "What are you doing tonight?"

"There's some kind of rehearsal dinner. I'm all spiffed out in black tie. We're all supposed to meet downstairs in a few minutes. Something tells me pre-lubrication will be on the agenda."

"Like I said, you must be in heaven," he snickered. "Well, I wish you were here in LA instead. Will just be a boring Friday night for me I guess."

"I have a hard time believing that one."

"Actually, I'm kind of looking forward to a relaxing evening on my own. I've got some things to do around the house. Do you think anyone will cause a big scene at the wedding?"

"I doubt it will be that interesting. This crowd likes everything in its place."

"Well, you never know. I've got to go because I have a meeting. Just wanted to say I missed you."

"I miss you too." I made a quick smooching sound before I hung up. I felt good inside. It was nice being missed.

I walked down the hall and headed down the staircase. In the foyer I saw Mr. Allingsworth looking rather agitated and chewing on an ice cube. Or maybe it was just annoyance at having to shell out truckloads of money for a wedding. As I approached him he shook the ice in his nearly empty glass.

"Scotch?" he asked as he held up his glass.

"No thank you sir. I'm going to hold off for now."

"You'll be regretting that decision soon enough," he said with a snarky smile. "These things bore the hell out of me. Really for the women you know."

"Probably so, sir." I said. I hardly ever used the word sir but it seemed appropriate with this guy.

Melanie's mother walked in from a hallway that I think led to the kitchen. She looked beautiful in a long green evening dress and the requisite diamonds.

"Good evening ma'am," I said.

"Well now, don't you look nice," she said with an approving smile. Before I had a chance to return the compliment she turned to her husband.

"Where's mother?"

"In the car where she belongs."

"How long has she been there?"

"One scotch," he said. "The driver was here when we came down and she was antsy to go."

Margaret looked at the clock on the wall and then turned to me.

"Thank you for being on time," she said.

"My pleasure ma'am." We turned our heads toward the top of the staircase at the sound of a slight giggle. Rand and Alison were on their way down. Rand was in his tux and Alison was wearing a vibrant red number that could have stopped traffic either from the low cut or the bright color.

"That dress," said Margaret under her breath in way that almost sounded like mock approval and left me wondering what her real thought was.

"Your grandmother is in the car waiting on us. Where's your sister?" barked Mr. Allingsworth.

"She was right behind us," said Alison.

"There she is," said Rand with a nod of his head to the second-floor landing.

Melanie was standing at the top of the staircase locking the clasp of her bracelet. Her black hair was swept back and up on her head and her body was caressed by a gown of pale dusty pink. Once it was fastened, she looked up and saw all of us looking up at her. Her face broke into a smile as she began to glide down the stairs. She was simply stunning, like a young Audrey Hepburn. She'd caught our attention and I couldn't think of a time she looked more incredible.

"That dress," said Margaret under her breath again but this time I could tell she meant something completely different than before.

CHAPTER THIRTY-SEVEN
CHAMPAGNE BUBBLES

They Go To Your Head

I WOKE UP OUT OF A DEAD SLEEP to find Rand stumbling into our room…drunk. He'd done his best to get me to stay at the rehearsal dinner longer and drink with his buddies but I used the excuse of jet-lag to go home with everyone else and get a good night's sleep before the big day.

"Sorry, dude," he said with a slur. "You should'a stayed and tied one on with us, it was fucking awesome." It was interesting how excessive alcohol made him sound a lot less well-bred than when I first met him. The clock said one-thirty. I'd only been asleep for about an hour and despite my exhaustion when I crawled into bed, I was wide awake now.

In the moonlight of the room I could see Rand take off his shirt and throw it in the corner. The pants went next and then the socks but thankfully he left on his boxers. He crashed into bed slurring a quick "good night" and in an incredibly short amount of time a guttural purr began to waffle from his mouth. This was weird. Here

I was lying in bed next to some straight guy I'd never met until a few hours before.

Sleep was going to be a challenge for me. I was wide awake and restless. It was then I realized I had forgotten to pack sleeping pills (Gay Scout Rule # 2…Always be prepared). Slipping quietly out of bed so as not to wake Rand I put on my pants and a shirt and decided to go in search of some milk. Or maybe a shot of vodka. God knows that would be easy to find in this house. Carefully slipping out of bed so as not to wake Rand, I put on the big terrycloth robe left in the room for guests. A nice touch and I had to marvel at how much this house was run like the Four Seasons.

The squeak of the stairs was muffled under the thick carpet runner as I made my decent. When I got to the foyer and turned left to go down the hallway towards the kitchen, I saw there was a light on. Drawing nearer I also heard voices. There's a weird feeling when you are in someone else's house and a simple goal to get some milk becomes filled with anxiety. Who was in there talking? Slowly I walked towards the kitchen careful to not make noise.

Standing in the shadows of the hallway I saw Melanie and Lottie sitting at the prep table. Their backs were to me. Lottie was in a bathrobe and Melanie was still wearing her dress from this evening. It was difficult to make out what Melanie was saying but I could tell she was crying. Lottie had her hand on Melanie's back in the way a mother would console an upset child. Melanie's hand went up to her eyes to stroke away tears. The awkwardness I felt at witnessing this situation killed my desire to get a glass of milk. Carefully, I backed up until I was out of the doorway and I silently made my way back to the base of the stairs. I paused there for a moment trying to decide what to do. Part of me felt like going back there and seeing what was wrong with Mel. But at the same time, I could sense she was in good hands and I didn't want to be an intruder on a private moment.

Before going upstairs however, I thought a shot of something would help me get back to sleep. I went through the first drawing room until I came to the room where earlier we had Bloody Marys. On one side of the room was a bar complete with heavy crystal decanters filled with booze. Glasses were neatly organized nearby. Lifting the stopper out of one of the decanters filled with clear liquid I took a sniff. Gin. The second one must be the vodka. As I took off the stopper, I realized that if I used a glass then someone would know I was hitting the bar cart. Couldn't wash it and return it because there was no sink nearby. So, I took a good long swig from the bottle, estimating two shots, then held back a choking cough as I replaced the bottle to its spot.

My journey took me back upstairs to the door of our room. When I entered I could hear Rand still purring away. The robe went back to its resting place on the chair by my side of the bed and I slid under the covers. Rand kept humming along. The warm restfulness of the vodka was starting to work, and I found it hard to think about Melanie and what was wrong. This had to have been a stressful day for her. I turned my head and looked at Rand's face, peaceful and content. Before I knew it, I was out like a light.

• • •

I was having the *best* sex dream. I was lying on my side and Glenn's hard body was pressed up against mine as he nuzzled that sweet spot behind my ear. With each exhalation of his hot breath on my bare neck and shoulder, a tingling sensation shot down my arm·and side and leg and out my toes. We were swirling in a sea of sleepy sensation and I could feel Glenn's hard cock rub against me.

"Wanna suck it?" he said.

"Sure," I replied. The room was spinning as we floated on top of his bed under the Los Angeles moon. I could feel him maneuvering around me, and in the background I heard the howl of a wolf and the sound of lawn sprinklers going chit chit chit chit. His muscled legs straddled my chest and then I felt his hard cock go into my mouth.

"Yeah, that's hot he said," as he continued to thrust.

I realized the wolf had come into the room and was standing at the side of the bed watching us have sex. The wolf howled again, and I opened my eyes to look at the expression on Glenn's face.

"God that feels good," said Rand. "Keep going." I turned my eyes to look at the wolf to help me with my confusion when I saw he wasn't there. Then I looked up at Rand looking down at me.

What the fuck?

There was just enough moonlight that I could see a mischievous yet satisfied smile on Tin Tin's face.

Oh my God...I was blowing the groom.

CHAPTER THIRTY-EIGHT

WEDDING DAY

Here Comes The Bride…
The Groom Already Came

NEEDLESS TO SAY, I DIDN'T SLEEP WELL but I can't say the same for Rand. He was snoring away; cocooned in contentment. I was up at the crack of dawn, showered and was putting on my pants when I heard my cell buzz with a text.

"Coffee?" said the message. It was from Mel.

"YES" I shot back.

"Meet hall 2 min." I put on a clean shirt, socks and some shoes before quietly slipping out the door so as not to wake Rand. Melanie was in the hallway.

"Morning," she whispered.

"Are we the only ones up?" I whispered back.

"Alison is in the shower. Let's go downstairs. Lottie has coffee ready for us."

We went down the stairs then walked through the dining room and then into a sunroom filled with huge plants and white wicker furniture. On a side table was a silver urn with coffee as well as breakfast pastries and fruit. The morning sun was dappling through the leaves of the trees outside providing morning glow without cooking us at the same time. A group of workers was already busy down by the wedding set up. We sat down. The coffee tasted great and I welcomed the fact I had Mel at my side instead of Rand.

"Did you sleep OK?" she asked.

"Sort of," I said. "Rand was a bit distracting."

"Alison said he's a real snorer."

"So, she's had sex with him?"

"I assume so. Unlike you and me she's a bit shier about that kind of stuff. She wouldn't tell me gory details." God knows I could.

"Mel...does Rand strike you as...uh..."

"Republican?" she said with a smirk. "I think that goes with the territory in case you hadn't noticed."

"That's not what I was thinking. More like gay."

"Rand?" she said with a surprised look. "I don't think so. Why, are you jealous Alison is getting him and you're not?"

"Hardly," I said. "But he does look hot naked."

"You don't have to tell me."

"Whoa, back up. The two of you have screwed around?"

"Get your mind out of the gutter. Back in high school some of us skinny dipped one summer. Even in the tenth grade he was packing. I can only imagine what he's like now."

"Does Alison know?"

"I never told her. Don't know if Rand did but I'd guess not. He's pretty conservative don't you think?"

"Yeah, maybe." She picked at her croissant in a way that was very unlike Mel. Normally she tore into her food with gusto.

"Now it's my turn to ask. You OK?"

"I'll be fine."

"It's just that I saw you last night with Lottie in the kitchen."

"When?" she seemed surprised and a little violated.

"I wasn't spying. I just came down to get some milk and when I saw you were upset I turned around and left. What's going on?"

"I don't know. It's being here, I think. It's so stressful. I don't feel like I belong with these people."

"You are sort of the black sheep."

"Lottie is the only one who understands me. It's pretty bad when I have a closer relationship with the maid as opposed to my own mother."

"Does Lottie know about your career?"

"No. I don't think she'd handle that one very well. But I was telling her the truth about you and me."

"You outed me to the servants!" I said with mock alarm.

"She had you figured out from the outset. Caught you checking out one of the gardeners when you were getting out of the limo."

"Force of habit, I guess. He was pretty hot."

"Anyway, I was just telling her about my real boyfriend and how I could never bring him here. They'd eat him alive."

"Well, maybe your grandmother would at least. She's intimidating."

"You're not the first person to say that," she smiled.

The bellow of a not-to-subtle yawn came from behind us and we turned to see Rand. He was barefoot and wearing his bathrobe and his casualness seemed out of character.

"Good morning," he said as he made his way over to the coffee. I could feel the tension creep into my muscles as he poured a cup for himself and then stood by the table.

"How'd you sleep Kyle?" he said.

"Good, I said."

"That's the way," he replied, giving my hair another quick tousle.

"Are you excited, Rand?" Melanie asked.

"Last hours of freedom," he said. "I guess I'd better go get showered and make the most of them. I'll see you two in a few." We watched him walk out of the room. I turned to Mel.

"He stuck his cock in my mouth while I was sleeping last night." She almost dropped her coffee cup. It was clearly the last thing she expected.

"No shit. Are you serious?"

"I feel like trash."

"Hey, you were asleep. What the hell happened?"

"I don't know. He came home drunk. I was asleep. Then I thought I was dreaming I was having sex with Glenn and bam!"

"Just goes to show that you can take the boy out of boarding school, but you can't take the boarding school out of the boy."

"What're you talking about?"

"I'm sure you're not the first guy he's fooled around with. Rand went to boarding school for six years. Any port in a storm...that kind of thing."

"You're awfully casual about all of this," I said, still upset that it happened in the first place although I had to admit it was rather thrilling on a certain level.

"All I'm saying Kyle, is that these things happen when guys get drunk. Now I see why you were asking if he was gay."

"Should we warn your sister?"

"About what? She'd probably just laugh it off. The Town & Country set knows guys screw around in boarding school. Even the straightest of the bunch. It's like polo. Put a person in the right environment and it's eventually a game that makes sense to play. Besides, you aren't the only one who's fooled around with him."

"You're kidding. Who else?"

"Well, that skinny dipping party was just me and Rand. I lost my virginity to him."

"Oh my God."

"So, I guess you're just part of the family at this point," she laughed.

CHAPTER THIRTY-NINE

POST NUPTIALS

Attack Of The Ice Sculpture

UNFORTUNATELY, THE ENORMOUS COST OF THE WEDDING didn't offset the sheer boredom I experienced during the ceremony. It was the usual drippy collection of poems, music and vows that seemed to go on forever. Routinely, when I find myself in that kind of situation I start to fantasize about what people look like without their clothes on…it's a way to pass the time…and pass it did…all 83 mind-numbing minutes. I was certain the applause at the end was generated more from relief that it was over as opposed to happiness for the newlyweds. Surprisingly enough Mel seemed to enjoy it. She was the last person I thought would want to sit, let alone stand, through a wedding but she beamed consistently throughout; resolutely standing by as Alison said "I do" to a cad.

The festivities that followed were actually rather fun. After a few glasses of champagne, Mel and I took a few turns around the dance floor while she joked in my ear that I should let her lead and I'd follow. Looking over Mel's shoulder as we danced, I spied

Margaret from the sidelines sipping Veuve Clicquot and watching us with a careful smile. Behind her was Mel's grandmother who was relentlessly stabbing at something on her plate with her fork, a look of disgust on her face.

"This ended up not being so bad after all," I said.

"You're right," said Mel and she jokingly swooped backwards and kicked up a heel as if she were auditioning for *Dancing with the Stars*. "It got off to a rough start but today has actually been fun."

"Do you think Alison is going to be happy?"

"Probably. Rand has what she's been looking for."

"Money?"

"Parental approval. He comes from a quote-quote *Right kind of family*. He may be a bit of a dingbat to us but he's on target for her and my parents. Even my grandmother likes him."

"Who would have thought that could happen."

"No kidding. I remember when I was in high school, I was going to go to a dance with this guy who my grandmother didn't approve of and she raised all holy hell like you can't even imagine."

"Knowing you I'm guessing you went anyway?" The band stopped playing and we headed back to our table.

"Are you kidding," said Melanie? "No one, and I mean no one, crosses her. A suitable date was arranged for me with a guy I could hardly stand but was the son of a good friend of my mother's. Welcome to Darien."

We stood off to the sidelines and people-watched while sipping champagne. Melanie kept pointing out various guests and then filled me in on some juicier aspects of their lives. She's having an affair with her cousin, he has testicular cancer, that one beat her husband with a fireplace poker after she found out he'd lost twenty million dollars on a bad real estate investment. On it went. On the surface it was a Ralph Lauren ad but underneath it was *The Real Housewives of Darien* and I loved the stories she was dispensing.

Margaret saw us laughing and walked over to where we were standing.

"Hello Mrs. Allingsworth," I said, hoping my good manners would win her over.

"The two of you look like you are enjoying yourselves."

"It's a beautiful wedding. You must be very proud of your daughter."

"I am."

"Alison looks beautiful today doesn't she mother," said Mel.

"A bride never looks prettier than on her wedding day," said Margaret. "Melanie, your grandmother was asking for you. Would you please go to her?"

"Sure," said Melanie as she handed me her empty champagne glass. "I'll be right back, Kyle."

Alone with Melanie's mother, I wondered if I should ask her to dance. She took a small sip of her champagne and then forced a smile.

"Have you been enjoying your stay with us, Kyle?"

"Yes ma'am. I've been made very comfortable."

"You're a handsome young man. I'm sure you have many ladies back in Los Angeles vying for your attention." If she only knew.

"Oh, I don't know about that," I said, feigning shyness.

"I can tell you have strong feelings for my daughter." My brain scrambled trying to guess what Melanie had told her mother.

"Melanie's amazing. There's no one else quite like her," I said.

"Yes. That she is." I could sense Margaret was on a mission. I started to wonder if she was going to ask me if I was planning on marrying her daughter. Thoughts of a second wedding had to be in the back of her mind. "I'm sure our life here in Darien is quite different than what you are used to in Los Angeles," she continued.

"LA is definitely its own beast," I said at a lame attempt to make her laugh.

"What I'm trying to say my dear, is that while you may understand life in Los Angeles, I can't help but think that you don't have a feel for what goes unsaid here." What the hell was she talking about? I had no idea how to respond.

"Ma'am?" My discomfort was increasing while Margaret took another mini sip from her glass.

"Let me put it more simply for you. I understand why you are attracted to my daughter...on multiple levels. Certainly, Melanie's father and I have appreciated the opportunity to meet you and have you in our home. But tomorrow, you will return to Los Angeles, and there your relationship with my daughter will come to an end. I've indulged her to an extent, in terms of wanting to live on the west coast, but I'm afraid the west coast will need to remain where it belongs."

I'm not sure what my face was saying but inside I felt a mixture of repulsion, amazement and fear. What did I have to fear about a skinny piece of cold fish rolled in a diamond Panko crust? Logically, nothing...intuitively, everything. She had the ability to intimidate.

Margaret put her spidery fingers gently on my shoulder. "You're a smart boy, I'm sure you understand." She shot me one last fake smile then walked off leaving me with a new understanding of why Melanie was dreading coming back here. I couldn't help but wonder what happened to the mother who enjoyed the pageant circuit with her little girl. In her place was a calculating monster.

I took a much-needed glass of champagne off a waiter's tray as he passed. The fun of this day was over, and I couldn't wait to get out of here. Our 10 a.m. departure seemed like an eternity away now.

The laughter, music and chatter continued. Melanie was nowhere to be found, so I stayed in my spot off to the sidelines figuring she'd eventually make it back here. Finally, I saw her come from around a hedge. The smile was gone from her face.

"What happened?" I asked.

"Just talking to my grandmother," she said. I could tell she was hiding the truth from me. "What did you and my mother talk about?" she asked in a tone that was somewhat nervous.

"Nothing much," I lied, and with that lie I saw a look of relief in her eyes. I wasn't about to make this situation worse for her now by telling her that Margaret tied a can to my ass. "Just wedding babble about how nice everything was; tasty hors d'oeuvres etcetera."

"She seems very happy with how everything turned out. I'm glad for Alison. It's what she wanted. Are you ready to head home?"

"Yeah. What about you?"

"Definitely. Kyle, I really appreciate that you did this for me."

"Of course. I'd do it again...maybe," I said with a gentle poke to her side. She laughed.

"Well, fuck it. We might as well get loaded and dance the night away," she said as she led me back out to the dance floor.

CHAPTER FORTY

LEAVING ON A JET PLANE

Carry-On Baggage

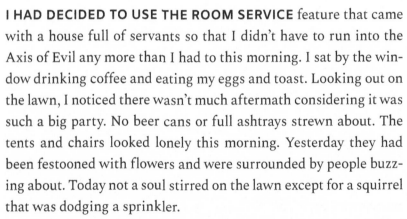

I HAD DECIDED TO USE THE ROOM SERVICE feature that came with a house full of servants so that I didn't have to run into the Axis of Evil any more than I had to this morning. I sat by the window drinking coffee and eating my eggs and toast. Looking out on the lawn, I noticed there wasn't much aftermath considering it was such a big party. No beer cans or full ashtrays strewn about. The tents and chairs looked lonely this morning. Yesterday they had been festooned with flowers and were surrounded by people buzzing about. Today not a soul stirred on the lawn except for a squirrel that was dodging a sprinkler.

I was showered, dressed and packed. My bag was by the door of my room in anticipation of a quick get away. I couldn't wait to get out of this silver spoon circus. At least I slept well last night because I had the bed to my self. By the time I retired, Rand and Alison had been whisked to a private jet headed for Bermuda and I was left to peace and quiet. No snoring and no penis in my face while I was trying to sleep.

I dreaded the departure because I was sure it meant having to be pleasant to Melanie's parents and grandmother. But at least I would never see them again. I felt bad for her. In a short amount of time I got to see a side of Melanie I'd never understood before this trip. I'd be spanking accountants from Encino too if it meant rebelling against this bullshit. Give me my crappy apartment and freedom any day over this life.

It was quarter to ten and I sent Mel a text. "Ready?"

"Two minutes," came the reply. I checked the room one last time and then got my bag and went into the hallway outside her door. Before I had a chance to knock she opened it up.

"All right, we are out of here," she said.

"Did you want to say goodbye to Lottie?"

"I did about an hour ago. She brought me breakfast. My parents are waiting for us downstairs." Wonderful I thought.

Just as we started down the hallway, the houseman magically appeared and took our luggage. We descended the staircase where Melanie's parents were staged for the departure ceremony. Her grandmother was noticeably absent, probably still asleep in her coffin.

Melanie hugged her father who warmly reciprocated. "Take care of yourself," he said. Melanie moved on to give her mother a hug which was my cue to extend my hand to her father. "Thank you for coming to our daughter's wedding young man," he said with a smile that just as easily could have been used with a mechanic who did a good job fixing his car. "Thank you for your hospitality," I said with equal bull-shittiness.

I turned to Margaret who had her hand extended and a phony smile lacquered on her face. "Mrs. Allingsworth, what can I say about your wonderful hospitality," I said with warmth and enthusiasm. I took her hand and gave it a bone crushing squeeze. He eyes widened and her mouth opened as I felt her diamond rings press into her flesh. I pulled her into me feigning a big hug and as soon as my lips were close to her ear I whispered, "*I blew the groom.*" I pulled back smiling warmly as I reveled in the emotional salad I'd just tossed. One part relief that I'd let go of her hand and one part complete horror at what I'd said. Her mouth agape, I could see the bridgework on her back molars. It hardly matched her Chanel suit.

• • •

The ride to the airport was full of meaningless conversation that was appropriate for the driver to hear. The Bentley was in use by another houseguest, so we were downsized to a Mercedes sedan driven by a gardener. The airport was the usual flurry of checking in and dealing with security. Once we'd taken some seats to wait for our flight Melanie turned to me.

"OK, I owe you big time for this weekend."

"Nah," I said. "I was happy to do it."

"Be honest with me. My mother had more to talk to you about than cake and appetizers yesterday."

"Slightly," I said.

"Did she tell you to scram?"

"She wasn't quite that succinct, but I got the point eventually."

"Well, why you were getting grilled by her my grandmother was raking me over the coals."

"What did you say?"

"I sat there and listened to her like I've always done. Like everyone has done. I can't imagine being able to do anything else. It was just awful, and I wanted it to be over. All of these things were running through my head that I wanted to scream at her, but I just sat there."

"Well, it's over now. Hate to tell you this but I'm breaking up with you because your family is one fucked up mess." We laughed in unison enjoying the release of tension.

"I'll second that," she said. "They're calling first class. Let's board."

"By the way, I think there's something I need to tell you."

"What?" she said as she gathered her things.

"I told your mother I blew Rand." Mel perked up in delight.

"I love it," she said. "The perfect wedding gift. I wish I'd thought of it first."

CHAPTER FORTY-ONE

SATURDAY MORNINGS

Waking Up To Sunshine

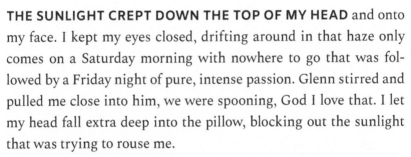

THE SUNLIGHT CREPT DOWN THE TOP OF MY HEAD and onto my face. I kept my eyes closed, drifting around in that haze only comes on a Saturday morning with nowhere to go that was followed by a Friday night of pure, intense passion. Glenn stirred and pulled me close into him, we were spooning, God I love that. I let my head fall extra deep into the pillow, blocking out the sunlight that was trying to rouse me.

This was contentment.

His paw came around and played with the hair on my chest. Reaching up, I held his hand close to me, squishing it into my heart. It sounds corny I know, but if I could have squashed him right into me, I would have. Gay mashed potatoes.

It had finally worked out the way I wanted.

He'd fallen in love with me. It had been a while since I'd felt that way about him, but I wasn't about to be the first one to say it. With guys like Glenn you had to hold back a little to make sure you got an accurate reading and it wasn't just a knee-jerk reaction to something you'd blathered out after too many glasses of wine.

Opening an eye, I stared at the fabric of the pillowcase. The fibers in the threads looked enormous up close. I rolled over and faced him, pushing my nose up against his. I could tell that he, like me, was trying not to exhale morning breath *too* hard.

"You feel nice," he said.

"Mmmmm."

"Glad you agree," he chuckled.

"You're good at convincing."

"Hungry?"

"For???" I was hoping he'd say sex. Despite last night's post 'I love you' marathon I was nonetheless ready to roll. I reached down and gave his penis an erection check. He was on the same page.

"Again? Don't you ever get enough?"

"Don't ask questions you know the answer to."

"You're insatiable Kyle."

"Well, if you weren't so hot maybe I could focus on other things."

"All right, if I told you that you could have French toast *or* sex what would you choose?"

"Can't I have both? It's not even 10:00 a.m. yet so there's plenty of time to work it all in."

"Don't be greedy, one or the other."

"OK, French toast." He sat up surprised.

"What?"

"Yeah, I'm hungry. French toast please."

"Boy, you're quick to cash me in for some diner food aren't you?"

"No, I'm just starved, and I know that sex on low blood sugar can be dangerous."

"You nut."

I looked into his eyes.

"You still love me?" I asked.

"If you make the French toast and let me sleep in."

"Hey! That's not fair."

"I'll say anything for French toast in bed."

"I bet."

We just kept lying there, snuggling and enjoying the morning.

"So?" he asked.

"So what?"

"You know."

"The answer is no. I'm not making you French toast unless you have sex with me first?"

"What happened to the low blood sugar advisory?"

"It's been postponed due to an incoming blowjob."

"You wish."

"I want a blowjob and French toast."

"In that order?"

"Yeah." He let out a fake sigh then grabbed me.

"All right you, here comes room service."

CHAPTER FORTY-TWO

DIRTY LAUNDRY

When Three Are Better Than Two

THERE'S SOMETHING ABOUT BREAKFAST WITH A LOVER that makes bacon taste that much better. But I guess when you are first in love even stale saltines taste great. I was on cloud nine with a full belly. It was a warm morning and the birds were chirping in the trees outside, the morning sun glistened across the pool. If it was anyone else sitting in my chair telling me about this, I'd be ready to gag, but when it's your own Hallmark Card moment, well, unbearably gooey turns into cant-get-enough wonderful.

"What should we do today?" I asked. It was Saturday, we were in love and all of Los Angeles was at our feet. It had seemed like we waited for ages to get together what with me being in Connecticut followed by a busy work week. I was ready to have some fun with him.

"I have to work."

"On a Saturday? You're kidding me." So much for Los Angeles at our feet.

"Sorry." It probably didn't take much for him to see the incredible disappointment on my face. I had envisioned us laying by the pool and going into the house every other hour to have hot sex. "I take it you had other plans?"

"Well, yeah. Ones that didn't involve you sitting behind a desk all day."

"Just *part* of the day." He shot me a big smile.

"Serious?"

"I just have to go in for meeting, drop by the set of a film that's shooting some pick up shots today and then I'll be back home...if you make it worth my time to come back that is."

"Leave that up to me."

"Promises, promises," he laughed. This was nice. This is how I wanted it to be. The two of us starting to get into our groove bantering back and forth and feeling comfortable with each other. God! That smile of his. His hairy chest combined with that damn smile just makes me crazy.

"How's this sound," he started. "I'll head into the studio, do my meeting and what not, while you lump around here like a boy toy of leisure, poolside...I'm sure, with a Bloody Mary."

"Sounds good so far," I smiled.

"Then I'll come home, and we'll flip a coin to see who gives it up for whom, and then have at it."

"Are you serious?"

"Sure, why not? Aren't you a gambling man? 'Fraid I'll fuck the daylights out of you?"

"Not if I toss that coin correctly."

"There you have it then." He got up and planted a kiss on the top of my head and headed off towards the bathroom. In a few minutes I heard the shower running and contemplated starting the coin toss before the official start of the game later this afternoon. But then I remembered that a sign of maturity is delayed gratification. Only, could I last that long?

You had to hand it to Glenn. He could get ready at the drop of a dime and be halfway to work before I even got the shower running. After he left, the rest of my morning went something like this:

Too lazy to shower so I just jumped in the pool and soaked my bed hair.

Hopped on a lounge chair and called Mel to give her the gory details.

Laid in the sun til I was hot.

Re-dipped.

Repeated steps three and four as needed.

I did this until my cell rang. It was Glenn.

"Hey, what are you up to?"

"I'm like a pig on a spit. I just keep basting and turning. How's the working world?"

"Over and done with. I'm leaving now. Hey, can you do me a favor?"

"Maybe."

"I need a phone number that's on a piece of paper I left in my slacks yesterday. They're in the laundry room. Can you check for me?"

"Sure, where's the laundry room?"

"Just go down the other hall, second door on the left."

"Hang on." I started walking towards the part of the house that I had never been in. Not because it was forbidden but because there was no reason to go there, and come to think of it, I had never been offered a tour. Down the hall, I opened the second door on the left. It was a large utility room with not one but two washers and get this… *three* dryers. Who needs three dryers? Hell, who needs two washers?

"Nothing excessive about this room," I chimed.

"Very funny. How many guys do you know who can do blacks and whites at the same time?"

"I've known a few."

"I was talking about socks."

Thinking it was best to change the subject, I said "Do you mean the slacks thrown on top of washer number one?"

"That would be them smart-ass."

I dug around in the pocket and found the paper with the number. "For someone named Kelly?"

"That's the one." I read him the number.

"Thanks so much. See you in fifteen." He hung up. Three dryers. I have to admit it would make laundry a breeze. I shut the door and looked across the hallway at another shut door. Curiosity got the best of me because I wanted to see what the guest room was like. I opened the door and looked in. What I saw made my jaw drop.

CHAPTER FORTY-THREE

PABLO

When Three Aren't Better Than Two

I WAS STANDING AT THE DOOR of the most magnificent bed-room I'd ever seen. Well, unless you count that guy I met two sum-mers ago who ran a porn business, but that had a lot to do with the company he kept. The room was expansive, and an entire wall was made of glass. The city stretched from one side of the room to the other and the best part was it was completely private. No one could see into this deco masterpiece of wall to wall, fluffy white carpet. At one end was a massive mahogany bed. It was flanked by match-ing silver art deco lamps sitting on really cool bedside tables right out of old Hollywood. The only thing missing was Jean Harlow sprawled out on the duvet. I walked closer. The sheen of the lamps reflected the light of the room, and when I looked closely, I saw the stamp Tiffany & Co. near each switch. On the wall opposite the bed was a large fireplace carved out of creamy white alabaster. The fire grate was also silver, and I noticed it matched the two lamps. Did Tiffany make fire grates too? This place was unbelievable.

Every detail was thought through. I looked above the fireplace and three eyes stared back at me.

It was the Picasso.

It was framed in a simple wood frame that had been lacquered a dull red color. The painting was, well, I'm only guessing here, a nude woman. Her face had three eyes, each of a different color staring back at me. In the bottom corner was the signature. Above the picture was one of those lighting bars that poor people only see in museums and rich people hang above the Picasso.

I felt hot and sweaty like when I was a kid and my mom caught me doing something I shouldn't have been.

The woman in the picture stared back at me. Clearly this was the master bedroom. Why hadn't I seen it before? I just stood there soaking it all in. I dialed Mel.

"Forget to tell me something?"

"He has a Picasso?"

"Are you serious? Oh, I want to hear every detail," she cooed.

"It's in the bedroom."

"And you just now noticed it?"

"There's another bedroom."

"He keeps it in the guest bedroom? That's unusual."

"No, it's the master bedroom."

"What are you talking about?"

"Mel, there's another bedroom; a big bedroom. It's clearly the master bedroom and the bedroom we've been in is clearly *not* the master bedroom."

"Are you sure?"

"You should see this place. It's like a hotel suite."

"That makes no sense. Does he fuck you in the guest room then retire to his own room when you leave?"

"I don't know. This is weird."

"I mean...is it the same size as the room you stay in?"

"No Mel, it's three, maybe four times the size. I'm telling you, it's a massive room that is decked out to the max."

"Well, maybe it's more of a show room than anything else. Maybe he doesn't feel comfortable because the room is too big."

"It's very sunny."

"Well there you go. Maybe he likes a darker room so he can sleep late."

"If you can afford a Picasso I think you can afford black-out drapes."

"Go into the bathroom."

"What?"

"Go into the bathroom and see if you find everyday items. You know, his razors and toothpaste and stuff."

I walked over to the bathroom. "I feel like I'm cheating."

"Oh, screw on some balls and look around. He'll never know."

The bathroom was amazing. All black marble with two sinks and matching art deco medicine mirrors. "Mel, you wouldn't believe this place."

"My God, this is like that scene out of that Hitchcock movie *Rebecca* where she finds the other wing to the house and that bedroom with those trippy drapes."

"This is so confusing. Should I look in a drawer?"

"Of course, idiot. Do it."

I opened the drawer. It was full of guy stuff. Toothpaste, shaving cream, razors that clearly had been used.

"Well?"

"It's his stuff. toiletries and what have you."

"Wow. Kyle, I don't understand."

"Yeah. I don't get it. I feel like I'm snooping."

"Uh, hello?"

"Yeah, guess I am, huh?"

"Well, you have a right."

"I do?"

"Sure, as soon as a guy says he loves you then the drawers and closets are fair game as far as I'm concerned." She had a point.

"I feel like I'm being watched."

"Do you think the room you sleep in with him is the designated fuck room?"

"It's not the kind *you're* used to. It's just a regular bedroom."

"Sounds like he has a hang-up."

"What do you mean?"

"Think about it Kyle. Maybe he has an issue with being gay and can't sleep with you in the master bedroom. Sex with you probably leaves him feeling dirty. I'm telling you I can spot a freak at fifty paces."

"OK, I've had enough."

"You have to go through the closets in the room you've been sleeping in."

"That's exactly where I'm headed." My pace quickened as I went down the hall to the other side of the house. I went into the room we slept in and walked over to the closet. When I put my hand on the closet door I froze.

"What am I doing? I can't go through his closet."

"Do it, damn it. I'm dying of curiosity."

"This man just told me he loved me."

"Exactly. All the more reason you should prove his love. Open the closet."

The door grabbed at first and then suddenly slid open. After inhaling a big clichéd breath, I exhaled and slid the door close again.

"It's full of clothes."

"You're kidding me."

"Nope. His stuff is here."

"Go back and check the closets in the other room."

"No."

"Why?"

"I can't do it Mel. I love the guy. I feel like I'm violating his trust by digging through his things. I'm sure that he has a reason for what he's doing. I just need to wait to find out what it is."

From the other end of the phone came a sigh of frustration.

CHAPTER FORTY-FOUR

GOING AT IT LIKE CATS

Post Picasso Coin Toss

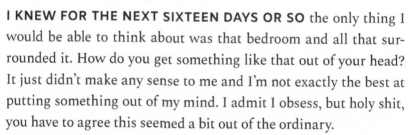

I KNEW FOR THE NEXT SIXTEEN DAYS OR SO the only thing I would be able to think about was that bedroom and all that surrounded it. How do you get something like that out of your head? It just didn't make any sense to me and I'm not exactly the best at putting something out of my mind. I admit I obsess, but holy shit, you have to agree this seemed a bit out of the ordinary.

After hanging up with Mel, a deep sense of cheap guilt swept over me. I felt like a schoolgirl for going through his stuff; it wasn't my business where he stored his clothes or what rooms he used in his house. Or was it? Maybe Mel had something with her claim that once the "I love yous" are said then all bets are off on the privacy front. Deep down I couldn't buy into that though and I worried I might have crossed a line. Was I pussing out? The bigger question was whether I should let this bother me. Hey, everything was going great; I just had the guy who I was in love with tell me he loved me.

I was on top of the world. I needed to accept the fact that I didn't have to have all the answers right away.

Deciding some exercise would clear my mind I hopped in the pool and swam laps until I was too tired to do any more. I toweled off, went into the kitchen to get a beer, and then plopped down on one of the cushy chaise lounges. The sun felt good on my naked body and no matter how many times I had seen the view from this vantage point it still took my breath away. How many times I had stood at the edge of the retaining wall, looking out over the city, yet not realizing that just around the wall of the house was a wall of glass hiding a huge mystery?

I heard the front door open and Glenn came out to the patio.

"Getting some sun, I see." He flicked his eyebrows up and down in approval.

"Hey there, how was work?" Should I ask him about the room?

"Is work ever good on a Saturday?" He took my beer and helped himself to a nice long swallow then he poured a bit onto my chest.

"Hey!"

"Is it time to fuck yet?"

"Don't let anyone say you aren't direct," I smirked.

"You look so fucking hot laying there all naked in the sun." He leaned and started to run his tongue over my belly and chest, lapping up the beer. I started laughing like hell.

"Stop it! That tickles."

"Come on, it's coin toss time. Who's giving it up for whom?" He put his arms around me and started to deep kiss me. What the hell got into him at work? Everything was delightfully intense, the sun, the sweat running down my body, Glenn. I put my hand on his crotch and big surprise…he was as hard as a rock.

"God damn it I want you, Kyle." He ripped off his shirt and started kissing me again, he was on fire...who cares about a Picasso; this was great.

When you're laying naked poolside in the hot sun making out with the man who makes you crazy-insane-hot, time just sort of stands stills. We kept at it until we finally went inside and one of us found a quarter and flipped it into the air.

I won't tell you who got tails...

CHAPTER FORTY-FIVE
HONEYMOON S OVER

Should've Kept My Mouth Shut

MY POST-PICASSO SEX ROMP with Glenn was just what the doctor ordered for a warm Saturday afternoon. We snoozed on and off while the breeze lapped at the blinds on the window. My stomach growled when I stretched my arms over my head.

"Someone's hungry, he said."

"Fried chicken sounds good."

"Are you serious?" Glenn propped himself up on his elbow so I could see him roll his eyes.

"Yeah, nothing like something fried and greasy after hot sex."

"Sort of a Southern Man's cigarette?" I laughed at his joke.

"I want fried chicken, mashed potatoes and a big wedge of apple pie." I looked over at him and smiled. "Bitch, get up and fry me some chicken."

"Who are you calling bitch?" He said this with mocked raised eyebrows and a quick poke to my ribs. "Come on, let's hit the shower."

We traipsed into the bathroom and I got the shower going while Glenn grabbed some towels. He joined me and we started to soap each other up. As much as I love getting him all sudsy I have to admit I prefer taking showers alone. Inevitably I'm the one who ends up with soap in his eyes or an elbow to the jaw while my partner is shampooing his hair. That's what I get for liking tall guys. Glenn squirted a ton of shampoo into his palm and then lathered his hair into a huge meringue. I started laughing.

"Funny."

He gave his hair another good whipping and then made a screwy face.

"You look like your Picasso." Oops, it just popped out. He gave me a funny look.

"What did you just say?" Well, I was busted now so I might as well run with it.

"I said you look like the Picasso in that other bedroom. Why didn't you ever show it to me?" Keep in mind how awkward this moment was. There we were naked in the shower and Glenn has his hair whipped up into a shampoo meringue with an angry and look on his face. There is nowhere to run. In a mere three seconds the moment went from fun and frisky to extremely uncomfortable.

"Is that what you were doing while I was at work? Snooping around?" He stuck his head under the shower head and started scrubbing the suds out as fast as he could. He was definitely angry.

"I wasn't snooping." Yeah, like he's going to believe that one. He didn't respond but just kept focusing on the rinse cycle until he stepped out of the shower and grabbed his towel. I finished as quickly as I could and shut off the nozzle. He wouldn't look me in the eye, and as soon as I stepped out of the shower, he walked out of the room continuing to dry himself. Great, more fucking drama.

I dried off and wrapped the towel around my waist. I found him out by the pool watering the plants. This is one of those agonizing relationship moments when you have to take a step back from your ego and apologize. Basically, you are wrong but you wished he wasn't such a big fucking baby that's making you grovel.

"I didn't mean to snoop."

He kept watering in silence for a moment, his back to me. Then he turned to me.

"I think it's time for you to go."

I didn't know what to say. I mean come on, what should I do? Tell him he's overreacting and get him even more angry? My skin felt hot and tingly and it reminded me of when I'd get in trouble when I was in grade school. I didn't really do anything that wrong for God's sake. It's not like I cheated on him or something.

"OK. I'm not sure I know what to say."

He turned back around to me and looked at me with the most disapproving look anyone has ever given me. I felt like a heel. After a few seconds of the two of us just staring at each other I turned around and went back in the house to get my things. I went into the bedroom and picked up my clothes from the floor, putting them on as fast as I could. I just wanted out of there. It suddenly wasn't fun anymore.

When I had what I figured was everything I went back out to the patio to say goodbye. Glenn was finished watering and was just lying in the sun with his eyes closed.

"OK, I'm leaving now." No response. "Like I said, I didn't mean to do anything to upset you. I'm really sorry." Still no response but I knew he wasn't asleep. OK, time to go. So I turned around and left. What an asshole.

CHAPTER FORTY-SIX
MEL TO THE RESCUE

This Is What Friends Are For

"HOLY SHIT!" I SAID, as my car swerved on the road.

"My God Kyle, what are you doing? You aren't trying to pull the plug on yourself are you?" Mel was on the other line. I had called her on my drive home from Glenn's thinking she was the best person, as usual, to sort out relationship stuff.

"Of course not. I was just trying to miss a squirrel that shot out into the road."

I was driving through the canyon on my way home from Glenn's giving Mel an earful. She was shopping on Melrose looking for some new stilettos and I was on my way to meet her at a halfway point so we could discuss my latest saga in person. Something this good deserved face-to-face time.

"I'm sure he's just overreacting. He probably has an enormous dildo in his dresser drawer he was worried you had found." She was doing her best, but I didn't buy it.

"Don't you think he overreacted a bit?" I asked.

"Gee, do you think? Of course, he did, I'm telling you this guy needs a good lay."

"He got that remember?"

"Well, regardless, he's got some balls to treat you this way. I mean what's up with him anyway? One minute he's red hot all over you and the next minute he's got a bug up his ass that just won't quit. I'm completely convinced that the only true way to manage men is via a leather strap. You all need a good crack on the ass to keep you in line."

"What would you have done in the same situation?"

"Told him to go fuck himself."

"I'm serious."

"Told him to go fuck himself. I *was* being serious. I'm telling you Kyle, this guy needs to grow up. Big deal. So you were snooping around where you shouldn't have been. He shouldn't have been trying to keep secrets from you. In most relationships guys try to hide porn or texts from old flames. In yours he's weirdly hiding a bedroom suite. This is *all* his fault when you really look at it."

"That's true isn't it?" This is why I wanted to call her. It's that feminine perspective on why I was justified from the get-go to snoop that I needed to hear most right now.

"I'm sure after he's had time to cool his jets and blue his balls a bit he'll be calling."

"Nice. You have such a way with words sometimes."

"Give it three days and you'll be hearing from him. Guaranteed. Most likely he's just unnerved that you found something he didn't want you to see."

"But the main question is why hide a master suite from someone?"

"Yeah, that is a bit odd. Maybe he thought you'd stain the sheets."

"You're disgusting."

"I may not be so far off. Think about it. He's very particular about his house, right? It's possible that he likes to keep that room all to himself. It could be his private sanctuary. You are a bit of a slob. If I had a white bedroom like his I'd want to sequester you to the guest room as well."

I wasn't so sure. There was something deeper about all of this that bothered me more than the fact that Glenn got so pissed. OK, so I screwed up and violated trust or what have you. But it was the look in Glenn's eyes when he wouldn't talk to me that really got to me. It had a cruel edge to it like he was trying to punish me or something. That didn't add up.

"So, what are you guys doing tonight?" I thought I'd change the subject. I can be a master avoider when I want to and now was as good a time as any.

"I don't know. Probably the dinner and movie thing. Are you going to be OK?"

"Oh yeah, don't cancel out on account of me. I'll be fine." My efforts to avoid my problems with Glenn instantly reminded me of my problem with Melanie and her boyfriend to which I still had not found a solution.

"It should be fun. I like the easiness of this guy, Kyle. He's not demanding, you know? We just have a good time doing the simple stuff in life. It's refreshing to have something so uncomplicated and straightforward. No pretensions."

Hardly, I thought.

"After meeting my family, you have to have a better understanding of why I'm attracted to him."

"Definitely," I said. "But Mel, how well do you know him?"

"I don't know. What are you getting at?"

"You just seem to be falling for him a little fast is all."

"I'm hearing this from you of all people?" She had a point.

"I just don't want you to get hurt." What a line. No one ever says that line and actually means it. It always has some greater level of subtext to it such as 'You're dating a loser,' 'He's not right for you,' or 'I slept with him after grocery shopping last year.'

"This doesn't feel like it's going too fast for me."

I tried another avenue. "I'm just wondering if you are interested in him because he would piss off your parents. How much of this is about getting back at them?"

"What? Kyle, this is a bullshit conversation. Peter is not my attempt to exact revenge on my parents."

"It wouldn't be such a stretch if he was."

"I like him because he's genuine."

Not exactly I thought.

CHAPTER FORTY-SEVEN

SPONTANEOUS COMBUSTION

... And The Loose Tongue Of Pandora The Twat

TYLER CONTACTED ALL OF US up to see if we wanted to come over and throw something on the grill. There's something great about how spontaneity can turn an otherwise dull Sunday afternoon into something fun. We'd all been lounging on our prospective couches when he texted…I was watching a ball game, Mickey was taking a nap, and Melanie was busy painting her nails.

Mickey swung by and picked me up and on our way we stopped off at Ralph's to grab some cold beer. When we pulled up in front of Tyler's house Melanie tooted her horn as she came rolling along and parked across the street from us.

"Hello boys," she said, struggling to drag a picnic basket out of her front seat.

"What did you bring?" said Mickey. Our beers in their plastic bag paled in comparison to her wooden basket with Burberry trim.

"A ham," she said.

"You brought an entire ham? And by the way, tell me you didn't actually *pay* for a Burberry picnic basket."

"Yes, it's a ham and no, I'd never be so stupid." It was a tip from a customer yesterday. Isn't it ridiculous?"

"What did he do with the ham?" said Mickey, lifting the lid of the basket to see what was inside.

"He had nothing to due with the ham. Just the picnic basket. It was a Red Riding Hood kind of scenario except that he wore a leather mask on his face."

"Did you play grandma?" smirked Mickey.

"No silly. The wolf of course. She said this as if it was the most obvious thing in the world. He was Red Riding Hood. Anyway, my next door neighbor left for Europe yesterday and she told me to take this ham out of her fridge because she didn't have room in her freezer and it would spoil by the time she got back."

"Amazing that she'd have an entire ham lying around," I said.

"I didn't ask questions…free ham." She had a point.

We walked round the side of Tyler's place and went through the gate that led to the backyard. He was furiously scraping crud off the grill.

"Hi kids!" he hollered. "Beers in the cooler."

We wandered over and gave our perfunctory hugs and kisses, set stuff down on the patio table, and then sifted through piles of ice to find an even colder one than we had purchased.

"I brought a ham," said Melanie, almost as an afterthought. She dug it out of the picnic basket and held it up like a trophy.

Tyler took a long drag on his Parliament. "What on earth for?"

"It was free," said Mickey.

"It's not for today. I just thought you'd like one. You always order it for breakfast so now you have one of your own." Tyler grinned.

"I'm going to put it in the fridge." As soon as she was in the house Tyler turned to me.

"Did you tell her about you and Peter doing the deed last summer?"

"Are you kidding? It's hardly come up."

"You need to get it over with Kyle, like rippin' off a band-aid," said Mickey.

"There hasn't been a right time. I've got enough going on with life right now."

"I don't know that there's ever a good time to tell someone news like that," said Tyler. "I imagine you've been fretting about it for some time now."

"How couldn't I? After all, how am I ever going to tell her what happened?"

Tyler gave me an understanding look and took another drag on his cig. "On another note, any word from Glenn? Mickey filled me in yesterday." Leave it to Mickey to get the word out. He always loved some good gossip.

"Nothing, but it's only been a day. Besides, screw him. I don't need someone acting like an asshole like that. Anyway, I'll probably hear from him tomorrow. I mean, how long can he stay mad at me? It was an honest mistake don't you think?"

"Rifling through his drawers?" said Tyler with a raised eyebrow.

"I didn't rifle."

"Well whatever you call it he had a reason for not showing you that bedroom."

"Yeah, but what do you think it was?" said Mickey just as Mel stepped back outside. "Maybe he'd thought you'd steal that painting," he said.

"Oh, don't be stupid Mickey," said Melanie. "I'm telling you the guy has a hang up about being gay. Plain and simple." She plopped herself down on a deck chair.

"Like Peter?" said Tyler.

Mickey and I both stiffened.

"What's that supposed to mean?" shot back Melanie with a half-laugh in her voice. "Peter's as straight as they come."

"Maybe with you but not when he's getting fucked by Kyle."

Holy shit! He didn't just say that. I felt hot and frozen at the same time. Melanie stood up from her chaise.

"Excuse me?" She looked over at me like Tyler was crazy but expecting me to say something. My mouth just hung open like an idiot.

"Oh, for God's sake Kyle I did the hard part for you, spill it," said Tyler.

"Melanie…"

"Spit it out Kyle, what are you trying to say."

"Peter's not as straight as you might think," I said.

"What do you mean?"

I paused again trying to find the words. "For God's sake Kyle," said Tyler. "Melanie, it went something like this. Kyle fucked around with Peter last summer. He's been freaking out ever since he met him because he didn't know how to tell you. So, there it is. Let's eat."

"No!" She had a look on her face that went right through me and I felt awful that it had come out this way. I was ready to kill Tyler. "This can't be. Is this true."

"Yeah. I'm sorry Mel. It's not like he was your boyfriend when we did anything."

"Stop it! I don't want to hear any more of this," she wailed. Creepy silence thickened the air.

"Thanks a lot Tyler."

"I only did what you didn't have the balls to do."

"Oh, fuck you, Tyler," said Melanie. "I can't believe this. You are just screwing with me, aren't you?" She said it with a nervous laugh.

"Mel, he has Snoopy tattooed on his ass, doesn't he?"

She gasped and her hand went to her bosom, just like a bad actress in a soap opera as she did a mental double-take. "I must have told you about his tattoo."

"No, you didn't," I said. But I'm surprised you didn't because it's the kind of thing I would have thought you'd mention.

"No, I *told* you. Or at the very least I told one of you two," she spat. "I can't believe you Kyle. I've finally got someone in my life, and you have to go fuck with it. Is it because things aren't going the way you want with Glenn, so you have to have someone in the same boat?"

"Mel, I'm not trying to wreck this for you. It's just that it happened, and I thought you had a right to know."

"You're a liar. You're just jealous and for some reason you're trying to screw this up for me. Damn you Kyle. You've got some balls." She grabbed her purse and headed towards the back gate. I shot up to follow her.

"Mel, come back here."

She stopped and turned toward me. "No. Go back to those two and have a good laugh. I bet you thought this was funny the whole time. Let's see what bullshit we can cook up to fuck with Melanie. Well, I don't think it's funny and I expected a lot more from you." She stormed out the gate. She was so mad as she walked that she wobbled on her heels.

"Mel!" It was no use, the last thing she was going to do was turn around and talk about this.

So much for a fun Sunday afternoon.

CHAPTER FORTY-EIGHT

MONDAY MORNING REALITY

Regroup

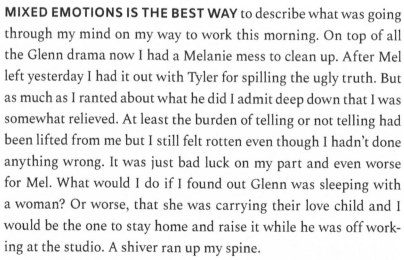

MIXED EMOTIONS IS THE BEST WAY to describe what was going through my mind on my way to work this morning. On top of all the Glenn drama now I had a Melanie mess to clean up. After Mel left yesterday I had it out with Tyler for spilling the ugly truth. But as much as I ranted about what he did I admit deep down that I was somewhat relieved. At least the burden of telling or not telling had been lifted from me but I still felt rotten even though I hadn't done anything wrong. It was just bad luck on my part and even worse for Mel. What would I do if I found out Glenn was sleeping with a woman? Or worse, that she was carrying their love child and I would be the one to stay home and raise it while he was off working at the studio. A shiver ran up my spine.

The flip side of the past few days was my instant hero status at work since the coup on *Candy*. I still had the "Congratulations

Kyle$$$" sign that someone had printed out using a clip-art template and posted on my door. I had since moved it to my bulletin board. I liked the nifty use of dollars signs replacing the exclamation points.

I went through my voice mail messages and looked over my e-mails. Nothing from either Glenn or Melanie, but there was an e-mail from Tyler apologizing for getting involved like he did and also from Mickey checking in on my morning.

"There you are!" It was Lucy and the suits at my door. They were all smiles. Lucy had just returned from a book convention in Denver, so I had not seen her since before I left for Chicago. While she'd gushed over the phone to me many times since Gordon's appearance I have to admit that I enjoyed seeing her smiling at me in person.

"Welcome to Monday morning."

"Congratulations *still* Kyle," said Dave. He was beaming like a kid on Christmas morning who'd gotten everything he wanted.

"It's so good to see you finally in person. I'm so proud of you. We just got an updated finance report. Sales are still through the roof on all of Gordon's books since the *Candy* appearance." Lucy looked like she was having an orgasm while she spoke. "The New York office thinks we're golden. They can hardly keep up with the print orders and Kindle sales are amazing. You did it, Kyle. We knew all along you'd come through in the end."

I'm not so sure I bought that but who cares? I was the hero on top of his game, and I loved it. After more congratulations and verbal accolades, the other suits headed out and Lucy took a chair across from my desk.

"Now," said Lucy. It's critical you follow this up with a new campaign. Get as much as you can for Gordon. *Candy* was just a door opener; the rest *has* to follow.

"Already on top of it," I said. "It's a good opportunity to go full-force." Between Melanie and Glenn being out of the picture it looked like I would have plenty of time to fill. "I'll give you a full reporting later today. I'm getting some great hits."

"You should at least get some more national bookings out of his appearance. The *New York Times* is long overdue to give us something decent."

"I was thinking a profile in *People* would be a good one. It would be a great follow-up; they could shoot it at his place in Taos."

"You could fly in first and make sure to hide the bottles. By the way, how drunk was he on the trip?" She pulled a cigarette case out of her jacket pocket and removed cigarette.

"Not too bad." I said as she lit up. I pulled an ashtray from my desk drawer and handed it to her.

"Did he keep it under control?"

"Kind of with the minor exception of his freaking out right before they went on the air."

"Did you cover?"

"I think they bought that it was just severe stage fright."

"How'd you get him to calm down?"

"I have my tricks."

"Well, thank God they didn't catch on. That was close. Oh, by the way...bad news. Tammy and Tom are arriving on Thursday."

"What for?"

"Who knows? Supposedly for some conference they are attending this week on Tantric sex. Tammy insisted on a sit-down meeting with us as long as they are in town. And she's also expecting some kind of mini-tour for Friday."

"Are you kidding me?" I asked. "That's only a few days away. What was Tom saying about all of this?"

"What do you think? She barks and he cowers. Nothing's changed. Don't knock yourself out, but you know, a couple of TV things and maybe an *LA Times* sit-down interview would be good."

Only? Was she crazy? I was always amazed by the way Lucy acted as if I could pull things out of thin air. "Let me see what I can pull off."

"Seriously Kyle, get something decent otherwise she's going to be on my ass. I hear inside rumbling that she's been complaining to New York and that's the last thing we need especially when we are finally on top with them."

For the publishing industry, which was mainly based in New York, we were both lucky and unusual to be isolated in the western expanse. We liked our distance from the main office because it allowed us a lot of latitude and we didn't have people watching our every move. However, there was always the pervasive fear that one day we'd get yanked back East and none of us had a desire to leave LA sunshine for New York winters.

"OK, let me see what I can do."

"Thanks Kyle, you're the best. I know you can do it."

I may be the hero of the day but now the expectations were that of hero for a lifetime. The downside of success I guess.

CHAPTER FORTY-NINE

ASS PINCHER

Doing My Part For Equality

"DON'T EAT THAT THEY TASTE DISGUSTIN'," said Mickey. I looked down at the hors d'oevre I had just taken off a waiter's tray.

"What is it?"

"I have no idea but it's somethin' like peanut butter mixed with anchovy."

"Great," I said as I crumpled it up in a cocktail napkin and threw it on a nearby abandoned plate. It's always a mistake to come to these things hungry I thought as I scouted the room for another waiter who might be able to provide some relief to the pains in my stomach. I had to skip dinner in order to make this fundraiser on time. Work had been a zoo the past two days so I'd come straight from the office with no chance to eat or change. Some wet paper towels to my face and an extra shot of cologne had done wonders. No one would guess that underneath my snappy exterior I was in reality a sweaty, smelly mess with my undies binding my balls in the worst way.

"How was work today?"

"Brutal, but I finally got a booking for Tammy and Tom."

"That's a relief I'm sure."

"You've no idea. They're such a pain in the ass."

"What's the interview?"

"Channel nine early morning news."

"That's cool."

"Trust me, I paid for this one."

"What do you mean?"

"I had to bribe the producer."

"Cash?"

"Worse, I said I'd fix him up with a friend of mine. By the way, I have a favor to ask you." I shot him a crafty look.

"Are you serious? I can't believe you pimped me out again."

"Come on, it will be good extra money for you, you only have to go out once, and you'll get a nice meal out of it."

"I'll think about it," he said. That's what I liked about Mickey. He had his moments when he could drive you crazy but in the clutch he was always willing to help provided there was something in it for him.

After scoring a couple of pieces of chicken-on-a-stick we surveyed the scene. It was your standard gay fundraiser with a demographic that skewed older and professional. Plus, lots of lesbians which always added to the mix.

"I kind of like the way these events have a mix of the boys with the girls," I said.

"I was thinking just the opposite," said Mickey. "There's half the scoring potential at this thing than there would have been on a regular night at this bar. Although…that guy checking you out over there is pretty hot."

"Really?" I said as I turned to see an old guy with a bad rug give me a creepy look once he caught my eye. His goatee has nicotine stains on it, and he was stuffed into what looked like a very expensive purple shirt. A nervous smile pasted on my face and I turned back to Mickey. "Thanks, you're a real pal."

"Just doin' my part to help you get laid during the Glenn interim. Still no word?"

"Nada. I'm trying to focus on other stuff and give him some space but it's driving me crazy. You know I want to call him."

"I'm sure it will blow over. If it doesn't then he's a complete ass-hole. I mean come on; it's not like you did anything *that* awful." A smile crossed his face which seemed to mismatch his last statement. Just then I felt my ass get pinched.

"OK, tell me it's not that guy in the purple shirt."

"You're safe. He's walking towards the bar."

"I turned around with a dirty look and saw the back of my letch's shirt as he wandered in search of libations. "How degrading; he doesn't even bother to say hi. I'm just a drive-by grope." We both started laughing.

We did our best to mingle. Mickey is really good at picking up people at these things to the point where he's turned it into an art form. It was fun watching him try to jockey for the best position to strike up with some hottie he had in his sights. After a couple of strikeouts, he buzzed back to where I was standing.

"Did I miss anything?"

"A few more questionable appetizers but that's about it."

"You speak tuh Mel yet?"

"Nothing. Have you spoken to her?"

"I left a message for her yesterday but didn't hear from her. I'm a sure she caught on I was trying to mine for info on what was going through that mind of hers."

"I don't think I'm the only one she's mad at."

"Come on, I wasn't the one who slept with her boyfriend, what does she have against me?"

"As far as Mel is concerned, you and Tyler are co-conspirators because you knew all about it. Sorry to have dragged you into it."

"Don't blame yourself for that. I would have asked for some advice if I were in your position. Talk about dumb luck. What are the odds?"

"I don't know. Everything in my job is going so well and my personal life is in the crapper. Go figure."

"Well, on the bright side at least he was a good lay. What if he'd been a let down like soggy French fries. At least he gave you some good masturbatory material in exchange for strife down the road. It's like buying something on credit where you pay after the fact."

Mickey had the kind of logic that could make your head split open if you weren't careful but in an odd way it made sense.

We scoped the room for about fifteen more minutes then hit the road when we felt we'd run out of interesting people to try to meet. I was starving and needed something substantial, so we hit a taco stand on the way home. The rest of the evening we talked about everything other than Melanie and Glenn and it felt good, almost therapeutic really. The evening waned away, and we covered every mindless topic we could wrap our minds around. Finally, around midnight we gave each other a hug and headed our separate ways.

CHAPTER FIFTY

MEL CALLS

Deny, Deny, Deny.

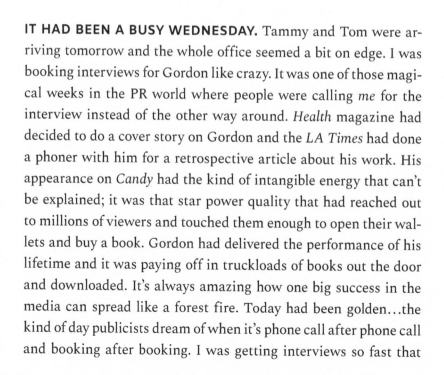

IT HAD BEEN A BUSY WEDNESDAY. Tammy and Tom were arriving tomorrow and the whole office seemed a bit on edge. I was booking interviews for Gordon like crazy. It was one of those magical weeks in the PR world where people were calling *me* for the interview instead of the other way around. *Health* magazine had decided to do a cover story on Gordon and the *LA Times* had done a phoner with him for a retrospective article about his work. His appearance on *Candy* had the kind of intangible energy that can't be explained; it was that star power quality that had reached out to millions of viewers and touched them enough to open their wallets and buy a book. Gordon had delivered the performance of his lifetime and it was paying off in truckloads of books out the door and downloaded. It's always amazing how one big success in the media can spread like a forest fire. Today had been golden...the kind of day publicists dream of when it's phone call after phone call and booking after booking. I was getting interviews so fast that

I only had time to jot down some notes and later tonight I would put together formal booking contracts and segment structures. So many days in this business were spent banging your head against the desk trying to figure out a fit between a client and a media outlet or getting the right kind of social media buzz. It had even been such a busy and fulfilling day that I didn't seem to care so much that there had been no word from Glenn or Melanie. OK, I admit to occasionally checking for e-mails or text messages, but it was what it was today. There were other things to keep me preoccupied and I was grateful for that. However, despite today's success, the downside had been having to spend time pitching Tammy and Tom's piece of crap when I had better things to do surrounding Gordon. However, I found that I could start off pitching T&T and once that was a turn-down I was able to make some headway regarding an angle on Gordon. Believe it or not I'd been able to book the two unholy monsters on a talk radio segment during the morning drive so thankfully that gave me one other media piece for them. If I could only get one more item, then I'd stop at three which would be a miracle considering the time I'd had to turn this around not to mention the subject matter on top of it.

I'd passed Lucy and the other suits in the hall and there seemed to be a tense kind of energy permeating the office. We were definitely busy; trying to keep up on what was going on with Gordon's books, but I sensed an air of uneasiness too. At one point when I was taking a leak Dave had taken the urinal next to me (which is always weird when you know that person) and started in about the Tammy and Tom meeting tomorrow. I wasn't the only one dreading all of this.

Just as I returned to my office my cell phone rang. It was Mel. I hesitated a moment before picking up.

"Hey there,"

"Hi Kyle."

"How are you? It's good to hear from you."

"Thanks, listen. I'm sorry to call you during work but I felt I needed to get something off my chest." Interesting she was apologizing for her timing since it was de rigueur for her to call me a couple of times during the day.

"Shoot."

"I had a talk with Peter, and I told him what you told me Sunday." Here it comes. "And?"

"He said you're lying. Actually, he said that after he stopped laughing. He couldn't believe you'd be so desperately jealous to have said something like that."

"Huh? Jealous of what?"

"Of my relationship with him. You know, this all makes sense after I talked to him. He told me about your conversation while I was in the restroom."

"Really, what did he say?"

"He told me about how you admitted you were jealous of the time he took me away from you and how our friendship was going to suffer if things got more serious. My God, Kyle, I have to say that after some of the things he told me I'm just completely stunned. Why can't you just be happy for me?" What a fucker. I couldn't believe that asshole pulled a maneuver like this.

"I *was* happy for you Melanie until I realized who you were dating."

"Bullshit. I just can't believe I couldn't see this clearly until now."

"Look Melanie, let me tell you something. This guy is a liar. I never said that over dinner."

"Yeah, right."

"Do you really think I would make up a story like this? That I would say something which would obviously be hurtful to you?"

"I wouldn't have until now."

"My stomach was in my mouth the minute I walked into your living room that night and saw Peter standing there. Except he had told me his name was Doug when I was with him last summer. And trust me, I remembered him quite well." How after all these years of fantastic friendship could Mel not believe anything I was saying? Could love make someone this blind?

"You're full of shit Kyle."

"No, you're dating a big homo who likes to take it up the ass and the sooner you face that fact the better." Screw this.

"Fuck you!" and she hung up on me.

"Damn!" I said out loud just as Dave popped his head in my office.

"You've got that right. Battle stations Kyle. Tammy and Tom just arrived a day early for their meeting. Lucy is gathering everyone in the conference room right now.

"Double damn."

CHAPTER FIFTY-ONE

TAMMY UNGLUED

Die Evil Bitch! Die!

IF YOU'VE EVER BEEN CAUGHT MASTURBATING then you know the feeling everyone in the office was feeling. Here we were, reveling in the wonderful glow of our Gordon success and Wham!...in walks mother. I grabbed my notes, pad and pen and started to head to the conference room. I didn't even have time to grab a cup of coffee because the last thing I wanted to do was to have everyone waiting for me. When I walked into the conference room there were Tammy, Tom and the always-not-lovely Leanne Bixner. Leanne was fervently texting something on her phone while Tammy sat there with an icy smile on her face. Tom looked up and gave me a weak nod but then glanced around the room in a nervous sort of way. Some of the other suits were there but Dave and Lucy were absent.

"Hello, Kyle," said Tammy. "We're just waiting on Dave to collect Lucy. I guess she was out having a nice jog this afternoon instead of being in the office."

Tammy had probably already alerted the New York office from a stall in the ladies' room about Lucy's exercise. I wanted to knock that smug smile right off of her face. Dave and Lucy swept into the room. Dave looked flustered and Lucy came in wearing ripped sweatpants and a sweaty T-shirt that revealed the outline of her athletic bra. I felt bad for her.

"Hello, everyone," said Lucy, trying to regain some sense of control. "I'm sorry but I thought this meeting was scheduled for tomorrow."

"It was, but we decided we wanted to attend one of the afternoon sessions at the *New Age LA* conference tomorrow. You do know we're speaking there tomorrow don't you?"

"Yes of course," we all mumbled.

"Can we expect to see *all* of you there?" said Tammy with a slight sneer.

"I'm afraid it's a crazy week here Tammy," said Lucy. We don't have the ability to send a contingency to your event."

"I find it hard to believe that when two best-selling authors, of whom you are publishing their current book, are speaking at the largest New Age conference in Los Angeles that you aren't going to send people for support," said Tammy.

"It would be nice to see some familiar faces in the audience," said Tom. You could tell he was trying to buffer some of Tammy's abrasiveness.

Leanne looked up from her texting. "I wonder what the New York office would have to say about this?"

"I didn't say no one was attending," said the backpedaling Lucy. "Kyle will be there tomorrow to root you on." I wanted to kick her.

"Just Kyle," that's it? said Tammy. What a bitch.

"I'll be there as well," said Lucy.

"That's better," said Tammy. "What about you Dave? You edited our book after all?"

"I'm afraid I can't," said Dave. "You have to understand that we are really swamped since Gordon Lempkin was on *Candy* last week."

"Yes," said Tammy. "We saw that. Congratulations, Kyle. I'm sure you're the one behind that booking."

I was starting to feel very uncomfortable. As if Tammy was a snake who had slithered into my campsite and was far enough away that she couldn't bite me right now but who might come closer and go on the attack. "Thanks," I said.

"Gordon is the most successful charlatan," said Tammy. We have mutual friends in Taos and spent a fascinating New Year's Eve with America's foremost former alcoholic. In fact, I'm pretty sure we have some video footage of Gordon staggering around and slurring his words. So tragic." Tom looked down at his notepad.

"Kyle," said Tom with an uneasy smile. "Did you get us some bookings for Friday? We took and extra day here in LA so that we could take advantage of some media time."

"Kyle worked very hard this week to get you some choice bookings, didn't you Kyle?" Thanks, Lucy.

"Well," I said. "On Friday I will personally pick you up at your hotel and take you over to channel nine where I have booked you on the early morning news. It should be a nice segment and they promised they'd plug your books big time."

"That sounds good," said Tom. Tammy just kept staring at me.

"Then after that we will go over to Air Talk 106.5 FM for a segment on the Jan Williams show. She has a talk program during drive time that is…"

"I'm familiar," said Tammy. "What's after that?"

This was one of those moments when the spotlight was shining not on me but in my eyes. "Well, as of now nothing but it's still Wednes…"

"WHAT?" shrieked Tammy? Everyone stiffened in their seats. Her face had become instantly red. "Are you telling me that's it?" You can book that drunk Gordon Lempkin on *Candy* but that's all we get?

"No, I'm saying it's still Wednesday and I need more time."

"THIS IS TOTALLY UNACCEPTABLE!" she screamed. Everyone had a shocked look on their faces including that pit bull of a woman Leanne Bixner. "DO YOU UNDERSTAND ME? DO YOU UNDERSTAND ME? DO YOU UNDERSTAND ME?" Tammy chanted as she pounded her notebook on the table. It was unnerving. The Tammy bomb had exploded.

Lucy spoke up. "Tammy, I don't think this is the way to discuss this…"

"SHUT UP!" snarled Tammy. "I DON'T WANT TO HEAR ANYMORE OF THIS LAME BULLSHIT FROM YOU PEOPLE!" No one could believe what was happening. "AAAAACCCCK!" She yelled at the top of her lungs, our ears almost splitting. She was encased in rage and suddenly she started to hyperventilate. Everyone remained frozen but Tom moved into action. He spun her around in her chair and grabbed her by the shoulders shaking her.

"Stop it woman, stop it!" Tammy continued to hyperventilate, and her eyes were rolling into her head.

"Get me a paper sack!" he demanded. Dave shot out of his chair like his ass was on fire and ran to the trash can where he pulled out a greasy McDonald's bag that had held someone's lunch earlier in the day. He dumped out some stray fries and handed it to Tom. Tammy had a look of horror on her face and started to shake her head "no" just as Tom shoved the filthy bag against her mouth and held it here. His arm muscles were bulging, and you had to hand it to him, he was in pretty good shape.

"Tammy, try to focus as I chant to help you," said Tom. "Tee ahhh, oh do. Tee ahhh, oh do. Tee ahhh, oh do," he chimed as Tammy's body breathed each heavy breath. The rest of us kept exchanging stunned looks including Leanne Bixner who almost looked apologetic.

"Tee ahhh, oh do. Tee ahhh, oh do."

"What should we do?" I whispered to Lucy.

"Hope she dies," she whispered back.

"Tee ahhh, oh do." Tammy's chest was expanding less and less, and her eyes started to loose some of their fire and roll back in her head.

"Tee ahhh, oh do. Are you ready for me to take the bag off?" Tammy nodded yes and Tom removed the bag. A pickle was stuck to the side of her chin and she wiped it off in horror.

"Are you OK?" I asked?

"I'll be fine," she snapped. "Responsive hyperventilation is very common," she added as if the shitshow we'd just witnessed was supposed to be considered normal behavior. Tammy started gathering her things into a neat pile, put them into her bag, and then stood up.

"Let me make something very clear to all of you," she said in a low, controlled voice that I swear she copied from Faye Dunaway in *Mommie Dearest*. "If you people don't get your act together pronto we will go public with the fact that Gordon is a drunk. Don't think for one minute you're going to fuck with our careers while you milk the tit of that cow. Come on Tom! We're leaving."

CHAPTER FIFTY-TWO

NEW AGE HELL

Granola And Patchouli

NEW AGE LA WAS THE BIGGEST NEW AGE CONVENTION on the West Coast. This massive event took over the entire LA convention center. It was Mecca for women who didn't believe in shaving their armpits and men who slathered themselves in patchouli oil. It was also a major money-maker for the book industry as long as you were a publishing company that had a New Age imprint.

I had picked up Lucy from her home near Wilshire and La Brea. She had a cool little Spanish Bungalow in a neighborhood that bordered on some sketchy streets but had remained picture perfect with manicured lawns and flowerbeds around the base of palm trees. Before she got into my car she took one last drag on her cigarette and then ground it into the gutter with the toe of her shoe.

"You can smoke in the car if you want," I said. "The top's down."

"Thanks, but I don't want to smell like cigarette smoke around a bunch of health nuts." I honestly didn't know how this would be possible considering her veins bled nicotine. I pulled onto Wilshire and we headed downtown.

"Can you believe we're having to go to this nonsense today?" said Lucy. "What a colossal waste of time."

"It should be an experience." I loved it when Lucy was in a cynical mood as long as the cynicism wasn't directed toward me.

"Have you ever seen one of their talks?" she asked while she reapplied her lipstick in the vanity mirror.

"No, but I can only imagine."

"You're in for a treat. I'll give you twenty bucks if you can make it all the way through without laughing out loud at an inappropriate place. Ha, it's bloody embarrassing some of the stuff I've seen these two do." Lucy had been around longer than I had, and she'd been involved with Tammy and Tom's other books.

"I'm just grateful I was able to get one more booking for tomorrow." I said.

"Great, what is it?"

"NBC. They're going to tape a segment with them to use sometime over the weekend."

"Well that should shut them up a bit." Lucy used her fingernail to pick at something in her teeth. "Can you believe that scene from yesterday?"

"It was incredible, I was actually getting scared."

"I know! The veins were popping off her forehead, weren't they? It was just creepy beyond belief. And then that chanting thing Tom was doing to calm her down!"

"Tee ah, doo wop wop, tee ah, doo wop wop," I started to crack up and Lucy followed suit. We spent the rest of the drive rehashing all of the good moments from yesterday's meltdown. I'd seen some real winners in my time but this one was beyond belief.

I pulled the car into the enormous parking lot complex of the convention center and we made our way into the exhibition halls. Lucy got our badges while I looked up the room number for Tammy and Tom's lecture. We worked our way up the escalators and found the room.

"Thank God it's not empty," said Lucy. "You know they would've blamed us if it was." We took some seats about halfway back and I did a quick head count.

"About two hundred; not bad. There's always the people who come in late too, so I bet they get about two-fifty by the end."

Lucy saw a few people she recognized and waived. Finally, it was time to begin and the lights dimmed. A spotlight came on illuminating the center of the platform stage just as cheesy music filled the air.

"Ladies and gentlemen, *New Age LA* is proud to present, Tammy and Tom!"

"Did I die and wake up in Reno?" smirked Lucy?

Tammy and Tom came running up the aisle and jumped on the dais. They were dressed in matching khaki Dockers and short-sleeved polo shirts. Tammy's was pale pink and Tom's was pale blue. They each wore a base ball cap with a double "T" logo...but this time Tom wore the pink hat and Tammy wore the blue.

"To think I fucked this man," said Lucy and she said it loud enough that the woman in front of her turned around and gave us a haughty look. "I bet you anything they start off with their Viagra routine."

Sure enough, more music started, and Tammy and Tom did a little song and dance number about erectile dysfunction and relationships. The crowd seemed to eat it up.

"You have to hand it them," I said. "They seem to know their target audience."

"Unnerving isn't it?" said Lucy.

The presentation was anything but boring. For the next hour and a half Tammy and Tom worked the room like a resurrected Regis and Kathy Lee; exposing old wounds of their own relationship, and even discussing Tom's former problem with premature ejaculation and how they had to work to overcome Tammy's disappointment at not getting sexually satisfied. Lucy and I kept kicking and poking each other at various "intimate" moments of the presentation such as the picture show from Tammy and Tom's wedding.

"He was a real hunk back then," I said.

"You're telling me," said Lucy. In the pictures Tammy looked like she had a softer edge to her which I never could've thought possible.

At the end of the presentation Lucy and I hung back a bit while fans crowded around Tammy and Tom asking them to sign copies of their books or give them free advice.

"Thank God they have some hangers-on to fawn over them," said Lucy.

"Should we offer to take them to lunch?" I said?

Lucy stiffened, "Oh, do we have to?"

"Something tells me it might be in our best interest."

"You're probably right. It's going to be unbearable though, not to say embarrassing with those stupid outfits they are wearing. Hopefully they will take off those hats before eating."

After twenty minutes or so the fan-base dissipated and we approached Tammy and Tom. Now it was our turn to fawn.

"Great job!" beamed Lucy.

"You had the audience absolutely riveted," I added.

Tammy and Tom were still glowing from their performance. If you didn't know what reality was, you'd swear that Tammy was this warm, wonderful person.

"Thank you, it was wonderful wasn't it?" said Tammy.

"It was good to see your friendly faces supporting us," said Tom.

"Can we take you to a celebratory lunch?" said Lucy

"Oh, we'd love to but we already made plans with some old friends who are coming to meet us here and then we're catching some of the other speakers this afternoon and evening."

"That's too bad," I lied.

"Well, I guess we should be heading out then," said Lucy. "Congratulations again. Everyone was just raving about your talk on the way out the door." Lucy was a good liar as well.

We said our goodbyes and then Tammy made me promise to not be late tomorrow morning for their interview. As soon as we got away, we made a beeline for the parking lot.

"I don't know about you Kyle, but I need a drink," said Lucy.

"Ditto. Want to hit the Pantry?"

"No, we might see them there. Let's go to one of the hotels."

We got into my car and drove to the Standard. Once we were inside and seated for lunch the first thing we did was order a round of martinis.

"Shouldn't I be back at the office getting more stuff for Gordon?" I smiled as we clinked glasses.

"Nah, we deserve it," said Lucy. She kicked hers back in one long gulp which while I'd seen plenty of times in the movies this was the first time I'd seen someone do it live.

Lunch was actually fun. Lucy was one of those people who could really be cool to hang with, but it usually took a ballgame or a cocktail. As we munched on crab salads and she was working her way through her third martini the conversation took an unexpected turn.

"Can you believe I actually had an affair with Tom?" she said. How do you respond to your boss telling you this? "I almost couldn't believe he was the same man up there on that platform," she said. "He was such a stud and now he's just a dick-less, pussy-whipped fool. What a waste." She pulled the olive out of her martini and popped it into her mouth.

"So what all happened?" I figured as long as she was letting loose I might as well get all the details.

"Don't you already know?" she said. "I thought Dave had blabbed to the whole office by now."

"I've only heard bits and pieces."

"Well, it was when I was working at the New York office that they came to us with their first book. They were newly married; for only about four months if I remember correctly. Anyway, they were both much different then. Tammy was softer, nicer, but still driven to succeed. That part hasn't changed. Tom was really handsome. He had that California tennis stud look that I've always been a sucker for and back then he was something to look at. He wasshh built like a brick shit house too." She was starting to slur her words around the edges.

"Anyway, he and I were editing the book together. Don't know if you know this but that woman is no writer. Even though both of their names are on the books he's the one that does all of the grunt work for them. She just comes up with the ideas. So, one thing led to another and before you knew it I was scheduling editing sessions in hotel rooms and we were having mind-blowing sex."

"Really," I said. I was riveted. This was great.

"Oh yeah. I was living with this dope at the time so we couldn't go to my place. If Tammy was busy in the evening sometimes we'd do it in the office too. And let me tell you somethin', all that bullshit 'bout him having a hair trigger is jus' that, bullshit. That man could fuck like a bull and go for hours."

OK, this was a bit more than I needed to know because it was creepy thinking about Lucy and Tom screwing on her desk. Still, does it get better than this?

"Then Tammy found out and all hell broke looshe. She tried to get me fired, I never saw Tom again and I swear that was the beginning of his trip to the land of dick-less men...no dick...too bad Tommy los' his big, fabuloush dick." She was clearly loaded at this point as she poked her toothpick into her empty martini glass.

I felt bad too because it was clear to me that Lucy had had some pretty strong feelings for Tom.

"He swould've been a diff'rent man wit' me," she said.

We paid the check and I drove her home so she could sleep off the lunch.

"You're a goot guy Kyle," she said as I deposited her at her front door. "Why don you take the affernoon off."

"Thanks, Lucy, maybe I will. Are you sure you're going to be OK?"

"I'll be fine. Old cougars never die," she said as she waved good-bye and shut her front door.

CHAPTER FIFTY-THREE

HOUSE OF CARDS

Living Life On Shaky Ground

AFTER DROPPING OFF LUCY I swung by the office just to check on things because a part of me felt a tad guilty knowing that I was getting an afternoon off due to her over consumption. Plus, I needed some copies of Tammy and Tom's book to take on their interviews tomorrow morning.

After the office I went to the gym and had a good workout. There's something wonderfully decadent about exercising at three in the afternoon when you should be at work. You might think that the gym would be empty but guess again...in West Hollywood my gym is busy all the time. Now that I was out of the office, I found my mind wandering back to Melanie and Glenn. Once I was done with the elliptical I went outside and got some sun by the pool. Maybe if I just spent some time meditating about everything that had gone on I would get some clarity on the situation and feel less frustrated.

The sun felt good. It was one of those almost hot days that LA is famous for. Great weather but not too hot. I felt the occasional droplet of water hit my body from some hunky swimmers doing laps. The inventory of my life started running through my head…work stuff was in control and going well. Tammy and Tom seemed satiated after a successful rah-rah event at the convention center and I got two decent interviews for them tomorrow morning. Everything else in the office was going fantastic so work was an item I could move to the "good" column.

The scenario with Melanie vexed me. The truth had come out and I was paying a price for that but deep down I felt that the honesty of the situation was truly the best thing. It had been eating me up that I knew something she didn't know so at least that part of the misery was over. However, I didn't expect Peter to pull the stunt he did. So now the question was how to manage that? Mel and I had been best friends for years so I could only hope that would win out in the long run over her temporary blindness. Eventually the truth would surface, she'd realize Peter was the liar, and our friendship would pick up again. It would just be a matter of when and how she'd find out. That was the problem. There was no one else I could turn to for help; even Mickey and Tyler were blamed in this relationship sabotage conspiracy she'd cooked up in her mind. Maybe after a while she'd miss our friendship and soften a bit but I knew that it was going to take some time.

In the meantime, what the hell do I do about the Glenn situation? Now that I didn't have the distraction of work I realized his silence hurt more than I thought it did. Since Saturday I'd heard nothing. Certainly, in the past he had an M.O. of letting days go by before I would hear from him. But this time was different. For a while now we had been speaking every day, things had been going great, hell, the "I love yous" had been said. Relationships *have* to be God's joke on mankind because they are so damn complicated.

I flipped over on my stomach so that I could braise my back for a few minutes. I opened my eyes and looked through the slats of the lounge chair at an ant walking along the concrete. Do ants have all of the relationship problems that people do? Considering how many of them lived together hell had to break loose once in a while. OK, so I figure I have three options: one was to not do anything and see how much longer this was going to go on. He might eventually call. The second option was to call or text him. Texting is a pain because then if I don't hear anything back I have to play the game in my head of wondering if the text actually went through or was deleted blah blah blah. I could call but If I got voicemail that would be a dead end. The third option was to just show up and ring his doorbell. At least there would be no caller id to trace me to the scene of the crime if he wasn't home and perhaps a face-to-face would be the best option to force us to deal with this incident and hopefully move on. He couldn't possibly be chucking everything over this one thing could he? That would be a bit extreme.

I opted to shower back at home so I wouldn't smell like gym soap. To kill some time waiting for Glenn to get home from work I ate a light dinner (in case we ended up going out later on) and vacuumed my apartment. After cleaning up I chose a shirt I look really hot in along with some killer jeans. No harm in stacking the deck in my favor.

Traffic was a nightmare on my way over the hill, but I finally reached Glenn's street and wound my way up the mountain. It was a nice evening as it was getting close to magic hour; that special last hour of daylight where everyone looks incredible and Hollywood films love scenes. I hoped that within the hour everything would be back on track with Glenn and we'd be enjoying the sunset together.

Rounding the corner before Glenn's place, his house came into view and I saw a Toyota Prius sitting in the driveway. Damn! After all this he has company. Who was over? I pulled my car into a parking spot across the street but far away enough that I could see his driveway, but he wouldn't notice my car if he looked out the window. There was an SUV in front of me adding some cover too. I sat there for a few minutes wondering what I should do.

Ten minutes passed and I started to feel like an idiot. Maybe I should go shopping for a while and come back later. This was stupid sitting here like a stalker. But just as I was getting ready to start up my car and leave, Glenn's front door opened. A tall, blond dude, maybe in his late thirties, walked out the front door. He was good-looking and he was wearing an airline pilot's uniform. He pulled a small rolling carry-on bag, the type that are issued to airline employees and put it into the trunk. Just then Glenn popped out of the front door. Quickly, I slid down in my seat so that I was peering through the steering wheel with only one eye fixed on what was going happening. The pilot closed the trunk and walked back to Glenn who was still in the doorway. Then I saw them kiss. Not just a peck on the cheek but the kind of kiss you give a lover when he is on his way out the door on a business trip. I instantly felt hot all over, and my mouth went dry. The pilot got into the Prius and Glenn went back into the house and closed the door. Once the front door shut I sat up a bit so I could get a close look at this pilot guy when he drove by me. He didn't see me sitting in the car and when he buzzed by I was able to tell he definitely was good looking up close as well as far away.

My chest felt really tight and my throat hurt. Suddenly the inside of my car felt stifling; like I was going to suffocate if I didn't get out of it immediately. The fresh air was a huge relief once I stepped into it. I took a deep breath and tried to calm myself. I was completely confused. Alright, what was going on? Who was this person? Was this some guy he hooked up with? Trying to get my head around all of this and let my brain take over instead of my emotions. OK, wouldn't be a hookup because it's seven o'clock on a Thursday evening. Glenn would've worked today and wouldn't have let a trick from last night just hang out at his place unsupervised all day. Plus, that kiss was the kind of kiss you give someone you've known a long time. This wasn't just friends because that kiss was definitely not a friend kiss.

Then it hit me.

It started to all make sense.

Glenn was living with someone.

CHAPTER FIFTY-FOUR

THE FIGHT

Burning Up

MY SKIN FELT LIKE IT WAS ON FIRE as I walked towards Glenn's front door. I rang his bell and then stepped out of view from the security camera. I wasn't going to let him avoid me. My heart started to pound as I heard his footsteps get closer to the other side of the door. He reached the threshold and I could hear his hand grabbing the doorknob. There was a slight hesitation and then the door flew open and he stuck his head out turning to see me. The look on his face told me everything I needed to know. Busted.

"Kyle!" he said. I just stood there. I wanted him to squirm a bit. "What're you doing here?"

"Hi," I said trying to act nonchalant as possible.

"Umm, do you want to come in?"

"Sure, I said." The tension was thick between us as I walked into his house. I felt like an intruder in a place I normally felt welcomed; a place I had envisioned possibly living in one day.

"I was just going to have a beer. Why don't you grab one with me?" I followed Glenn into the kitchen and set my keys and cell phone on the counter while he pulled two beers out of the fridge.

"Here you go," he said as he handed one to me.

"Thanks, I said." Now that I was here I didn't know how to begin. My mind was racing, and I felt uncomfortable.

"So?" he said, putting the ball in my court.

What should I say? It felt awkward doing this in the kitchen. "Do you want to go into the living room?" I asked with uncertainty.

"OK, sure," he said. I led the way and we went into the living room. Only thing was, once I was there I realized I felt just as awkward as I did in the kitchen, so I stopped.

"Don't you want to sit down?" asked Glenn.

I took a swig of my beer to lubricate my dry mouth and throat.

"Who was that guy?" I did it! I got it out there but now I braced myself. This was one of those times when I knew the answer to the question was not going to be what I wanted to hear, that the end had come, and that this whole conversation was going to be about validating what I'd already come to realize.

"What guy?"

"The pilot I saw leaving here five minutes ago!" I said in a frustrated tone. "Don't pretend you don't know what I'm talking about."

Glenn bristled at my tone and hesitated a moment before saying: "That's Larry."

My God, *an airline pilot.* This was pure homo tragedy.

"A pilot named Larry. So that's who you're fucking."

"I don't appreciate your tone of voice Kyle."

"I don't care; you're living with this guy aren't you."

I could tell by his reaction that I had caught him completely off guard. I'd guessed right.

"That's none of your business!" I could see anger start to rise in Glenn.

"Answer me. You're living with this guy, aren't you?" I was really getting upset.

"OK fine, yeah. We're living together and have been for a long time."

There it was…the validation I was fishing for.

"Now it all makes sense," I said. "That's why you were so upset when I found your master bedroom because all along you've been fucking me in the guest room." It sounded so cheap.

"Kyle, your problem is you always have to keep messing with things."

"Don't try to turn this around on me. How dare you. I'm not the one fucking someone else and then lying about it."

"I never lied about anything to you."

"Are you kidding? You kept a door shut that led to another part of your house. You made up excuses for statues that suddenly appear that weren't there before. You move some of your clothes into the guest room to make it look like your bedroom."

"You and I never had any kind of commitment." Glenn's face was red.

"You told me you loved me."

"That's something I regret now."

That drove right through me.

"You son of a bitch," I said under my breath; trying to hold back.

"You should have left it alone!" yelled Glenn.

"Fuck you!" I said. How did it all come to this?

"No fuck you, Kyle!" he yelled back, poking me in the chest with his index finger. I shoved his hand away from me.

"You're a lying piece of shit. You're a scared, miserable child," I yelled.

"You brought this on yourself," he said poking me in the chest again with his finger.

"FUCK YOU!" I screamed, smacking his hand away from me again.

"FUCK YOU!" I heard. And like a cold Chicago wind it hit me; or rather he did. There was this blur of pink and then this numbness along with what I think was a loud crack. I saw the look in his eyes, cold mixed with fire, as my feet came out from underneath me. There was a shattering sound that came from behind me, I think, or was it from both sides? Something hard was at the back of my head and I wondered if I had been run over by a car. More clinking and there was rain coming down on me which didn't make any sense. Were we outside? Where was I? What was going on? A tingling sensation engulfed my entire body. I could feel electricity running down my fingertips and my legs and my toes. I felt completely alive but like I was wrapped in tight clear plastic so that I could see out but still feel pressure on every part of my body and I couldn't breathe.

I don't understand.

CHAPTER FIFTY-FIVE
FIGHTING BACK

Glass Houses

I SAT THERE ON THE FLOOR STUNNED. Warm liquid was filling my mouth and the back of my neck was wet. My head felt dizzy. I blinked my eyes a couple of times thinking maybe I had gotten stuck in someone else's nightmare but unfortunately it seemed to belong to me. Glenn stood there looking somewhat stunned himself but not enough to unclench his fist. He was breathing hard.

I didn't see this coming to be sure. The side of my face was numb, and it was hard to move my jaw. Pain was shooting up my back. Blood started to trickle out my mouth and down my chin onto my shirt. Another rivulet ran down the back of my throat and I coughed hard shooting it onto his Burber carpet. Should I be scared or angry? Am I in danger or was this a freak event and it was over now? I wasn't sure what was gong on or what I should do. I noticed there was shattered glass all around me and I realized I must have fallen back into the glass doors of the bookcase behind me.

I coughed more blood all over myself and the pain in my back seemed to be getting worse. Looking up at him I saw compassion and concern commingle on his face. He squatted down and I reeled back expecting another blow smacking the back of my head into the bookcase.

"No, no, no…it's OK," he said.

OK? *You just hit me…*

I wanted someone to tell me this didn't just happen; that it was all in my imagination. That he didn't just pound me like I was nothing to him; that it wasn't real.

But it *was* real. He certainly wasn't telling me otherwise and I was sitting here not sure what to do.

He got up and hustled to the kitchen. I could hear the faucet running and supposed he was getting a wet towel to clean up the mess. Which was the higher priority, the carpet or my face? He came back into the living room and knelt down to my level. For some reason I trusted him enough to start mopping the blood off me, but when the dishtowel hit my face the nerves came alive and I shot back away from him, back into the bookcase. I hit it so hard that a glass sculpture came crashing down and shattered right next to us.

"God damn it," he said. Fear shot through my eyes as I expected another blow from his fist. My heart was pounding so hard I couldn't catch my breath. I think he saw the fear in my eyes and it somehow affected him. He got up and went back into the kitchen. It was time to get the hell out of here. I almost screamed out loud from the pain as I forced myself into a standing position. I finally got over to the front door and let myself out. Walking was painful but I got over to my car as quickly as I was able to, head pounding, and then realized I didn't have my keys with me. I'd left them on the kitchen counter with my phone.

I was afraid and needed to get away, so I started to walk down the hill. I wasn't thinking clearly just that I needed to regroup somehow and figure out what to do next. When I got around the corner and out of sight I heard him calling for me. I picked up the pace and kept working my way down the road; adrenaline pushing me along.

Halfway down the hill a woman in a dusty-blue Jaguar was coming up the road. Her car slowed and by the expression on her face I could tell I must look like a nightmare. More blood trickled down my face and back of my neck. I must have a cut on the back of my head from the glass doors of the bookcase. She stopped her car in front of me and I just looked at her, stunned, like a hurt animal who wonders if this creature is going to harm or help. She lowered her window.

"My God, were you in an accident?"

Was I? I'm not sure. Does a fist meeting my face qualify as an accident or planned destruction? I started coughing up more blood and she looked horrified.

"What happened to you? My God, you're bleeding all over." She got out of the car and came over to me. In a city known for self-centeredness I was surprised she was actually trying to help.

Looking down, I saw my shirt was now covered in blood. I brought my hand up to my mouth and it was sticky and wet. I looked at her not sure what to do. There I was standing in the middle of the road in an affluent neighborhood bleeding like someone leaving a gang fight in the hood. I was violated, scared and dazed and I wanted to cry but everything felt crushed down inside of me. My chest heaved and then anger came over me. I was pissed. I had had enough, and I was ready to fight.

"I need you to call the police for me."

Her heel slipped on the pavement as she raced to her car rummaging in her bag for her cell phone.

Ten minutes later two officers arrived with lights flashing followed by paramedics.

The officers parked their cars and walked over to me just as I started coughing up more blood and finally throwing up a bloody mucus-covered mess from my stomach. Questions were being thrown at me, but I didn't have the energy to answer them. Every time I tried to get a word out my throat clenched, and I felt trapped in my own body. The paramedics slapped on latex gloves and started mopping me up.

I pushed one paramedic's hand away and looked up at him. Under different circumstances I would have been turned on by this guy: strong, dark hair, Italian muscles everywhere. I looked at him expecting him to be able to read my mind, I guess. It was time to do this.

"What?" he said. I just kept looking at him. "It's OK, he said. "Just tell me."

"I've been assaulted."

"Do you know who did this?"

I shook my head yes. "It's the guy I…was dating."

The paramedic went and got one of the officers and I filled them in on what had happened. The officer took notes and then started up the street in his car with his partner. Another office came over to me and after a few minutes she was radioed by the first two.

"Do you feel like you can ride in my car and ID this guy?" she said as I was being led to the ambulance.

"Yeah," I said.

"We need to get him to the hospital," said the paramedic. He's cut pretty badly in the back of his head and mouth."

After a quick negotiation I was put into the ambulance and we drove up the hill across from Glenn's. The officer rode along inside the ambulance. What a surreal experience this was.

The ambulance slowed down, and the officer had me sit up and look out the window. There was Glenn in his driveway...in handcuffs. He looked really enraged as police questioned him. Several neighbors had come out of their houses to watch the action.

"Is this the guy who did this to you?"

"Yes."

She radioed confirmation and I saw them lead Glenn into the back of their patrol car as the ambulance went on its way.

"Is he being arrested?"

"Yes."

"Will he go to jail?"

"Yes, he's going to be automatically charged but you still need to give a statement.

I lay there quiet for a moment while the paramedic put an IV in my arm.

"I need my keys and phone. They're on the table in his kitchen."

The officer had the ambulance stop while she hopped out. She said she'd deliver the keys and phone to the hospital.

"Is there someone we can call for you?" asked the paramedic?

"Yeah, I said," and gave him the number.

CHAPTER FIFTY-SIX

ER

Just Like On TV

AS THEY WHEELED ME INTO THE EMERGENCY ROOM at Saint Joseph's I found it amusing that my vantage point was the same camera angle I'd seen in countless TV shows. Cheap ceiling tiles rolled by as frantic doctors, nurses and my hunky paramedic chattered details back and forth. Unfortunately, I was assigned the ugliest Dr. on the planet but you can't have everything. One of the nurses looked like my third-grade teacher, Mrs. Lowell.

I was wide awake. I guess from the oxygen they'd given me or the adrenaline in my system. I was also sort of high so they must have given me some kind of pain killer. When they moved me from the gurney to the exam table I saw stars from all the pain.

A flurry of events happened at lightening speed. Quick X-rays were taken of my head, neck and back, blood pressure, IV's etc. Someone spread cool lubey stuff on my belly and ran a sonogram. Fingers went into my mouth, lights in my eyes etc. A police officer was taking pictures.

Due to everyone's reactions I wondered if I was going to die? That would be a shitty way to go...from some asshole hitting me. I thought about my parents having to come collect my body; my Dad shaking his head that my end had come as a result of my being gay and if only I'd joined the military I could have been straight. Then I thought of the old porn DVDs I had in the third drawer of my dresser and suddenly I had a pretty strong reason to live. It was one thing for my parents to sign for the body bag but quite another to find *Palm Springs Ass Fest 3*.

"Am I going to die?" I asked.

The nurse laughed, "Probably not tonight Honey."

"You've got a couple of nasty cuts on the back of your head and one in your mouth," said the Dr. I'm going to have to stitch them up.

I felt the sting of a syringe going into my mouth and I could hear the gurgling of that sucker thing the dentist uses to pull spit and blood out while they work. After a while I was turned over on my side while the doctor started working on the back of my head.

"Kyle, your friend has arrived," said one of the nurses. It felt good to know someone was there for me. "He can see you as soon as we finish patching you up." I smiled back at her, afraid to nod my head while a needle was being inserted into the back of it.

When it was finally over they moved me onto a bed that wasn't covered with bloody sheets and then rolled me into another area. About a minute later Mickey came into the room followed by Tyler.

"Oh my Gawd, Kyle. What the hell happened to you?" said Mickey. He came over and gingerly took my hand. I squeezed hard.

"It's a long story," I said, too tired to give him the whole nasty truth.

"Are you going to be OK?" Tyler asked?

"Yeah," I mumbled, but it hurt to talk much from the cut in my mouth.

A nurse came in and explained the morphine drip to me. Mickey bombarded her with questions and Tyler looked envious he didn't have a drip of his own.

"By the way," said the nurse. "There's a very loud, outlandishly dressed woman in the lobby demanding to be let back here."

I could feel a smile come over my face even though it hurt like hell. I gave Mickey a little nod.

"Yeah, she's with us," he said. "Go ahead and let her back."

"Good," said the nurse. "Because I think we were going to have to get security to remove her otherwise. We get allllll kinds in the ER."

Mickey laughed.

After she left Tyler said: "We missed a great opportunity to have her manhandled and thrown out on the street."

A minute later Mel came bursting into the room. She was wearing a Cat Woman outfit made of black latex. Her hood had little black ears and we could see a fluffy tail hanging from her backside. The capper was that she also had on her bright pink, thigh-high patent leather boots.

"Oh Jesus, are you OK?" said Mel? She rushed over to my bed. I could tell she'd been crying because mascara was smeared down her face.

"He's going to be fine," said Tyler. What the hell are you wearing?

"I'm Cat Woman, you idiot," as if he had asked the most obvious question he could have possible asked. "I rushed here from work."

"Kyle, are you sure you're going to be OK?"

I nodded a weak 'yes' and gave her a crooked smile.

"What happened to you," said Tyler?

I could tell they were dying to put the pieces together; after all, this was going to be the story of the year when we looked back on it. 'Remember that time you landed in the hospital?' Yeah, I certainly didn't expect for the day to end up like this but when all was said and done, I felt surprisingly fortunate. I guess lucky that I didn't die but maybe more so that I realized I was loved. You always can tell people's true colors when push comes to shove. And here I was surrounded by three people who loved me. I lay there looking at them and realized that despite everything that had transpired I was going to be OK.

This morphine's not bad stuff...and with that I closed my eyes and relaxed.

CHAPTER FIFTY-SEVEN

JELLO

Where's Mine?

THE NURSE POKED ME AWAKE.

"Time to wake up, Kyle. You need to try to eat some food honey." She was a big woman with arms the size of my legs and a friendly face. Her nametag said 'Donna.'

"I feel hung over."

She pointed to a tray which was set up in front of me and gave me a look that said 'Don't mess with me and eat your breakfast.' She started to take my blood pressure.

Melanie was asleep in the chair across the room. She was no longer in the cat suit but instead was dressed in doctors' scrubs. The nurse noticed I saw her. "She's been here the whole time. We got her some scrubs to change into because that outfit was causing a commotion. That must have been some party she was at all dressed like she was." I smiled and perused my breakfast tray.

"No Jello?"

"Maybe if you'd had your ass stitched instead of your head," I couldn't help but laugh which hurt like hell by the way. She ripped the armband off of me and put her stethoscope back around her neck. "Eat up," she said and as she walked by Mel's chair giving her a poke as well. "Your friend's awake girl," she said.

Melanie came to life and darted over to my bed. "Oh God, Kyle, are you OK?"

"Yeah, I guess so."

"He's going to be fine," said Donna. "By the way young man, the doctor said he's going to release you after you eat. No residual signs of concussion. He'll be by in a while or so to poke and prod." I waved goodbye and Donna was out the door. Mel leapt into action.

"Spill it. What the hell happened?"

"You're never going to believe this one," I said.

"It was Glenn, we know that much."

I was disappointed I didn't get to see the look on her face when she found out. "How'd you know that?" I asked.

"That cop interviewed us about him. You were passed out from the drugs. I got her to fill me in on part of it. What the hell did you do to make him hit you? The boys and I have been guessing at it all night."

Over my Jello-free breakfast I told her all the grim details; bit by bit. At least from what I could remember. I was surprised at how difficult it was to recall certain things and then the more I told her the more other details started popping back into my mind.

"I wonder what happened to Glenn?" I said.

"I hope he's getting gang raped in some slimy jail right now," said Mel.

"He'd like that though."

"What an asshole," she countered.

"I'm sure he's out on bail by now. You should have seen the look on his face when they cuffed him and threw him into the back of that car." As rotten as I felt I had to laugh.

"What happened after I fell asleep last night?"

"Not much, they moved you into this room around two in the morning. A doctor came by a little bit later and said they were going to keep you overnight just to observe what was going on with your concussion blah, blah, blah. You know doctors. They tell you the least they can about anything."

I just smiled and looked around the room. It was surprisingly well decorated for a hospital and my window looked out over Burbank.

"Not exactly the way you wanted to spend your Friday morning, I'm sure, but it could have been worse," said Mel. The minute she said it I bolted upright in bed.

"Oh my God, what day is it?"

"Why it's Christmas day sir!" she said in a fake *Christmas Carol* English accent.

"This isn't funny," I said. "What the hell day is it?"

She gave me a cautious look. "It's Friday morning Kyle. The time is nine a.m. and the year is…"

"Damn!" I said and my head started to pound as I tried to look for a phone. "Where's a phone? Where's a phone? I need to call the office."

"Kyle what the hell is going on? You need to lie back down."

"Mel you don't understand. Give me a phone *now!* I was supposed to pick up Tammy and Tom this morning at quarter to six for their interview. God, I'm so screwed."

Melanie grabbed the phone from behind the headboard and handed it to me. I almost threw it across the room in frustration until I figured out how to get an outside line. I knew I was in for it when Joyce the receptionist gave me a mini lecture that Lucy had been trying to reach me all morning. My head pounded while I waited for her to pick up.

"Where the hell are you?" Lucy demanded. "I can't believe you fucked this up. Tammy and Tom have been shitting bricks for the past three hours. Answer me, where the hell are you?"

"I'm in the hospital."

"Yeah right," she responded. Wow, she was a tough nut to crack.

"I'm serious, Lucy. I'm in Saint Joseph's in Burbank. I was assaulted last night, and I was pretty messed up."

Her tone changed instantly. "Serious? Oh my God, what happened?" I filled her in on my night and how I wasn't able to call until now because I'd been sleeping off the morphine.

"Kyle, I'm heading over there right now," she said.

"No, Lucy, I appreciate it but you don't have to do that."

"Don't be an ass," she said as she hung up the phone.

I turned to Mel. "Lucy's on her way."

"Are you kidding me? Probably just to see if you're telling the truth. Well, one look at that shiner and swollen jaw and that should set your story straight. I hate to tell you this but don't expect a date anytime soon." We sat there for a moment in the silence. It felt good to have her by my side.

"I'm glad you're here, Mel. Thanks for being here for me."

"Of course," she said. "By the way I owe you an apology."

"It's OK," I said.

"No, listen. What you guys said stuck and so, well, I started doing a little investigating and I found gay porn on his ipad."

"Wow, what'd you do?"

"Kicked him in the balls of course. It was quite cathartic. Honestly, this relationship stuff sucks."

"I hear you," I smiled the best I could even though my mouth hurt like hell. I reached over and held her hand.

We didn't talk much after that. Just kind of sat there in silence. Maybe it was just the aftereffects from the morphine drip, but when I thought about it, isn't that what you are able to do when you are really close to someone? You don't need to talk...they just understand along with you.

CHAPTER FIFTY-EIGHT

LUCY TO THE RESCUE

Just What I Needed

ABOUT AN HOUR LATER LUCY CAME IN with a flourish. Her arms were filled with a big bouquet of flowers and a bottle of gin. Since I had a visitor Mel took the opportunity to get some breakfast. I examined the bottle of gin recognizing it as a gift one of our authors had sent Lucy a few months back. I can't believe she was re-gifting me when I was in the hospital and wondered if she'd swiped the flowers from someone else's room while they were in surgery.

"Thanks for coming."

"Of course, I mean, how could I not? Everyone in the office is of course frantic with worry about you."

"I'm sorry about the screw up today."

"I found a solution to quiet the fire. When do you get out of here?" she added quickly.

"Later on today. Just waiting to be discharged."

"Were you mugged?"

"Yeah," I lied. I wasn't about to get into my relationship problems with Lucy. There's need-to-know and then there's never-need-to-know.

"Well, I'm glad you're going to be all right." She seemed nervous but I figured it was all about being in the role of caretaker.

"What ended up happening this morning?" I asked.

"Well, saying it was ugly is probably an understatement. I received the first call when you were five minutes late and it went downhill from there."

"Did Tammy need another paper sack?"

"Surprisingly no. I mean, she was screaming bloody hell over the phone but by the time I got there she was eerily cool. I had them take a cab over to the studio and I met them there. I didn't even have time to put on make up."

"Did they make it on time?"

"No, they missed the segment by ten minutes and there was no turning back for the show. I tried to see if they would tape the segment to use later but it was a no go. The producer was livid too. We owe him a gift basket of some kind."

Nice...and I'd pimped Mickey out for this as well, I thought.

"I tried reaching you over and over on your cell to find out the next interview location. Luckily Tammy had remembered the name of the show and we made it to the radio station in time for that one. Missed breakfast though which caused Tom to have blood sugar issues. I went out for muffins and juice while they were on the air."

"Well, at least they got the second interview in. I guess I'm going to have to call and explain what happened."

"I don't think that's going to be necessary," said Lucy.

"Really?" Lucy looked uncomfortable as she shifted her weight in her chair.

"Kyle, there's only one way to say this. You're fired."

"What?" I was floored.

"It's nothing personal; just business. Tammy made it very clear that she was going to go public with Gordon being a drunk unless we got rid of you. I tried to offer up simply moving the account to a PR person in the New York office, but she wouldn't go for it. She wants your head."

Wow, I couldn't believe this. After all the money I'd made for the company recently I was being tossed away like trash.

Lucy continued. "Of course, I'll give you a fantastic reference don't worry one minute about that." I just looked at her. "And with your experience you'll find another job in no time." She gave my arm a little squeeze of reassurance.

I didn't know what to say and Lucy clearly wanted to get the hell out of here.

"So, take care of yourself and get some rest young man. Don't worry about your things. I'll have someone clear out your office and we'll messenger everything over to you." She smoothed her skirt as she stood up and grabbed her purse off the table by the bed. "And listen, we'll have to do a Dodgers game as soon as you're back on your feet."

"Thanks," I said weakly, still stunned from what had just gone down.

And with that she gave me one last awkward smile and walked out of the room.

CHAPTER FIFTY-NINE
EXHAUSTION

Disposable Human Beings

I LOOKED AT MY FACE IN MY BATHROOM MIRROR. It was a wreck. My jaw was swollen, and I had bruising under my eyes. Peeling up my lip I was able to look at the stitch job on the inside of my mouth. It was pretty creepy looking.

Melanie had gotten me home and right now she was out picking up some groceries. The doctor had released me before lunch, and I was grateful to get the hell out of the hospital. At least I was home, but it was really lonely here. It would have been nice to have had a dog; someone to greet me with excitement when I came through the door and who understood the true meaning of unconditional love.

I'm not exactly sure what it was I felt. The longer I looked in the mirror the more I realized I was experiencing a lot of confusing feelings. I was numb and exhausted from all of this and I couldn't help not feeling like a disposable human being. How could Glenn have done what he did to me? In the end was that how little he cared for me? Complete disregard? How else could he have just laid me out like that? Contempt for Lucy and Shitty Books Inc. had started to rise in my throat the minute Lucy walked out of my hospital room this morning. At least her motivation for doing what she did was clear to me so in one respect that was helpful.

I shifted my ass onto the counter, trying to see the back of my head where they had allegedly put about forty stitches. It didn't look as bad as I expected. I guess they were tiny stitches and my hair was long enough to fall back over the place they shaved. I could cover it with a baseball cap too for a few weeks.

Exhaustion. Yeah, that's what I'm feeling. I thought I was tired of all the bullshit previously but the past twenty-four hours had taken me to a new plane altogether. What was the point of all of this? Life. How many times had I been the one to give and give and give and in the end what did it get me anything? A.K. had walked out, Glenn smashed up my face, and a job I'd slaved away at for too many years tossed me aside as well. What is it about me that makes me so disposable or what it that I just ended up attracting bad scenarios?

I'd spent years of my life trying to get people to see the person I was and to value that person. My friends could see that but why not anyone else? The job situation left me feeling angry but the fact that everything came crashing down with Glenn, that I was back to square one of being single and alone, well, that just made me feel empty. There was a deep hurt inside me, like a stalk of something awful that had grown from my stomach up through my chest and into my throat and head. There was a tightness in me; that feeling which comes when you want to cry but can't. When you want to let it all out, but it's bottled down inside so tightly that the pressure is unbearable. It would be a lot easier if I could just start crying.

I heard Melanie knocking on the front door, so I hobbled into the living room to let her in. My back was really stiff, but the doctor had said nothing was broken, just some aggravated muscles from crashing into the bookcase. I opened the door and she was overloaded with grocery sacks and a big bouquet of pink roses.

"Let me help you," I said.

"That's OK, don't strain yourself," she said as she plopped everything down on the counter.

"My God, what did you get?"

"I shot by Gelsen's and picked up all kinds of things for you. You won't need to go to the store for a while."

I could see. "I really appreciate it."

"Don't worry about it. That's what friends are for right?"

Thank God for my friends.

"I picked up some roses to cheer this dump up a bit," she said as she pulled a vase from the cabinet and threw them in all at once.

"Heard from Mickey or Tyler?"

"Yeah, they both called while you were out to check on me. Tyler is going to come over this evening and watch a movie or something."

"You know, he drives me crazy sometimes but deep down he's a great guy."

"Yeah, you all are. By the way, how are *you* holding up?"

She continued to fiddle with the bags on the counter, putting stuff away, and getting something ready for our lunch while I sat down at the table.

"I don't know. Between dealing with asshole and you getting hurt I think I've cried about all I can for a while. It is what it is I guess." She wiped away a tear from one of her eyes. "I'm just so tired from all of this," she said. "I mean, God damn it, Kyle!" she turned to face me. "When it is going to be our turn? Huh?" I could see the anger and frustration in her.

"I don't know."

"I mean, at what point am I going to be able to have someone for me in my life? Why is this so fucking hard?" She swung the utensil drawer open, grabbed a soup ladle out of it, and slammed it on the counter."

"Don't kill lunch," I said, trying to break the mood. She laughed.

"Matzo ball soup."

"Are you kidding? It's ninety degrees out today."

"It kept the Jews going for a gazillion years. I figured we could give it a try. Believe it or not they even had apricot humentash."

"If your mother could see you now," I added. She turned from the counter and headed to the table. In her hands were two bowls of matzo ball soup that she set down. Stuck in each matzo ball was one of those little umbrellas they serve with piña coladas.

"What's with the umbrellas?" I asked.

"Miami."

"Huh?"

"Miami. We're going to Miami."

"I'm a bit lost. What're you talking about."

"Matzo ball soup and plane tickets to Miami. I think it's called a Jewish first aid kit. I called United while I was shopping for groceries and booked us on a flight to Miami. We leave on Friday and get back a week later. I figured after the bullshit we've both been through that we could use a break."

"Are you kidding?"

"Don't worry princess. Your bruises will be gone by the time we leave. And I mean, come on, it's not like you have a job to go to next week. What the hell's stopping you?"

She had a point. This is why I love Mel.

CHAPTER SIXTY
ANGER

Cold Sweaty Reality

THE COKE FUCKED ME UP. Sweat is rolling down my chest as the music is beating in the background. Sweat fills the air, hanging there like a cloud of sex. My heart is pounding as we grind up against each other, my fist grabbing the back of his hair, shoving his face down into the pillow. His arm reaches back behind him and he cups my jaw with his hand putting just enough pressure to cause a certain amount of erotic pain. I can feel the sweat of his palm against the roughness of my unshaven face. I can hear him breathing harder and harder as the sinews of our bodies crash into each other. I jam myself up into him, controlling him. Pheromones, sweat and force. As the tempo builds with each guttural sigh so does the anger inside of me. The anger that I'm here, doing this, that it's not Glenn but just a hot fuck I used to see from time to time. The anger that I'm doing this to myself again, that my life isn't changing, that I'm repeating the same God damn mother-fucking thing over and over and over and over and over and yet still…it feels good. It feels hot. It has a rightness to it for this moment in time. There's an organic magic to sex between men; an animal passion that is surpassed by no other. Pule male. Pure sex. Pure passion. Pure anger. Pure frustration. Pure sweat. Pure pounding. Pure release. Pure.

Maybe base but it's pure. No words. We can feel the blood rushing through our veins as we lay there holding tight. Coming back down to Mother Earth. I drop my head down to the back of his shoulder and close my eyes, our breathing still intense, almost as if we are trying to gasp to stay alive. The sweat and saliva and fluid trickles down my chest; gravity taking control. Primal release.

Release from my life. Release from the fact that it didn't work out again and I'm so fucking angry and frustrated. Sex is control, it's power, it's force. Fuck love. It just fucks you back. I want to let the anger out.

"My God. That was amazing…you're amazing," he says. He flips over onto his back and tries to pull me close to him, but I maneuver away and just lay beside him on my back looking up to the ceiling. I don't have anything to say, don't want to fake anything, so I just continue to lay there and stare, trying to find truth in this moment. Trying to justify it for what it is but can't help realize what it isn't.

I look over at him and he turns his head to me, and I give him a weak smile. "I need to go," I say.

I slide into my jeans and T-shirt, put my shoes on and head to the door.

"It was good seeing you after all this time," he said. "Call me next time you want to get off." I nod a goodbye and another weak smile and head outside. It's pouring down rain.

But the rain feels good. It's unusually warm for a rainstorm and by the time I get to my car I'm soaked to the skin. I sit there for a while just listening to the rain pattering away.

My emotions are running all over the place. I am both physically and emotionally drained both in a good and bad way. Satiation, satisfaction and emptiness. While the rain patters away my breath slowly starts to fog the windows blurring the outside world. I'm trying to find meaning in it all; there has to be some kind of purpose that I'm just not getting. Right? This can't be all that life is about; an endless search for something that I don't seem to be finding. Or did I find it in A.K. and that was my chance? Or maybe Tyler has it right all along, that I don't need to find someone to complete me, that I have to be able to be complete on my own. I don't know. That's a hard concept for me to swallow.

A.K. I don't event know where to begin with all of that. And with Glenn I couldn't help facing the irony of it all. How many nights feeling safe by his side, feeling his breath on my shoulder, only to find myself picking my carcass off his Burber rug. I hope he never gets the bloodstains out. I'd heard nothing from him and certainly didn't expect to. I told the police I wanted nothing more to do with it. I needed to wash it off of me.

Splat, splat, splat went the rain. The humidity was building in the car and I was beginning to feel sleepy despite the coke still in my system. I should go home now but there was something captivating by the sound of the rain. A water womb holding everything at bay, and I didn't want to go right now. Maybe if I stayed listening long enough I would hear the answers or at least one of the answers I'd been searching for all this time.

And then I felt it. It just started welling up inside of me and came bubbling to the surface. Years of pain and frustration and anger forced the tears up and out. My chest was heaving, rain on my face now. I was so tired. Tired of holding all this inside. I just wanted it all out of me so I could go forward with a light load. It had weighed me down for so long and I needed to be rid of it. But with the tears, with the exit of all that pain, also came many happy memories flooding back and mixing in with the sorrow. It was a cruel mix of good and bad that seemed to exacerbate the physicality of it all. I cried until there was nothing left inside of me, I have no idea for how long. I was drained both inside and out and just wanted to go to sleep. At least when I was asleep I was at peace.

CHAPTER SIXTY-ONE
MIAMI

Mojito Madness

WE SAT IN THE OUTDOOR BAR of the Pelican looking out over the Atlantic at a pink sky which had come with dusk. Thank God for South Beach. Salsa music blared over the sound system and I couldn't soak in the beautiful people and Mojitos fast enough. The flight had been fantastic. Mel cashed in miles, so we were able to upgrade to business class and after five hours of warmed nuts, free cocktails and a good meal we finally found ourselves having the ability to breathe.

"I don't know about you," said Mel. "But I could sleep with half the guys in this city."

"Well said. There is something hot about Cuban men isn't there?"

She tried to spear a mint leaf with her straw. "This is going to be one great week. We have time, we have no commitments, we have plenty of money to spend, and best of all…we don't have two assholes to screw it all up."

"Miami here we come!" I said as I raised my glass for what had to be our sixth toast that day. We'd toasted everything from naked Cuban men with big Cohibas, to old friends, to business class seats. It was a great start to what we both hoped would be a week away from everything.

We'd made a pact to not discuss relationships but that ended somewhere over Arizona.

"You know," said Mel. "I'm sure there was a lesson to be learned from all this."

"You think?" I said skeptically. "What?"

"Beats me. But it can't be as simple as we just got royally screwed."

"I think that's exactly what it was. Call me dumb as a brick wall but I don't think this was a learning experience in the least. Except maybe I need to stop looking for love anywhere. I think I'm ready to give up on the notion that I'm going to find someone to grow old with; someone who will be there when I die."

"When you think of everyone around us," said Mel. "Look at who is the happiest. It's Tyler. It's not you or me or Mickey. It's the guy who we always think is pitiable and lonely because he's happy to just screw around and travel the globe."

"I don't want to admit it because that would mean he's been right all along. But don't you think deep down, despite what he always says, that he'd rather have a traveling companion on all those trips?"

"I don't know," she said.

"When I look at Tyler, yeah, on the surface in his own quirky way he seems to have it together but I can't help believe that his endless restlessness is because he's in search of the very same thing we at least *admit* to looking for."

"Maybe," she said, finally spearing the mint leaf she was after.

"But even so, I just feel so jaded that I can't help but think I need to switch gears all together. It's scary though. I don't want to end up alone."

"Yeah," she said. "It's one of those things in life where some people just get really lucky and the rest of us want to chase after the dream of having what they have. But it *is* scary. Who's going to be there for me when I die? I don't have any kids. I can hardly stand to be around my family. I certainly can't depend on them for anything let alone holding my hand as I gasp my last breath." A look of frustration and concern crossed her face.

I swirled the ice around in my drink and looked back out over the ocean. It was a paradox having such a depressing conversation against such an amazing backdrop. The pink sky had darkened, and lights were beginning to pop on up and down Ocean Drive. Good looking couples were walking up and down the sidewalk; holding hands and perusing menus trying to decide where to land for dinner.

Two choices: either we keep down this depressing road or we do something about it. "I vote for finding the best nightclub nearby and having the time of our life tonight. What do you say?"

"Good idea," said Mel. "I can always worry about dying later."

CHAPTER SIXTY-TWO
GLORIA

The Sun Also Rises On Miami

MIAMI HAD BEEN JUST WHAT WE NEEDED. The week had been amazing: fun clubs, sun on the beach, shopping and enough Cuban food to last us a lifetime. It was our last day there and we were walking along Collins Avenue from our hotel to what had become our favorite little spot to have breakfast. On the way there we walked past the coolest Art Deco apartment building. It was painted pink and was three stories tall. It was built around a nifty little courtyard blocked off with an iron gate. The courtyard was loaded with flowers and in the center was a fountain which burbled away; the brick sidewalk skating either side as it met again in front of the entrance.

"What a cool place," said Melanie.

"Yeah, it's great isn't it?"

"Now this is the kind of place I'd live in if I moved here," she said. "Look at that top floor window with the fancy glass panes." A nifty little window was opened to South Beach below. After a few additional minutes of marveling at this little gem, we kept walking until we reached our destination.

Our last breakfast had been somewhat ceremonial with Café Cubanos and some spicy eggs that we had come to love over the course of just a few days. We had arrived losers and we were leaving winners. OK, maybe not winners, but at least we'd had a chance to do a lot of thinking and to let go of some of the emotional baggage with which we'd arrived. It had gone the wayside of pink skies over the beach and the dinner of Ropas Viejas I'd thrown up in someone's bush after a night of a few too many Mojitos. We were leaving as newly empowered people: me ready to find a new job, Mel ready to add new sparkle to the way she could crack a whip, and both of us swearing off men.

Sitting back in my chair, I inhaled the sea air deeply and contently.

"What is it about this place?" I asked.

"I know exactly what you mean," said Mel. "It's as if I'm coming home when I come here. Not that it makes any sense."

"It doesn't have to. I don't know if it's the music or the men or the humidity, but I feel energized here."

"Well," said Mel. "Time to say goodbye to our little spot and start heading back."

Our return walk to the hotel was a slow one and I could tell neither one of us wanted it to end. As we retraced our steps we came back upon on our little pink palace. In front of the gate a kooky looking older woman in a flowered house dress was tying a 'For Rent' sign onto the cast iron with pieces of yarn. Mel and I stopped dead in our tracks.

"You have a place to rent?" I said.

"Yes," said the landlady. "It's the top unit." She pointed in the direction of the window Mel had been mooning over earlier.

I looked at Mel. "Want to take a look?" and gave her one of those 'You know, just for fun' kind of shrugs so the landlady wouldn't think we were just looky-loos.

"Sure," said Mel. "How big is the place?"

"Enormous," said the landlady. It was the owner's apartment when the building was built back in the twenties. It has three bedrooms. My name's Doris." We introduced ourselves as we shook her hand.

An electric zing went up my spine as we stepped over the threshold of the gate and into the cool shade of the courtyard. Once inside, the sound of the fountain seemed almost magical as it blocked out the traffic on the street.

"Look, Kyle. Birds of Paradise, your favorites." She pointed to one side of the building where it was fronted with blooming birds of paradise.

"It's a great building," said the landlady. "I've lived here for thirty years and it's very well maintained." She opened the front door and we went up the stairs to the second floor. She unlocked the door and we stepped inside.

An odd feeling that I'd somehow come home washed over me. The place was amazing. Hardwood floors and arched windows with long white gauzy curtains which billowed from the ocean breeze wafting into the rooms. We could hear the fountain from the courtyard inside the apartment. The kitchen had all the original Art Deco tiles and cool new appliances. There was a dining room off of the living room and the walls had sconces that the landlady swore were original but had been rewired during the last renovation. The rooms were large, spacious and well lit. Against one wall was a staircase that led to the upper floor. Even the banister had an art deco flair.

"The bedrooms are upstairs," said Doris. We climbed the stairs and at the top landing found ourselves looking out of the window

Mel loved. It looked down on the fountain and we could even it hear it from this high up.

"My God, Kyle. Look at the size of these bedrooms." They were indeed big. One bedroom had a bathroom off of it done in pink tiles and fixtures and the other bathroom connected both to a bedroom and the hallway and had mint green tiles and white fixtures.

"The basins are original as are the tiles, toilets and tubs, but the tubs were re-glazed. You could use the third bedroom as an office of course and that still gives you a room for kids."

Mel and I looked at each other and smiled. We stopped in one of the bedrooms and looked down on the courtyard. Neither one of us wanted to move.

"I have to tell you that if you're interested in this place you'd better grab it, I usually don't keep these places vacant for more than a few days. Not in this kind of building. Everyone wants in." As she said this, Doris kept swatting a fly that buzzed around her head.

"How much are you asking?" said Mel

Doris told us her price.

Mel and I looked at each other.

"This is crazy" I said, knowing what Mel was thinking.

"It's not like we haven't done crazy before," she said.

"We're just going to pick up and move?"

She stood there for a bit. "Yeah, why not? I mean really, what's keeping us in LA? Boyfriends?"

"There's Tyler and Mickey."

"There are also planes and phones. It's a chance to start over Kyle. Your lease is almost up anyway, and I can always rent out my condo."

We stood there in silence for a bit somewhat paralyzed by the possibility of the future.

"What do you say, Kyle?" Melanie looked at me and gave me a loving smile. It was a look you give someone you care for deeply, someone you understand fully, and someone you love unconditionally. It's the kind of smile you hope to see on someone's face as you take your last breath, give their hand that final squeeze, and know that you made it to the end and someone was there for you.

"Fuck it," I said. "What do we have to lose?"

The pink palace was ours.

EPILOGUE

ON THE FLIGHT HOME, we spent a lot of time chatting about our new adventure. The stuff we needed to take care of to move, what we'd keep and what we'd sell, and how we'd decorate. Also, how we'd break the news to Tyler and Mickey which was the one downside of leaving Los Angeles. But that was the only downside. We were leaving behind a life that had become unfulfilling and hopefully were heading to something that was going to be great. LA wasn't going to change anytime soon, so we might as well make the changes ourselves. Like the Phoenix rising from the ashes we would leave the land of plastic for a chance at something new.

After a while Mel fell asleep; her head nestled on my shoulder. Careful not to wake her, I gazed out my window at the lights from different cities passing below. It had been a long journey to get where I was now. I thought back to so much, what I had learned, what was good, and what was bad. It wasn't like it was all bad by any means. There were a lot of happy times and some good fortune along the way but somehow it wasn't what I wanted it to be.

I don't know, maybe it wouldn't ever be what I hoped for. But when all was said and done, when I thought of all the bullshit and the frustration and the pain that had led up to this point, I knew one thing. I knew that no matter what, I was still standing, and I was still fighting for what I wanted. Because most importantly, if there's one thing we *have* to hold onto, one thing to always remember, one thing to keep us going, it's Gay Scout Rule # 1...We *will* survive.

— End —

ACKNOWLEDGEMENTS

THIS BOOK WAS A 17-YEAR PROJECT from the first word that hit the page to the first sale. Life repeatedly got in the way of completion, but my Irish tenacity refused to give up on it. In part, what never allowed me to shelve it was the number of people who spurred me on and have believed in my writing—for past works written under a different name and of course this book. I would especially like to thank Calder Lowe who served as mentor on this book's journey. Her guidance, expertise, cheerleading and occasional kick in the ass have left me indebted. To Laura Fitler who read the first drafts and told me I was onto something. To Betsy Behr who provided key advice on the main character at the beginning stages. Laurie Blazek who spent summer afternoons laughing out loud when I read it to her, insisting I get it to print one day. Amanda Pisani for her expert editorial guidance and enthusiasm. Russ Carthy who told me I had to write something again after directing my stage play. Friends who encouraged me to put my collection of short stories into print—it was one of those that was the seed for this book. Kostis Pavlou who brought the spirit of the book to life with his amazing cover and Tara Mayberry for the beautiful interior work. Matt Wadland who pushed me one last time. A special note of thanks to the judges at the contests I entered who gave my book its prizes. Those were immensely exciting and validating.

Many times, when I was discouraged this would never happen, I remembered praise from a number of people who championed my other written works including my brother, Joan Benedict, Shelley Winters, Rod Steiger, and Laura Linney. That past support nagged at me to not give up on this project.

And finally, Leslie Hazan, who gave me another shot at life via her caring generosity. Her action allowed me, like the phoenix, to rise from my own ashes. She would have been the first to have bought a copy and laughed out loud.

—Kyle McGraw

Made in the USA
Monee, IL
03 July 2020